HADRIAN THE SEVENTH

Frederick Rolfe was born of a respectable Dissenting family in 1860, in Cheapside, and until 1886 worked as a schoolmaster, at which he was successful and well liked. He then became a Roman Catholic and attended college with a view to entering the priesthood. He was rejected, however, as a result of the extremely 'difficult' temperament and eccentricities that he displayed. In 1890 he went to Rome, where he was again refused ordination, but where he acquired a considerable knowledge of medieval history and possibly also the title Baron Corvo. From 1891 until 1898 he worked as an artist in Christchurch, Aberdeen, Holywell, and Oxford, living largely on credit.

In 1900, after the publication of his first large work, *Stories Toto Told Me*, he met a publisher for whom he agreed to write *Chronicles of the House of Borgia*. He devoted the next six years to writing, and in this period produced, among other works, his two best-known novels *Hadrian the Seventh* and *Don Tarquinio*. But his way of life and his relations with his friends and publishers remained most unstable, and in 1907 he left for Venice. Here the 'man demon', as D. H. Lawrence called him, continued his way of life, and wrote *The Desire and Pursuit of the Whole*. He died in Venice in 1913. In 1968–9 the play adapted from *Hadrian the Seventh* had a highly successful run both in London and New York.

NEVE ME IMPEDIAS NEVE LONGIUS PERSEQUARIS

ὅπως μήτε ἀντιστήσει μόι μήτε ἕψει
πορρωτέρω

FR. ROLFE

(Frederick Baron Corvo)

+>-<+->-><+->-><+->-><+->-><+->-><+->-><+->-<+->-

HADRIAN THE
SEVENTH

Penguin Books

Penguin Books Ltd, Harmondsworth, Middlesex, England
Penguin Books, 625 Madison Avenue, New York, New York 10022, U.S.A.
Penguin Books Australia Ltd, Ringwood, Victoria, Australia
Penguin Books Canada Ltd, 2801 John Street, Markham, Ontario, Canada L3R 1B4
Penguin Books (N.Z.) Ltd, 182–190 Wairau Road, Auckland 10, New Zealand

—

First published by Chatto & Windus 1904
Published in Penguin Books 1963
Reprinted 1969, 1982

—

—

**Printed in Great Britain by
Richard Clay (The Chaucer Press) Ltd,
Bungay, Suffolk
Set in Monotype Bembo**

TO MOTHER

Prooimion

IN mind he was tired, worn out, by years of hope deferred, of loneliness, of unrewarded toil. In body he was almost prostrate by the pain of an arm on the tenth day of vaccination. Bodily pain stung him like a personal affront. 'Someone will have to be made miserable for this,' he once said during the throes of a toothache. He was no stranger to mental fatigue: but, when to that was added corporeal anguish, he came near collapse. His capacity for work was constricted: the mere sight of his writing materials filled him with disgust. But, because he had a horror of being discovered in a state of inaction, after breakfast he sat down as usual and tried to write. Dazed in a torrent of ideas, he painfully halted for words: stumbling in a maze of words, he frequently lost the thread of his argument: now and then, in sheer exhaustion, his pen remained immobile. He sat in a small low armchair which was covered with shabby brocade, dull-red and green. An old drawing-board, of the large size denominated Antiquarian, rested on his knees. The lower edge frayed the brocade on the arms of the chair. His little yellow cat Flavio lay asleep on the tilted board, nestling in the bend of his left elbow. That was the only living creature to whom he ever spoke with affection as well as with politeness. His left hand steadied his MS., the sheets of which were clipped together at the top by a metal clip. At the upper edge of the board a couple of publishers' dummies reposed, having the outward similitude of six-shilling novels: but he had filled their pages with his archaic handwriting. The first contained thoughts – not great thoughts, nor thoughts selected on any particular principle, but phrases and opinions such as Sophocles' denunciation,

'Ὦ μιαρὸν ἦθος καὶ γυναικὸς ὕστερον,

or Gabriele d'Annunzio's sentence,

Old legitimate monarchies are everywhere declining, and Demos stands ready to swallow them down its miry throat.

The second was his private dictionary which (as an artificer in verbal expression) he had compiled, taking Greek words from Liddell and Scott and Latin words from Andrews, enlarging his English vocabulary with such simple but pregnant formations as the adjective 'hybrist' from ὑβριστης, or the noun 'gingilism' from *gingilismus*.

He was looking askance at his MS. In two hours, he had written no more than fourteen lines; and these were deformed by erasures of words and sentences, by substitutions and additions. He struck an upward line from left to right across the sheet: laid down his pen: lifted board, cat, books, and MS. from his knees; and laid them by. He could not work.

He poked the little fire burning in the corner of a fire-clayed grate. He was shivering: for, though March was going out like nine lions, he was very lightly clad in a blue linen suit such as is worn over all by engineers. He had an impish predilection for that garb since a cantankerous red-nosed prelate, anxious to sneer at unhaloed poverty, inanely had said that he looked like a Neapolitan. He brushed the accumulation of cigarette-ash from the front of his jacket and seized a pair of spring dumb-bells: but at once returned them, warned by the pain of his left arm-pit. He took up the newspaper which he had brought with him after breakfast, and read again the news from Rome and the news of Russia. The former, he could see, was merely the kind of subterfuge which farthing journalists are wont to use when they are excluded from a view of facts. It said much, and signified nothing. 'Our Special Correspondent' was being hoodwinked; and knew it: but did not like to confess it; and so indulged his imagination. Something was occurring in Rome: something mysterious was occurring in Rome. That could be deduced from the dispatch: but nothing more. The news of Russia was a tale of unparalleled ghastliness. It emanated from Berlin: no direct communication with Russia having taken place for a fortnight.

'How exquisitely horrible it is,' he said to Flavio; 'and I believe it's perfectly true. The Tsar – well, that was to be expected. But the Tsaritsa – though, if ever a woman bore her fate in her face, she did, poor creature. Those dreadful haunted eyes of hers! That hard old young soft face! The innocent babies! How abominably cynically cruel! Yet there have been omens and portents of just such a tragedy as this any time these last few years. They must have known it was coming. Or is this another example of the onlookers seeing most of the game?' He fetched a book of newspaper cuttings, and turned the pages. 'Here you are, Flavio,' he said to the sleeping cat; 'and here – and here. If these are not forewarnings – well!'

He sat down again, and studied certain paragraphs attentively.

EDUCATION BY THE KNOUT

PETERSBURG – All Russia is in a state of unrest and seething with discontent. The very air is alive with the rumours of tumults on the one hand and of *coups d'état* on the other. The strangest stories are being bandied about as to what is taking place at Kiev, Sula, and all parts of the Empire, in fact, but especially in Moscow. There, it seems, while students and members of the higher classes are being thrown into prison by the hundred – not a few of them being packed off to Siberia – the workers are being treated with quite extraordinary consideration. They are even allowed to say their say and hold public meetings without let or hindrance, a thing unheard of in Russia. In Petersburg itself an ominous state of things prevails, and the city is completely in the hands of the police and the military. The streets are thronged with gendarmes; even private houses are packed with soldiers; and never a week passes without some disorder arising or some public demonstration being made. In February a terrible scene occurred in the house of Nicholas II, a sort of People's Palace. In the course of a theatrical performance there some students threw down from the gallery into the body of the hall leaflets in which they demanded redress of their grievances. The place was crowded with law-abiding people for the most part; nevertheless the gendarmerie who are always within hail, rushed in and simply trampled under foot all who came in their way. One great fellow was seen to deliberately stamp on the face of a poor lad who had fallen, cracking it like a nut. How many were injured is unknown and probably will remain so. On Sunday the state of things was even worse. During the previous week the students had sent to the leading journals, and even to the police, a formal announcement that they intended to hold a demonstration in the Nevsky Prospect to demand in constitutional fashion the redress of their grievances. It was taken for granted that measures would be taken to prevent the meeting, and the Nevsky was crowded for the occasion with the usual loungers and pleasure-seekers. But so far as everyone was aware the police seemed to have done nothing in the matter, and it was known only to a few that the courtyards of the great houses of the neighbourhood were filled with gendarmes and soldiers. Up to twelve o'clock all went well; then quite suddenly not only students but working men began to stream into the Nevsky from every side-street; and within a very few minutes the place was one vast crowd. In the square before the Kazan Cathedral alone there were 3,000 at least. Suddenly seditious cries were raised, red flags were waved, stones were thrown, and in the midst of it all the gendarmes began a mad gallop through the crowd. It was a ghastly sight, for they slashed right and left with their swords, even at the bystanders bent only on escaping. Many were wounded, some were killed – how many no two accounts agree – and in the course of the following week hundreds of arrests were made. Since then other demonstrations of the same kind have been held, and will continue to be held, let the cost be what it may, the students declare, until a clean sweep has been made of the police regime under which Russia is groaning.

THE GATHERING OF THE STORM

M. Baltaicheff's murder has drawn the world's attention to the present state of things in Russia – which is much worse than most people imagine. The present movement is not confined to the students alone, though it is that class which makes most noise. The revolutionary fever has gained a hold of the lower classes – Brains and Brawn as we said yesterday have combined, and the combination is formidable. More significant, however, than anything else, if it be true, is the statement of the *Neue Freie Presse* that during the demonstrations in the Kazan Square in Petersburg a detachment of infantry was called upon to fire upon the crowd, the men thrice refused to obey, were marched back to barracks, no inquiry being subsequently held, and that similar incidents have occurred elsewhere. With universal service the Army is only the people in uniform. Any popular feeling must sooner or later touch the Army, and if the soldiers cannot be depended upon to shoot, the game of absolutism is up. The great cataclysm may be nearer at hand than is generally supposed.

SIGNS OF SMOULDERING REVOLT

PETERSBURG – In two of the districts of the Poltava Government workmen's riots have occurred in consequence of the systematic repression of 'Little Russia' by 'Greater Russia'. The journal *Pridzheprovski Krai* gave the first intimation of the state of affairs, and was promptly suspended for eight months.

PETERSBURG – The murder of the Procurator of the Holy Synod is regarded in a measure as the symptom of the general situation in Russia. It is reported that the château of the Duke of Mecklenburgh in S.E. Russia has been pillaged and destroyed by rioters.

BERLIN – On the arrival of the express train from Berlin at Wirballen on the Russian frontier today, a passenger was arrested, and Nihilist documents were discovered in his trunks. This is the third Nihilist arrest within the fortnight. The Berlin police have received information from Petersburg of numerous revolutionists having recently left France. They are now maintaining from Berlin a vigorous agitation against the Tsar's Government. From London, too, the whereabouts of several suspects have been reported. In most cases the Berlin authorities are powerless to effect arrests, but they always supply full information to Russia, so that suspicious characters are always detained in passing the frontier.

ANARCHY ADVANCING

The *Kreuzzeitung*, which is unusually well-informed in Russian affairs, expresses the opinion that one of the immediate consequences of the triumph of Japan will be a general rising of the Russian peasants against their landlords, and of the army against the aristocracy. The same paper declares that revolutionary agents of Social Democratic tendencies have long been systematically poisoning the minds of the people.

He turned back to THE GATHERING OF THE STORM, and read the ominous paragraph again.

'Warning enough, in all conscience,' he said: 'first, the Public

Prosecutor assassinated at Odessa, then the Chief of Secret Police of Petersburg, then the Procurator of the Holy Synod; and now a hecatombe, sovereign, royalty, aristocracy, government, bureaucracy, all annihilated, and Anarchy *in excelsis*. France will take fire at any minute now, that's absolutely certain. Oh, how horrible! But we're all Christians, Flavio; and this is only one of the many funny ways in which we love one another.'

He rose and went to the window. The yellow cat deliberately stretched himself, yawned, and followed; and proceeded to carry out a wonderful scheme of feints and ambuscades in regard to a ping-pong ball which was kept for his proper diversion. The man looked on almost lovingly. Flavio at length captured the ball, took it between his forepaws, and posed with all the majesty of a lion of Trafalgar Square. Anon he uttered a little low gurgle of endearment, fixing the great eloquent mystery of amber and black velvet eyes, tardy, grave, upon his human friend. No notice was vouchsafed. Flavio got up; and gently rubbed his head against the nearest hand.

'My boy!' the man murmured; and he lifted the little cat on to his shoulder. He went downstairs. He could not work; and he was going to take an easy; and he wanted a novel, he said to his landlady. He feared that he had read all the books in the house. Yes, and those in the drawing-room too. After a quarter of an hour, application to a neighbour produced three miserable derelicts, a nameless sixpenny shudder, a Braddon, and an Edna Lyall. Not to seem ungracious, he took them upstairs; and pitched them into a corner, to be returned upon occasion. That salient trait of his character, the desire not to be ungracious, the readiness to be unselfish and self-sacrificing, had done him incalculable injury. This world is infested by innumerable packs of half-licked cubs and quarter-cultivated mediocrities who seem to have nothing better to do than to buzz about harassing and interfering with their betters. Out of courtesy, out of kindness, he was used to give way; but all the same he tenaciously knew and clung to his original purpose. He knew that delay was his enemy: yet he invariably would stand aside and let himself be delayed. And now towards the end of his youth, he was poor, lonely, a misanthropic altruist.

He returned to his armchair, breathing a long sigh of irritation and exhaustion: broke up three cigarette dottels (for a tobacco famine was afflicting him), rolled them in a fresh paper, and applied a match. Flavio, with an indulgent protestant mew, bounded from his knee to a bedroom chair; and coiled himself up to sleep.

The armchair was placed directly in front of the fireplace, the ordinary garret-coloured iron fireplace and mantel of a suburban lodging-house attic. To the grey wall above the mantel a large sheet of brown packing-paper was tacked. On this background were pinned photographs of the Hermes of Herculaneum, the terracotta Sebastian of South Kensington, Donatello's liparose David and the vivid David of Verrocchio, the wax model of Cellini's Perseys, an unknown Rugger XV prized for a single example of the rare feline-human type, and the O.U.D.S. Sebastian of *Twelfth Night* of 1900. Tucked into the edges of these were Italian picture postcards presenting Andrea del Sarto's young St John, Alessandro Filipepi's Primavera, a page from an old Salon catalogue showing Friant's Wrestlers, another from an old *Harper's Magazine* showing Boucher's Runners, a cheap and lovely chromo of an olive-skinned black-haired cornflower-crowned Pancratius in white on a gold ground, the visiting-cards of five literary agents, and a postcard tersely inscribed *Verro precipitevolissimevolmente*'. The mantel-shelf contained stone bottles of ink, pipes, a miniature in a closed morocco case, a cast of Cardinal Andrea della Valle's seal from Oxford, two pairs of silver spectacles in shagreen cases, four tiny ingots of pure copper, a sponge gum bottle, and an open book with painted covers showing Eros at the knees of Psyche and a mysterious group of divers in the clear of the moon. The door was at a yard to the left of the fireplace, at a right-angle. Uncared for clothes, black serge and blue linen, hung upon it. A small wooden washstand stood between the door and the armchair, convenient to the writer's hand. A straw-board covered the hole in its top; and supported ink-bottles, pens, penknife, scissors, a lamp, a biscuit-tin of cigarette-dottels, sixteen exquisite Greek intagli. On the lower shelf stood a row of books of reference. Between the washstand and the fire was the chair whereon Flavio slumbered (if one may use so indelicate a word of so delicate a cat). About four feet of wall extended on the right of the fireplace. Pinned there were a pencil design for a *Diamastigosis*, a black and white panel of young Sophocles as Choregos after Salamis done on the back of an Admiralty chart, a water colour of Tarquinio Santacroce and Alexander VI, a pair of foils and fencing masks, and a curious Greco-Italian seal showing St George as a wing-footed Perseys wearing what looked like the Garter Mantle and labelled φυλαξ ἀρχης. Substitutes for shelves stood against the lower part of the wall. A rush-basket, closed and full of letters, set up on end, supported files of the *American Saturday Review*, the *Author*, the *Outlook*, the *Salpinx*, *Reynards's*, and the *Pall Mall Gazette*, and a feather broom for dusting books and papers or for correcting Flavio when obstreperous. Another rush-basket, placed length-wise on a bedroom chair, held a row of books, MS. notebooks, duodecimo classics of Plantin, Estienne, Maittaire, with English and American editions of the writer's own works. The third wall was pierced by two small windows, wide open to the full always. A chest of drawers protruded endways into the room. Its top was used as a standing desk. The drawers opened towards the fourth wall. Sheaves of letters in metal clips hung at the end. Between it and the armchair, more shelves were contrived of rush-baskets placed beneath and upon a small wooden table. Books of reference, lexicons, and a box of blank paper, congregated here convenient to the writer's hand. The little table drawer contained notepaper, envelopes, sealing-wax, and stamps. The whole was arranged so that, when once ensconced in the armchair before the fire with his writing-board on his knees, the digladiator could reach all his weapons by a simple extension of his arms. The attic was eleven feet square, low-pitched, and with half the ceiling slanting to the fourth foot from the floor on the fourth wall. Here was a camp-bed, a small mirror, and a towel-rail, three pairs of two-, six-, and ten-pound dumb-bells, a pair of boots on trees, a bottle of eucalyptus, and a spray-producer.

His eyes, as they wandered round the room, met these things. He took a towel, and went downstairs to the bathroom to wash his hands. On returning he enticed Flavio with a bit of string. The cat was unwilling to play: gazed at him with innocent imperscrutable round eyes: elaborately yawned and requested permission to retire. The odour of the kitchen-dinner was perceptible. The door was opened; and shut.

He put the butt of his cigarette in an earthenware jar on his left for future use. The maid appeared with his lunch, a basinful of bread and milk. Following some subconscious train of thought, he stretched himself, took the little mirror from the wall, and went to the window.

'It's one of your bad days, my friend,' he commented, regarding his own image. 'You look all your age, and twelve years more. Draw down those feathered brows, man. Never mind the upright furrow which makes you look stern. Draw them down; and open your eyes; and look alert. Do something to counteract the tender thin line of that mouth. You mustn't let yourself relax like this. It brings out your wrinkles, and shows the sparseness of your hair. If you had an inch more thigh, and say a couple of inches more shin, you might look people down a little more: but with that meek subservient aspect – how Luckock used to chaff about it! – no wonder everyone takes advantage of you. What's the good of having your fastidious mind clearly written on that fastidious mouth if you don't insist on behaving fastidiously. Cultivate the art of looking as though you were about to say No. You always can say Yes after No. But, if you begin with Yes, as you always do, you prevent yourself from ever saying No. That's why everyone can swindle you. You're far too anxious to give way. Buck up a bit, you ugly little thing! Ugly as you are, you're neither vulgar nor commonplace. Straighten your back, and open your eyes wide, and pull yourself together.'

He put the mirror in its place; and again cast a glance round the room, seeking something to read, something, anything that was not too recent in his mind. He picked up at random one of the rejected novels. It was called *Donovan*. He remembered having seen (in an ex–tea–pedlar's magazine) a print of the writer thereof. He also remembered that he had found her self-conscious pose and labial conformation intensely antipathetic. His sense of beauty was a great deal more than acute. Let his predilection (which was for reticent expert virtue in the male and for innate delicate modesty in the female) once be satisfied, and the door to his favour lay open.

'However,' he argued with himself, 'she sells her books by tens of thousands while we don't sell ours by tens of hundreds. We'll have a look at her work, and see how she does it.'

He ate his bread and milk; and seriously and deliberately set himself to dissect and analyse the book.

The manner of the portrayal of a youth, of an abnormal type of youth, the Sentient-Modest type, at once disgusted him by its inadequacy and superficiality. The male human animal is omnipresent: it is not difficult for an observant and careful writer to describe the γνωριμωτερον φυσει, things as they appear. But the author's sex had prevented her from knowing, and therefore from describing, the γνωριμωτερον ἡμιν, things as they are. It is doubtful whether Man ever mentally knew Woman. It is certain that Woman never knew Man: except in cases of occession – the author of *The Gadfly* for example. He found the image of Donovan fairly convincing: not so the real. Donovan, in his eponymous history, obviously was the creation of a good sweet-minded woman, who created him in her own image.

The student several times was at the point of closing the book from sheer annoyance. Only the knowledge that he had nothing else to do, and the desire to gain instruction, caused him to persevere. His temper only was logical in so far as it endowed him with the faculty of pursuance. He began many things: he followed them: oftentimes the influence of Luna on his environment obliged him to pause: but invariably he returned to them – even after long years he returned to them – ; and then, slowly, surely, he concluded what he had begun. He had tenacity – the feline pertinacity of vigorous untainted English blood. Cigarette after cigarette he rolled, and smoked. He frequently turned back and read a chapter over again. Flavio mewed for admittance. He took him on his knee: and continued reading, stroking the little cat meanwhile, tickling his larynx till he purred content. So the dull March afternoon passed. At five, the maid brought a tray containing black coffee and dripping toast. At half past six, he took a bath and attended to his appearance, execrating the pain of his swollen arm and the difficulty of keeping it out of the water. He dined at half past seven on some soup, and haricot-beans with butter, and a baked apple. Meanwhile he counted the split infinitives in the day's *Pall Mall Gazette*. When he was adolescent, an Oxford tutor had said of him that he possessed a critical faculty of no mean order. At the time, he had not understood the saying perfectly: but he cultivated the faculty. He taught himself in a very bitter school, the arts of selection and discrimination, and the art of annihilating rubbish. To this perhaps was due his complete psychical detachment from other men. He trod upon so many worms. And few things are more exasperating than a man of whom it truly may be said 'A chiel's amang ye takin' notes'. After dinner, he returned to his attic with his cup and the coffee-pot: and resumed his task. In time, he forgot the pain of his arm: he even forgot the usual terrified anticipation of the late postman's knock, such was his faculty for concentration. He smoked cigarettes and sipped black coffee now and then, oblivious of Flavio who returned from a walk about eleven and promptly went to sleep on the foot of the bed. A little after midnight, he reached the end of the book: turned back and examined the last chapter again; and put it down.

'Yes,' he said, 'she's a dear good woman. Her book – well – her book is cheap, awkward, vulgar – but it's good. It's unpalteringly ugly and simple and good. Evidently it's best to be good. It pays. . . . Anyhow it's bound to pay in the long run.'

He pushed Flavio's chair to the wall near the door: by its

side he placed the washstand from the left of his armchair. He disposed the armchair also against the wall, leaving a cleared space of garret-coloured drugget between the dead fire and the bed. This was his gymnasium.

'If a book like that pays,' he reflected, 'it must be that there's a lot of people who care for books about the Good. Why not do one of that sort instead of casting folk-lore and history before the publishers who turn and rend you? The pity is that the Good should be so dreadfully dowdy. Evidently $\tau o \ \kappa \alpha \lambda o \nu$ and $\tau o \ \dot{\alpha} \gamma \alpha \theta o \nu$ are just as distinct as they were in the days of the Broad-browed One. Sophisms again! Why can't you be honest and simple instead of subtle and complex? You're just like your own cat ambuscading a ping-pong ball as strategically and as scrupulously as though it were a mouse. For goodness' sake don't try to deceive yourself. It's all very well to pose before the world: but there's no one here to see you now. Strip, man, strip stark. You perfectly know that the Good always is admirable, whether it be dowdy or chic; and that what you call the Beautiful is no more than a matter of opinion, worth – well, generally speaking, not worth six and eightpence.'

He threw all his clothes on the armchair: picked his trousers out of the heap and folded them lengthwise over the towel-rail: powdered his arm with borax and bound cotton-wool over it: looked at his dumb-bells while he brushed his hair: sprayed the room with eucalyptus; and got into bed. Extreme fatigue and pain rendered him almost hysterical. His thoughts expressed themselves in ejaculations when he had tied a handkerchief over his eyes, straightened his legs, and laid his right cheek on the pillow.

'Yes! It pays to be good – just simple goodness pays. I know, oh I know. I always knew it.

God, if ever You loved me, hear me, hear me. *De profundis ad Te, ad Te clamavi.* Don't I want to be good and clean and happy? What desire have I cherished since my boyhood save to serve in the number of Your mystics? What but that have I asked– of You Who made me?

Not a chance do You give me – ever – ever –

Listen! How can I serve You? How be happy, clean, or good, while You keep me so sequestered?

Oh I know of that psalm where it is written that You set apart for Yourself the godly. Am I godly? Ah no: nor even goodly. I'm Your prisoner writhing in my fetters, fettered, impotent, utterly unhappy.

Only he, who is good and clean, is happy. I am clean, God, but neither good nor happy. Not alone can a man be good or happy. Force, which generates no one thing, is not force. All intelligence must be active, potent. I'm intelligent. So, O God, You made me. Therefore I must be active. Of my nature I must act. For the chance to act, I languish. I am impotent and inactive always. He, who wishes to be good, strives to do good. Deeds must be done to others by the doer. Therefore I, in my loneliness, am futile. Friends? And which of them have You left me faithful these twelve years of my solitude, God? Not one. Andrews, faithless; and Aubrey, faithless; Brander, faithless; Lancaster, faithless; Strages, faithless and perfidious; Scuttle also; Fareham, Roole, and Nicholas, faithless; Tatham, faithless; that detestable and deceitful Blackcote who came fawning upon me crying "Courage! You shall suffer no more as you have suffered!" and then robbed me of months and years of labour. Ah! and Lawrence, my little Lawrence, faithless.

Women? What do I know of women. Nothing.

Fiat justitia – well, there's Caerleon. But a bishop is very far above me; and his friendship is only condescension – honest, genial, kind, but – condescension. Still, he wishes me well. I truly think it. But if only he would believe me, trust me, show faith in me, and absolutely trust me – I might do what the mouse did for the lion.

Strong? But why do I name my splendid master. Strong of nature and Strong of name and station, Strong of body and Strong of mind, immensely my superior altogether, knowing all my weakness and all my imperfection: who, to me, is as much like You as any man can be! It is only grand indulgence and urbanity on his part which make him know me; and, when the sun lacks splendour, only then will Megaloprepes need me, only then Kalos Kagathos perchance may need me.

Why, O God, have You made me strange, uncommon, such a mystery to my fellow-creatures, not a "man among men" like other people?

Do I want to appear like other people?

No, no, certainly not: but – Lord God, am I such a ruffian as to merit exile?

Oh of course I'm a sinner, vile and shameful. But, God, look at the wreck which You have let them make of me and my life. You have some purpose in it all. Oh you must have, if You are, God; and I know that You are. O God, I thank You.

But look – haven't I tried and toiled and suffered? Yet You never allow me any satisfaction, any gain or reward for all my trouble. No: but You always let some shameless brigand rob me, snatching the fair fruit of my labours.

Yes: I know how I dream of certain pleasures, certain luxuries, cleanness, whiteness, freshness, and simplicity, and the life of quiet healthful vigorous and serene well-doing, all in secret, and all unostentatious, which, when once I achieve success, I will have. I know all about that. But You know also that I never should use success in that way, if You gave it to me. Now did I ever use success for myself and not for others? No: I couldn't endure the eternal silent wistful vision of Your Maiden-Mother.

You know why I want freedom, power and money – just to make a few people happy, just to put things right a bit, just to make things easy, just to straighten out tangled lives whose tangles make me rage because I myself am helpless. Is that wrong? No – I swear my aim is single and unselfish. I don't want credit even. You well know that you made me all-denuded of the power of loving anybody, of the power of being loved by any. Self-contained, You have made me. I shall always be detached and apart from others.

Murmur? No. I never have murmured – nor will murmur.

Truly, though, I should like to love, to be loved: but, so long I have been alone and lonely, I suppose I must go on like that always till the end. They are frightened of me, even when they come to the very verge of loving. They are frightened because of certain labels which I frequently use to put on others: frightened lest I should fit them also some day with a label. Oh, often they have told me that they wouldn't like me to be against them.

I will stop that, O God, if You desire it. But, instead of it, what? I think You mean me not to waste the one talent. You have given. Then, I beg of You, give me scope. I must act.

No: I am not doing well at present – not my best. Oh, I know it, and I loathe it. All my life is a pose. Somehow or other I have taken the pose, or stolid stupids force me into the pose, of strange recondite haughty genius, very subtle, very learned, inaccessible – everything that's foolish. God, You know what a sham I am: how silly this is: how very little I know really. Don't I know it too? Don't I always tell them? Then they say that I'm modest – me – ha! – modest!

Here's the truth, by my One Hope of Salvation. I am frightened of all men, known and unknown; and of women I go in violent terror: though I always do say superb and hard things to the one, and pretty gentle soft things to the other, while writing pitilessly of them both: for I'm frightened of them, frightened; and I want to avoid them; and to keep them off me. Therefore I pose. And, therefore also, I provide an image which they can worship, like, or loathe, as it pleases, or displeases, or strikes awe – and they generally loathe it. All the time, while they manifest their feelings, I look on like a child at Punch and Judy.

Oh, it's wrong, very wrong, wrong altogether. But what can I do? God, tell me, clearly unmistakably and distinctly tell me, tell me what I must do – and make me do it.'

He got out of bed: took his rosary from his trouser-pocket; and returned. During the fifth meditation on the Finding of The Lord in the Temple, he fell asleep.

*

'Dr Courtleigh and Dr Talacryn?' he repeated as a query, in the tone of one to whom Beelzebub and the Archangel Periel

23

have been announced at eleven o'clock on the morning of a working day.

'Yes,' the maid replied. 'Clergymen. One is that bishop who came before.'

'The bishop who came before! And – What's the other like?'

'Oh, quite old and feeble – rather stoutish – but he's been a fine handsome man in his day. He wears a red neck-tie under his collar.'

'Well – I – am! . . . Thanks. I'll be down in a minute.'

George put his writing-board away and brushed the front of his blue linen jacket, mentally and corporeally pulling himself together.

'Flavio, I should just like to know the meaning of this. I rather wish that I had Iulo here to back me up. If they are meditating mischief, an athletic and quarrelsome youngster, with an eye like a basilisk and a mouth full of torrential English, would be an excellent trump to play. Mischief? What nonsense! Don't you give way to your nerves, man. Respectable epistatai do not habitually engage in mischief, as you are well aware. You have nothing to fear: so put on a mask – the superior one with a tinge of disdain in it – and brace yourself up to resist the devil; and go downstairs at once to see him flee.'

The two visitors were in the dining-room, a confined drab and aniline room rather over-filled with indistinct but useful furniture. When George entered, they stood up – grave important men, of over forty and seventy years respectively, dark-haired and robust, white-haired and of picturesque and supercilious mien. George went straight to the younger prelate: kneeled; and kissed the episcopal ring.

'Your Eminency will understand that I do not wish to be disrespectful,' he said to the senior, with as much quiet antipathy as could be crowded into one man's voice: 'but the Bishop of Caerleon calls himself my friend; and I am at a loss to know to what I may attribute the honour of Your Eminency's presence, or the manner in which you will allow me to receive you.'

'I hope, Mr Rose, that you will accept my blessing as well as Dr Talacryn's,' the Cardinal-Archbishop replied in a voice where hauteur strangely struggled with timidity. He extended his hand. George instantly took it; and respectfully kneeled again, noting that this ring contained a cameo instead of the cardinalitial sapphire. Then he caused his guests to become seated. The atmosphere seemed to him laden with the invigorating aroma of possibilities.

'Zmnts* wishes to ask you a few questions,' the young bishop began; 'and he thought you would not take it amiss if I were present as your friend.'

George shot a glance of would-be affectionate gratitude at the speaker; and turned, saying 'I have been imagining Your Eminency in Rome – in the Conclave.'

'I was there until a fortnight ago; and then – well, you are said to be an expert in the annals of conclaves, Mr Rose, so it will interest you to know that we stand adjourned.'

'For the removal of the Conclave from Rome?'

'Oh dear no! There is no need for removal. The Piedmontese usurpers treat us with profound respect, I'm bound to say. No. We simply stand adjourned.'

'But this is extremely interesting!' George exclaimed. 'Surely it's unique? And may I ask – no, I would not venture to inquire the cause; but, is this generally known? I have seen nothing of it in the papers; and I am not on speaking terms with any Roman Catholics except the –'

'No. It is not generally known; and it is not intended to make an official announcement, for reasons which you will understand, and which, I believe, you will respect.'

'I am much honoured by Your Eminency's confidence,' George purred.

'Certain affairs required my personal presence in England;' the cardinal continued. He was a feeble aged man, almost senile sometimes. He hesitated. He stumbled. But he maintained the progression of the conversation on its hands and

* This onomatopoeia presents the English Catholic pronunciation of 'His Eminency'.

knees, as it were, with 'These are very pregnant times, Mr Rose.'

George went to the door: admitted his cat who was mewing outside; and resumed his seat. Flavio brushed by cardinalitial and episcopal gaiters turn by turn: bounded to his friend's knee: couched; and became still, save for twinkling ears. The prelates exchanged glances.

'But perhaps you will let me say no more on that subject, and come directly to the point I wished to consult you upon.' The cardinal now seemed to have cleared the obstacles; and he archiepiscopally pranced along. 'It has recently been brought very forcibly to my remembrance that you were at one time a candidate for Holy Orders, Mr Rose. I am cognizant of all the unpleasantness which attended that portion of your career: but it is only lately that I have realized the fact that you yourself have never accepted, acquiesced in, the adverse verdict of your superiors.'

'I never have accepted it. I never have acquiesced in it. I never will accept it. I never will acquiesce in it.'

'Would you mind telling me your reasons?'

'I should have to say very disagreeable things, Eminency.'

'Never mind. Tell me all the truth. Try to feel that you are confiding in your spiritual father, whose only desire is to do justice – I may even say to do justice at the eleventh hour.'

'I am inclined indeed to believe that, because you yourself have condescended to come to me. I wish, in fact, to believe that. But – is it advisable to rake up old grievances? Is it desirable to scarify half-healed wounds? And, how did Your Eminency find me after all these years?' The feline temper of him produced dalliance.

'It certainly was a difficult matter at first. You had completely disappeared –'

'I object to that,' George interrupted. He suddenly saw that this was the one chance of his life of saying the right thing to the right person; and he determined to fight every step of the way with this cardinal before death claimed him. 'I object to that,' he repeated. 'I neither disappeared nor hid myself in any way. There was no question of concealment whatever. I found myself most perfidiously deserted; and I went on my way alone, neither altering my habits, nor changing my appearance –'

'There was no implication of that kind, Mr Rose.'

'I am very glad to hear Your Eminency say so. But such things are said. They are the formulae which spite or indolence or foolishness uses of a man whom it has not seen for a month. Sometimes they are detrimental. To me they are offensive; and I am not in a mood to tolerate them.'

The cardinal swallowed the cachet; and proceeded, 'I first wrote to your publishers; and my letters were returned un-opened, and marked *Refused*.'

'That was in accordance with my own explicit directions. A few years ago, the opportunity was given me of drawing a sharp line across my life –'

'You mean –'

'I allude to a series of libels which were directed against me in the newspapers, especially in Catholic newspapers – dirty Celtic wood-pulp –'

'Precisely. But why was that an occasion for drawing what you call a sharp line across your life?'

'Eminency,' said George, calming down and setting out to be concise and categorical, 'scores of people who had known me all my life must have seen that those attacks were libellous, and false. You yourself just have seen that.' He stretched out a hand and opened and shut it, as though claws protruded from velvet and retired. 'Yet only a single one out of all those scores came forward to assure me of friendship in that dreadful moment. All the rest spewed their bile or licked their lips in unctuous silence. I was left to bear the brunt alone, except for that one; and he was not a Catholic. Except from him. I had no sympathy and no comfort whatever. I don't know any case in all my reading, to say nothing of my experience, where a man had a better or a clearer or a more convincing test of the trueness and the falseness of his friends. Not to do any man an injustice, and that no one might call me rash or precipitate in my decision, I waited two years – two whole years. The Bishop of Caerleon came to me in this period of isolation; and one other Catholic, a man of my own trade. Later, that one betrayed me again, so I will say no more of him. Women, of course, I neglect. And the rest unanimously held aloof. Then I published a book; and I told my publishers to refuse all letters which might be addressed to them for me. The sharp line was drawn. I wanted no more fair-weather friends, afraid to stand by me in storms. If, after those two awful years, I had received overtures from my former acquaintances, I really think I should have fulminated at them St Matthew xxv: 41–3 –'

'What is that?'

'"I was an hungred and ye gave me no meat" down to "Depart from me, ye cursed, into aeonial fire". Yes, the sharp line was drawn across my life. I had one true friend, a Protestant. As for the Faith, I found it comfortable. As for the Faithful, I found them intolerable. The Bishop of Caerleon at present is the exception which proves the rule, because he came to me in the teeth of calumny.'

'You are hard, Mr Rose, very hard.'

'I am what you and your Catholics have made me.'

'Poor child – poor child,' the cardinal adjected.

'I request that Your Eminency will not speak to me in that tone. I disdain your pity at this date. The catastrophe is complete. I nourish no grudge, and seek no revenge, no, nor even justice. I am content to live my own life, avoiding all my brother-Catholics, or treating them with severe forbearance when circumstances throw them in my path. I don't squash cockroaches.'

'The effect on your own soul?'

'The effect on my own soul is perfectly ghastly. I positively loathe and distrust all Catholics, known and unknown, with one exception. I have become a rudderless derelict. I have lost all faith in man and I have lost the power of loving.'

'How terrible!' the cardinal sighed. 'And are there none of us for whom you have a kindly feeling? At times, I mean? You cannot always be in a state of white-hot rage, you know.

There must be intervals when the tension of your anger is relaxed, perhaps from sheer fatigue: for anger is deliberate, the effect of exertion. And, in those intervals, have you never caught yourself thinking kindly of any of your former friends?'

'Yes, Eminency, there are very many, clerks and laics both, with whom, strange to say, when my anger is not dynamic, I sometimes wish to be reconciled. However, I myself never will approach them; and they afford me no opportunity. They do not come to me, as you have come.' His voice softened a little; and his smile was an alluring illumination.

'But you would meet them with vituperation; and naturally they don't want to expose themselves to affronts?'

'Oh, of course if their sense of duty (to say nothing of decency) does not teach them to risk affronts – But I will not say before hand how I should meet them beyond this: it would depend on their demeanour to me. I should do as I am done by. For example,' he turned to the ruddy bishop, 'did I heave chairs or china-ware at Your Lordship?'

'Indeed you did not, although I thoroughly deserved both. Yrmnts,'* the young prelate continued, 'I believe I understand Mr Rose's frame of mind. He has been hit very hard; and he's badly bruised. He is a burnt child; and he dreads the fire. It's only natural. I'm firmly convinced that he has been more sinned against than sinning; and, though I'm sorry to see him practically keeping us at arms' length, I really don't know what else we can expect until we treat him as we ourselves would like to be treated.'

'True, true,' the cardinal conceded.

'But it's a pity all the same,' the bishop concluded.

The cardinal audibly thought, 'You have perhaps not many very kindly feelings towards me personally, Mr Rose.'

'I have no kindly feelings at all toward Your Eminency; and I believe you to be aware of my reasons. I trust that I never should be found wanting in reverence to your Sacred Purple:

* This onomatopoeia presents the English Catholic pronunciation of 'Your Eminency'.

but apart from that –' indignant recollection stiffened and inflamed the speaker – 'indeed I only am speaking civilly to you now because you are the successor of Augustine and Theodore and Dunstan and Anselm and Chichele and Chichester, and because my friend the Bishop of Caerleon has made you my guest for the nonce. My Lord Cardinal, I do not know what you want of me, nor why you have come to me: but let me tell you that you shall not entangle me again in my talk. You are going the Catholic way to work with me; and that is the wrong way. Frankness and open honesty is the only way to win me – if you want me.'

'Well, well! You were going to give me your own view of your Vocation.'

'Your Eminency first was about to tell me how you found me after your letters to my publishers had been returned.'

'I applied to several Catholics who, formerly, had been your friends; and, when they could tell me nothing, I had a letter sent to all the bishops of my province directing inquisition to be made among the clergy. Your personality, if not your name, was certain to be known to at least one of these if you still remained Catholic, you know.'

'If I still remained Catholic!' George growled with contemptuous ire.

'People in your position, Mr Rose, have been known to commit apostasy.'

'And it is precisely because people in my position habitually commit apostasy that I decline to do what is expected of me. No. I'll follow my cat's example of exclusive singularity. It would be too obliging and too silly to give you Catholics that weapon to use against me. No, no, Eminency, rest assured that I rather will be a nuisance and poor, as I am, than an apostate and rich, as I might be.'

The cardinal raised his eyebrows. 'I trust you have a worthier motive than that!'

'I mentioned that I was not in revolt against the Faith, but against the Faithful.'

'And the Grace of God?'

'Oh, of course the Grace of God,' George hastened in common courtesy conventionally to adjoin.

The fine dark brows came down again, and the cardinal continued, 'As soon as I had issued the mandate to my suffragans, Dr Talacryn at once furnished the desired information.'

'I see,' said George. Then, 'Where would Your Eminency like me to begin?'

'Tell me your own tale in your own way, dear child.'

George softly and swiftly stroked his little cat. He compelled himself to think intensely, to marshal salient facts on which he had brooded day and night unceasingly for years, and to try to eliminate traces of the acerbity, of the devouring fury, with which they still inspired him.

'Perhaps I'd better tell Mr Rose, Yrmnts, that we've already gone very deeply into his case,' the bishop said. 'It will make it easier for him to speak when he knows that it is not information we're seeking, but his personal point of view.'

'Indeed it will,' said George; 'and I sincerely thank Your Lordship. If you already know the facts, you will be able to check my narrative; and all I have to do is to state the said facts to the best of my knowledge and belief. I will begin with my career at Maryvale, where I was during a scholastic year of eight months as an ecclesiastical subject of the Bishop of Claughton, and where I received the Tonsure. At the end of those eight months, my diocesan wrote that he was unable to make any further plans for me, because there was not (I quote his words) an unanimous verdict of the superiors in favour of my Vocation. This was like a bolt from the blue: for the four superiors verbally had testified the exact contrary to me. Instantly I wrote, inviting them to explain the discrepancy. It was the Long Vacation. In reply, the President averred inability to understand my diocesan's statement: advised me to change my diocese; and volunteered an introduction to the Bishop of Lambeth, in which he declared that my talents and energy (I am quoting again) would make me a very valuable priest. The Vice-president declined to add anything to what he already had told me. A dark man, he was, who hid inability under a guise of austerity. The Professor of Dogmatic Theology said that he never had been asked for, and never had volunteered, an opinion. The Professor of Moral Theology, who was my confessor, said the same; and, further, he superintended my subsequent correspondence with my bishop. You will mark the intentions of that act of his. However, all came to nothing. The Bishop of Claughton refused to explain, to recede, to afford me satisfaction. The Bishop of Lambeth refused to look at me, because the Bishop of Claughton had rejected me. It was my first introduction to the inexorability of the Roman Machine, inexorable in iniquity as in righteousness.'

'Did you form any opinion at this juncture?' the cardinal inquired, waving a white hand.

'I formed the opinion that someone carelessly had lied: that someone clumsily had blundered; and that all concerned were determined not to own themselves, or anyone else but me, to be in the wrong. A mistake had been made; and, by quibbles, by evasions, by threats, by every hole-and-corner means conceivable, the mistake was going to be perpetuated. Had the case been one of the ordinary type of ecclesiastical student (the hebete and half-licked Celtic class I mean) either I furiously should have apostatized, or I mildly should have acquiesced, and should have started in as a pork-butcher or a cheesemonger. But those intellectually myopic authorities were unable to discriminate; and they quite gaily wrecked a life. Oh yes: I formed an opinion; and I very freely stated it.'

'I mean did you form any opinion of your own concerning your Vocation?'

'No. My opinion concerning my Vocation, such as it was and is, had been formed when I was a boy of fifteen. I was very fervent about that time. I frankly admit that I played the fool from seventeen to twenty, sowed my wild oats if you like. But I never relinquished my Divine Gift. I just neglected it, and said "*Domani*" like any Roman. And at twenty-four I became extremely earnest about it. Yes, my opinion was as now, unchanged, unchangeable.'

'Continue,' the cardinal said.

'A year after I left Maryvale, the Archbishop of Agneda was instigated by one of his priests, a Varsity man who knew me well, to invite me to volunteer for his archdiocese. I was only too glad. His Grace sent me to St Andrew's College in Rome. The priest who recommended me, and Canon Dugdale, assured me that, in return for my services, my expenses would be borne by the archbishop. They never were. I was more than one hundred and twenty pounds out of pocket. After four months in College I was expelled suddenly and brutally. No reason ever has been given to me; and I never have been aware of a reason which could justify so atrocious an outrage. My archbishop maintained absolute silence. I did hear it said that I had no Vocation. That was the gossip of my fellow-students, immature cubs mostly, hybrid larrikins given to false quantities and nasal cacophonies. I took, and take, no account of such gossip. If my legitimate superiors had had grounds for their action, grounds which they durst expose to daylight; and, if they frankly had stated the same to me, I believe I should have given very little trouble. As it is, I am of course a thorn, or a pest or a firebrand, or a rodent and purulent ulcer – *vous en faites votre choix*. The case is a mystery to me, inexplicable, except by an hypothesis connected with the character of the rector of St Andrew's College. I remember the Marquess of Mountstuart reading a leading article about him out of the *Scotsman* to me in 1886, and remarking that he was "an awful little liar". But perhaps the right reverend gentleman is known to Your Eminency?'

'Well known, Mr Rose, well known. And now tell me of your subsequent proceedings.'

'I made haste to offer my services to other bishops. When I found every door shut against me, I firmly deliberated never to recede from my grade of tonsured clerk under any circumstances whatever; and I determined to occupy my energies with some pursuit for which my nature fitted me, until the Divine Giver of my Vocation should deign to manifest it to others as well as to myself. I chose the trade of a painter. I was just beginning to make headway when the defalcations of a

Catholic ruined me. All that I ever possessed was swallowed up. Even my tools of trade illegally were seized. I began life again, with no more than the clothes on my back, a book of hours and eight shillings in my pocket. I obtained, from a certain prelate, whose name I need not mention, a commission for a series of pictures to illustrate a scheme which he had conceived for the confounding of Anglicans. He saw specimens of my handicraft, was satisfied with my ability, provided me with materials for a beginning and a disused skittle-alley for a studio; and, a few weeks later (I quote his secretary), he altered his mind and determined to put his money in the building of a cathedral. I think that I need not trouble Your Eminency with further details.'

'Quite unnecessary, Mr Rose.'

'I don't know how I kept alive until I got my next commission. I only remember that I endured that frightful winter of 1894-5 in light summer clothes unchanged. But I did not die; and, by odds and ends of work, I managed to recover a great deal of my lost ground. Then a hare-brained and degenerate priest asked me to undertake another series of pictures. I worked two years for him: and he valued my productions at fifteen hundred pounds: in fact he sold them at that rate. Well, he never paid me. Again I lost all my apparatus, all my work; and was reduced to the last extreme of penury. Then I began to write, simply because of the imperious necessity of expressing myself. And I had much to say. Note please that I asked nothing better than to be a humble chantry-priest, saying Mass for the dead. It was denied me. I turned to express beautiful and holy ideals on canvas. Again I was prevented. I must and will have scope, an outlet for what the President of Maryvale called my "talent and energy". Literature is the only outlet which you Catholics have left me. Blame yourselves: not me. Oh yes, I have very much to say.'

He paused. The cardinal evaded his glance; and intently gazed at the under-side of well-manicured pink-onyx fingernails.

'And about your Vocation, Mr Rose. What is your present opinion?'

George wrenched himself from retrospection. 'My opinion, Eminency, as I already have had the honour of telling you, is the same as it always has been.'

'That is to say?'

'That I have a Divine Vocation to the Priesthood.'

'You persist?'

'Eminency, I am not one of your low Erse or pseudo Gaels, flippertigibbets of frothy flighty fervour, whom you can blow hither and thither with a sixpence for a fan. Thank The Lord I'm English, born under Cancer, tenacious, slow and sure. Naturally I persist.'

Cardinalitial eyebrows reascended. 'The man, to whom Divine Providence vouchsafes a Vocation, is bound to prosecute it.'

'I am prosecuting it. I never for one moment have ceased from prosecuting it.'

'But now you have attained a position as an author.'

'Yes; in the teeth of you all; and no thanks to anyone but myself. However that is only the means to an end.'

'In what way?'

'In this way. When I shall have earned enough to pay certain debts, which I incurred on the strength of my faith in the honour of a parcel of archiepiscopal and episcopal and clerical sharpers, and also a sum sufficient to produce a small and certain annuity, then I shall go straight to Rome and square the rector of St Andrew's College.'

'Sh-h!' the bishop sibilated. The cardinal threw up delicate hands.

'Yrmnts mustn't be offended by Mr Rose's satirical way of putting it,' the bishop hastily put in. 'He's a regular phrase-maker. It's his trade, you know. But at the bottom of his good heart I'm sure he means nothing but what is right and proper. And, George, you're not the man to smite the fallen. Monsignor Cateran was deposed seven years ago and more.'

'I beg Your Eminency's pardon if I have spoken inurbanely; and I thank Your Lordship for interpreting me so generously. I didn't know that Cateran had come to his Cannae. Really I'm sorry: but, I've been stabbed and stung so many years that, now I am able to retaliate, I am as touchy as a hornet with a brand-new sting. I can't help it. I seem to take an impish delight in making my brother-Catholics, especially clerks, smart and wince and squirm as I myself have squirmed and winced and smarted. I'm sorry. I simply meant to say that, when I have made myself free and independent, then I will try again to give you evidence of my Vocation.'

'Have you approached your diocesan recently?' the cardinal inquired.

'His Grace died soon after my expulsion from St Andrew's College. I approached his successor, who refused to hear me; and is dead. I never have approached the present archbishop, beyond giving him notice of my existence and persistence; for I certainly will not come before him with chains on my hands.'

'Chains?'

'Debts.'

'Have you any special reason for belonging to the archdiocese of Agneda?'

'There is a certain fascination in the idea of administering to a horde of unspeakable barbarians, "the horrible and ultimate Britons, ferocious to strangers". Otherwise I have no special reason. I had no choice. I happen to have been made an ecclesiastical subject of Agneda at the instance of Mr George Semphill and at the invitation of the late Archbishop Smithson. That is all.'

'Would you be inclined to offer your services to another bishop now?'

'Eminency, "it is not I who have lost the Athenians: it is the Athenians who have lost me". I would say that in Greek if I thought you would understand me. When the Athenians want me, they will not have much difficulty in finding me. But to tell you the truth, I find these bishop-johnnies excessively tiresome. As I said just now, when Agneda silently relieved himself of his obligations to me, I offered my services to half a dozen of them, more or less, plainly telling them my history and my circumstances. What a fool they must have thought me – or what a brazen and dangerous scoundrel! Yes, I do believe they thought me that. I was astonishingly unsophisticate then. I didn't know a tithe of what I know now; and I solemnly assever that I believe those owl-like hierarchs to have been completely flabbergasted because I neither whimpered penitence, nor whined for mercy, but actually had the effrontery to tell them the blind and naked truth about myself. Truth, nude and unadorned, is such a rare commodity among Catholics, as you know, and especially among the clergy; and I suppose, as long as we continue to draw the majority of our spiritual pastors from the hooligan class, from the scum of the gutter, that the man who tells the truth in his own despite always emphatically will be condemned as mad, or bad, or both.'

'Really, Mr Rose!' the cardinal interjected.

'Yes, Eminency: we teach little children that there are three kinds of lies; and that the Officiose Lie, which is told to excuse oneself or another – the meanest lie of the lot, I say – is only a Venial Sin. It's in the catechism. Well, naturally enough the miserable little wretches, who can't possibly grasp the subtlety of a *distinguo*, put undue importance on that abominable word "only"; and they grow up as the most despicable of all liars. Ouf! I learned all this from a thin thing named Danielson, just after my return to the faith of my forefathers. He lied to me. In my innocence I took his word. Then I found him out; and preached on the enormity of his crime. "Well, sir," says he as bold as brass, "it's only a Venial Sin!"'

'George, you're beside the point,' the bishop said.

'His Eminency will indulge me. What was I saying? Oh – that I had had enough of being rebuffed by bishops. I came to that conclusion when His Lordship of Chadsee blandly told me that I never would get a bishop to accept my services as long as I continued to tell the truth about my experiences. I stopped competing for rebuffs then. I do not propose to begin again until I am the possessor of a cheque-book.'

The cardinal was gazing through the leaves of an india-rubber plant out of the window; his magnificent eyes were drained of all expression. When the nervose deliberately hardened and pathetic voice of the speaker ceased, he brought the argument to a focus with these words, 'George Arthur Rose, I summon you to offer yourself to me.'

'I am not ready to offer myself to Your Eminency.'

'Not ready?'

'I hoped that I had made it clear to you that, in regard to my Vocation, I am "marking time", until I shall have earned enough to pay my debts incurred on the strength of my faith in the honour of a parcel of archiepiscopal and episcopal and clerical sharpers, and also a sum sufficient to produce me a small and certain annuity –'

'You keep harping upon that string,' the cardinal complained.

'It is the only string which you have left unbroken on my lute.'

'I see you are a very sensitive subject, Mr Rose. I think that long brooding over your wrongs has fixed in you some such pagan and erroneous idea as that which Juvenal expresses in the verse where he says that poverty makes a man ridiculous.'

'Nothing of the kind,' George retorted with all his claws out. 'On the contrary, it is I – the creature of you, my Lord Cardinal, and your Catholics – who make Holy Poverty look ridiculous!'

'A clever paradox!' The cardinal let a tinge of his normal sneer affect his voice.

'Not even a paradox. A poor thing: but mine own,' George flung in, glaring through his great-great-grandfather's silver spectacles which he used indoors.

'Well, well: the money-question need not trouble you,' said the cardinal, turning again to the window. Indifference was his pose.

'But it does trouble me. It vitally troubles me. And your amazing summons troubles me as well – now. Why do you come to me after all these years?'

'Precisely, Mr Rose, after all these years, as you say. It has been suggested to me, and I am bound to say that I agree with the suggestion, that we ought to take your singular persistency during all these years – how many years?'

'Say twenty.'

'That we must take your singular persistency during twenty years as a proof of the genuineness of your Vocation.'

George turned his face to the little yellow cat, who had climbed to and was nestling on his shoulder.

'And therefore,' the cardinal continued, 'I am here today to summon you to accept Holy Order with no delay beyond the canonical intervals.'

'I will respond to that summons within two years.'

'Within two years? Life is uncertain, Mr Rose. We who are here today may be in our graves by then. I myself am an old man.'

'I know. Your Eminency is an old man. I, by the grace of God, the virtue of my ancestors, and my own attention to my physique, am still a young man; and younger by far than my years. I have not been preserved in the vigour and freshness of youth by miracle after miracle during twenty years for nothing. And, when I shall have published three more books, I will respond to your summons. Not till then.'

'I told you that the money-question need not hinder you.'

'Yes, Eminency; and my late diocesan said the same thing several years ago.'

'You are suspicious, Mr Rose.'

'I have reason to be suspicacious, Eminency.'

The cardinal threw up his hands. The gesture wedded irritation to despair. 'You doubt me?' he all but gasped.

'I trusted Your Eminency in 1894; and – '

The bishop intervened: for cardinalitial human nature burst out in vermilion flames.

'George,' he said, 'I am witness of Zmnts's words.'

'What's the good of that? Suppose that I take His Eminency's word! Suppose that in a couple of months he alters his mind, determines to mistake the large for the great and to perpetrate another pea-soup-and-streaky-bacon-coloured caricature of an electric-light station! What then would be my remedy?

Where would be my contract again? And could I hale a prince of the church before a secular tribunal? Would I? Could I subpoena Your Lordship to testify against your Metropolitan and Provincial? Would I? Would you? My Lord Cardinal, I must speak, and you must hear me, as man to man. You are offering me Holy Orders on good grounds, on right and legitimate grounds, on grounds which I knew would be conceded sooner or later. I thank God for conceding them now.... You also are offering something in the shape of money.' In his agitation, he suddenly rose, to Flavio's supreme discomfiture; and began to roll a cigarette from dottels in a tray on the mantelpiece.

'If I correctly interpret you, you are offering to me, who will be no man's pensioner, who will accept no man's gifts, a gift, a pension –'

'No,' the cardinal very mildly interjected: 'but restitution.'

'Oh!' George ejaculated, suddenly sitting down, and staring like the martyr who, while yet the pagan pincers were at work upon his tenderest internals, beheld the angel-bearers of his amaranthine coronal.

'Amends and restitution,' the cardinal repeated.

'What am I to say?' George addressed his cat and the bishop.

'You are simply to say in what form you will accept this act of justice from us,' the cardinal responded, taking the question to himself.

'Oh, I must have time to think. You must afford me time to think.'

'No, George,' said the bishop: 'take no time at all. Speak your mind now. Do make an effort to believe that we are sincerely in earnest; and that in this matter we are in your hands. I may say that, Yrmnts?' he inquired.

'Certainly: we place ourselves in Mr Rose's hands – unreservedly – ha!' the cardinal affirmed, and gasped with the exertion.

George concentrated his faculties; and recited, rather than spoke, demurely and deliberately and dynamically. 'I must have a written expression of regret for the wrongs which have been done to me both by Your Eminency and by others who have followed your advice, command, or example.'

'It is here,' the cardinal said, taking a folded paper from the fascicule of his breviary. 'We knew that you would want that. I may point out that I have written in my own name, and also as the mouthpiece of the Catholic body.'

George took the paper and carefully read it two or three times, with some flickering of his thin fastidious lips. It certainly was very handsome. Then he said, 'I thank Your Eminency and my brother-Catholics,' and put the document in the fire, where in a moment it was burned to ash.

'Man alive!' cried the bishop.

'I do not care to preserve a record of my superiors' humiliation,' said George, again in his didactic recitative.

'I see that Mr Rose knows how to behave nobly, as you said, Frank,' the cardinal commented.

'Only now and then, Eminency. One cannot be always posing. But I long ago had arranged to do that, if you ever should give me the opportunity. And now,' he paused – and continued, 'you concede my facts?'

'We may not deny them, Mr Rose.'

'Then, now that I in my turn have placed myself in your hands' (again he was reciting), 'I must have a sum of money' – (that paradoxical 'must' was quite in his best manner) – 'I must have a sum of money equal to the value of all the work which I have done since 1892, and of which I have been – for which I have not been paid. I must have five thousand pounds.'

'And the amount of your debts, and a solatium for the sufferings – '

'You no more can solace me for my sufferings than you can revest me with ability to love my neighbour. The paltry amount of my debts concerns me and my creditors, and no one else. If I had been paid for my work I should have had no debts. When I am paid, I shall pay.'

'The five thousand pounds are yours, Mr Rose.'

'But who is being robbed – '

'My dear child!' from the cardinal; and 'George!' from the bishop.

'Robbed, Eminency. Don't we all know the Catholic manner of robbing Peter to pay Paul? I repeat, who is being robbed that I may be paid? For I refuse to touch a farthing diverted from religious funds, or extracted from the innocuous devout.'

'You need not be alarmed on that score. Your history is well known to many of us, as you know: latterly it has deeply concerned some of us, as perhaps you do not know. And one who used to call himself your friend who – ha – promised never to let you sink – and let you sink – one who acquiesced when others wronged you, has now been moved to place ten thousand pounds at my disposal, in retribution, as a sort of sin-offering. I intend to use it for your rehabilitation, Mr Rose – well then for your enfranchisement. Now that we understand each other, I shall open an account – have you a banking account though? – very good: I will open an account in your name at Coutts's on my way back to Pimlico.'

'I must know the name of that penitent sinner: for quite a score have said as much as Your Eminency has quoted.'

'Edward Lancaster.'

'I might have guessed it. Well, he never will miss it – it's just a drop of his ocean – I think I can do as much with it as he can – Eminency, give him my love and say that I will take five thousand pounds: not more. The rest – oh, I know: I hand it to Your Eminency to give to converted clergymen who are harassed with wives, or to a sensible secular home for working boys, or to the Bishop of Caerleon for his dreadful diocese. Yes, divide it between them.'

The prelates stood up to go. George kneeled; and received benedictions.

'We shall see you at Archbishop's House, Mr Rose,' said the cardinal on the doorstep.

'If Your Eminency will telegraph to Agneda at once, you will be able to get my dimissorials to your archdiocese by tomorrow morning's post. I will be at Archbishop's House at half past seven to confess to the Bishop of Caerleon. Your Eminency says mass at eight, and will admit me to Holy Communion. At half past eight the post will be in; and you will give me the four minor orders. Then – well, *then*, Eminency' (with a dear smile). . . . 'You see I am not anxious for delay now. And, meanwhile, I will go and have a Turkish Bath, and buy a Roman collar, and think myself back into my new – no – my old life.'

*

'What does Yrmnts make of him?' the bishop inquired as the shabby brougham moved away.

'God knows! God only knows!' the cardinal responded. 'I hope – Well we've done what we set out to do: haven't we? What a most extraordinary, what a most incomprehensible creature to be sure! I don't of course like his paganism, nor his flippancy, nor his slang, nor his readiness to dictate; and he is certainly sadly lacking in humility. He treated both of us with scant respect, you must admit, Frank. What was it he called us – ha – "bishop-johnnies" – now you can't defend that. And "owl-like hierarchs" too!'

'Indeed no. I believe he hasn't a scrap of reverence for any of us. After all I don't exactly see that we can expect it. But it may come in time.'

'Do you really think so?' said the cardinal; and the four eyes in the carriage turned together, met, and struck the spark of a recondite and mutual smile.

'For my part,' the younger prelate continued, 'I'm going to try to make amends for the immense wrong I did him by neglecting him. I can't get over the feeling of distrust I have of him yet. But I confess I'm strangely drawn to him. It is such a treat to come across a man who's not above treating a bishop as his equal.'

'Did it strike you that he was acting a part?'

'Indeed yes: I think he was acting a part nearly all the time. But I'm sure he wasn't conscious of it. He's as transparent and guileless as a child, whatever.'

'It seemed to me that he had all these pungent little speeches cut and dried. He said them like a lesson.'

'Well, poor fellow, he's thought of nothing else for years; and I find, Yrmnts, that mental concentration, carried to anything like that extreme, gives a sort of power of prevision. I really believe that he had foreseen something, and was quite prepared for us.'

'Strange,' said the cardinal, whose supercilious oblique regard indicated dearth of interest in ideas that were out of his depth.

'He behaved very well about the money though?'

'Very well indeed. But, what a fool! Well, Frank, we can only pray that he may turn out well. I think he will. I really think he will. I hope and trust that we shall find the material of sanctity there. An unpleasant kind of sanctity perhaps. He will be difficult. That singular character, and the force which all those self-concentrated years have given him: oh, he'll never submit to management, depend upon it. Frank, I've seen just that type of face among academic anarchists. It will be our business to watch him, for he will go his own way; and his way will have to be our way. It won't be the wrong way: but – oh yes, he will be very difficult. Well. God only knows! Will you be on the look-out for a telegraph office, Frank, while I get through my Little Hours? Perhaps we had better –'

The cardinal opened his breviary at Sext; and made the sign of the cross.

*

George returned to the dining-room; and sat down in the cane folding-chair which the cardinal had vacated. He lighted the cigarette rolled during conversation. Flavio had taken possession of the seat lately occupied by the bishop, a deep-cushioned, wickerwork armchair; and was very majestically posed, haunches broad and high and yellow as a cocoon, the beautiful brush displayed at length, forepaws daintily tucked inward under the paler breast, the grand head guardant.

A shameless female began to shriek scales and roulades in an

The bishop locked the parlour door: took the crucifix from the mantel and stood it on the table: kissed the cross embroidered on the little violet stole which he had brought with him, and put it over his shoulders. He sat down rectangularly to the end of the table, his left cheek toward the crucifix, his back to the penitent. George kneeled on the floor by the side of the table, in face of the crucifix: made the sign of the cross; and began,

'Bless me, O father, for I have sinned.'

'May The Lord be in thine heart and on thy lips, that thou with truth and with humility mayest confess thy sins, ✠ in the Name of the Father and of the Son and of the Holy Ghost. Amen.'

'I confess to God Almighty, to Blessed Mary Ever-Virgin, to Blessed Michael Archangel, to Blessed John Baptist, to the Holy Apostles Peter and Paul, to all Saints, and to thee, O Father, that I excessively have sinned in thought, in word, and in deed, through my fault, through my fault, through my very great fault. I last confessed five days ago: received absolution: performed my penance. Since then I broke the first commandment, once, by being superstitiously silly enough to come downstairs in socks because I accidentally put on my left shoe before my right: twice, by speaking scornfully of and to God's ministers. I broke the third commandment, once, by omitting to hear mass on Sunday: twice, by permitting my mind to be distracted by the brogue of the priest who said mass on Saturday. I broke the fourth commandment, once, by being pertly pertinacious to my superior: twice, by saying things to grieve him –'

'Was that wilful?'

'Partly. But I was annoyed by his manner to me.'

'What had you to complain of in his manner?'

'Side. He had used me rather badly: he came to make amends: I took umbrage at what I considered to be the arrogance of his manner. I was wrong. I confess an ebullition of my own critical intolerant impatient temper, which I ought to have curbed.'

'Is there anything more on your conscience, my son?'

'Lots. I confess that I have broken the sixth commandment, once, by continuing to read an epigram in the Anthology after I had found out that it was obscene. I have broken the eighth commandment, once, by telling a story defamatory of a royal personage now dead: I don't know whether it was true or false: it was a common story, which I had heard; and I ought not to have repeated it. I have broken the third commandment of the Church, once, by eating dripping-toast at tea on Friday: I was hungry: it was very nice: I made a good meal of it and couldn't eat any dinner: this was thoughtless at first, then wilful.'

'Are you bound to fast this Lent?'

'Yes, Father. . . . Those are all the sins of which I am conscious since my last confession. I should like to make a general confession of the chief sins of my life as well. I am guilty of inattention and half-heartedness in my spiritual exercises. Sometimes I can concentrate upon them: sometimes I allow the most paltry things to distract me. My mind has a twist towards frivolity, towards perversity. I know the sane; and I love and admire it: but I don't control myself as I ought to do. I say my prayers at irregular hours. Sometimes I forget them altogether.'

'How many times a week on an average?'

'Not so often as that: not more than once a month, I think. The same with my Office.'

'What Office? You haven't that obligation?'

'Well no: not in a way. But several years ago, when I received the tonsure, I immediately began to say the Divine Office –'

'Did you make any vow?'

'No, Father: it was one of my private fads. I was awfully anxious to get on to the priesthood as quickly as possible; and, as soon as I was admitted to the clerical estate, I busied myself in acquiring ecclesiastical habits. I wrote the necessary parts of the Liturgy on large sheets of paper, and pinned them on my bedroom walls; and I used to learn them by heart while I was

48

dressing. The Office was another thing. I said it fairly regularly for about three years. Sometimes a bit of nasty vulgar Latin, for which someone merited a swishing, shocked me; and I stopped in the middle of a lection – it generally was a lection – but I never relinquished the practice for more than a day. Circumstances deprived me of my breviary: but I kept a little book of hours; and I went on, saying all but mattins and lauds. It wasn't satisfactory; and I had no *Ordo*; and, after a month or two I gave it up. Then I began to say the *Little Office*; and that is of obligation, because I have made my profession in the Third Order of St Francis. I added to it the *Office for the Dead* to make up a decent quantity. But I have not been regular. The same with my duties. Generally, I go to confession and communion once a week: but sometimes I don't go on the proper days. Sometimes I miss mass on holidays for absurd reasons. Yes, often. I generally hear mass every day; and, when I fail, it always is on a holiday – '

'Explain, my son.'

'I live between two churches: the one is half an hour away: the other, a quarter – '

'Have you been obliged to live where you do?'

'Yes: as far as one is obliged to do a detestable inconvenient thing. I did not choose the place. A false friend enticed me there, absconded with some papers of mine, and obliged me to stay there, and rot there – '

'Continue, my son.'

'When I am well disposed, I go to the distant church. When I am lazy, I don't go at all – this only refers to holidays – because at the near one I should have to encounter the scowls of a purse-proud family who knew me when I was well-off, and who glare at me now as though I committed some impertinence in using a church which they have decorated with a chromo-lithograph. Also I detest kneeling in a pew like a Protestant, with somebody's breath oozing down the back of my collar. I can hear mass with devotion as well as with aesthetic pleasure in a church which has dark corners and no pews. I've never seen one in this country where I can be unconscious of the

49

hideous persons and outrageous costumes of the congregation, the appalling substitute for ecclesiastical music, the tawdry insolence of the place, the pretentious demeanour of the ministers. Things like these distract me; and sometimes keep me away altogether. I like to worship my Maker, alone, from a distance, unseen of all save Him. You see, among the laity, I am as a fish out of water: because I am a clerk, whose place is not without but within the *cancelli*. However, I confess that I habitually more or less am guilty of neglect of duty, on grounds which I know to be fantastic and sensuous and indefensible. I confess that I have used irreverent expletives, such as 'O my God' and 'Damn'. Not very often. . . . I confess that I am imperfectly resigned to the Will of God. I very often think that I do not know and cannot know what is God's Will. I generally follow my instincts: not, of course, when I know them to be sinful. I generally resist those. But, in planning my life, in trial, when I really want to know God's Will, I have no test which I can apply to the operations of my intellect. I am not alluding to dogma. I implicitly take that from the Church. I mean life's little quandaries. Years ago, I used to consult my confessor. I never got an apt or an illuminating or even an intelligent response. Time was short: there were a lot of people waiting outside the confessional: or His Reverence had been interrupted in the middle of his Office. An inapplicable platitude was pitched at me; and of course I went away in a rage. Later, I grew to think that man ought not to shirk his personal responsibility: that he ought to be prepared to decide for himself and face the consequence. I gave up consulting the clergy, except upon technical points. I do my best, by myself; and I pray God to be merciful to my mistakes. I earnestly desire to do His Will in all things: but I often fail. For example, I can't stand pain. It makes me savage, literally. I don't bear chastisement submissively. I confess all my failures. I was lacking in filial respect towards my parents. I have been irreverent and disobedient to my superiors. I have argued with them, instead of meekly submitting my will to theirs. I have given them nicknames, labels that stick, that annoy them by revealing mental and corporeal characteristics of which they are not proud. For example, I said that the violet legs of my college rector were formed like little Jacobean communion-rails; and I nicknamed a certain domestic prelate the Greek for 'Muddy-Mind', βορβοροθυμος. I haven't done these things out of really vicious wanton cruelty: but out of pride in my own powers of penetration and perception, or out of culpable frivolity. I confess that I have been wanting in love, patience, sincerity, justice, towards my neighbour. Selfishness, self-will, and a fatuous desire to be distinct from other people, have caused these breaches of God's law. That desire nearly always is unconscious or subconscious: seldom deliberate. I am un-kind with my bitter tongue and pen: for example, I made a jibe of the scrofula of a publisher. I am impatient with mental or natural weakness: for example I brought tears into a school-boy's eyes by my remarks when he recorded Edward III's words to Philippa in reference to the six burgesses of Calais as 'Damn, I can deny you nothing, but I wish you had been otherwhere'. I am insincere, sinfully not criminally. I mean that I delight in bewildering others by posing as a monument of complex erudition, when I really am a very silly simpleton. I am unjust, in my readiness to judge on insufficient evidence: by my habit of believing all I hear – that's a tremendously salient fault of mine – and by telling or repeating detrimental stories. I confess the sin of detraction. I have told improper stories: not of the ordinary revolting kind, but those which are exquisite or witty or recondite. The coprolalian kind, those which are common in colleges and among the clergy, I have had the injustice to label 'Roman Catholic Stories'. If it were necessary to designate them with particularity, the classic epithet 'Milesian' would serve: but it is never necessary. I have not often offended in this way: but now and then, according to the company in which I have happened to be. I confess that I have sinned against myself – for example, I have not avoided ease and luxury. I have only been too glad to enjoy them when they came in my way. I have been fastidious in my person, my tastes, my dress, affecting delicate habits, likes, and dislikes. I hate getting up early in the morning; and do it with a bad grace. I am dainty in my diet. I never have conquered my natural antipathy to flesh-meat, especially to entrails such as sweet-breads and kidneys. I abhor fish-meat on account of its abominable stench. Formerly, I never would sit at a table where fish-meat was served. I can do that now, with an effort of will: but I could not eat fish without physical nausea. I never will eat it. Once I made a man sick by the filthy comparison which I used in regard to some oysters which he was about to eat. . . . I have not avoided dangerous occasions of sin: I have not been prompt to resist temptation. For example, my desire to improve my knowledge leads me to minute appreciation and analysis of everything which interests me. In regard to the fine arts, I study the nude, human anatomy, generally with no emotion beyond passionate admiration for beauty. I never have been able to find beauty shameful: ugliness, yes. In regard to literature, I have read prohibited books and magazines – the *Nineteenth Century*, and books ancient and modern which are of a certain kind. My motive always has been to inform myself. I perfectly have known into what areas of temptation I was straying. As a rule, no effect has been produced on me, save the feeling of disgust at writers who write grossly for the sake of writing grossly, like Straton, or Pontano. I confess that two or three times in my life I have delighted in impure thoughts inspired by some lines in Cicero's Oration for M. Coelius: and, perhaps half a dozen·times, by a verse of John Addington Symonds in the *Artist*. I confess that I have dallied with these thoughts for an instant before dismissing them. There is one thing which I never have mentioned in confession to my satisfaction. I mean that I have mentioned it in vague terms only. I have not felt quite sure about it. I know that I cannot think of it and of the stainless purity of the Mother-Maid at the same time. Hence I conclude that I am guilty – '

'Relieve your mind, my son.'

'About fourteen years ago, I dined with a woman whose husband was a great friend of mine. Her two children dined with us – a girl of fifteen, a boy of thirteen. Her husband was away on business for a few months. Soon after dinner, she sent the children to bed, A few minutes later she went to say good night to them: she was an excellent mother. I remained in the drawing-room. When she returned, I was standing to take my departure. As she entered, she closed the door and switched off the electric light. I instinctively struck a match. She laughed, apologizing for being absent-minded. I said the usual polite idioms and went away. A fortnight later, I dined there again by invitation. All went on as before: but this time, when she came back from saying good night to the children, she was wearing a violet flannel dressing-gown. I said nothing at all; and instantly left her. Afterwards, I gave her the cut direct in the street. I never have spoken to her since. Her husband was a good man, a martyr, and I immensely admired him. He died a few years later. I have no feeling for her except detestation. She was wickedly ugly. Vague thoughts ensued from these incidents; thoughts not connected with her but with some sensuous idea, some phasma of my imagination. They never were more than thoughts. I think that I must have delighted in them, because they returned to me perhaps twelve or fourteen times in as many years. I confess these sins of thought. Also, I think that I ought to confess myself lacking in alacrity after the first switching off of the electric light; and that I never ought to have remained alone with that woman again. I was ridiculously dense: for, only after the second event, did I see what the first had portended. I confess that I have not kept my senses in proper custody. I place no restraint whatever upon sight, hearing, taste, smell, touch, except in so far as my natural sympathies or antipathies direct me. I cultivate them and refine them and sharpen them: but never mortify them. I hardly ever practise self-denial. Even when I do, I catch myself extracting elements of aesthetic enjoyment from it. For example, I was present at the amputation of a leg. Under anaesthetics, directly the saw touched the marrow of the thigh bone, the other leg began to kick. I was next to it; and the surgeon told me to hold it still. It was ghastly: but I did. And then I actually caught myself admiring the exquisite silky texture of human skin. . . . Father, I am my Master's most unfaithful servant. I am a very sorry Christian. I confess all these sins, all the sins which I cannot remember, all the sins of my life. I implore pardon of God; and from thee, O Father, penance and absolution. Therefore I beseech blessed Mary Ever-Virgin, blessed Michael Archangel, Blessed John Baptist, the Holy Apostles Peter and Paul, all Saints, and thee, O Father, to pray for me to The Lord our God.'

'My son, do you love God?'

From silence, tardily the response emerged, 'I don't know. I really don't know. He is Δημιουργός, Maker of the World to me. He is Το 'Αγαθον to me, Truth and Righteousness and Beauty. He is Πανταναξ, Lord of All to me. He is First. He is Last. He is Perfect. He is Supreme. I believe in God, the Father Almighty; I believe in God the Son, Redeemer of the World; I believe in God the Holy Ghost, the Lord, the Life-giver; One God in Trinity and Trinity in Unity. I absolutely believe in Him. There isn't in my mind the slightest shade of a question about Him. I unconditionally trust Him. I am not afraid of Him, because I can't think of Him as anything but righteous and merciful. To think otherwise would be both absurd and unfair to myself. And I'm quite sure that I'm ready and willing and delighted to make any kind of sacrifice for Him. I don't know why. So far, I clearly see. Then, in my mind, there comes a great gap – filled with fog.'

'Do you love your neighbour?'

'No, I frankly detest him, and her. Let me explain. Most people are repulsive to me, because they are ugly in person: more, because they are ugly in manner: many, because they are ugly in mind. Not that I never met people different to these. I have. People have occurred to me with whom I should like to be in sympathy. But I have been unable to get near enough to them. I seem to be a thing apart. I can't understand my neighbour. What satisfies him does not satisfy me. Once I induced a young lover to let me read his love-letters. He brought them every day for a week. His love had appeared to be a perfect idyll, pure and lovely as a flower.

Well – I never read such rot in my life: simply categories of features and infantile gibberish done in the style of a housemaid's novelette. It made me sick. This kind of thing annoys me, terrifies me. You see, I want to understand my neighbour in order to love him. But I don't think I know what love is. But I want to – badly.'

'Do you love yourself?'

'Father, do you mean the essence of me, or the form?'

'Yourself?'

'Well, of course I look after my body and cultivate my mind: I'm afraid I don't pay enough attention to my soul. I certainly don't admire my person. That's all wrong. I can pick out a hundred deviations from the canon of proportion in it. Lysippos would have had a fit. And the tint is not quite pure. I make the best of it: but I don't think it matters much. As for my mind, I suppose I'm clever in a way, compared with other people: but I'm not half as clever as I'm supposed to be, or as I should like to be. In fact I'm rather more of a stupid ignoramus than otherwise. Naturally I stick up for myself, when I care to, against others: but, to myself, I despise myself. Oh I'm not interesting. On the whole, I think that I despise myself, body, mind, and soul. If I thought that they would be any good to anyone else, I'd throw them away tomorrow – if I could do it neatly and tidily and completely and with no one there to make remarks. They're no particular pleasure to me –'

'My son, tell me what would give you pleasure.'

'Nothing. Father, I'm tired. Really nothing – except to flee away and be at rest.'

'My son, that is actually the longing of your soul for God whatever. Cultivate that longing, oh cultivate it with all your powers. It will lead you to love Him; and then your longing will be satisfied, for God is love, as St John tells us. Thank Him with all your heart for this great gift of longing: besiege Him day and night for an increase of it. At the same time, remember the words of Christ our Saviour, how He said, *If ye love Me, keep My Commandments*. Remember that He definitely commands you to love your neighbour. *This is My*

Commandment, that ye love one another as I have loved you.
Mortify those keen senses of that vile body, which by God's
grace you are already moved to despise. In the words of St
Paul, keep it under and bring it into subjection. And do try
to love your neighbour. Lay yourself out to be his servant: for
Love is Service. Serve the servants of God; and you will learn
to love God; and His servants for His sake. You have tasted the
pleasures of the world, and they are as ashes in your mouth.
You say that there is nothing to give you pleasure. That is a
good sign. Cultivate that detachment from the world which is
but for a moment and then passeth away. In the tremendous
dignity to which you are about to be called – the dignity of the priesthood – be ever mindful of the vanity of
worldly things. As a priest, you will be subject to fiercer tempta-
tions than those which assault you now. Brace up the great
natural strength of your will to resist them. Continue to
despise yourself. Begin to love your neighbour. Continue –
yes, continue – unconsciously, but soon consciously, to love
God. My son, the key to all your difficulties, present and to
come, is Love. . . . For your penance you will say – well, the
penance for minor orders is rather long – for your penance
you will say the Divine Praises with the celebrant after mass.
Now renew your sorrow for all your past sins, and say after
me, "O my God – because by my sins I have deserved hell – and
have lost my claim to heaven – I am truly sorry that I have
offended Thee – and I firmly resolve – by Thy Grace – to avoid
sin for the time to come. O my God – because Thou art infinitely
Good – and Most Worthy of all love – I grieve from my heart
for having sinned against Thee – and I purpose – by Thy Grace
– never more to offend Thee for the time to come" . . . *ego te
absolvo* ✠ *in Nomine Patris et Filii et Spiritus Sancti*. Amen. Go
in peace and pray for me.'

*

When, a couple of hours later, George actually found himself
door-keeper, reader, exorcist, and acolyth, he noted also with
some exasperation that he was in his usual nasty morning tem-

56

per. He sat down to breakfast with the cardinal and the bishop in anything but a cheerful frame of mind. They had said a few civil kind-like words to him after the ceremonies: *ad multos annos* and a sixpenny rosary emanated from his new ordinary: but, in the refectory, they left him to himself while they ate their eggs and bacon discussing the news of the day. He chose a cup of coffee, and soaked some fingers of toast in it. His idea was to bring himself into harmony with his novel environment. Environment meant so much to him. Now, he no longer was an irresponsible vagrant atom, floating in the void at his own will, or driven into the wilderness by some irresistible human cyclone: but an officer of a potent corporation, subject to rule, a man under authority. His pose was to be as simple and innocuous as possible, alertly to wait for orders; and, at the present moment, to win a merit from a contemplation of the honour which was his in being received as a guest at the cardin-alitial table. He turned his head to the left, wondering whether mere accident had placed him at His Eminency's right hand where the light from the window fell full upon him. He studied the singularly distinct features of his diocesan, who was reading from *The Times* of the outbreak of revolution in France, where General André's army reforms of 1902, the blatant scandalous venality of Combes and Pelletan, and the influence of that frightful society of school-boys called Les Frères de la Côte, had thrown the military power into the hands of Jaurès and his anarchists, revived the Commune, and broken off diplomatic relations with the Powers. Dreadful! His Eminency feared that he would be obliged to return to Rome by the sea-route, unless, perhaps, he could go comfortably through Germany. Oh, very dreadful!

George listened, regretting that he had not the paper and a cigarette all to himself: but the coffee was not bad; and the ponderous irritation of his matutinal headache was disappearing. He took another cup. He remembered how he had laughed at an Occ. Note in the *Pall Mall Gazette* some few months before, to the effect that the old tradition of antipathy between the two peoples separated by the Channel was as dead as

Georgian England and the era of the Bien-Aimé, and suggesting that the two leading democracies of the world – (England a democracy indeed!) – ought to live on terms of good understanding and neighbourliness, or some such tomfoolery. How could two walk together unless they were agreed? And on what single permanent and vital essential were England and France agreed? George could think of none, any more than Nelson could. Commerce? Yes, perhaps some fools thought so, forgetful that commerce fluctuates from day to day, and that it is the spawning-bed of individual and international rivalry. No. He had no confidence in France. She openly had been accumulating combustibility these five years; and here was the conflagration. This seemed to be a thoroughly French revolution, sudden, sanguinary, flamboyant, engendered by self-esteem on instability, and produced with *élan* and theatrical effect. Brisk and prompt to war, soft and not in the least able to resist calamity, fickle in catching at schemes, and always striving after novelties – French characteristics remained unaltered twenty centuries after Julius Caesar made a note of them for all time.

George detected himself in the very act of affixing a label to a nation. He brought down his will with a thud on his critical faculty. The bishop looked at the cardinal, suggesting that Mr Rose was accustomed to smoke over his meals.

'Don't you find it bad for the digestion?' the cardinal inquired in the tone of an archbishop to an acolyth. An access of genial gentlehood, and something else, to which George at the moment was unable to put a name, suddenly infused his manner when he had spoken.

'I don't think I have a digestion. At least it never manifests itself to me.'

'Happy man!' the cardinal exclaimed to no one in particular: adding, 'Well perhaps we might go upstairs; and Mr Rose can have his cigarette and listen to me at the same time.'

The room to which they went was a private cabinet, a very vermilion and gold room, large, airy, princely. The cardinal took a long envelope from the bureau.

'I think you will find that correct, Mr Rose,' he said. 'You had better open it before we go any further.'

The contents were a blank cheque-book, and a bank-book containing Messrs Coutts's acknowledgement of the credit of ten thousand pounds to the current account of the Reverend George Arthur Rose.

Notwithstanding his natural hypersensibility, that peculiar individual did not become the plaything of his emotions until some time after the event which brought them into action. At the moment when blows or blessings fell upon him, he rarely was conscious of more than a crab is conscious of when its shell is struck or stroked. Later, when he deliberately set himself to analyse consequences, all his senses throbbed and tingled. But, at first, he was wont to act, on the impulse certainly – but to act. Having acquainted himself with the contents of the envelope, he took out his beloved Waterman, saying

'I'm sure Your Eminency will let me have the pleasure of writing my first cheque here.'

He handed to the cardinal a draft for five thousand pounds, payable to bearer. It afterwards occurred to him that he could have taken no more cynical way of testing the reality of this fortune. He felt ashamed of himself, for he hated cynicism. The act itself merely was the act of a man awakening from a vivid dream and automatically doing what he had resolved, before falling asleep, to do. In effect, it was by way of being a pinch of a kind to himself. There was no doubt whatever but that it was a pinch of another kind to the cardinal. Followed alternately disclaimers, stolidity, embarrassment, humility, unction: the cheque went into the bureau, the cheque-book and the bank-book into the pocket of George's jacket.

And now, what was the extent of his theological studies? His general knowledge of course was unexceptional; but special knowledge – theology? Well, in Dogma he had done the treatises *On Grace* – 'a very difficult treatise, Mr Rose' – and *On the Church* – 'a very important treatise, Mr Rose'; – and in Moral Theology he had read Lehmkuhl, especially *On the*

Eucharist and *On Penance* – 'nothing could be better, Mr Rose'. These had been the subjects of the professorial lectures at Maryvale. During the years which had elapsed since then, he had read them again and again, until he thought he had them at his fingers' ends. As for Cardinal Franzelin's *De Ecclesia* (that was the Maryvale text-book), he found it one of the most fascinating books in the world. In fact, it was a regular bedside book of his: and by this time he knew it by heart. Being a man of letters, of course he would like to enlarge it a little, to put a gloss upon it here and there, perhaps even to expand the thesis at certain points. St Augustine's *Enchiridion* was another favourite book. And St Anselm's *Cur Deus Homo* was another. His reading was extensive and curious: but, sad to say, desultory and unsystematic, because undirected. He had read the standard works as a matter of duty: but he had made a far more exhaustive study of obscure writers. The occult, white magic *bien entendue*, was intensely interesting, the book on *Demoniality* by Fr Sinistrari of Ameno, for example. Perhaps it would be desirable for him to tabulate the sum of his studies, that His Eminency might decide whether to have him examined in those or to submit him to a fresh course.

'Quite unnecessary, Mr Rose. And now touching the matter of ceremonial.'

He had made a point of mastering Martinucci, practice as well as theory. It was astonishing what a lot could be done with a guide-book, a few household implements, and imagination. He was aware that he had practised under difficulties: but a few rehearsals beneath the eye of an expert –

'And Canon Law?'

'Nothing at all.'

'Well, well, just those few treatises in Dogmatic and Moral Theology in particular, and a large amount of random reading in general. Of course the Grace of God can supply all our deficiencies. I myself – Things which are hidden from the wise and prudent oft-times are revealed unto – oh yes! Well, Mr Rose, it is not a large, or, humanly speaking, an adequate equipment for – for the priesthood, certainly. But we must

60

consider the years which you have waited. Yes. Well, perhaps we had better waste no more time now. Go home and pack your bag: and come and stay with me for a little till we can settle on your future. I shall give you the subdiaconate to-morrow morning; and you can arrange to say your first mass on Sunday in the cathedral.'

'My first mass must be a black mass, Eminency.'

The cardinalitial eyebrows would go up.

'It is a long-planned intention, Eminency: it is all I can do.'

'I quite understand, Mr Rose. You would wish to say your first mass quietly and alone. You shall say it in the private chapel. The Bishop of Caerleon would like to be your assistant; and – ha – I shall be very glad if you will allow me to serve you.'

George looked from the cardinal to the bishop; and back again. After storm, this was calm and peace, with a vengeance.

CHAPTER I

WHAT was causing the special correspondents in Rome to exude the subterfuges, with which (as a *pis aller*) they are accustomed to gain their daily bread, was no such recondite matter after all.

Just as Jews are less commercial, and Jesuits less cunning, so journalists are less capable than they are supposed to be. As a matter of fact, they are quite unscientific persons, in that they go about their business in a fortuitous manner trusting to the human element called 'smartness' for producing their effects. They have not yet realized the instability of all human elements. The superhuman is a sealed book to them. They mean oh so well: but they have no knowledge of first principles. They invariably commit the unpardonable error of confounding universals with particulars: because the influence of fragile or unworthy authority, custom, the imperfection of undisciplined senses, and concealment of ignorance by ostentation of seeming wisdom, are as stumbling-blocks which obstruct their path to Truth. Add to this a lack of sympathetic intuition and of an historical knowledge of their subject. They take no end of pains to acquire a fluid style of writing; and it may be admitted that, within their limitations, they can describe the superficies of almost anything which may be shoved under their noses. But, as for giving a scientific description (under such heads, for example, as the Material, Formal, Efficient, and Final Causes,) so that one can derive a satisfactory understanding of the thing described – that is beyond their power. And, as for proceeding in a scientific manner, whether by means of the liberal or the so-called occult arts, to what on the whole is the essence of their business, viz. the collection of news, why Sir Notyet Apeer's young men, or Sir Uriah Tepeddle's criminal-investigators, or the 'yearnest' exoletes who fill the *Daily Anagraph* with food for literary lionlets and Roman Catholic clergy and nonconforming philanthropists, have no such adequate ideal of their branch of literature. Their aim is to please editors or proprietors; and, so, to earn an as-near-as-may-be-legally honest living. No more.

Consequently, when (during March and April) a score or so of these good gentlemen found themselves in Rome, with the doors of the Conclave bricked-up in their faces, the windows boarded and canvas-covered, and even the chimneys (with one exception) capped, they knew no better than to curse quite quietly all to themselves, to say that nothing was happening because they could not see what was happening, and to write dicaculous descriptions of the crowd, and the seven puffs of smoke (which on seven separate occasions distracted the said crowd), in the square of St Peter's.

For, if there be one place in all this orb of earth where a secret is a Secret, that place is a Roman Conclave. It is due to the superlative incompetency of the spies. Ignorant of their subject, they cannot seize its saliencies: they cannot move a hair's breadth out of their conventional groove, notwith-standing that common sense should teach them the imperative necessity for applying unconventional methods to uncon-ventional cases. When once we have emerged from the banal blinding stifling paralysing obfuscation of the nineteenth century (and that should be in about ten years' time) it will be obligatory for 'Our Special Correspondent' to add two things to his professional apparatus. The first is the power of mind-projection, as well as that other power of will-projection which, already, up-to-date practical common-sense men of the world like the Jesuits use to such advantage. The second is a round matter, of about two pounds ten ounces' avoirdupois weight including its black-velvet wrapper, which costs forty-two pounds sterling at the mineralogists' in Regent Street.

CHAPTER 2

WELL: this is what was happening in the Roman Conclave.

Cursors had shouted *Extra omnes*: fifty-seven cardinals and three hundred and eleven conclavists had been immured in three galleries of the Vatican. All the ceremonies ordained in 1274 at the Council of Lyons by the Bull of Gregory X had been observed.

The Sacred College was divided into factions. There were five candidates for the paparchy: Orezzo, Serafino-Vagellaio, cardinal-bishops: Ragna, Gentilotto, Fiamma, cardinal-presbyters. Then came groups representing divers nationalities. The French were Desbiens, Coucheur, Lanifère, Goëland, Perron, Mâteur, Légat, Labeur, cardinal-presbyters; and Vaghemestre, cardinal-deacon. The Germans were Rugscha, Zarvasy, Popk, Niazk, cardinal-presbyters. The Spaniards were Nascha, Sañasca, Harrera, cardinal-presbyters. The Erse were O'Dromgoole, O'Tuohy, cardinal-presbyters. The Italians were Moccolo, Agnello, Vincenzo-Vagellaio, cardinal-bishops: Sarda, Ferraio, Saviolli, Manco, Ferita, Creta, Anziano, Cassia, Portolano, Respiro, Riciso, Zafferano, Mantenuti, Gennaio, Bosso, Conella, del Drudo, di Petra, di Bonti, cardinal-presbyters: Macca, Sega, Pietratta, Pepato, della Volta, cardinal-deacons. The English and American cardinal-presbyters Courtleigh and Grace agreed to vote together: so did the Benedictine cardinal-presbyter Cacciatore, and the Capuchin and Jesuit cardinal-deacons Vivole and Berstein. The Portuguese cardinal-prior-presbyter Mundo, and the Bohemian cardinal-presbyter Nefski (who was carried in a litter) posed as independent votes. Cardinal-presbyter Capacitato was absent through the infirmities of age; and, as common report (to say nothing of common knowledge) credited him with the possession of the Evil Eye, Their Eminencies were thankful to think that the fingers, which they would need for inscribing their suffrages, need not be employed in making perpetual horns.

Once walled-up, and the conclavists having been satisfied about their comical constitutional privileges, the cardinals spent the evening in visiting one another in their cells, in discussing the prospects of the five candidates, in canvassing for and promising suffrages. The five themselves were divided into two parties which Ferraio, who was a bit of a wag, denominated in an abstruse jest the Snarlers and the Mewers. A Roman tradition alleges that the letter R (the *litera canina*) exercises an indefinable influence over an election, in that it occurs in the family names of alternate pontiffs. Others declared this tradition to be grounded upon no more sure warranty than old wives' fables (*anicularum lucubrationes*), Serafino-Vagellaio, Gentilotto, Fiamma, gave expression to that theory. Circumlocution aside, there was little to choose between the five. Luigi Orezzo was Cardinal-Bishop, Dean of the Sacred College, Chamberlain of the Holy Roman Church. Mariano Ragna was Secretary of State. Serafino-Vagellaio had been the favourite of a pontiff who had had all the world from which to choose. Hieronimo Gentilotto, nicknamed 'The Red Pope' because he was Prefect of the Society for the Propagation of the Gospel in Foreign Parts, only had the Successor of the Fisherman as his superior. Domenico Fiamma, Archbishop of Bologna, was in the prime of vigorous life and famous for his brilliant intellect and noble mind.

A cardinal is prohibited from voting for himself. Orezzo promised his suffrage to Ragna: Ragna, his to Orezzo: Snarlers should snarl at each other. Serafino-Vagellaio also promised his suffrage to Ragna, having the idea that an official is worthy of observance. But Gentilotto supported Fiamma: and Fiamma, Gentilotto.

Morning saw mass and communion in the Pauline Chapel, and Their Eminencies proceeding to their thrones in the Cystine Chapel. A long silence came to pass. Fat wax tapers glimmered on the altar, on the screen, on the desk before each throne. So the cardinals waited, smoothing violet robes and the white uncovered rochets which indicated that supreme spiritual authority was devolved into their hands. No one was moved to speak. Election was not to be accomplished by the Way of Inspiration.

Masters-of-ceremonies placed, on the table before the altar, two silver basons containing little paper billets. The names of the fifty-seven cardinals were written each on a little snip of parchment. The snips, rolled up, were tucked in holes in fifty-seven lead balls. The balls were dropped into a huge violet burse, one by one, counted by the electors. The burse was well shaken; and Vaghemestre drew out three. The first bore the name Moccolo: the second, Popk: the third Harrera. Thus were elected the Cardinal-Scrutators.

In turn, each cardinal provided himself with a blank billet from the silver basons: retired to his desk: and set about recording his suffrage. At the top of the billet, he wrote 'I, Cardinal' and his name: folded it over: sealed it at each side. At the bottom he wrote his motto: folded it over: sealed it at each side. In the middle, he wrote 'elect to the Supreme Pontificate the Most Reverend Lord my Lord Cardinal' and the name of the candidate to whom he gave his suffrage. Scratching of quills, splashing of scattered pounce, punctuated momentous silence. In obedience to the Bull of Gregory X, some made efforts to disguise their script. The results were hideous. Last, all folded their billets to about the breadth of an inch; and, in turn, each cardinal approached the altar, alone, holding his suffrage at arm's length between the index and middle fingers of his right hand: bent his knee: rising, swore 'I attest, before Christ, Who is to be my judge, that I choose him whom I think fittest to be chosen if it be according to God's will'. A great gold chalice covered by a paten stood on the altar. Each cardinal laid his suffrage on the paten: tipped it until the suffrage slid into the chalice: replaced the paten; and returned to his throne.

Cardinal-Scrutator Moccolo took the chalice by the foot: placed one hand on the paten: and shook, thoroughly to mix the suffrages. The Cardinal-Dean, the Cardinal-Prior-Priest, and the Cardinal-Archdeacon brought down the chalice to the table from which the billet-basons now had been removed. A ciborium stood there. The three Scrutators sat at one side of the table in face of the Sacred College. Harrera counted the suffrages, one by one, from the chalice into the ciborium. There were fifty-seven. A grateful sigh went up. A hitch would have invalidated the scrutiny, giving Their Eminencies the pains of voting and sealing and swearing over again. Moccolo drew out one suffrage: unfolded it without violating the sealed ends: discovered the name of the candidate to whom the vote was given; and passed it to Popk, who also looked at the name; and passed it to Harrera, who read the name aloud.

Each cardinal had on his desk a printed list of the Sacred College. The names ran down the middle of the sheets. To right and left were horizontal lines on which a tally of the votes was kept. As Harrera published the names, he filed each billet, piercing the word 'elect' with a needle through which a skein of violet silk was threaded. When all were filed, he tied a knot in the silk; and laid the bunch of suffrages on the altar.

The Way of Scrutiny at first produced the usual result. The fifty-seven suffrages were so evenly distributed among the five candidates that no one was elected. Orezzo had eight, viz. Ragna, Moccolo, Agnello, Manco, Sarda, Macca, Pepato, di Petra. Ragna had thirteen, viz. Orezzo, Serafino-Vagellaio, Cacciatore, Vivole, Berstein, Nascha, Sañasca, Harrera, Ferita, Pietratta, Bosso, Sega, Conella. Serafino-Vagellaio had eleven, viz. his brother Vincenzo, Rugscha, Zarvasy, Popk, Niask, Gennaio, Cassia, Anziano, Portolano, Creta, di Bonti. Gentilotto had twelve, viz. Fiamma, Desbiens, Coucheur, Lanifère, Goëland, Mâteur, Légat, Perron, Labeur, Vaghemestre, Zafferano, Mantenuti. Fiamma had thirteen, viz. Gentilotto, Courtleigh, Grace, O'Dromgoole, O'Tuohy, Saviolli, della Volta, del Drudo, Respiro, Riciso, Nefski, Ferraio, Mundo. The Way of Access showed that all still were of the same opinion; and that each expected the others to change theirs. A bundle of straw in the stove, the files of pierced suffrages laid thereon, and fire applied, produced the puff of smoke from the chimney in the Square of St Peter's which announced that the Lord God had sent no Pope to Rome that morning.

The cardinals went to dine in their separate cells. After siesta and before prayers those who could walk took exercise in the galleries: others read the *Daily Office* with their chaplains. There was conversation, canvassing. In the evening, they sang

Veni Creator and went to work again. Orezzo gained Anziano and Portolano, raising his total to ten. The nine French and the two Erse, with Ferita, Bosso, Pietratta, Sega, Conella, acceded to Ragna, raising his total to twenty-four. Serafino-Vagellaio kept but five supporters, viz. his brother and the four Germans. Gentilotto lost the nine French: but gained Gennaio, di Bonti, Cassia, Creta, bringing his total to seven. The defection of the two Erse reduced Fiamma's adherents to eleven. And once more the puff of smoke emptied the Square of St Peter's.

Private conferences occupied time: candles burned late into the night. Violet silk robes sussurated between violet serge curtains everywhere. There were colloquies, hints, exhortations, arguments, promises, promises dictated, suggested, given. Ragna took the opinion of his friends concerning a commodious pontifical name. Vivole offered him 'Formosus the Second' and a pinch of Capuchin snuff out of the pages of his breviary: but Berstein preferred 'Aloysius the First'. The Secretary of State would bear both in mind. Cohesion in clots began. The French, Germans, Spaniards, and Erse, already were united in four groups. What the leader of each group would do, the nine, the four, the three, and the two would do. By demonstrating that cardinal-deacons occasionally were raised to Titles, or Suburban sees, by Popes Whom they had elected, Cardinal-Archdeacon Macca collected a little diaconal fraction of four, himself, Pietratti, Sega, and Pepato. Ten Italians, viz. Conella, Manco, di Petra, Ferita, Creta, Cassia, Gennaio, di Bonti, Sarda, Bosso, agreed to vote together. Mundo refused to join the Spaniards; and Nevski, the Germans, on account of sundry events in Poland. Ferraio, Archbishop of Milan, would stick to Fiamma under all circumstances, because they both had been raised to the cardinalature together. Saviolli threw in his lot with the Celtic and American cardinals. Della Volta was in sympathy with Saviolli and his friends. Del Drudo delivered himself of the cryptic sentence that one who had been a major-domo ought to know a fresh egg from a stale one. And Cardinal-Vicar Respiro, and Riciso, Archbishop of Turin, agreed with del Drudo.

So in the morning the third capitular assembly revealed an extraordinary state of affairs. Orezzo lost all his supporters but four, viz. Moccolo, Agnello, Anziano, Portolano. Serafino-Vagellaio lost all votes except his brother's. Gentilotto lost all but three, viz. Fiamma, Zafferano, Mantenuti. Fiamma retained his loyal eleven. And Ragna began to score. First, he kept Orezzo and Serafino-Vagellaio, the Benedictine, the Capuchin, the Jesuit, and the three Spaniards. The nine French (for a wonder) remained constant to him for two consecutive days. So did the two Erse: indeed O'Tuohy, who as a student had vowed that he never would look a woman in the face (and kept his vow) was as persistent as he had been when Leo XIII had tried to force him into the primacy of Eblana in the teeth of electors who rejected him. The four Germans, the four deacons, and the decade of Italians also joined Ragna, whose tally went in jumps (so to speak from two, to five, and eight, and seventeen, and nineteen, and twenty-three, and twenty-seven, and thirty-seven –

According to the Constitution of Alexander III, made at the Council of Lateran in the year of the Fructiferous Incarnation of the Son of God MCLXXX, and confirmed by subsequent Bulls of Gregory XV and Urban VIII, the votes of two thirds of the cardinals present at the Scrutiny are required for the election of a Pope. Not one of Their Eminencies was ignorant of the fact that two thirds of fifty-seven is thirty-eight. Wherefore, when the tallies showed thirty-seven votes for Ragna, and the Junior Scrutator stood up with just one more billet in his hand, some began stertorously to breathe through their noses: some went mauve and some magenta: while those of a phlegmatic habit of body reached for the cords of the canopies above their thrones, which descend at the manifestation of Christ's Vicar.

Harrera read the name 'Ragna'.

What happened next happened very quickly. The Scrutators broke the seals of the billets one by one; and Harrera read aloud the names of the electors as well as the name of the elected. At the thirteenth, he read, *I, Cardinal Mariano Ragna, elect to the*

Supreme Pontificate the Most Reverend Lord my Lord Cardinal Mariano Ragna.

This was a horrid example of the clever strong man, who loses control of his directive faculty, in the moment of excitement. No one could have done such a thing out of wilful wickedness: for the stringency of conclavial regulations effectually denies success to nefarious practices. Everyone knows that. The Secretary of State, by voting for himself just when he was on the verge of achieving the most tremendous of all ambitions, forfeited his own suffrage; and his election was nulled by defect of a single vote. What passions dilacerated his breast, God only knows. He shut up himself in his cell during the rest of the day, horribly snarling. Orezzo, who injudiciously went to sympathize, suddenly came away mouthing and tottering.

The fourth Scrutiny began to show how unpardonable a mistake is. Ragna's ten Italians and four Germans fled to the faction of Fiamma. Ragna himself voted for Serafino-Vagellaio. The tally gave Orezzo, four: Ragna, twenty-three: Serafino-Vagellaio, two: Gentilotto, three: Fiamma, twenty-five.

In the fifth Scrutiny, desertions from Ragna continued. The French nine voted for Orezzo: the three Spaniards for Gentilotto. The tally gave Orezzo thirteen: Ragna eleven: Serafino-Vagellaio, two: Gentilotto, six: Fiamma, twenty-five.

And now the French began to be flighty. In the sixth Scrutiny, they were seen to have dashed from Orezzo to Gentilotto, making the tally of Orezzo four: of Ragna, eleven: of Serafino-Vagellaio, two: of Gentilotto, fifteen: of Fiamma, twenty-five.

Little suburban boys formerly used to satiate their emotions with a phrenetic and turbulent pastime called General Post. The seventh Scrutiny indicated a conclavial propensity for a verisimilar species of energetic dissipation. The four cardinal-deacons, evidently despairing of Ragna, left him. So did the two Erse cardinal-presbyters. The diaconate went over to Gentilotto who lost the French to Serafino-Vagellaio. The Erse voted for the Cardinal-Chamberlain. The seventh puff of smoke from the chimney in the Square of St Peter's was caused by the burning of fifty-seven suffrages allotted thus: Orezzo six: Ragna five: Serafino-Vagellaio eleven: Gentilotto ten: Fiamma twenty-five.

Confabulations, to say naught of protocols, became the order of the day and night. No new candidate was forthcoming. The five candidates flatly refused to retire, or to alter the disposition of their suffrages. Moccolo, Agnello, Anziano, Portolano, refused to desert Orezzo. Zafferano and Mantenuti refused to abandon Gentilotto. Vincenzo-Vagellaio refused to be false to his brother. The Benedictine, the Capuchin, and the Jesuit, refused to forsake Ragna. Fiamma's stalwart twenty-five excited disgust. Ringed and middle fingers were protruded at it. Although there was not a single clean-bred Englishman in its ranks, it was said to be getting 'quite English'; and that is a very bitter taunt in the Vatican when the Quirinale is notoriously Anglophile. As for the Portugal Mundo, its leader – well, everyone knows that Portugal has been in the King of England's pocket since the Lisbon extravaganza, said Sañasca. As for the Germans – well, everybody knows that Prussians are just as bestially cynical as Jonbulls, said Coucheur. The Franco–Hispano–Erse faction was quite ready to go anywhere and vote for anybody who was not 'English'. The deacons, on the contrary, remembered that England was very much the fashion; and began to have respect unto the twenty-five. But the Way of Scrutiny failed, and the Way of Access also failed, to produce a pontiff. Fiamma's tally rose to twenty-nine by the accession of the diaconate. The Franco–Hispano–Erse alliance attached itself by fits and starts to Orezzo, to Ragna, to Serafino-Vagellaio, to Gentilotto: but the indispensable two thirds of fifty-seven never was attained. And, after a week of errancy, Their Eminencies thought that the whole affair was rather tiresome.

Ragna's massive prognathous jaw, the colour of porphyry, bulged in emitting a suggestion. As the College seemed unlikely to come to any agreement, why not elect an old man, who, in the course of nature, only could live a year or two and whose demise would necessitate another Conclave at an early date? He unselfishly would designate Orezzo. There, for example, was a cardinal to whom the paparchy was by way of being owed since 1878, when he actually had lost it to Leo. Let Orezzo now be elected; and, during his brief pontificature, let the Most Eminent Lords devote their energies towards arrangements for giving him a generous glorious and enlightened successor, who, in this reactionary age, was experienced in all the devious subtilties of secular diplomacy, and who was under sixty-five years old.

The Sacred College rejected the bare idea. What! Elect a Pope who, out of sheer personal antipathy, would make it his business to annul the policy of Leo? What! elect a Pope who had spent more than a quarter of a century in composing and reciting litanies of complaints against Leo's management of the Church? What! Elect a Pope who had proved himself to be purely barbarian by the ferocity of his ritual tapping on the forehead of the dead Leo? *Di meliora!*

Ragna adroitly disclaimed a personal predilection for Orezzo. That idea was dismissed.

'Then what?' was the general question.

'The Way of Compromise,' cooed Vincenzo-Vagellaio.

There was another capitular session in the Cystine Chapel. By means of the snips of parchment, the lead balls, the huge violet burse, nine cardinals were chosen by lot and appointed as Cardinal-Compromissaries. Singularly enough they were Courtleigh, Mundo, Fiamma, Grace, Ferraio, Saviolli, Nefski, Gentilotto, and della Volta. The College executed a compromise in writing, no one contradicting or opposing it, whereby these nine were invested with absolute power and faculty to make provision of a pastor for the Holy Roman Church.

The Compromissaries conferred. To begin with, they mutually protested that they would not be understood to give their consent by all sorts of words or expressions which might fall from them in the heat of debate, unless they expressly set the same down in writing. Then, they looked whole inquisitions one at another, saying nothing. And, after half an hour they adjourned till the morrow: gathered up their trains; and swept each to his separate cell. Stupid conclavists tried to read their expressions. As well try to find out his thoughts from the sole of his unworn shoe as from the face of a cardinal. The cardinalitial mask is as superior (in impenetrable pachydermatosity) to that of the proverbial public-schoolboy, as is the cuticle of a crocodile to that of *pulex irritans*.

The task of the Compromissaries was too onerous to be begun until a chaos of ideas had been set in order. Gentilotto and Fiamma paced up and down the galleries together. Acceptance of their present office had nullified their chances of the triple crown. Either would have worn that gladly and well: neither was inclined to struggle for it. The Scrutinies dreadfully had annoyed their dignity, the pure and gentle dignity of Gentilotto, the radiant opulent dignity of Fiamma. To have escaped from the sweaty turmoil of competition satisfied them. Ferraio joined them in their perambulation: joined his ideas and sympathies to theirs. Mundo paid a visit to Courtleigh, and heard his confession: the Cardinal of Pimlico had no use for the conclavial confessor, who was a Jesuit. Nefski, pallid and wan, tried a little walk by the aid of the arm of della Volta: and afterwards, those two said mattins and lauds together. Saviolli sat out the evening in Grace's cell, chatting about the Munroe Doctrine. Courtleigh sat alone in his cell: his hands were on the arms of his chair: his gaze was fixed on the flame of the candle. His thoughts whirled: eddyed: and were still. He fell asleep. His brother, who was his chaplain, peered through the violet curtains, inquiring his needs. He needed nothing – perhaps he would do a little writing before saying his nightprayers. Monsignor John placed a dispatch-box on the table, a couple of new candles on the prickets; and retired. Anon, His Eminency opened the box with a miniature gold key hinged to the underside of the bezel of his cameo ring; and meditatively turned over and over his archiepiscopal correspondence. One packet of letters seemed to fascinate him. He held it in his hands for a long time, fixedly regarding it. He untied the vermilion ribbon; and began to read. He had read these letters before, just before he entered the Conclave. He would read them again now: reading helps thought: it is as a strong arm supporting feeble steps: it is as the pinions upon which thought can fly: or it is inspiration. Cardinal Courtleigh read a dozen pages or so. Then he sat with his chin in his hand, gazing again at the candle-flame. His thoughts were flying. They were quite personal, quite unconnected with his present situation or his present office. Orezzo, Ragna, and Serafino-Vagellaio, engaged the Compromissaries in conversations wherever they met them, in doorways, on promenades: quite often they called to make perfectly certain that they lacked no conveniences in their cells.

Morning and evening conferences were occupied by long discussions on the merits of the three remaining candidates, and of the other five-and-forty cardinals. The predilections of the Powers were passed in review. The ambassador of the Emperor had notified that Austria would look favourably upon Rugscha. But to think of that old man – born in 1818 – nearly ninety years old – oh, quite impossible. The Siege of Peter needed no more senility, but rather juvence. Old men were so obstinate, much more obstinate than headstrong youth. The ambassador of the Catholic King had urged the claims of the Archbishop of Compostella. True, that one was not so old – but, three-score years and ten – is it not the Psalmist's limit? And did any of Their Eminencies desire to assist at another Conclave (say) within the next five years? Their Eminencies had had enough Conclaves to last them for the span of their mortal lives. The French ambassador had made no recommendation, seeing that the Commune had recalled him, torn him out of the train at Modane on the French frontier, and sliced him in pieces. Portugal had plumped for Mundo, who declared himself unwilling to accept, and as Compromissary incapable of accepting, the paparchy.

Italy – m-ym-ym-ym-ym – well, Italy? A geographical expression: no more. Now then the others. The German Emperor? His Majesty had nominated Courtleigh. Now why? The Cardinal of Pimlico, smiling, really did not know. He was much obliged, he was sure. Perhaps the young man thought

75

that by nominating one of his own uncle's subjects (and a very unworthy one) he would induce his said uncle to return the compliment and nominate a German. And would the uncle so oblige? Courtleigh thought not. The aforesaid uncle was quite as self-willed as, and infinitely more tactful than, and the last person in the world to let his leg be pulled by his imperial nephew. Well then what was the King of England's attitude? Courtleigh did not know: but he believed – indeed he had had it from Mr Chamberlain – Yes, and the Lord Chamberlain said? – Not the Lord Chamberlain – Mr Chamberlain – the Prime Minister – had said that His Majesty was not by way of meddling with matters which did not concern him. The Compromissaries pronounced the King of England's conduct to be most observable. And the Cardinal of Pimlico added that in any case he (as a Compromissary) was ineligible: while the Cardinal of Baltimore calculated that America also would stand out of this deal.

A definite decision evaded capture. Satisfaction seemed to be such a very long way up in the air. Not one of the nine was sensible of an overwhelming irresistible impulse to select any particular individual as Pope. That is such an invidious under-taking: the spirit faints at its immensity. But the Compromis-saries subconsciously were drawing near and nearer to each other and away from the rest, who, in their turn cohered in curiosity. The fourth conference was an unusually futile one. Mundo frankly and abruptly stated his conviction that the Lord God was not intending Himself to take a vicegerent out of the Sacred College: whereat Their Eminencies laughed; and adjourned, conversing of other and secular affairs.

Courtleigh went out on della Volta's arm. 'Eminency,' he said, 'I have known you now for nearly twenty years: and, whenever I see you, I always fancy that I have met you some-where in other circumstances. You have never been in London? I thought not. And I suppose you haven't what they call a Double? I don't mean that your type is common. Far from it. But, at times, I seem – You remind me of – And yet I do not know of whom – '

And another night enshrouded the palace on the Vatican Hill.

As Cardinal Courtleigh was trying to shave himself next morning, the phantom of his friend della Volta invaded his mental vision: suddenly, resemblance and remembrance clashed together striking a spark. By the light of it, he saw and knew – something. He laughed shortly: and grew grave. He was deeply engrossed with his dispatch-box until the hour of conference. The matters which he laid before the other Compromissaries caused several precedents to be set aside and some to be created. And, at 9 p.m., forty-two cardinals, wearing the habits of ordinary priests, drove away in cabs towards the railway station: while the Cardinal-Chamberlain unlocked the inside of the door of the Conclave. Hereditary-marshal Ghici, summoned from his watching chamber to unlock the outside, was flabbergasted by an invitation to declare whether the Vatican was a prison for cardinals as well as for popes? He did hate being mocked by a boiled lobster!

Fifteen comparatively speechless Eminencies spent a few weeks there in quiet leisure, reading in the library, admiring the pictures and the sculptures, sometimes strolling in the gardens. One of them seriously began to study botany; and the Cardinal-Dean, with a view to a future Bull, composed a very scathing indictment of that hypocritical anomaly called Christian Socialism. And all the time the pontifical army guarded the inside of every entrance, fraternizing through the gratings with the national army outside. But special correspondents of the London newspapers in Rome munched vacuity and excreted fibs, after their kind.

By twos and threes, plain (but very dignified) priests arrived: were admitted; and changed black for violet. One did not change. He was only Cardinal Courtleigh's new chaplain. The door of the Conclave was locked on both sides and bricked-up again.

Ensued another session of the Compromissaries, when their authentic act was put into prescribed form by apostolic protonotaries. Ensued a final capitular assembly, in which the Act of the Compromise was published. Ensued a tempest of tongues and manners, dissolving (as storms do) in muttered thunders, less and less convulsive upheavals, a parcel of broken boughs and chimney-pots, stillness, peace, relief, and sun-bright April smiles.

CHAPTER 3

WHEN their lords had entered the Cystine Chapel for this last exercise, the conclavists went away about their own affairs; and the door was shut. The Reverend George Arthur Rose departed with the Bishop of Caerleon who was acting-chaplain to Cardinal Mundo. They walked in the royal gallery between the Cystine and the Pauline Chapels. George was in a mood of silence. His mind (as usual) was receiving impressions: the historic scene being enacted under his notice: the magnificent masks veiling the humanity of the actors: the mysterious gloom of the stage, its smallness, its air of cavernous confinement: the sour oppressive septic odour of architectural and waxen and human antiquity. He had been told that he would have to say mass before noon; and his head ached from fasting in that indescribably stifling effluvia. He remembered that, in former days, necessity frequently had forced him to abstain from all food for a hundred hours at a time. Often, during four days in the week, he had eaten nothing: but that was in the open air, on the shore of a northern sea, or among the heather on moors and mountains, where the wind and the spray gave life. Here, the fast of less than twenty hours made him sick and sulky. However, it had to be tolerated. Semphill once had told him that a course in an ecclesiastical college, and the first few years of clerical life, were as disgusting as ten years' penal servitude. He took it at that with his eyes open. It was part of the business. He determined to go through with it. Still, he was in a better position now than he ever had been before. He no longer was alone. Dr Talacryn had seemed anxious for his company since that day in London; and George was inclined to value kindness.

The Bishop of Caerleon appeared to be precisely what the new-fledged priest knew himself to need – a sympathetic expert subintelligent walking-stick, honest and sturdy as oak. Oh, for the certainty of fidelity! Presently George took out his cherished edition of Theocritos by Estienne. In spare moments, he was introducing his companion to the melody of Greek; and together they read and analysed the twelfth idyll.

An hour later, the bishop suggested that they should go into the Pauline Chapel and say some prayers. George followed him. Prayer is a mind-cleanser – the best: anyhow it is an effort always due. They looked for a clean four-feet-of-floor: kneeled side by side; and got into communication with the Unseen. George's method was intellectual rather than formal. To him, with his keen and carefully cultivated sense of the ridiculous, the absurdity of a human individual composing complacent criticisms of Divine decrees, hashing up scriptural and liturgical tags with a proper and essentially sensuous pleasure in patchwork, seemed like gratuitous impertinence. 'Dear Jesus, be not to me a Judge, but a Saviour,' was all the form of words which he used. It included everything, as far as he could see. He repeated it over and over again and again like a wonderful incantation; and anon it had its psychic effect. He became in direct communication with the Invisible Omniscient, to Whom all hearts are open, from Whom no secrets are hid. It was just his own method, compiled from bitter-sweet experience. In time, he began to finger his moonstone rosary, concentrating his meditation on the Mystery of the Annunciation: his mind strenuously went to work on that: his lips swiftly enunciated the prayers. After five decades he said *Salve Regina*: and examined his conscience. Was there any difference in him? He felt more clear: he felt that he had effected some kind of a difference. That was relief. But was it worth anything? Wasn't it stained? Was he really strengthened by the exercise? For example, was he now filled and inflamed with pure Love? No. Was he any nearer to pure Love, fit to be thought of, even harshly, by pure Love? No. Well: he had done his best: it would come some day. God be merciful to us all poor sinners.

He looked at the bishop, two weeks his junior in years, two centuries his senior in worth of every kind. The cheerful satisfied stolidity of that one, turning from his prayers and meeting George's gaze with a homely smile, was something astounding. How different men are! Here was one envying the other his stolidity, and the other half afraid of the agility of the one. George realized that this bishop never had had embarrassments of any kind: nor could have. He saw the great gulph which is fixed between the simple and the complex.

There was a stir at the door of the chapel. 'I think perhaps we'd better be getting back,' said Dr Talacryn.

Two masters of ceremonies appeared in attendance upon Cardinal-Archdeacon Macca and Cardinal-Deacon Berstein. As George and his companion approached them, they turned and retraced their steps. George wished them anywhere but there, impeding him when he ought to be running off to the service of his diocesan. They completely blocked the path as they went before him with superb unconcern. 'How stiff, how antipathetic the elder one looks!' he whispered with acerbity.

'Sh-h-h!' the bishop sibilated.

The door of the Cystine Chapel was open. Conclavists from all quarters hurried towards it. George and his friend found themselves impelled through the portals. Beyond the delicate marble screen, gleamed the six steady flamelets of the candles on the altar. The protentous figures in the Doom appeared to writhe. Inside the screen Macca and Berstein went; and paused; and faced the crowd which followed them.

George was looking about him, vehemently alert. He had felt like this three times in his life before, at the exsequies of the Queen of England, at the incoronation of the King of England, at the foot of the first grave which had opened in his path through life. It was the feeling of the cognoscente who is permitted, during sixty seconds, to do his own pleasure in a treasure-chest filled to the brim with inestimable intagliate gems. It was the feeling of absolute acquisitiveness. Here was history in the making; and he was in the front rank of the spectators. There was no time to think of effects. This was

80

a case of causes; and every detail must be seized and stored. Selection could come later: appreciation afterwards: but now he must collect. First, his glance flashed upward to the little square canopies: they all were in position. Then, to the occupants of the five and fifty thrones: they were sitting as still as the conscript-fathers sat in their curule chairs, turned to and watching the crowd which oozed through the screen-gates. Unconsciously, George was urged further and further in. His demeanour was abstrusely unemotional: he continued violently absorbent of the spectacle. Presently, he whispered to the bishop, 'What is it? What is happening?'

'I think God has given us a Pope.'

'Oh! Whom?'

'Wait. We shall know in a minute.'

The silence, the stillness, the dim light, where motionless forms of cardinals curved like the frozen crests of waves carved in white jade and old ivory on a sea of amethyst, were more than marvellous.

A voice came out of the gloom, an intense voice, reciting some formula.

George did not take the Latin easily from an Italian tongue: he found himself tralating, *Reverend Lord, the Sacred College has elected thee to be the Successor of St Peter. Wilt thou accept pontificality?*

'Reverend'? he thought. Why not 'Most Eminent'? He instantly turned to the bishop, with another question on his tongue. The bishop was kneeling behind him. The crowd also was kneeling. Why in the world did not he kneel too? Why should he hesitate for a moment? He faced round once more, a single black figure with an alert weary white face, alone and erect in the splendour of violet. He glanced again at the canopies.

It was on him, on him, that all eyes were. Why did he not kneel?

Again the voice of the Cardinal-Archdeacon intoned, 'Reverend Lord, the Sacred College has elected thee to be the Successor of St Peter. Wilt thou accept pontificality?'

There was no mistake. The awful tremendous question was addressed to him.

A murmur from the bishop prompted him, 'The response is *Volo* – or *Nolo*.'

The surging in his temples, the booming in his ears, miraculously ceased. He took one long slow breath: crossed right hand over left upon his breast: became like a piece of a pageant; and responded 'I will.'

Two hands clapped, and the canopies came down rustling and flapping. The Sacred College struggled to its feet, as God's Vicegerent passed to the rear of the high altar.

They offered Him three suits of pontifical white, large, medium, and small. The large was too large: the small, too small: but the medium would serve for the present. He began to undress, among the throng of assistants, with the noncurance of one accustomed to swim in Sandford Lasher. He forbade all help, refusing to be touched. When He had assumed the white hosen, cassock, sash, rochet, cape, and cap, the crimson shoes and stole, the great new gold Ring of The Fisherman, He went through His former pockets leaving nothing behind: tucked His handkerchief into His left sleeve; and asked for the Bishop of Caerleon. While masters-of-ceremonies and the Augustinian sacristan hurried to prepare altars for the episcopal consecration of the Pope, Dr Talacryn was admitted to the Apostolic presence. He made obeisance: the moment was too enormous for words, but eyes spoke.

'A glass of water,' then the Pontiff said.

'The fast, Holy Father – '

'Will not be broken. Remain always close at hand, please.' He felt as though the whole world suddenly had left Him. Not that He Himself had moved, or changed: but the world, the past, was entirely gone and blotted out: the future was obscure: the present was all strange. His unrelated idea was to steady Himself by this one link with the past. Water was brought. He dipped half His handkerchief: wrang it out: pressed it on His hot dry eyes.

All through the long ceremony of consecration, He carried

Himself with enigmatical equanimity. Though His eyes saw nothing but the matters of each moment, and though His bearing seemed to indicate an aloof indifference, yet, within, His sensibilities were at their tensest. Nothing escaped Him. And He was mobilizing His forces: planning His campaign. He was looking down, He was surveying, the opening vista. Two or three moves on the apostolic chess-board He already could foresee.

At the conferring of the episcopal ring, He drew back His hand; and demanded an amethyst instead of the proffered emerald. The ceremony halted till the canonical stone came. Cardinals noted the first manifestation of pontifical will, with much concern, and with some annoyance. Ragna muttered of ignoble upstarts: Vivole, of boyish arrogance: Berstein, of beggars on horseback. 'He, who is born of a hen, always scratches the ground,' asserted the Benedictine Cacciatore: and 'He, who was a frog, is now a king,' Labeur quoted from the *Satyricon* of Petronius Arbiter.

They brought Him before the altar; and set Him in a crimson-velvet chair, asking what pontifical name He would choose.

'Hadrian the Seventh:' the response came unhesitatingly, undemonstratively.

'Your Holiness would perhaps prefer to be called Leo, or Pius, or Gregory, as is the modern manner?' the Cardinal-Dean inquired with imperious suavity.

'The previous English pontiff was Hadrian the Fourth: the present English pontiff is Hadrian the Seventh. It pleases Us; and so, by Our Own impulse, We command.'

Then there was no more to be said. The election of Hadrian the Seventh was proclaimed in the Conclave. They came to the ceremony of adoration. One by one, Their Eminencies kissed the Supreme Pontiff's foot and hand and cheek. Contact with senile humanity made His juvenile soul shudder. All the time he was saying in His mind 'Not unto Us, O Lord, not unto Us. . . .' Yet that seemed such a silly inadequate thing to say. It was not humility, it was physical loathing which nauseated Him all secretly. Some had the breaths of bustards, and all but one were hot. He would have liked to tear off His Own cheek with clawed tongs. By a peculiar mental gymnastic, He vaulted to the verse, 'Who sweeps an house as in Thy Sight makes that and the action fine.' He clutched the thought and clung to it. 'Greatest and Best, or by what other Name Thou wishest to be called, I am only Thy means. This horrible osculation is no more than a chance for them to benefit themselves by honouring Thee through me. Let them. I will be the means – Thy means to all men. Ouf! How it hurts!' His external serenity was unflinchingly feline. He just tolerated attention. The arrows of cardinalitial eyes impinged upon Him; and glanced off the ice of His mail. He withdrew His sensibilities from the surface; and concentrated them in the inmost recesses of his soul, foreseeing, forescheming. 'One step's enough for me' was another tag, which became detached from the bundles of His memory to float in the ocean of His counsels. He made sure of the one step: fearlessly strode and stood; and prepared for the next. He never looked behind. The amethyst, the pontifical name, and now – ? Yes! 'Begin as you mean to go on,' He advised Himself.

When the huge princes of the church bourgeoned in ermine and vermilion, Hadrian, mitred and coped in silver and gold, followed Macca who bore the triple cross. Tumultuous sumptuous splendour proceeded through the Conclave into the gallery of benediction over the Porch of St Peter's. Masons were removing brickwork from a blocked window leading to a balcony on the right hand, half-way down the long gallery. The Supreme Pontiff beckoned Orezzo.

'Lord Cardinal, this balcony looks into the church?'

'Into the church, Holiness.'

'Which window looks out over the City?'

'The window on the left.'

'Let the window on the left be opened.'

The Sacred College swung together as to a scrum.

Pressure never had influenced George Arthur Rose. He used to say that you might squash him to death, if you could: but you never should make him do what you were too lazy, or too proud, or too silly, to persuade him to do. He would wait a century for his own way; and, unless you actually and literally had removed him from the face of the earth by the usual methods of assassination, you would find him still implacably persistent at the end of the said century. He had learned the trick from Flavio: observing that, if he would not open the door when the cat mewed to go out, the creature remained in the room, but would not come and sit on his friend's neck, nor agree to anything except the opening of the door. And Hadrian the Seventh was quite prepared to be hustled and hullabaloed at, as Leo the Thirteenth had been hullabaloed at and hustled in 1878: but no earthly power should extort Apostolic Benediction from His hand and lips, except at a place and a time of His Own choosing. They might push this Pope on to the inner balcony; and they might lead a horse to the water: but not even the College of Cardinals arrayed in all its glory could make the one drink, the other bless.

'Holiness, that window was bricked up in 1870; and has not been opened since.'

'Let it now be opened.'

Ragna snarled and burst out of the phalanx. There was a tinge of truculence about him. 'Holiness, Pope Leo had wished to have it opened on the day of His Own election; but it was impossible. Impossible! *Capisce?* The rust of the stanchions, the solidity of the cement –'

'All that We know. The gentleness of Pope Leo was persuaded. We are not gentle; and We are not to be persuaded by violence.'

Orezzo, though secretly enchanted that anyone should act differently to his one antipathy, Pope Leo, was rather shocked at the notion of blessing the City and the World while (what he held to be) the Piedmontese Usurper was occupying Peter's so-called Patrimony and Intangible Rome. It is an ingrained idea with his school that peoples should excruciate for the petty spites of potentates. But he tried urbanity. 'Holy Father have pity upon us; and deliver us as soon as possible from the miseries which afflict us in this Conclave. Deign blessings to the faithful in the church today; and we will see what can be done about the one affair tomorrow.'

Hadrian looked a little amused. The Bishop of Caerleon thought that he never had seen more cruelly dispassionate inflexibility. At a sign from the Pope, the master-mason came forward and fell on his knees. Hadrian stooped.

'Son, open that window.'

Through and through vermilion billows the masons dived and thrust across the breadth of the gallery, conveying ladders, crowbars, hammers. Conclavial porters threw down rolls of carpet which they were about to spread, and sat upon them. Berstein squawked and expectorated. Hadrian winced: and marked the man. At the clang of hammers, masonry began to fall: a white dust hovered in the air: the vermilion college swept away with the white Pope. Some went to the end of the gallery, where loud voices became protestant: midway, the Germans halted with most of the Italians: they conversed more moderately. A few paces beyond the range of operations, the Pope remained quite still: by His side, He detained Macca with His cross: behind Him, congregated the Bishop of Caerleon and the nine Cardinal-Compromissaries.

In a break of the clang of the hammers, Hadrian intoned 'Kyrie eleison'. Mundo gave prompt response. The assemblage at first failed to catch the idea: but, by degrees, voice acceded to voice; and the Litanies of the Saints magniloquently reverberated through the gallery.

Outside, in the Square of St Peter's, only a few hundreds of people were collected. Interest in the proceedings of the Conclave was nearly dead; and several special correspondents were beginning to think seriously of the superior excitements of a murder trial at New Bailey. But many old-fashioned Romans wished to be able to tell their grandchildren that they themselves had been in the square when the Pope was proclaimed in the church; and, again, on the morning of St George's Day, no smoke had been vomited from the Cystine chimney. The affair was very mysterious! What combinations behind those white walls!

Inside the basilica, there were thousands of expectant people, officials of the Vatican, cardinalitial familiars, prelates, penitentiaries, beneficiaries, who had not been immured in the Conclave. Also there were lords and ladies of eminent quality belonging to the Black (or clerical) Party, who had been admitted with meticulous secrecy (in broad daylight and in face of all Rome) by a privy door. Every day for weeks, they had come and waited, hoping to be among the first to salute the Pope. To go to St Peter's in the morning before dinner, and in the evening before supper, had become the mode in a society which has few and futile dissipations of its own and to which the comity of the Quirinale and White Society is forbidden fruit. Some, who were near the great doorway, thought they heard faint tappings in the gallery overhead. Rumour protruded her tongue: certainly there were tappings, more ponderous, more insistent. Certainly the balcony was being opened. Then the crashing ceased. In the hush, surmises were born; and stifled: or nurtured. A loose Benedictine with a face of a flesher, who was leaning against one of the great piers, suddenly asseverated that the tapping had begun again: but in another place – further away, he said. An honorary decurial chamberlain-of-the-cloak-and-sword sniffed long-nosedly, picking a vandyke beardlet; and stuttered, 'They're n-n-never o-opening the outer b-b-b-b-b-b-b-b-balcony.' That notion resembled the spark between negative and positive poles. It vibrated and glittered; and fell upon a heap of human combustibles.

'Then what are we waiting here for?' shouted Prince Clenalotti; and he made a dash at the door by which he had entered. Naturally he led a stampede.

The crowd in the Square stood obliquely to the church, with all its eyes directed to the Vatican: when, round from Via della Sagrestia poured a stream of half-wild creatures, shooting instant glances at the vacant balcony, and bringing amazing news. The two crowds flew together, thronging the wide stone steps and the open space beneath. The military rigesced to attention. The special correspondents (as one man) made for the obelisk in the centre, or the basins of the fountains, and set up portable pairs of steps. And, of course, motor-cars and cabs, and Caio and Tizio and also Sempronio, not to mention Maria and Elena and Yolanda and also Margherita, began to issue from every Borgo avenue.

There was nothing to be seen, except the empty balcony over the porch. It was neither canopied nor decorated: but someone said that there was movement behind the window. That was concisely true. More. The window itself was moving. The sun-flashed panes of glass turned dull, as it swung on its hinges, inward. The Italian army presented arms. Rome kneeled on the stones. The special correspondents ascended their pairs of steps: directed phonographic and cinematographic machines: pressed buttons and revolved wheels.

A tiny figure splashed a web of cloth-of-gold over the balcony; and a tiny ermine and vermilion figure ascended, placing a tiny triple cross. Came in a stentorian megaphonic roar a proclamation by the Cardinal-Archdeacon,

'I announce to you great joy. We have for a Pope the Lord George of the Roses of England, Who has imposed upon Himself the name of Hadrian the Seventh.'

He gave place to another tiny figure, silver and gold, irradiant in the sun. A clear thin thread of a voice sang,

'Our help is in the Name of the Lord.'

Phonographs recorded the sonorous response,

'Who hath made heaven and earth.'

Hadrian the Seventh raised His hand and sang again,

'May Almighty God, ✠✠✠ Father, ✠✠✠ Son, ✠✠✠ and Holy Ghost, bless you.'

It was the Apostolic Benediction of the City and the World.

CHAPTER 4

Now things went briskly. There was a brain which schemed and a will to be obeyed. The hands began to realize that they would have to act manually. Dear deliberate Rome simply gasped at a Pontiff Who said 'Tomorrow' and meant it. The

Sacred College found that it had no option. Naturally it looked as black as night. But the Cardinal-Archdeacon could not refuse point-blank to crown; and, when Hadrian announced that His incoronation would take place in the morning on the steps of St Peter's, futile effort suggested difficulty preventing possibility. That was the only course open to the opposition. Three cardinals in turn alleged that there would not be time to give notice of the ceremony, to arrange the church, to issue tickets of admission. Hadrian swept these ideas aside, as rubbish. Another courted catastrophe saying that there was no time to summon the proper officials. He heard that there were sixteen hours in which to summon those who actually were indispensable. A fifth said that, owing to the antichristian tendencies of the times, no representatives of the King of France, of the Holy Roman Emperor, of the First Conservator of the Roman people, were forthcoming; and he politely inquired how the quadruplex lavation could be performed in their absence? The Pope responded that He was capable of washing His hands four times without any assistance, in the absence of legitimate assistants: but the General of the Church was not to seek: the modern Syndic of Rome was the equivalent of the ancient First Conservator: the Austrian Ambassador could represent the Empire: while, as for wretched kingless unkingly France – let someone instantly go out into the streets of Rome and catch the first Christian Frenchman there encountered. Anyhow, the quadruplex lavation was accidental. The essential was that the Supreme Pontiff should sing a pontifical mass at the high altar of St Peter's, and should receive the triple crown. These things would be done at eight o'clock on the following morning. All the doors of the basilica were to be fixed open at midnight; and so remain. No official notice need be published. And that was all. Then the Pope shut up Himself in His predecessor's gorgeous rooms, inspecting them till they gave him a pain in His eyes. Luckily He had secured his pouch-full of tobacco and a book of cigarette-papers: He smoked, and thought, looking out of the windows over Rome.

After sunset, He ate some cutlets and a salad: placed two

chairs face to face near the right-hand window; and sent for the Bishop of Caerleon and a large jug of milk. His interior arrangements were as disreputably healthy as those of a schoolboy.

Dr Talacryn came, and observed the forms. Hadrian sent him to clear the antechambers and to close the doors. He returned and remained standing. The Pope was sitting in one of the splendidly uncomfortable red chairs.

'We have sent for Your Lordship because We have occasion for your special services.'

'I am at all times very ready and willing to serve Your Holiness.'

Hadrian was attracted to this bishop. Lots of his acts He loathed: but He liked the man, and believed him honest. The bishop was attracted to the Pope. He liked Him: but he could not understand Him, and was a little frightened of Him: but still – it was as well to know all that could be known and that might be useful.

'We placed this chair for Your Lordship,' said Hadrian.

Dr Talacryn was astonished: but not more than much. His trained placid nature stood him in good stead at a mark of favour which would have abashed many, and rendered others presumptuous.

'I thank Your Holiness,' he simply said. It appeared that the ship was cleared for action.

The Pope continued in His usual concise monotone. He spoke in the key of Eb minor, very quickly indeed, slurring the letter r, clipping some words and every final g, enunciating others with emphasis, in a manner curiously suggestive of fur and india rubber and talons. As for His matter, He seemed to be arguing with Himself by the way in which He arrayed His ideas, disclosing His process of thought.

'We have very much to do, and We are confronted by the physical impossibility of carrying out Our schemes. We find Ourself surprisingly placed at the head of affairs. We believe that We should not have been placed there unless the service, which We are able to do, had been deemed desirable. Therefore

We feel bound to act. But, though We know (or shall know) what to do, yet We cannot do it with this one pair of hands. We must have assistants with whom we can be intimate, and who themselves can be sympathetic. First of all, We wish to have Your Lordship.'

The bishop was quite honest enough to get a little rosier with pleasure.

'Very pleased, whatever,' he said.

'Next, We need information. Do you know the circumstances which led to Our election?'

'In the main they are known to me, Holiness. Indeed, I may say that they are generally known – except to the Supreme Pontiff Himself,' the bishop added, with an episcopally roguish smile.

Hadrian enjoyed the point. 'Please bear this dogma carefully and continually in mind: the Pope well-informed is wiser than the Pope ill-informed. Remember also that Hadrian at all times desires to know everything. At present He wishes to know what you know about His election. Briefly: the details can be given later.'

'Briefly, the Conclave found no Pope by the ordinary means and committed the task to certain Cardinal-Compromissaries. These chose Your Holiness.'

'But why?'

'Cardinal Courtleigh – '

'Was he a Compromissary? How many were there?'

'He was one of nine. The others were – '

'Never mind their names for the moment. Now We take it that these nine cardinals are well-disposed toward Us?'

'Most assuredly, Holy Father.'

'Good! Nine! The names please?'

'Courtleigh, Grace – '

'Archbishop of Baltimore. Yes?'

'Saviolli – '

'What is he? He formerly was nuncio or something in America, was he not? Please give the status of each.'

'He was Archbishop of Lepanto and Pontifical Ablegate to

the United States of America. Now he is one of the curia. Then came della Volta, formerly Major-domo, also of the curia: he, by the bye, is Your Holiness's Double, according to Cardinal Courtfield.'

'How delicious!' Hadrian vivaciously put in.

'Mundo, who led the Compromissaries, is Patriarch of Lisbon. Nefski is Archbishop of Prague, poor fellow – '

'Why "poor fellow"?'

'Oh he was nearly killed by the anarchists – Well then, Ferraio is Archbishop of Milan: Gentilotto is Prefect-General of the Society for the Propagation of the Faith, and Fiamma is Archbishop of Bologna. The two last were candidates at first, but gave it up by consenting to become Compromissaries.'

'These, you say, are well-disposed to Us?'

'Yes, Holy Father.'

'A Celt: an American: a Portugal: five Italians: and a Pole.'

'No, a Bohemian, Holiness.'

'Oh?' Hadrian directed the bishop to a writing-table. 'Now, whether this be in accordance with regulations or not, We neither know nor care. Please write' – He sipped a glass of milk; and began to dictate – '"Hadrian VII – Bishop – Servant of the servants of God – wills that you immediately shall come – to Him – in the Vatican Palace – at Rome. Nothing – except the gravest physical inability – or your duty to your family – if such there be – is to impede you. All Catholics – are to afford you – the comfort – conveyance – and assistance – of which you may stand in need." Please sign it with your own name and make five copies of it.'

The bishop, sighing for his typewriter, diligently wrote in an angular oblique almost illegible hand. Electric lights sprang up in the City. The Pope lighted candles, closed the curtains, and rolled a cigarette. Then He came and sat by the table, looking at the manuscripts – considering the huge ring on His Own index finger. Smiling to Himself, He took a taper and a stick of sealing-wax; and produced the *Little-Peter-in-a-Boat* at the foot of the six sheets.

'Address them,' He continued, 'to the Reverend George Semphill, St Gowff's, North Britain; Reverend James Sterling, Oakheath, Stafford; Reverend George Leighton, Shorham, Sussex; Reverend Gerald Whitehead, Wilton, Warwick; Reverend Robert Carvale, Duntellin, Ayrshire; and – yes, do you know that eighteen years ago he had the most exquisitely beautiful face and the most exquisitely beautiful soul and the most exquisitely horrible voice of any boy in the college – address the sixth to Percy Van Kristen, 2023 Madison Avenue, New York.'

While Dr Talacryn was closing the envelopes, the Pope Himself wrote on a sheet of paper which, also, He sealed:

Hadrianus P. M. VII. dilectissimo filio Francisco Talacryni Caerleonis Episcopo.

Te in cardinalem Designamus et Approbamus: quod tamen sub silentio tenebis donec tempus idoneum aderit.

Datum Romae. Sub annulo Piscatoris. Anno pontificatus Nostri I., a.d. viiii Kal. Mai.

'Now please come and kneel here,' He said.

The bishop looked an inquiry: but he came round the table, and kneeled before the Pope, Who addressed him in these words:

'Well-beloved son, Francis Talacryn, Bishop of Caerleon, We appoint thee to, and confirm thee in, the cardinalature. But thou shalt not disclose the fact until the proper time.'

So saying, He lightly pinched together the bishop's lips, putting the breve into his hand.

'Silence,' the Pontiff continued. 'Now will you yourself go to San Silvestro – not to the post office here – and stamp and post those letters. One thing more. There will be no hitch tomorrow? Right. Then, after leaving San Silvestro, will you find Prince Pilastro and Prince Orso, and tell them – We certainly shall have the support of these nine? Good – Well, quite informally let those princes (as Princes-Assistant at the Pontifical Throne) know of Our insuing incoronation. When you have named that to Prince Pilastro, say, also informally, that the Supreme Pontiff wishes the Syndic of Rome to know that, when He has received the crowns, He intends to go to Lateran to take possession of His episcopal see. No. There is to be no fuss. We will go as simply as possible and on foot. Will you always be quite near? We name you train-bearer; and will make your office a sinecure. God bless you. *Da B'och a dibechod.*'

Hadrian remained standing at the antechamber-door, watching the bishop's big figure disappear along the corridor. He thought it a pity that a tendency to corpulency was not checked by healthy physical exercise. A detachment of the Swiss Guard stood armed and motionless at regular intervals. 'For me,' was His plebeian thought. A small man appeared, bowing. He had a servile air. Hadrian's second glance recognized him.

'Is there an apartment on the top storey above this?' He inquired.

'But yes, Holiness, a large apartment of smaller rooms not having the altitude of these.'

'You will cause them to be emptied by noon tomorrow. Now you can go to bed. Please take care that no one comes inside this door until the morning.'

The Pope closed the door: and returned through the antechambers and the throne-room to the table where He had been working. He sat on the edge of the table for about an hour, swinging a leg, thinking, and sipping milk. Then He took a candle, and went into a dressing-room with huge oak clothes-presses. Opening their doors, He looked for a cloak among piles and festoons of new clothes. There were several of crimson velvet. After vainly searching for something plain, He put on one of these and proceeded to the outer door, taking a breviary from the table on the way. Out in the corridor, He signed to the nearest guard. The black-red-yellow-and-steel figure came and kneeled.

'Do you know the way into St Peter's?' the Pope said.

'But yes, Most Holy Father.'

'Procure what keys are necessary and conduct Us thither, son.'

94

'But securely, Most Holy Father.'

The Swiss went on before. Hadrian followed, feeling annoyed by the salutes with which He was received along the way. He had been so long unnoted that notice irritated and abashed Him. Life would be unbearable if trumpets and quaint halberds greeted every movement. He had not the stolidity of born personages. Presently, He threw back His cloak and kept head and hand raised in a gesture which petrified. They passed through innumerable passages and descended stairs, emerging in a chapel where lights burned about a tabernacle of gilded bronze and lapis lazuli. Here He paused, while His escort unlocked the gates of the screen. Once through that, He sent back the guard to his station: but He Himself went on into the vast obscurity of the basilica. He walked very slowly: it was as though His eyes were wrapped in clear black velvet, so intense and so immense was the darkness. Then, very far away to the right, He saw as it were a coronal of dim stars glimmering – on the floor, they seemed to be. He was in the mighty nave; and the stars were the ever-burning lamps surrounding the Confession. He slowly approached them. As He passed within them, He took one from its golden branch and descended the marble steps. Here, He spread the cloak on the floor; placed the lamp beside it: and fell to prayer. Outside, in the City and the World, men played, or worked, or sinned, or slept. Inside at the very tomb of the Apostle the Apostle prayed.

At midnight, bolts of great doors clanged, and fell. A cool air crept in. Subsacristans set up iron candlesticks, huge, antique, here and there upon the marmoreal pavement. The burning torch of each made a little oasis of light in the immeasurable gloom. From far away, a slim white form which carried a crimson cloak swiftly came, shedding benedictions on the startled beholders; and disappeared in the chapel of the Sacrament.

On returning to His apartment, Hadrian went straight to bed, invoking the souls in purgatory to awaken Him at six o'clock. He slept instantly and well.

At seven o'clock He had paid His debt with the *De Profundis*;

and was dressed and waiting in the throne-room. Entered to Him a dozen cardinals, two by two. Opening their ranks, they disclosed the Cardinal-Prior-Priest solemnly ostending the image of a cock in silver-gilt. Hadrian stood on the steps of the throne, still erect, vivid. He seemed so brimming over with restrained energy that He resembled a white flame. Not a sound was uttered. In silence they came; and they went away in silence. When the Pontiff was alone again, He strode and stopped in the middle of the floor.

'No, Lord, I never will deny Thee – never!' He exclaimed with tremendous emphasis. 'But keep me and teach me and govern me, that I may govern and teach and keep Thy Flock, O Thou Shepherd of the people.'

When the Bishop of Caerleon conveyed the extraordinary news to the Syndic of Rome, Prince Pilastro at once inquired what arrangements were made.

'No arrangements are made.'

'But look here,' said Marcantonio, who affected English brusqueness, 'of course we are very happy that the Holy Father should come among us: but, you know, we are bound by our own guarantees to give Him all the honours of a sovereign-regnant. We shall be shamed in the eyes of Europe if we omit those. What I mean by that is this is a state-progress; and we shall have to turn out the troops, and stop the traffic and line the streets – '

'I don't think His Holiness expects you to do all that, Prince. I'm not speaking officially; and I'm not bringing you an official request for anything of the kind which you name. The Holy Father says He is going quite simply – on foot, in fact.'

'Now I should just like to know what the devil (if Your Splendour will excuse the French) that means.'

'Perhaps His Holiness thinks that the movement of the sedia gestatoria, or of a litter, will make Him sick. It did with Leo, you know.'

'What's the matter with a white mule?'

'I happen to know that He cannot ride.'

'Peuh! No sportsman, then! And yet He's English?'

'Yes: but not the kind of sportsman you mean, Prince.'

'Well: what does He want me to do?'

'Let's say that I am sent to warn you of His intention, in order that you may arrest Him for disturbing the traffic, if you choose.'

'Of course we shan't do that.'

'No: of course you won't. That's only my way of putting it. I think He really means to advise you beforehand, so that it can never be said that He played you a trick, took you unawares, stole a march on you, so to speak.'

'I see. Well, this is one of the amazing things which you English do as a matter of course. It's either frantic madness, or – Will His Holiness go in any sort of state?'

'I think not. You see time is short; and (between ourselves) I'm not at all sure that we're all of one mind over there.'

'By rights, you know, I ought to walk with Orso, just before the ambassadors. Does Orso know about this walking business?'

'No. Only of the incoronation.'

'That means that there will be no formal procession. It is well. You see, as Pilastro, I walk with Orso in the Pope's progress: while, as Syndic of Rome, I ought to walk at the head of the pontifical pages who precede His Blessedness. I can't do both, can I? Well, I request Your Splendour to convey my respects to our Holy Father; and to say that Prince Pilastro will assist at the throne during the incoronation, and the Syndic of Rome will go before the Pope to Lateran.'

'You will not take the chance of coming to blows with Prince Orso on the question of precedence then?' joked the bishop.

'But no. During the incoronation I shall secure the right hand; and the Pope will be between us. Afterward, no question of precedence will arise, because Orso may or may not join in this promenade to Lateran; and in each case the Syndic will have the more honourable position. I may not be the rose: but at least I shall be near the Rose – a great deal nearer than Orso,' punned the versatile Marcantonio.

At eight in the morning, Hadrian descended to St Peter's. Miscellaneous multitudes paved the spaces with tumultuous eyes. He came down in ruddy vesture, gleaming with rubies and garnets and carbuncles like a fire borne high above the crowd, slowly, deliberately, dropping benedictions. His English phlegm was much admired. They roared at Him, 'Long live the Pope-King'. Instantly He stopped His bearers; and the very air of Him struck sudden silence. People stared, and forgot to shout: the wave of acclamation ebbed in the great nave and transepts. He moved onward, sitting erect, god-like, with a frozen mien prohibiting personal homage. Mitred and enthroned, He was the servant of those who would serve Him: that was the import of His demeanour. A child acolyth of the lowest rank held up before him a salver containing flax: set it on fire; and shrilled,

'Behold most Holy Father, how that the glory of this world passeth away.'

His features showed no emotion. He well knew all about that. He was accepting, even insisting on, the observance of all rites to consolidate Him in the Supreme Pontificature: not that He cared for them, but that He might be free to act. It was not the glory of the world which He craved: but the combat, the combat – because one rests so much more sweetly after strife.

Slowly, and with all the unspeakable solemnity accumulated during centuries, the mass was sung. The Apostle elevated the Host to the four quarters of the globe. Cardinals ruffled like huge flamingoes round Him. He always was white and still. At the end, the Cardinal-Archpriest of St Peter's brought Him a damask purse containing twenty-five gold coins, honorarium for a mass well-sung. He bestowed it on della Volta and Sega, who had intoned the Gospel in Greek and Latin; and they passed it to their train-bearers. Down the nave, He went again toward the great porch. Out of the crowd a voice cried 'Christus regnat'. As He sat enthroned amid the surging peoples, Macca crowned Him, saying,

'Receive this tiara adorned with three crowns, and know

Thyself to be the Ruler of the World, the Father of Princes and Kings, the earthly Vicar of Jesus Christ our Saviour.'

Hadrian understood the formula in no metaphorical, but in the plain and literal, sense of the words. He neither minimized nor magnified their significance. He had an opportunity which was entirely grateful to Him. He was Ruler, Father, Vicar. And He was altogether unafraid. He stood up, and blessed the City and the World.

In the Cystine Chapel, they relieved Him of the pontifical regalia, and the voluminous far-flowing petticoat of white taffetas, which is so sumptuous to the eye of the beholden and so ridiculously cumbersome to the legs of the wearer; and He ate some apples while Orezzo, on behalf of the Sacred College, recited time-honoured compliments.

'Lord Cardinals,' said Hadrian, 'We thank you for your service: and We invite those of you who are able and willing to attend Us, now, when We go to take possession of Our episcopal see.'

He moved towards the door. The short train of His cassock trailed behind Him, and the Bishop of Caerleon stooped to it.

Ragna had something to howl.

'Holiness, this is suicide for You and murder for us. The City is full of Jews and Freemasons; and we shall most assuredly be stabbed, or shot, or shattered to pieces with bombs, or drenched with vitriol –'

'The Church wants a martyr badly. Your Eminency is invited, not commanded.'

Berstein muttered to Vivole, in a scandalized tone, that the Pope was courting popularity. Pepato, with a note of admiration, commented on the mad English. Word of the invitation rushed on ahead. Of the crowd of officials, many began to arrange themselves in a certain order: others had pressing calls elsewhere. Masters of ceremonies, wracking their brains for long-forgotten details, flew hither and thither with instructions and pushes. Poor old Grani sat down in a recess; and wept to think that there was no time to get out the white gennets annually presented by the King of Spain. Hadrian came on slowly, chatting with Caerleon, giving people a chance of making up their minds. When He emerged from the colonnade in the Square of St Peter's, the Syndic of Rome fell into the ranks just before the Pope; and a royal escort of the Praetorian Guard surrounded Him. Hadrian stopped; and beckoned Prince Pilastro.

'Sir Syndic, are We free?' He mewed.

'But free, Holy Father.'

'Let your soldiers precede and not surround Us; and let no one come within ten paces of Us. We go by Via Giulia and Monte Celio.'

The squadron moved to the head of the line. The Pope took His train from the Bishop: threw it over His left arm: and came on alone. Acting as though the ideal were real, He made it real. If Jews and Freemasons would slay Him, well and good: it was part of the day's work, no doubt. He was by no means anxious to be martyred; and He sincerely hoped that, if it should come to Him, it would not be very painful or distorting. But, as it was His Own affair, a piece of the part He was fulfilling, He displayed Himself alone. Ten paces before Him went Prince Pilastro, looking back from time to time. Ten paces behind Him came the bishop, ruddy and strong in white and purple, wondering. The vermilion nine followed in a compact phalanx, very venerable and grand; and, after a great deal of bustle and noise, seventeen other cardinals added their magnificence. A motley of patriarchs, archbishops, bishops, prelates, and pontifical guards closed the rear.

A tremendous shout greeted Hadrian's first appearance in the square. It was quite incoherent: for the real significance of the pageant was not immediately realized. No Pope had set His foot in Rome since 1870: but here undoubtedly was the Pope, with a gentle inflexible face – a lonely white figure Whose left hand lay on the little cross on His breast, Whose right hand gravely scattered the same sign. This crowd was not the even human parallels which authority is wont to describe on streets when the Great go by. It was a concurrence from side-ways coalescing with loafers and ordinary passers-by, suddenly dipping its knees, gazing, panting, and emitting howls of delirious onomatopes. Cabs and carts swept to the side of the road; and the drivers kneeled on the boxes.

Here and there, some dowdy alien said, 'What mockery' and patronizingly explained that the Salvation Army did these things much more properly. Here and there, some sour sorry incapable stood spitting in praise of secret societies. Here and there some godless worldling scoffed in an undertone. But Hadrian went on, walking at that deceptive pace of His, which seemed so leisurely and was so swift. His movements resembled the running of a perfectly geared machine: they had the smooth and forceful grace of the athlete whose muscles are supple and strong: even the occasional impulse had no jerkiness. It was the manner with which He disguised His natural timidity. He sometimes glanced from side to side. Once He smiled at a barelegged rascalt of brown boys who kneeled by one of Bernini's angels on the parapet of the bridge. He adored children, although He was so desperately afraid of them. Going up the hill by the Church of Sts John and Paul, a little girl dabbed an indescribable rag on her head: rushed into the road, dashing primroses; and remained transfixed by her own audacity. He led her by the hand to her mother; and blessed them both. All His life long He had yearned to be giving. Now, under any circumstances, He always had something to give, ten words and a gesture; and people seemed so thankful for it. He was glad.

In the porch of the Mother and Mistress of All Churches in the City and the World, He sat on the low throne while canons made shift to intone, *He raiseth up the poor out of the dust, and lifteth the needy out of the dung-hill; that He may set Him with the Princes, even with the princes of His people*. They gave Him gold and silver keys. They attended Him to the throne of precious marbles in the centre of the apse. They intoned *Te Deum*. Ascending to the lodge of benediction, He blessed the mobile vulgar in the Square of St John; and anon returned in the way by which He came, Bishop of Rome in act and deed, and Supreme Pontiff.

CHAPTER 5

BEING physically tired with the exertion of withstanding the concentrated gaze of Rome, He rested all the afternoon. The palace was a scene of commotion. Cardinals and their familiars cackled and cooed and squeaked and growled in corners: or arranged for return to their distant sees. Workmen cleared away the structure of the Conclave. Hadrian made an attempt to get into the gardens with a book: but, obsequious black velvet chamberlains with their heads in frills like saucers made themselves so extremely necessary, and Auditors of the Ruota scudded along by-paths with such obvious secrecy and bounded out of box-hedges before Him by carefully calculated accident so very frequently, that at last He took refuge in the pontifical apartment. He rang the gong and sent for Caerleon.

'We have a more or less distinct remembrance of a place on the Lake of Albano, called Castel something.'

'Castel Gandolfo, Holiness.'

'Yes. And it used to be a pontifical villa?'

'It is a pontifical villa now: but since 1870 an order of religious women have used part of it as a convent.'

'Which part?'

'They, I believe, keep the pontifical suite in *statu quo*, hoping for the day when the Holy Father shall come to His Own again.'

'Good. Now will you at once telegraph to those nuns that the Pope is coming to His Own tomorrow for the inside of a week. And please arrange everything on a plain and private scale. That is the first thing.'

'Perhaps I'd better do that at once whatever.'

'Yes, but don't be long.'

When the bishop returned, Hadrian invited him to take a tour of observation round the rooms. They were accentedly antipathetic, too red, too ormolu, too floridly renascent, too distractingly rococo. He could not work in them. Yes, work –

nothing was going to interfere with that. How, in the name of heaven, could anyone work under these painted ceilings, among all these violently ineffectual curves? Now that He was able, He must have what He wanted. He was going to move on to the top floor, where people could not stamp on His head, and where there was a better view from the windows. He would have clean bare spaces and simplicity without frippery. Then His mind could move. By the clothes presses, He damned red velvet. That should go. The feeling of it made Him squirm. The sight of it on His person reminded Him of the barking of malodorous dogs and the braying of assertive donkeys. White was all right, if it fitted properly. He would stick to white, soft flannelly white, not this shiny cloth: with a decent surplice (which did not resemble the garments of David's servants after the attentions of the children of Ammon) – a surplice and the pallium, and the pontifical red stole in public: but no lace – that should be left to ladies. How delicious to have plenty of white clothes to wear! How delicious to wear white in the sun! Well, He was going to work to earn all these amenities. And now, talking of work, something would have to be done to the rooms upstairs: and certain things would have to be settled regarding the domestic arrangements. To what official ought directions to be given?

'The Major-domo is the head of the household; and the Master of the Chamber has immediate charge of Your Holiness's person.'

'That set man? Look now, he shall continue to be Master of the Chamber. We will not repeat the mistake of Pius IX, or interfere with any of their offices. But he must not come near Us. We should feel bound to assist his decrepitude; and Our idea is to be so free from secular cares that We can concentrate undivided attention upon Our Apostolature. There is the root of the matter. That man is a stranger: his age makes it certain that he has got into a groove: he is full of prior experiences and opinions which he cannot, and ought not to be expected to, change for a newcomer. But, if he remains here, it will be Ourself Who will have to obey him. That would distract Us. Therefore We must interpose someone whom We know – someone who is young enough to suit himself to Us. There are two young ruffians of about twenty-five years old, who, like most of his other acquaintances, formerly loved and hated George Arthur Rose. Their circumstances are disagreeable: they never had a chance: they are hot-headed passionate people, always in love with some woman or other, because they have no means of amusing themselves innocently, being tied and bound with the chains of respectable poverty. They really have no opportunity of leading godly righteous and sober lives. They're insane, unhealthy, because civilization gives them no opportunity to live sane healthy lives unless they crush all the most salient and most admirable characteristics of their individuality. Please send for them – John Devine, 107 Arkwright Street, Preston – Iulo Carrino, 95 Bloomsbury Square, London – and let Us give them some service and much freedom, and a little wholesome neglect to strengthen and develop their characters and to give play to their individual natures, as good old Jowett says. We believe in making it, not difficult but, easy to be good – Look, Frank, tell Iulo Carrino to bring with him that yellow cat which you may remember. By the bye, both these men cannot move without money. Take this cheque for George Arthur Rose's balance at Coutts's: use what is generous – generous, mind you – and account to Us later. And now, about the other things, We had better see Centrina and the Major-domo upstairs.'

The Pope and the bishop inspected a series of empty rooms on the top floor. They occupied the N.E. and the S.E. sides of the palace. Hadrian chose the large room in the angle with windows on two sides for the secret chamber. It was approached from the N.E. corridor by way of fifteen antechambers and a large room suitable for private receptions. Beyond the antechambers there was another series of apartments which He also took. The private room in the angle, sitting-room, or workshop (as He called it), led into some smaller rooms on the S.E. face of the palace. Here he fixed upon a bedroom, bathroom, dressing-room, oratory, and sundry store-rooms, accessible by a single door in the last room which led into the corridor overlooking the court of St Damasus.

The Major-domo and the Master-of-the-Chamber attended. The latter was quaking about his situation. Hadrian rapidly reassured him and came to the point. 'You are confirmed in your benefice until such time as you choose to retire. The emoluments and the pension are at your disposal. In a few days, two gentlemen will arrive from England. You will prepare a parlour and a bedroom for each, adjoining the first ante-chamber. Fix a bell in each parlour communicating with this room.' (They were standing in the room which had been selected as a workshop.) 'You will provide two servants for them. They will take their meals in their parlours. After their arrival, Our commandments will come to you through them.' (He turned and addressed Himself to the Major-domo.) 'These two gentlemen must be given some official status.'

'If I understand aright, Your Holiness is appointing two Gentlemen-in-Waiting-in-the-Apostolic-Chamber.'

'That will do. When they arrive, see that they have diplomas of appointment as Gentlemen of the Apostolic Chamber. The Bishop of Caerleon will arrange with you about their emoluments. Now, let Us furnish these rooms.'

They went out into the corridor; and re-entered the apartment by the first antechamber.

'Cover all the walls and ceilings with brown-packing paper – yes, brown-packing paper – *carta straccia*,' the Pope repeated. 'Stain all the woodwork with a darker shade of brown. The gilding of the cornices can remain as it is. No carpets. These small greenish-blue tiles are clean; and they soothe the eye. Curtains? You may hang very voluminous linen curtains on the doors and windows, greenish-blue linen to match the tiles, and without borders. Furnish all those ante-chambers with rush chairs and oaken tables. Remember that everything is to be plain, without ornament – In this room you may place the usual throne and canopy: and that crucifix from downstairs – (how exquisite the mother-of-pearl Figure is!) – and the stools, and twelve large candlesticks – iron or brass –

Now this room is to be a workshop. Let Us have a couch and three armchairs, all large and low and well-cushioned, covered with undyed leather. Get some of those large plain wooden tables which are used in kitchens, about three yards long and one and a half wide. Put writing-materials on one of them, there, on the right of the window. Leave the middle of the room empty. Put three small bookcases against that wall and a cup-board here – Make a bedroom of this room. Let the bed be narrow and long, with a husk mattress; and let the back of the head be toward the window. Put one of the large wooden tables here and a dozen rush-chairs –' (He spoke to the bishop) 'Do you know that there is no water here at all, except in little jugs?' (He continued to the Major-domo) 'Line the walls of this room with greenish-blue tiles, like those on the floor. Put several pegs on both doors. In this corner put a drainpipe covered with a grating; and, six feet above it, let a waterpipe and a tap project rectangularly two feet from the wall. Yes. Six feet from the floor, two feet from the wall; and let there be a constant and copious supply of water – rain water, if possible. Do you understand?'

The Major-domo understood. The Master-of-the-Chamber shivered.

'And lamps. Get two plain oil-lamps for each room, with copper shades: large lamps, to give a very strong light. Paint over both doors of the bedroom, on the outside of each, *Intrantes excommunicantur ipso facto*. When We have finished here,' He addressed the Master-of-the-Chamber again, 'you will parade your staff; and We will select one person and pro-vide him with a dispensation from that rule as long as he be-haves himself well. He will have charge of the bedroom and the sole right to enter it.' (The Pope passed into the next room: paused, and whispered explicit directions to the Major-domo; and moved on to the farther room.) 'The clothes-presses from downstairs can be moved into this room. They will serve. And you had better make a door here, so that it can be entered from the corridor.' (He went on again.) 'This room is to be the vestry – and this the oratory. Let Us have a plain stone altar and the stations, and the bare necessaries for mass, all of the simplest. Let everything, walls, floor, ceiling, everything, be white – natural white, not painted; and make a door here, also leading into the corridor, a large double door convenient for the faithful who assist at the pontifical mass. The rooms beyond – you will take order about them at a convenient occasion.'

Hadrian and the bishop returned to the pontifical apartments downstairs.

'Your Holiness will excuse me –'

'Yes?'

'– but have You ever contemplated the present situation?'

'No. Why?'

'Well, Your Holiness seems to have everything cut and dried.'

The Pope laughed. 'You shall know that George Arthur Rose has had plenty of time for thinking and scheming. His schemes never came to anything, except once; and he certainly never schemed for this. But you understand perhaps that the last twenty years have rendered Hadrian conscious both of His abilities and His limitations, as well as of His requirements; and hence He is able at a glance to describe in detail what He wants. When He wants something, without knowing what He wants, He asks questions. For example, what is that hinged arrangement under Cardinal Courtleigh's ring?'

'A master-key, Holiness; I have just got one too.' The bishop showed his own ring.

'What is that?'

'I have several places which I have to keep locked, safes, cupboards, and that sort of thing; and the keys, which are all different, have to be entrusted to my various chaplains, and so on. Well, each of these can only open the lock of the thing which concerns him: but, with that master-key, I can unlock everything and no one else in the world can do that.'

'Capital? Where do you get these things made?'

'At a place in Bond Street – Bramah I think the name is.'

'Tell them to –' The voice sank, for some scarlet gentleman began to bring in tables with the sealed dishes of the pontifical supper. Hadrian's eyes lingered on the intruders for a moment. They were so slim, so robust, so deft, so grave, so Roman. He drew the bishop into the embrasure of a window.

'Aren't they lovely?' He said. 'Isn't the world full of lovely things, lovely live things? It's the dead and the stagnant that are ugly.'

This was so rapid a change of mood that Talacryn could not follow it. As soon as the servants were gone, Hadrian continued, returning the episcopal ring, 'Tell your Bramah people to fit all the doors upstairs with locks which have separate keys, and to send another score of locks also with separate keys; and also to send a man here who is capable of making an episcopal ring for Us which shall contain a master-key to all those locks.'

'Very well, Holy Father.'

'Don't go. Supper can wait a minute. Look here: We desire to be in direct communication with the Sacred College. We chiefly are curious to know the nine Compromissaries: but distinctions sometimes are invidious. At all events, We must have a long and secret conference with Cardinal Courtleigh. So will you please make it known to Their Eminencies that We will receive them after supper. Ask Pimlico to remain after the others. And – who manages the finances here?'

'The Cardinal-Deacon of Santa Maria Nuova is Apostolic Treasurer; and the Major-domo is responsible for the household expenses.'

'Ask the Treasurer particularly to come. Don't come yourself. Good night: God bless you.'

Caerleon firmly had believed that he knew George Arthur Rose to be charming – perhaps somewhat incomprehensible, and therefore perhaps somewhat dangerous. But as for Hadrian – Caerleon felt about him as M. and Mme Curie felt when they first put a penny on a piece of radium and observed the penetrative energy incessantly thrown off from a source which was both concrete and inexhaustible.

The Pope's evening party was well attended. Some of the older members of the Sacred College, who really had suffered from the discomforts of the Conclave, had left the Vatican.

Most of the French absented themselves, as they had every right to do in view of the informality of the invitation. The Secretary of State stayed away on a plea of business. But a mixed motive, in which inquisitiveness was the dominant ingredient, impelled thirty-two vermilion princes into the Pontiff's throne room. The Cardinal-Dean, notwithstanding his age and infirmity, came with glee. Next to succeeding to the paparchy himself, nothing suited him better than to have a perfect stranger for a Pope, Who evidently was about to subvert every single act of Leo's. He said almost as much to Hadrian, bustling up to the throne and using a stool.

'We take it very kindly that Your Eminency should come to Us; and We let you know that We summon Our first consistory to meet on the thirtieth day of April,' said the Pope, in a tone which was a skilful blend of the World's Ruler's with that of youth to age, of a newcomer to an old stager.

Orezzo was pleased. He took the ball of conversation and set it rolling. 'It is a fortunate event, Holiness,' he said, 'that the Divine Leo – may His soul rest in a cool place – never carried out His intention of nominating His successors.'

'Ah!' the Pope responded. 'We remember reading about that in an English newspaper, the *Pall Mall Gazette*, a few years back. Perhaps Your Eminency can tell Us what truth there was in the report?'

'The facts, Holy Father, were these. Leo so firmly believed that the policy, which He had seen fit to pursue during His long reign, was essential to the welfare of the Church, that He wished to be assured of its continuance; and He would have had each of us to promise Him that, upon election, we would not depart from His example. Some of us – I name no names – were unwilling to bind ourselves; and, being unable to secure unanimous assurance, Leo declared that He would use the plenitude of the apostolic power and nominate His successors.'

The other cardinals, attracted by these words, drew nearer to the throne. Some sat on stools: others remained standing: all intently listened to Orezzo: all intently gazed at Hadrian.

The aspect of the Pontiff did not give satisfaction. It was not listless: it was not inattentive, for, as a matter of fact, it indicated very vivid ardent studiose concern, a perfect perception of being 'among the Doctors': but Hadrian seemed to be treating the matter too impersonally, too much from the viewpoint of the outsider. He gave no sign whatever that He was conscious how very nearly this thing touched Himself.

'He reminds one of a surgeon probing for a bullet in a body which is not his,' said Mundo to Fiamma.

'And He will find that bullet,' the Archbishop of Bologna replied.

Hadrian (Who could see as far through a brick wall as most men, and a great deal further than some) was not by any means unconscious of the situation, and was avidly curious after information. He pursued the inquiry. Many thought it would have been more delicate to drop it.

'Yes. That was the gist of the statement in the paper,' He continued to Orezzo. 'We remember it well: because We wondered whether or not such a privilege was included in that "plenitude of apostolic power". We could not find a precedent; and none of the authorities whom We consulted could provide one. Advise Us, Lord Cardinal.'

If Orezzo had not been Cardinal-Bishop of Ostia and Velletri, Dean of the Sacred College, and Chamberlain of the Holy Roman Church, he would have grinned. He found the moment unmitigatedly delectable.

'Holiness, there is a pious opinion, represented (I believe) by the Cardinal-Penitentiary' – (Serafino-Vagellaio violently flushed) – 'to the effect that the Divine Leo was not in error. Also, there is another pious opinion, represented (I happen to know) by the rest of the College, that on this point the said Divine Leo erred as infallibly as possible.'

This was thin ice indeed.

'Your Eminency's exposition hath been most sound. The matter is one for the theologians,' said Hadrian, ceasing to lean forward. 'But why, Lord Cardinal, do you call it fortunate that the nomination was not effected?'

'Because if it had been effected, we might not have experienced the pleasure of saluting a Pontiff, Who, according to the Cardinal of Pimlico, is an academic anarchist.'

Hadrian candidly and simply laughed, with a friendly look at Courtleigh, who did not at all like being the second victim of Orezzo's caustic tongue.

'His Eminency has taken that bad habit of labelling people from Us,' He said. 'But, although We give due weight to the epithet "academic", We abhor from and cannot away with the term "anarchist". Aristocrat We are not: the mere word Democrat fills Us with repugnance. Such as it is, Our philosophy is individualistic altruism. But, Eminencies, is not the labelling of matter which is in a state of flux, humanity for example, somewhat futile? Even supposing the labelled matter to be static, do not the very words on the label change their meaning with the course of time? But deeds remain; and the motive of a deed is that by which it must, and will, be judged. Give Us then the benefit of your holy prayers, Lord Cardinals, that Our motives may be pure, and Our acts acceptable to Him Who has deigned to Our unworthy hands the awful office of His Vicegerent here on earth.'

He leaned back in His chair for the moment after this little outburst. The sense of His enormous responsibility was upon Him. In an indefinite shadowy sort of way, it had been in His mind to utter some such allocution to the cardinals by way of explaining to them His Own conception of His task: but He had intended to make it more of a deliberate formal pronouncement. The instant when the words had passed His lips, however, He perceived that in one sentence He had said all. He also perceived that the gaiety of the beginning, and the solemnity of the conclusion, sufficed to give His utterance distinction. He said no more. There was no doubt but that He had created an impression: an impression which differed, it is true, according to the temper of the impressed – but still He had created an impression. Those Eminencies, who were more formal than vital, assumed that professional abstraction of demeanour which marks a conference of clergy while one of their number is 'talking shop'. Those two or three, who were devout enthusiasts, blessed themselves and exhibited the white cornea beneath the iris of their eyes. The majority (who combined the qualities of the dignified fine-gentleman-of-the-old-school, with those of the scholar, the teacher, and the practical Christian) beamed instant approbation. Their verdict was that the utterance was very correct and proper. Nothing could be more true.

The assemblage split up into groups; and separate conversations were begun. The Pope sat, still and grave. Orezzo gracefully pleaded his age and the hour of night: kissed the Apostle's knee; and retired.

Hadrian beckoned the Cardinal-Deacon of Santa Maria Nuova; and addressed him in a confidential manner.

'We understand that the expenses of Our household pass through the hands of the Major-domo. Are they paid from some fund particularly allotted to the purpose?'

'Yes, Most Holy Lord; from –'

'The details are unimportant. And the expenses of the paparchy in general?'

'There are numerous funds, Most Holy Lord, which are administered by numerous departments under my supervision.'

'And those funds – Some suffice; and some do not suffice. They vary, no doubt?'

'Most Holy Lord, they vary.'

'Is there any particular fund over which We have exclusive control?'

'The whole revenue, Most Holy Lord, is subject to Your pleasure: but Peter's Pence belong to the pontiff-regnant personally. They are His private property – salary – honorarium, I should say.'

'In eight days, Your Eminency will be good enough to let Us know the annual average of that income, say, for the last twenty years.'

'It shall be done, Most Holy Lord.'

'Meanwhile, what money is at Our disposal at this moment?'

'There has been accumulated a large reserve, the exact

amount of which is known only to the bankers. It is Yours, Most Holy Lord.'

'What approximately is the sum?'

'In round numbers, Most Holy Lord, it cannot be less than five millions.'

'Lire?'

'Pounds sterling, Most Holy Lord.'

Hadrian's eyes sparkled. 'Where is it?'

'The bulk is in the Bank of England, Most Holy Lord: but there is much gold in the safe.'

'Which safe?'

'The safe in the bedroom wall, Most Holy Lord.'

'Where is the key?'

'The Cardinal-Chamberlain holds all keys, Most Holy Lord.'

'Tomorrow Your Eminency will be good enough to cause the safe in the bedroom wall to be removed to a similar position in the bedroom which We have instructed the Major-domo to prepare on the upper storey. And now please follow the Cardinal-Chamberlain: obtain the key of the safe; and bring it to Us.'

The Apostolic Treasurer rose; and went out. Hadrian also stood up. The company, understanding that the reception was ended, made obeisance and began to move away. The Pope detained Courtleigh.

'Eminency,' He said, 'We have many things to say to you: but We will not detain you now. Tomorrow We go to Castel Gandolfo. Come with Us. A few tired priests are sure of a hospitable welcome there. Yes, come with Us. Who is that young cardinal by the door?'

'That is Monsignor Nefski, Holiness -- the Archbishop of Prague.'

'He is marked by some fearful sorrow?'

'A most fearful sorrow indeed.'

'Once, in a man's rooms at Oxford, a young undergraduate happened to enter. He had just that deadly pallor, that dense black hair, that rigidity of feature, that bleached bleak fixity of gaze. When he was gone, We remarked on his appearance. Our host said that he had been seeing his best friend drowned. They were on a cliff, somewhere in Your Eminency's native land, taking photographs of breakers in the height of a storm. The friend was on the very verge. Suddenly the cliff gave way; and he fell into the raging sea. He was a magnificent swimmer. He struggled with the billows for more than half an hour. There was no help within five miles; and, finally, the breath was battered out of him. The other perforce had to stand by, and watch it all. It indelibly marked him. Cardinal Nefski, you say, is marked by a fearful experience. Lately? Was it as fearful as that?'

'Ten weeks ago, Holiness; and a much more fearful experience.'

'Eminency, bring him also to Castel Gandolfo. Some of you must attend the Pope. Let Us have those to whom We can be useful.'

When he was alone, Hadrian examined the safe in the bedroom wall. It added to His consciousness of His immense potentiality. What a number of long-planned things He could do now! With its contents, He would open a current account at the Bank of Italy. With that, and another at the Bank of England – He acquainted Himself with the tools of His new trade. Truly, Caerleon did not altogether err in calling Him an incomprehensible creature. On the one hand, with His principle of giving He could not even grasp a problem which involved taking: while, on the other hand, He utterly failed to realize that most people are averse from giving. As for Himself, He took freely; and, as freely, He was going to give. As for the Bishop of Caerleon's opinion – it is so easy and so satisfactory to call a man 'an incomprehensible creature', when one is mentally incapable of comprehending, or unwilling to try to comprehend, the 'creature'.

CHAPTER 6

HE spent the first day at Castel Gandolfo in the garden, writing, enjoying the loveliness of late spring. He produced a score of sheets of swiftly scribbled manuscript bristling with emendations. The second day He summoned Cardinal Courtleigh directly after breakfast; and addressed him with some formality.

'We desire to establish relations with Your Eminency, chiefly because You hold so responsible a position in England, a country dear above all countries to Us which We design to treat with singular favour. In pursuance of Our intention, and of Our desire, certain matters must be defined. If Our words are unpleasing. Your Eminency must take them in the light of Our said intention and desire.'

The cardinal put on his cardinalitial mask. He was to hear and note this rash young man. If anything needed to be said, he was there to say it.

'It is Our wish to make England "a people prepared for The Lord". We will attempt it of the whole world; and for this reason We begin with the race which dominates the world. We find Ourself impeded at the outset by the present habitude and conduct of English Catholics, especially of the aboriginal English Catholics.'

At this unexpected fulguration, this feline scratch, the cardinalitial eyebrows shot upward with a jerk and horizontally came down again. His Eminency slightly bowed, and attended. The Pope fingered a volume of cuts from English newspapers: selected a cut; and continued,

'Kindly let Us have your opinion of this statement: – *A remarkable petition has been prepared for presentation to Parliament. The petitioners are the Roman Catholic laity resident in England; and they pray Parliament to set up some control over Roman Catholic moneys and interests. It is pointed out that the total capital invested in the Roman Catholic clergy in the United Kingdom must amount to nearly £50,000,000. It is alleged that no account is afforded by the*

Roman Catholic bishops of the management or disbursements of such property and moneys. And the petitioners also call attention to gross injustices which are of daily occurrence.'

'That emanated from a priest of my archdiocese, Holiness. It was a terrible scandal: but we were successful in preventing it from spreading.'

'Then there was such a petition? At first, We were prepared to ascribe it to the imagination of one of Sir Notyet Apeer's young men. And really were there many supporters of the petition?'

'Unfortunately, yes.'

'Then you have rebellion within the camp. And was there any ground for these statements?'

'There was no ground whatever for the insinuation that we habitually misuse our trusteeship. The man had a grievance. His agitation was merely a means to compel us to solace him. He trusted, by making himself unpleasant to us, to make us pleasant to him. So he attacked our financial arrangements. It was a wicked stroke: for, you know, Holy Father, that we cannot be expected to account to any Tom-Dick-and-Harry for bequests and endowments which we administer.'

'Your accounts are properly audited, no doubt?'

'To a great extent, yes.'

'But not invariably? You trust much to the honesty and the financial ability of individual clerks? We do not presume for a moment that there is any systematic malversation of trust. You have had a lesson on that subject.'

'Lesson?'

'Yes: in 1886: after the notorious Carvale Case, when the infatuated imbecility of the Gaelic and Pictish bishops was shown to render them undesirable as trustees, the clergy simply dare not stray into illegal paths. Oh no. But are the clergy actually capable of financial administration?'

'As capable, I suppose, as other men.'

'Priests are not "as other men". However, We take it that you all believe yourselves to have acted conscientiously. We also take it that, in view of the power and influence which the position of trustee affords, your clergy eagerly become trustees and are unwilling to submit to supervision or to criticism. That is quite human. We entirely disapprove of it.'

'But what would your Holiness have?'

'We cannot say it in one sentence. You must collect Our mind from Our conduct as well as from Our words. We entirely disapprove of the clergy competing for or using any secular power or dominance whatever, especially such power as in-heres in the command of money. The clergy are ministers – ministers – not masters. And as to the other charge – "the gross injustices which are of daily occurrence"?'

'That, of course, is simply the scream of an opponent. It is spite.'

'Does Your Eminency mean that there are no injustices? Don't you know of gross injustices?'

'"It needs must that offences come."'

'"But woe to him by whom the offence cometh." Emin-ency, why not frankly face the predicament? The clergy are more than less human; and they certainly are not even the pick of humanity. Now, don't they attempt too much in the first instance; and, in the second, don't they invariably refuse to admit or amend their blunders? Listen to this. The *Pall Mall Gazette* states, on the authority of the *Missiones Catholicae* that, in Australia, during the last five years, we have increased our numbers from 3,008,399 to 4,507,980. But the government census taken last year gives the total population of Australia at 4,555,803. That leaves only 47,823 for the other religious and irreligious bodies. As a matter of fact, the latest Roman Catholic record is 916,880. Therefore an overstatement of 3,591,100 has been made. Which is absurd. And perpetuated. Which is damnable.'

'I do not precisely see Your Holiness's point.'

'No? Well, let us go to another.' The Pope produced a small green ticket on which was printed, *Church of the Sacred Heart – Quest Road – Admit Bearer to – Midnight Service – New Year's Eve 1900 – Middle Seat 6d*. 'This comes from Your Eminency's archdiocese,' he said.

The cardinal looked at the thing, as one looks at the grass of the field. There it is. One has seen it all before.

'We disapprove of that,' said the Pope.

'What would Your Holiness suggest then to prevent improper persons from attending these services?'

'Improper persons should be encouraged to attend. No obstacle should be placed in their way.'

The cardinal was irritated. 'Then we should have scenes of disorder, to say nothing of profanation.'

'That is where Your Eminency and all the aboriginals err. Your opinion is formed upon the apprehensive sentimentality of pious old-ladies-of-both-sexes whose ideal of Right is the Not-obviously Wrong. When a thing is unpleasant, they go up a turning: wipe their mouths; and mistake evasion for annihilation. They don't annihilate the evil: they avoid it. Now, we are here to seek and to save that which was lost: and our churches must be more free to the lost than to the saved – if any be saved. Experience proves that your pious fears have no sure warranty. Wesleyan schismatics have performed Watch-night services for more than a century. Anglican schismatics have done the same: and, in later years, they have celebrated their mysteries at midnight on Christmas Eve. We Ourself have assisted at these functions. The temples were open and free: and We never saw or heard a sign of the profanation of which you speak. Sots and harlots undoubtedly were present: but they were not disorderly: they were cowed, they were sleepy, they were curious, but they made no noise. Even though they had shouted, it only would have been in protest against some human ordinance; and a human ordinance must give way the moment it becomes a barrier between one soul and that soul's Creator. Supposing means of grace to be obtainable in a church, who durst deny them to those who chiefly need them? The position which you clergy take up is an essentially false one. We are not here to establish conventions, or to enforce conformity. We are here to serve – only to serve. We especially disapprove of any system which bars access to the church, or which makes it difficult – this admission-fee, for example.'

'Holy Father, the clergy must live.'

'You lead Us to infer that they cannot live without these sixpences?'

'We are so poor: we have no endowments: the fee is no more than a pew-rent for a single service –'

'Lord Cardinal, be accurate. You have endowments: not equal to those of which you are thinking, the "stolen property" enjoyed by the Church-of-England-as-by-Law-Established: but you have endowments. You mean that they are meagre. But pew-rents are abominable: so are pews, for that matter. Abolish them both.'

'I am bound to obey Your Holiness: but I must say that this quixotic impossible idealism will be the ruin of the Church –'

'That is impossible: because Her Founder promised to be with Her always even unto the end of the world.'

'God helps those who help themselves –'

'But not those who help themselves out of other people's pockets.'

'The workman is worthy of his hire –'

'Perfectly. But he accepts the wage: he does not dictate it. The builder of London's new concert-hall in Denambrose Avenue did not let his masons domineer. He offered work at a certain wage. They took it, or left it. You confuse the functions of the buyer with those of the seller, as the clergy always do. Besides, as you seem fond of Scripture, "provide neither gold nor silver nor brass in your purses", and "take no thought for the morrow –"'

'This is simply Tolstoy!'

'No. We never have read a line of Tolstoy. We studiously avoid doing so. We give you the commands of Christ Himself as reported by St Matthew. Lord Cardinal, you are all wrong –'

'Your Holiness speaks as though You were not one of us.'

'Oh no! The head looks down at the hands; and says "Your knuckles and your nails are dirty".'

The cardinal really was angry. Hadrian paused: fixed him with a taming look: and continued 'Is it right or even desirable that the clergy should engage in trade – actually engage in trade? Look at your *Catholic Directory*; and see the advertisement of a priest who, with archiepiscopal sanction, is prepared to pay bank interest on investments, in plain words to borrow money upon usury in direct contravention of St Luke's statement of The Lord's words on this subject. Look at the *Catholic Hour*; and see the advertisement of a priest who actually trades as a tobacconist. Look in the precincts of your churches; and see the tables of the Fenian-literature sellers and the seats of them that sell tickets for stage-plays and bazaars where palmistry is practised –'

'I merely interrupt to remind Your Holiness that Your august predecessor traded as a fisherman.'

'Very neat,' the Pope applauded, enjoying the retort: 'but not neat enough. A fisherman's trade is an open-air trade, and a healthy trade, by the way: but – did Our predecessor St Peter trade as a fisherman after He had entered upon the work of the apostolature? We think not. No, Lord Cardinal, the clergy attempt too much. They might be excellent priests. As tradesmen, variety-entertainers, entrepreneurs, they are failures. As a combination, they are catastrophes. These two things must be kept apart, the clerical and the secular, God and Mammon. The difference must be emphasized. By attempts at compromise, the clergy fail in both. As priests, they are mocked: and as for their penny-farthing peddling –'

'But Holy Father, do think for one minute. What are the clergy to live on?'

'The free-will offerings of the faithful; and one must keep the other.'

'But suppose the faithful do not give free-will offerings?'

'Then starve and go to Heaven, as Ruskin says. That is what We are going to do, if possible.'

'How are we to build our churches?'

'Don't build them, unless you have the means freely given. Avoid beggary. That way you sicken the faithful – you prevent generosity –'

'How shall we keep up those we have? For example, the cathedral –'

'Yes, the cathedral – a futile monument of one vain man's desire for notoriety. How many lives has it ruined? One, at least, We know. How many evil passions has it inspired? – the passion for advertisement by means of the farthing journalist, the critical passion which is destroying our creative faculty, the passions of envy and covetousness, the passion of competition, the passion of derision – for you know that the world is mocking the ugly veneered pretentious monstrosity now. Better that it never had been. As it is, and in regard to the churches which exist, you must do what you can. If the faithful freely give you enough, then let them stand. If not, you must let them go. England never will lack altars. In any case, encumber yourselves with no more unpaid for buildings. Accept what is given: but ask for nothing and suggest nothing. Lord Cardinal, the clergy do not act as though they trusted the Divine Disposer of Events. They mean well: but their whole aim and object seems to be to serve God by conciliating Mammon. There is nothing more criminally futile. Instead of winning England's admiration, you secure Her scornful toleration. Instead of consolidating the faithful, multitudes have become disaffected, and multitudes leave you day by day. Instead of improving the clerical character (and, by consequence, the character of all who look to the clergy for example) the clergy ever more and more assimilate themselves to the laity. The clergy should cultivate the virtues, not the vices, of humanity. Not one of us can tell which of our actions is important or unimportant. By a thoughtless word or deed, we may lead astray a brother for whom Christ died. That is what is to be feared from your worldly clergy. Teach them that *magna ars* which St Thomas of Aquino says *est conversari Jesu*. Teach them to rise above the world.'

'Surely, Holy Father, they do.'

'Some members of the clergy do, no doubt. We never met them. The tone of the clergy is distinctly worldly. Here is an illustration from your own newspaper. The very first thing which the *Slab* thinks worthy of note is *How Monsignor Cateran signally vindicated his honour and suitably punished his traducer, the proprietor of the* Fatherland. *The terms of the apology which Sir*

Frederick Smithers has had to publish in his own journal are set forth as a warning to evil-doers. It is on p. 397. You know the particulars?'

'I have read them.'

'You cannot approve of the savage triumph of the letter on p. 416, in which Monsignor Cateran describes his victory: you cannot approve of the sneer at his enemy who *could not be punished by damages – he has no means to pay*, or the gibe at the freemasonry of the libeller, or the vicious malignant spite of the whole disgraceful document –'

'But, Holiness, the libel was a dreadful one and grossly unjust.'

'But, Eminency, the accused was bound by his Christianity to suffer revilings and persecutions and the saying of all manner of evil falsely. He forgot that. In vindicating himself, he behaved, not as a minister of God but, as a common human animal. However, besides the so-called triumphant vindication of Monsignor Cateran, which the *Slab* glorifies in three separate columns, this same number bristles with improprieties. On p. 415, you have Dominican and Jesuit controversialists calling each other liars, and otherwise politely hating and abusing one another –'

'Oh, Jesuits and Dominicans!'

The Pope put down the paper, and looked. The cardinal collected himself for a sally in force.

'Your Holiness will permit me to say that all this is extremely unusual. I myself was consecrated bishop in 1872, fourteen years before You were a Christian; and it seems to me that You should give Your seniors credit for having consciences at least –'

'Dear Lord Cardinal, if We had seen a sign of the said consciences –'

The cardinal tottered: but made one more thrust.

'I am not the only member of the Sacred College who thinks that Your Holiness's attitude partakes of – shall I say singularity – and – ha – arrogance.'

'Singularity? Oh, We sincerely hope so. But arrogance –

We cannot call it arrogance to assume that We know more of a particular subject, which We eagerly have studied from Our childhood, than those do who never have studied it at all. Eminency, We began by saying that We desired to establish relations with you. Now, have We shown you something of Our frame of mind?'

'Certainly, Holy Father: You wish me to –'

'We wish you to act upon the sum of Our words and conduct, in order that England may have a good and not a bad example from English Catholics. No more than that. We may call Ourselves Christendom till We are black in the face: but the true character of a Christendom is wanting to Us because the great promises of prophecy still lack fulfilment. The Barque of Peter has been trying to reach harbour. Mutiny within, storms without, have driven Her hither and thither. Is She as far off from port today as ever? Who knows? But the new captain is trying to set the course again from the old chart. His look is no longer backward but onward. Lord Cardinal, can the captain count on the loyal support of his lieutenant?'

'Holy Father, I assure You that You may count on me.' It was an immense effort: but, when it came to so fine a point, the nature and the pride of the man gave way to the grace of his Divine Vocation.

'Well now, only one more blow from the flail, and then We will take up the crook. Do stop your Catholics from toadying the German Emperor. Read that. It's perfectly absurd for them to tell him that *the whole Catholic world would be delighted if the protection of Catholics in the Orient were confided to him*. He's an admirable person: but We are not going to confide the protection of Catholics in the Orient to him. England is the only power which can manage Orientals. And what right have these Erse and Gaelic Catholics to speak for "the whole Catholic world"? Do neither England nor Italy count? Do make these pious fat-wits mind their own business – make them understand that when they tell the Kaiser that *they will exert themselves to remove all misunderstandings between Germany and England* – England last, you note – they would be comical if they were not impertinent and entirely stupid – and of course disloyal as usual.'

Hadrian collected His documents and the book of newspaper cuts: swept them all into a portfolio; and abruptly changed the subject.

'Will Your Eminency be good enough to tell Us the circumstances which led to Our extraordinary election?'

Barely recovered from his commotion of mind, and posed point-blank like this, Cardinal Courtleigh hesitated and said something about the Acts of the Conclave. His aboriginally tardy temperament was incapable of keeping pace with the feline agility of the Pontiff. Hadrian perceived his difficulty, and intently pursued the inquiry from another footing.

'We know all about the Acts of the Conclave, which We shall read at Our leisure. But We want the more human light which Your Eminency can throw upon the subject. Perhaps it will be simpler if We use the Socratic method. By what means did Our name, did the mere fact of Our existence become known to the Sacred College?'

'By my means, Holiness.'

'We understand that Your Eminency actually proposed us to the Conclave?'

'That is so.'

'And We infer that you also recommended Us: or at least described Us in such a way that the cardinals knew whom they were electing?'

'Yes, Holy Father.'

'Why did Your Eminency propose Us?' the Pope purred.

The cardinal seemed to be at a loss again. He appeared to have a difficulty in expression, not a lack of material for expression. Hadrian made a dash for the rudiments.

'There were other names before the College? Why were none of their owners chosen?'

'It was impossible to agree about their merits, Holiness.'

'Several attempts, no doubt, were made?'

'The Ways of Scrutiny and Access were tried seven times.'

'And then?'

'And then came a deadlock. None of the candidates obtained a sufficiency of suffrages: and none of the electors were willing to change their opinion.'

'And then?'

'The Way of Compromise was tried.'

'And, through Your Eminency's means, the Compromissaries were induced to impose Us on the Sacred College?'

'Yes, Holiness.'

'Eminency, at the time when the Conclave first was immured, We hardly can have been in Your mind. It is improbable that you could have thought of Us then in this connexion. At what point did We come into your calculations?'

'I ought perhaps to say that Your name had been brought before me some weeks before the demise of Holiness's predecessor.'

'That would be in connexion with the matter of which we treated in London.'

'Yes.'

'Precisely in what way was Our name brought before Your Eminency?'

'It was brought before me in a letter from Edward Lancaster – a perfectly frantic letter accusing himself of all sorts of crimes. Your Holiness perhaps is aware what a queer person he is, rather inclined to be scrupulous, and most impulsive.'

'Yes, We know him. We Ourself would have said "unscrupulous": Your Eminency uses the word "scrupulous" in the Catholic sense, whereas We prefer frank English.'

'I mean that he is given to tormenting himself about fancied sins –'

'And We mean that, as a rule, he does nothing of the kind: but, like a good many others, is singularly successful in lulling his conscience. At least, for fifteen years he contrived to do so in this case. However, he now has made amends; and there is nothing more to be said. Let us continue. You received a self-accusing letter from Edward Lancaster. And then?'

'Not one letter, Holiness: a dozen at least. The injustice, of which You had been the victim, was on his nerves. He wrote me several letters; and came to see me several times. He is, as you know, a person of some importance and a great benefactor to the Church; and so I was obliged to take the matter up. I promised to investigate the case myself.'

'Yes. And you did.'

'I instituted an inquisitorial process among some of the persons who had had to do with Your Holiness; and I am bound to say that their replies gave me grounds for thought.'

'Why?'

'They differed materially as to the details of Your history; and yet their opinion of You seemed to be fairly unanimous.'

'It was not a desirable opinion.'

'No, Holiness.'

'It would not be. We never were able to arrange to be loved. To be disagreeable was a sort of habit of Ours. But is Your Eminency able, from memory, to give Us an idea of these differences in regard to facts? Opinions do not matter.'

The cardinal pondered for a minute. 'Yes, Holiness, I can give you three examples from Oxford. Fr Benedict Bart said that he had met You twice personally: but that he had heard much of You from his friends, priests as well as laymen. He stated that all that could be done for You had been done; and that You were – ha – Your Holiness will pardon me – a very incapable and ungrateful person.'

The Pope gave the little leaden weight of His pallium a swing: and beamed with delight. The cardinal went on.

'Fr Perkins who received You into the Church said "I'm afraid he's a genius, poor fellow!"'

'What rank blasphemy!'

'Blasphemy, Holiness?'

'Yes: blasphemy. Almighty God happens to make something a little out of the common; and, instead of praising Him for the privilege of tending a singular work of His, Fr Perkins actually bewails the fact! But continue.'

'I confess I never thought of it in that light before –'

'No: nor did Fr Perkins. Continue.'

'I also took the opinion of a certain Dr Strong who appears to be one of the superiors of the university.'

'He was senior Public Examiner in Honour Greats, if you know what that means.'

'Quite so. Well: he said that You had been his intimate and valued friend for more than twenty years, that You had had no influential friends to encourage You, and that Your abilities were no less distinguished than Your moral character.'

The Pope laughed again. 'Dr Strong is an experienced writer of testimonials.'

'But I should hardly think that a man in his position –'

'Certainly not. Dr Strong is one of the two honest men known to Us. Well: and how did the discrepancy between his statement and Fr Benedict's strike you?'

'It struck me in this way. How did so many worthy priests arrive at practically the same opinion (for what Fr Benedict said, others said also) when their knowledge of facts seemed to be so superficial and so doubtful. I mean, Fr Benedict and the rest spoke from an exceedingly casual acquaintance: but Dr Strong from more than twenty years' intimacy. However, just when I was pondering these contradictory statements, Your Holiness's predecessor died; and I was obliged to come to Rome.'

'Did Your Eminency ever note that very few clergymen are capable – capable – of forming an unprejudiced proper original opinion – of judging on the evidence before them and on nothing else.'

'I have excellent reason to believe that what Your Holiness says is correct.'

'It is so much easier to echo than to discriminate. Now, if you please, we will go back to the Compromise. What brought Us again to Your Eminency's remembrance in the Conclave?'

'Holy Father, that was most strange. We Compromissaries were quite as unable to agree as the Sacred College had been. And then, at the end of one of our sessions, I was struck by the extraordinary likeness of Cardinal della Volta to someone whom I remembered having seen, but whose name I had forgotten. It was the merest accident: but I came away wracking my brains about it. Another curious thing happened the same night. Having some papers to sign, I happened to go to my dispatch-box; and, quite by accident, I came across Edward Lancaster's letters about Your Holiness –'

'We do not call these things "accidents".'

'Nor do I, Holy Father, now. Well: for want of something better to do, I suppose, I looked over half a dozen of the letters: and I determined to go further into the matter on my return to England. But, early the very next morning, it suddenly flashed across my mind that I myself had seen Your Holiness –'

'In 1894.'

'Ah yes, in 1894; and that Cardinal della Volta was Your Holiness's Double. This sent me back to the letters again; and I became more and more convinced that an immense and almost irreparable wrong had been done. I cannot tell You how strongly I felt that, Holy Father.'

'But what made you – well, practically impose Us on the Compromissaries?'

'That I cannot say: although in my own mind there is very little doubt but that – However, these are the facts. I was so full of the case, that I narrated it at our morning conference as an instance of the fallibility of what – I think it was Your Holiness Who gave it the name – yes, it was – as an instance of the fallibility of the Machine. I shall never forget the effect of my words upon Cardinal Mundo. It was most extraordinary. He said – I shall remember what he said as long as I live – he said, "My Lord Cardinal, you owe it to that man to propose him for the paparchy; yes you owe it!" He rather upset me. I replied that Your Holiness was not even in sacred orders. He answered "Whose fault is that?" I may say that the point was a very keen one. No one could fail to perceive its relevancy. To use a vulgar expression, it touched the thing with a needle. The others did not help me at all; and I considered the matter for a few minutes. Mundo went on, "If that man had a real Vocation, he will have persevered: if he has persevered, the twenty years or more of waiting will have purified –'''

'Pray do not quote Cardinal Mundo.'

'Well, in short, I was irresistibly moved to propose Your Holiness – '

'And then, because no other candidate was forthcoming: because – We understand. You came to Us, found Us persistent –'

'Yes, Holiness.'

'Well: shall we take a little stroll in the garden, and say some Office?'

Cardinal Courtleigh jumped. 'I'm sure – if Your Holiness doesn't mind walking by the side of my bathchair –'

'Oh, but We do. It is Our invariable custom to walk behind bathchairs and push them.'

'Indeed I could not for one moment permit –'

'No: but for an hour you will submit. Nonsense man, do you suppose that one never has pushed a bathchair before! Now sit down quietly and open your breviary and read the Office; and We will look over your shoulder and make the responses. It's awfully good exercise, you know.'

CHAPTER 7

AFTER His morning's exertions in the way of taming and domesticating a prince of the church, Hadrian was conscious that He required a change of emotions. His thoughts went to the next thing on His list – the matter of Cardinal Nefski. That would be an exceedingly interesting experience. He did not want to intrude upon grief: but He was attracted by all singular phenomena; and the pathos of the pale young prelate seemed to be quite exemplary. Once in His secular life, George Arthur Rose had been taken by a doctor to see a man who had severed his throat in an unusual manner, using a broken penknife and cutting a jagged triangle, of which the apex missed the larynx, and the base the sterno-kleido-mastoid, avoiding by a hair's breadth carotid and jugular. The doctor wanted a diagram of the wound made for the enlightenment of the jury which was to pronounce upon attempted suicide; and George had made the sketch from the staring speechless life, noted the furniture of the room and the aspect of his model, quite untouched by the man's sensations or the horror of the event. Hadrian approached Cardinal Nefski with similar feelings. He was curious, He was psychically apart: but, at the same time, something of subconscious sympathy in His manner elicited the desired revelation. It was a ghastly one. Nefski, Cardinal Archbishop, had rushed to a little city in Russian Poland, occupied by anarchists, for the purpose of pleading with them. He arrived at sunset. There was a college there where a hundred and twenty lads of noble birth were being educated: among them, his own youngest brother, just seventeen years old. The cardinal was seized and crucified with ropes to the fountain in the market square. Anarchists burst into the college: stripped its inmates naked; and flung them into the street before his eyes. He absolved each one dashed from the lofty windows. Some instantly were smashed and killed: others, who fell on others, were broken and shattered, but not killed outright. All night long, Nefski remained crucified. The anarchists must have forgotten him: for they left him; and at dawn someone, whom he did not know, came and cut him down. He remembered nothing more, until he found himself paralysed, in a waggon with two priests, *en route* for Prague. Then he came on to Rome, hoping to lose the phantasm which continually occupied his sight and hearing – the heap in the dark night, the growing groaning heap on red stones of white young bodies and writhing limbs like maggots in cheese, the pale forms strained and curved, the flying hair, the fixed eyes, continually falling, the cut-off shrieks, the thudding bounding ooze of that falling, the interminable white writhing. It was a ghastly tale, quite unimpassionately told. The young man still was in that stupor which benignant Nature sends by the side of extreme pain. His paralysis was passing away. He could walk easily now – only he saw and heard. He spoke affectionately of his murdered brother: but he did not mourn for him.

Hadrian was moved. He put all the human kindness which he had, and it was not much, into His voice and manner. He really tried to comfort the cardinal. He quoted the splendid verses of the herald in the *Seven Against Thebes*,

'being pure in respect to the sacred rites of his country,
blameless hath he fallen, where 'tis glorious for the young to fall.'

Nefski seemed grateful. The Pontiff offered to remove him from Prague; and to attach him to the Court of Rome: but he preferred to return to his archbishopric for the present, at least, he said, until this tyranny be overpast. And, anon, he asked permission to retire. The sunlight dazzled him.

During the rest of the time at Castel Gandolfo, the Pope seldom was seen. A boatman rowed Him out on Lake Albano for an hour or two in the afternoon, while He occupied Himself in pencilling corrections on manuscript. But the white figure, set in the blaze of the sunny blue water, did not escape the notice of passers by on the high road near the Riformati; and, finding Himself under observation, He returned to the seclusion of the garden. His memory flew back to the time when people used to jeer at Him for His habit of writing letters, letters which explained a great deal too much, to blind men who could not see, to deaf adders who would not hear. He chuckled at the thought that those same people would read, mark, learn, and inwardly digest, every word and every dotted *i* of His letters now – letters which were not going to be painfully voluminously conscientiously persuasive any more: but dictatorial. He wrote sheet after sheet; and emended them: He returned to His room and burned all the rejected preliminaries; and He took a fair copy with Him to Rome on the night of the twenty-eighth of April.

Early on the morning of the thirtieth, at a secret audience in the new throne-room, Caerleon introduced five rather startled very dishevelled and travel-stained priests, five priests who had undergone a mental shock. Mr Semphill, with a white close-cropped head and the face of a clean pink school-boy, contrived to remind himself that he was in the presence of the most amusing man he ever had met. He bucked up; and made his obeisance with an aplomb which was a combination of the Service, Teddy Hall, an Anglican curacy, and a Pictish rectory. Mr Sterling, a stalwart brown schoolmaster, very handsome except for a mole on his nose, hid his feelings in calm inscrutability. Mr Whitehead, a level-headed common-sense Saxon, golden-hearted, who never had had any wild oats for sowing, observed reticence in a matter which was beyond his comprehension. Mr Leighton, plump, clean, curly-haired, blinked genially and waited. Mr Carvale, a lithe intense little Gael, with the black hair and rose-white skin and the delicate lips and self-contained mien of a dreamer, looked upon his old college acquaintance with clear eyes of burning blue. Some of the five had the remembrance of sins of omission at the back of their minds. None remembered sins of commission. All were wondering what was required of them – what the devil it all meant, as Semphill secularly put it. If any of them expected allusion to the past, they must have been disappointed. Hadrian gave them no sign of recognition. It was the Supreme Pontiff Who very apostolically received them and addressed them.

'Reverend Sirs, Our will is to have such assistance in the work of Our Apostolature as the organs of sense can render to the mind, or as the experimentalist can render to the theorist. For reasons known unto Ourself, We have selected you. Believing you to be single-hearted in this one thing, namely the service of God, We call upon you to devote yourselves actually to the service of His Vicegerent. To this end, We would attach you to Our Person in a singular and intimate connexion, by raising you to the cardinal-diaconate. Those of you who believe yourselves unable to do God service better in this than in your present capacity, can depart without forfeiting Our goodwill. The conscience of each man is his own sole true light. Far be it from Us to interfere with any man's prerogative as his own director in so grave a matter.'

The five remained standing, saying nothing. Semphill was sincerely delighted: the literary quality, the tops-i'-th'-turfy straightforwardness of the allocution gave him the keenest joy. The others felt obedience to be their plain duty: for George

Arthur Rose never had been wantonly fantastic, there always had been a fundamental element of reason about his eccentricities, he never had revolved at random but always round some deliberately fixed point. And, to plain priests, the voice of the Successor of St Peter was a call, to be answered, and obeyed.

The Pope addressed Semphill. 'Your Reverency quite legitimately hoped to end your days at St Gowff's?'

'True – (hum!) – Holiness: but I may be translated elsewhere by a telegraph's notice from my diocesan.'

'You are not yet a missionary rector?'

'Merely a poor master of arts of Oxford.'

'But you have been at St Gowff's as long as We can remember.'

Mr Semphill choked a chuckle. 'Having a little patrimony, Holiness, I made my will in favour of the archdiocese of St Gowff's and Agneda; and I did not omit to mention the fact to my archbishop. I happened also to say that, in the event of my being moved from St Gowff's, I should be compelled to make another will: but of course I did not contemplate being moved as far as Rome.'

Hadrian turned to Mr Sterling. 'The last words, which We said to Your Reverency, were that you had cause to be ashamed of yourself.'

'One had cause, Holy Father.'

'To you, Our invitation is a means of repairing a single small defect in a praiseworthy career.'

'It shall be repaired, Holy Father.'

To the others the Pope said nothing: for He saw their clean souls.

In the Sacred Consistory, the Supreme Pontiff dictated to consistorial advocates a pontifical act, denouncing the Lord Francis Talacryn, Bishop of Caerleon, as Cardinal-presbyter of the Title of the Four Holy Crowned Ones: the Lord George Semphill as Cardinal-deacon of St Mary-in-Broad Street: the Lord James Sterling as Cardinal-deacon of St Nicholas-in-the-Jail-of-Tully: the Lord George Leighton as Cardinal-deacon of

The Holy Angel-in-the-Fish-Market: the Lord Gerald White-head as Cardinal-deacon of St George-of-the-Golden-Sail: the Lord Robert Carvale as Cardinal-deacon of St Cosmas and St Damian. Then the six were brought in, and sworn of the College: their heads were hatted, their fingers ringed with sapphires, their mouths were closed and opened by the Pope; and they retired in ermine and vermilion.

What their emotions were, need not be inquired. Indeed, they had little time for emotion, seeing that during the rest of the day they sat in the secret chamber, writing writing writing from Hadrian's dictation. In the evening, Whitehead and Carvale put on their old cassocks and posted a carriage-full of letters at San Silvestro. These all were sealed with the Fisherman's Ring; and, as they were addressed to kings, emperors, prime ministers, editors of newspapers, and heads of various religious denominations, it was considered undesirable to trouble Prince Minimo, the pontifical postmaster, with material for gossip. Meanwhile Hadrian and Cardinal Semphill sat in the Vatican marconigraph office alone with the operators; and the Pope dictated, while the experts' fingers expressed His words in dots and dashes in London and New York. By consequence, what His Holiness called 'the five decent newspapers' came out on the first of May with an apostolic epistle, a pontifical bull, and editorial leaders thereupon.

The world found the *Epistle to All Christians* very piquant, not on account of novelty, but because of the nude vivid candour with which old and trite truths were enunciated dogmatically. Christianity, the Pope proclaimed, was a great deal more than a mere ritual service. It extended to every part of human life; and its rules must regulate Christians in all matters of principle and practice. He laid great stress on the assertion of the principle of the Personal Responsibility of the Individual. It was quite unavoidable, quite incapable of being shifted on to societies or servants. Each soul would have to render its own account to its Creator. In connexion with the last doctrine, He denounced as damnable nonsense the fashionable heresy which is crystallized in the Quatrains of Edward Fitzgerald,

'O Thou, Who didst with pitfall and with gin
Beset the road I was to wander in,
    Thou wilt not, with predestined evil, round
Enmesh; and then impute my fall to sin.
O Thou, Who man of baser earth didst make;
And, e'en with paradise, devise the snake; –
    For all the sin, wherewith the face of man
Is blackened, man's forgiveness give – and take.'

He described those lines as the whine of a whimpering coward: pertinently inquiring whether a human father would be blameable, who, having taught his boy to swim, should fling him into the sea that he might have the merit of fighting his own way to shore where the rope was ready at hand? He condemned all attempts at uniformity as unnatural crimes, because they insulted the Divine intelligence Which had deigned to differentiate His creatures. He declared that God's servants were to be known by their broad minds, generous hearts, and staunch wills.

The Church of God is not narrow, nor 'Liberal', but Catholic with room for all: for 'there are diversities of gifts'.

It was the individual soul which must be saved; and it was that which was addressed in the Evangel. He considered the immense strength of the single verse,

Let every man be fully persuaded in his own mind.

Hence He would have no barrier erected between Christians of the Roman Obedience and Christians of other denominations. The following passage, containing His Own idea of His relation to other men, attracted much attention:

It is in no man's power to believe what he list. No man is to be blamed for reasoning in support of his own religion: for he only is accountable. 'Other sheep I have, which are not of this fold'; and these deserve more care and love, but not cheap pity, nor insulting patronage, nor irritated persecution: for if, as has been said, a man shall follow Christ's Law, and shall believe His Words according to his conscientious sense of their meaning, he will be a member of Christ's Flock although he be not within the Fold. And, though We know that he understands

Christ's Words amiss, yet that is no reason for Our Claiming any kind of superiority over an honest man, the purpose of whose heart and mind is to obey and to be guided by Christ. Such an one is a Christian and Our good brother, a servant of God; and, if he will have Us, We, by virtue of Our Apostolature, are his servant also.

The conclusion of the *Epistle* contained a very striking admonition addressed to members of His Own communion, to the effect that the being Christian did not confer any title to physical or external dominion, but rather the contrary. Perhaps the peroration is worthy of quotation:

Persuade, if ye can persuade, and if the world will permit you to persuade: but seek not to persuade. Better to live so that men will convince themselves through the contemplation of your ensample. That way only satisfaction lies. Accept, but claim not, obedience. Seek not suffering, nor avoid it: but, when it is deigned to you, most stringently conceal it and tolerate it with jubilation, remembering the words of Plato where it is written 'Help cometh through pain and suffering, nor can we be freed from our iniquity by any other means!' Scorn not the trite. Scorn no brother man. Scorn no thing. Yet, if ye (being men) must scorn, then scorn the enemies of God and the King which be the Devil and Dishonour and Death.

An even greater sensation, than that caused by the *Epistle to All Christians,* attended the simultaneous publication of the Bull *Regnum Meum.* It personally was addressed to the very last person in all the world by whom, under ordinary circumstances, a communication from the Vatican might have been expected. Hadrian VII, Bishop, Servant of the servants of God, sent Greeting and Apostolic Benediction to His Well-beloved Son – the Majesty of Victor Emanuel III, King of Italy. 'My Kingdom is not of this world' was the text of the Bull, which the Pope began with an unwavering defence of the Divine Revelation, the Church, Peter, and the Power of the Keys. So far, He spoke as a theologian. Then, with lightning swiftness, He assumed the role of the historian. His theme was the Forged Decretals or Donation of Constantine, which first were promulgated in a breve which His Holiness's predecessor, Hadrian I, addressed to His Majesty's predecessor (in a certain sense), the

Emperor Charlemagne. He recited the well-known facts that these Decretals, though undoubtedly forged, had been forged merely as the intellectual pastime of an exiled archbishop's idle hours, and with no nefarious intent whatever. He showed how that, during four centuries, no doubt as to their authenticity had been entertained; and how that three more centuries had elapsed before evidence had been collected sufficing to justify their being thrown overboard from the Barque of Peter to lighten the ship. Then, He continued, the Pope was the sovereign of a patrimony of which He held no title-deeds. A right more inexpugnable than prescriptive right was deemed desirable; and Alexander VI and Julius II bound the Patrimony to Peter by military conquest. So it remained until the unification of Italy under the House of Savoy, when those territories, formerly known as the States of the Church, were absorbed by the new kingdom. Thus far Hadrian pursued the argument; and then turned to a disquisition on the worldly rights of Christians, the purport of which perhaps most luminously is expressed in the following sentences:

We use worldly things till they are wanted by the world: then we will relinquish them without even so much as a backward thought. For we all are clearly marked to get that which we give. Nothing is irrevocable on the orb of earth. Nothing is final: for, after this world is the world to come. Therefore, let us move, let us gladly move, move with the times, really move. God always is merciful.

Hence, as Supreme Pontiff, Hadrian would practise the principle of renunciation. He would renounce everything which another would take, because 'My Kingdom is not of this world'. And, first of all, in order to remove a bone of contention, He made a formal and unconditional renunciation of the claim to temporal sovereignty and of the civil list provided by the Law of Guarantees. At the same time, He would not be understood as casting any slight upon His predecessors Who had followed other counsels:

They were responsible to God: They knew it: He and They were the judges of Their acts. We, on Our part, in Our turn, act as We deem best. We know Our responsibility and shrink not. We are God's Vicegerent; and this is Our will. Given at Rome, at St Peter's by the Vatican, on this ninth day of Our Supreme Pontificate.

The formal publication of the *Epistle* and the Bull occurred in the second consistory which met at the abnormal hour of 6 a.m. on May Day. Hadrian read the two documents in that distinct minor monotone of His which was so intensely and yet so impersonally magisterial. By itself the tone was aggravating. The matter also was exasperating; and the pontifical manner added exacerbation. He seemed to be expecting opposition. That came from Ragna. If the Pope no longer was a sovereign, where did the Secretary of State come in? Was he dismissed? Oh dear no, he certainly was not dismissed: only, instead of playing at statesmanship in regard to states over which he had no control at all, and which were really rather commodiously managed by the secular power, he was requested to turn his attention to the increase of business which inevitably now would come into his department.

'The world is sick for the Church,' said Hadrian; but She never would confess it as long as the Church posed as Her rival.

Nevertheless the thing was a blow, a blow that was heavy and strong. Half the College put on an indifferent noncommittal air: the other half roared anathemas and execrations. And Ragna howled,

'Judas, Judas, this shall not be!'

In a lull, Hadrian coldly mewed 'It is; and it shall be.'

He flung down the steps of the throne a bundle of advance copies of the Roman morning journals. Vermilion faces stooped to them. There were the *Epistle* and the Bull in the vernacular. Serafino-Vagellaio pounced upon an announcement in *Il Popolo Romano* to the effect that

by the courteous condescension of the Holy Father Himself, we are enabled to present to our readers these authentic and momentous acts simultaneously with *The Times*, the *Morning Post*, the *Globe*, the *St James's Gazette*, and the *New York Times*, the splendid journals of the magnanimous English, to which race (the sempiternal friend of Italy) we owe so grand and so enlightened a pontiff.

Undoubtedly the thing was done: for the world knew it; and, knowing it, would not let it be undone. There was no cardinal, however infuriated, who was not sufficiently serpentine to recognize the columbine as the attitude most appropriate to the circumstances. The first mad idea which had seized the rebellious ones, the ideas of suppressing the pontifical decrees by physical force, was laid aside. There no doubt were other means of nullifying them later. And Their Eminencies dispersed to say their masses with an air which made the Pope feel like a very naughty tiresome little boy indeed, said Hadrian to Cardinal Leighton.

The question of Edward Lancaster worried Hadrian considerably: for the simple reason that, while He did not want to tire Himself by a renewal of relations with this individual, decency demanded something. He discussed the position with Courtleigh and Talacryn, neither of whom were able to appreciate His difficulty. Thrown back upon His Own resources, He made a cigarette very carefully, a long fat one with the tobacco tucked into the paper cylinder with a pencil, and with neatly twisted ends, resembling a small white sausage; and smoked it through. Then He wrote a letter, telling Lancaster that his offering had been accepted and applied, assuring him of the pontifical goodwill and of a pleasant reception in case he should feel bound to present himself in Rome, and conferring Apostolic Benediction and a plenary indulgence at the hour of death. This, He enclosed in a gold snuff box with a device of diamonds on the lid, which the recipient might put upon his mantelpiece with other curious monstrosities.

Orezzo and Ragna appeared to have exchanged ethics: for, whereas the latter had been a pontifical right hand while Orezzo had shut up himself in the Chancery, now it was Orezzo who watched the Pope while Ragna kept aloof in vermilion sulks. It was not that his occupation was gone: but he wished to emphasize (by withdrawing it) his indispensability. As for the others, they wonderfully retired into their shells. Hadrian kept his new creatures in fairly close attendance; and the nine Compromissaries always were ready to make themselves agreeable when they were in Rome. The Pope wished and tried to be on friendly terms with them; and failed, as He always failed. He could not show Himself friendly.

Crowds of English visitors appeared; and would have been distracting. They dotted themselves about the Ducal Hall and Hadrian walked among them. At one of these receptions, the pontifical glance lighted, on entering, on a dark gaunt Titan seamed with concealed pain, who was accompanied by a quiet fastidious English lady (wife and mother), and three children, two glorious girls and a proud shy English boy. They were a typical group, typical of all that is best – trial, culture, moderate success, and English quality. Hadrian at once shook hands with them.

'Please wait till the others are gone,' He said; and passed on to a cocky little gentleman with a pink eye, and a plump bare-faced party who tried to stand easily in the cross-legged pose of the male photograph of 1864. These sank to their knees, but stood up again at a word.

'Well, Holy Father, who would have thought,' etcetera, from the first; and 'Oh, I'm sure I shall never dare to call Your Holiness "Boffin" again' from the second.

'Yes you do,' replied Hadrian; and gave them a blessing, to which the plump one nervously responded,

'Quite so, I'm sure, as it were!'

Another couple kneeled, a weird brief-bodied man in pince-nez and a small suppressed woman with beautiful short-sighted eyes. They were raised; and the man would chatter like a hail storm, wittily and with Gallic gesticulation, and quite in-sincerely. They were blessed; and the Pontiff went on (with some elevation of gait) to the others.

When the audience was over a slim gentleman in scarlet, with the delicate pensive beauty of a St John the Divine by Gian Bellini, conducted the English family to the apostolic antechamber. Here Hadrian offered them some fruit and wine; and showed them the view from the windows.

'Now perhaps Mrs Strong would like to see the garden,' He presently said.

It was a very happy thought. His Holiness carried His little yellow cat, and they all went down together; and strolled about the woods and the box alleys and the vineyards. They picked the flowers; and the children picked the fruit. They admired the peacocks: and rested on white marble hemicycles in the sun-flecked shade of cypresses; and they talked of this, that, and the other, as well as these and those. A chamberlain came through the trees, and delivered a small veiled salver to the gentleman who followed the pontifical party at fifty paces. At the moment of departure he came near. The salver contained five little crosses of gold and chrysoberyls set in diamonds. Three were elaborate and two severely plain. Hadrian presented them to His guests.

'You will accept a memorial of this happy day; and of course' (with that rare dear smile of His) 'you will not expect the Pope to give you anything but popery. Good-bye, dear friends, good-bye.'

'How He has improved!' said the dark girl, as they went out.

'O mother, and did you see the buckles on His shoes!' said the fair one.

'I call Him a topper,' said the boy.

'He isn't a bit changed,' said the wife to the silent husband.

'I think that He has found His proper niche at last,' the great man answered.

Percy Van Kristen arrived; and was brought into the secret chamber. Though only a little over thirty, he looked as old as Hadrian. The glowing freshness of his olive skin had faded: but his superb eyes were as brightly expectant and his small round head as cleanly black as ever. He looked tired, but wholesome; and he was immaculately groomed. The Pope said a few words of greeting and of remembrance; and asked him to speak of himself. Van Kristen was shy: but not unwilling. Leading questions elicited that he was one of that pitiable class of men for whom the gods have provided everything but a career. Majority had brought him three quarters of a million sterling. There was no necessity for him to go into commerce. Politics were

141

impossible for respectable persons. He was too old for the services. The fact was, he had not the natural energy which would have hewn out a career – a career in the worldly sense – for himself; and by consequence, the world had shoved him aside on to the shelf of objects whose functions are purely decorative. His mode of life was that of a man of fashion, simple, exquisite. Perhaps he read a great deal; and, of course, his home took up most of his time – but that was a secret. Hadrian deftly extracted from him that he had founded and was maintaining a home for a hundred boys of his city, where he provided a complete training in electrical engineering and a fair start in life. His splendid eyes glittered as he spoke of this. It seemed that he had kept his own world in entire ignorance of his ardent effort to be useful; and one naturally enjoys talking of one's own affairs when the proper listener at last is encountered. No: he never had felt inclined to marry and rear a family of his own. He did not think that that sort of thing was much in his line. Yes: after leaving Oxford, he had had some thoughts of the priesthood. But Archbishop Corrie had laughed him out of that. He was not clever enough for the priesthood. That was the real truth, in his private opinion. Oh yes, he would like it very well – as much as anything: but really he hardly felt himself equal to it. He didn't want to seem to push himself forward in any way. Yes: the Dynam House could get on quite well without him. They were fortunate in having a capable manager whom everyone liked; and his own share didn't amount to much more than playing fives with the boys, and paying the bills, and finding out and getting all the latest dodges. If he could run over and look round the place, say twice a year, say two months in the year, he was quite willing to take up his abode with Hadrian, if His Holiness really wanted him. As a cardinal-deacon? Oh, that would be a daisy! But – sorry: he never did understand chaff. Hadrian was serious. Van Kristen's grand virginal eyes attentively considered the Pontiff. Then, with that strangely courtly gracious manner which was his natural gift (and due to the perfect proportion of his skeleton) contrasting so weirdly with the normal nasality of his speech, he said

'Wal: I expect I won't be much good to You: but You're the master; and, if You really want me, I guess I'll have a try.'

And he went straight into retreat at the Passionists' on the Celian Hill.

CHAPTER 8

'THE key to all your difficulties, present and to come, is Love.' Hadrian was at His old self-analytical games again; and the aphorism, which He had gleaned in the most memorable confession of His life-time, suddenly came back to Him. He went over a lot of things once more. He was convinced that, so far, He did not even know what Love was. People seemed to like Him. Up to a point there were certain people whom He liked. But, Love – He admitted to Himself that men mostly were quite unknown to Him. Perhaps that was His fault. Perhaps He could not get near enough to them to love them simply because He did not admit them to sufficient intimacy – did not study them closely enough. That was a fault which could be mended. He summoned His fifteen cardinals to spend an hour with Him in the Vineyard of Leo. The day was a glorious Roman day of opening summer. The Pope desired to use Their Eminencies for the discussion of affairs, to sharpen His wits against theirs, to pick their brains in order to assist in the formation of His Own opinions.

Gentilotto gently remarked that, if His Holiness would state a case, they would do their best to help Him. He designated the renunciation of the temporal power; and struck them dumb. Of course, in most of their own minds, they disapproved of it. It had shocked them. One and all of them had been brought up in the fatuous notion that the success of the Church was to be gauged by the extent of Her temporalities. An idea of that species, especially when it is inherited, is not dug up by the roots and tossed out in a moment, even by a Pontifical Bull. Hadrian understood that His supporters (as well as His opponents) disliked that audacity of His.

'Holiness, we don't presume to condemn it: but we don't praise it. Yet You must have had reasons?' Fiamma at length said.

The Pope had not His reasons ready on the surface: they were fundamental. And the temper of Him used to lead Him to disguise the sacrosanct with a veil of frivolity: that is to say, when His arcana seemed likely to be violated, He was wont to divert attention by some gay paradox or witticism. A little roguish glimmer lit His thin lips; and a suspicion of a merry little twinkle came in the corners of His half-shut eyes.

'Once upon a time We used to know a certain writer of amatory novels. The sentimental balderdash, which he put into the mouths of his marionettes (he only had one set of them), influenced Us greatly. He had a living to get. He thought he could get it by recommending the Temporal Power. He was a very clever worldly Catholic indeed: but the arguments, which he produced in so vital a matter as the earning of his living, were so sterile and so curatical, that We summed up the Temporal Power as negligible. Then there was the disgracefully spiteful tone of the Catholic newspapers – gloating over the misfortunes of hard-working well-meaning people, prophesying revolution and national bankruptcy for this dear Italy, and so on. Well: Our sympathy naturally went, not to the malignant but, to the maligned. Oh yes, We had reasons.'

'That is enough. One's hands obey one's head,' said Sterling.

'For my part, I think that if the Temporal Power is worth having it is worth fighting for. Lord Ralph Kerrison, who's a British general, once told me that, if the Pope cares to call upon Catholics throughout the world and order military operations, he is quite ready to throw up his commission tomorrow and enlist in the pontifical army,' Semphill asserted.

'No?' Mundo with big eyes inquired.

'Fact: I assure you,' Semphill asservated.

'But is it worth fighting for?'

'Of course, Holy Father, the possession would confer a certain status,' put in Saviolli.

The Pope smiled. '"Certain" – and "status"? Oh really!'

Talacryn was annoyed. He considered the query too sarcastic.

'His Holiness perhaps leans upon the theory that the Church never was more powerful than She is now,' della Volta ventured.

'I calculate that's fact, not theory!' exclaimed Grace.

'Well then?'

'I see. In these thirty-odd years without the Temporal Power, the Church has increased in power. It might be argued on that that Temporal Power is not essential.'

'Prosecute that argument, and – '

'Has anyone a theory as to what precisely is the chief obstacle in Our way here in Italy?' the Pope interpolated.

'The secret societies.'

'Atheism.'

'Poverty.'

'Socialism.'

'Corrupt politicians.'

'What do we newcomers know of Italy?' asked Whitehead of Leighton, who had made the last remark.

'The newspapers say – '

'The newspapers!' Carvale ejaculated. 'Don't we know how the newspapers are written? Has no one of us ever contributed a paragraph? Well then – '

'Please view the question from this stand-point. On the one side, you have the Paparchy and the Kingdom, Church and State, Soul and Body. On the other, you have the enemies of those. What is necessary?'

'The destruction of the enemies.'

'Or the conversion of them into friends. But how?'

'How shall two walk together unless they be agreed?' the Pope inquired.

'The Paparchy and the Kingdom are not agreed,' said Courtleigh.

'Your Holiness means that they should be agreed: that they should unite forces?' Ferraio asked.

'It is Our will and Our hope to be reconciled with the King of Italy.'

'But is His Majesty willing?'

'We know not: but We have shown that We will not block the way.'

'Certainly the Pope and the King together would have almost unbounded influence for good,' Ferraio reflected.

'Then Your Holiness does not think the Temporal Power to be worth fighting for?' Sterling concluded.

Hadrian's eyes no longer were half-shut. 'No,' He answered. 'Try, Venerable Fathers, to believe that the time has come for stripping. We have added and added; and yet we have not converted the world. Ask yourselves whether we really are as successful as we ought to be: or whether, on the whole, we really are not abject and lamentable failures. If we are the latter, then let us try the other road, the road of simplicity, of apostolic simplicity. At least let us try. It's an idea; and for Our Own part We are glad to have a chance of realizing it, the idea of simplicity, going to the root of the matter.'

'Your Holiness is not afraid of going too far?' inquired Talacryn.

'William Blake says that truth lies in extremes. To the humdrum champion of the so-called golden mean (which generally is a great deal more mean than golden), that maxim is nothing less than scandalous. All the same, it is as sound as a bell, Eminency, and nowhere does it ring more soundly than in the principle of the union of Church with State.'

As they were going in to dinner, Mundo whispered to Fiamma, 'Have we a saint or a madman for a Pope?'

'Two thirds of the one and one third of the other,' replied the radiant Archbishop of Bologna.

After one of the receptions of English pilgrims, Hadrian privately received an unusual visitor in the last antechamber. She was brought in by a gentleman, who remained outside one of the doors during the interview, while his fellow guarded the outside of the other. It was as secret an audience as ever has been deigned to a sovereign; and it was accorded to a woman of the lower-middle class, about sixty years old, who looked like an excessively worthy cook. She flopped on her knees when the

Pontiff came to her: mentioned her joints when assisted to rise; and made bones about using the chair which He placed for her. Hadrian's manner was absolutely divested of pontificality. No one would have taken him for anything but a plain English-man, perhaps of a slightly superior type, and perhaps rather oddly attired. He spoke kindly and easily; and gradually brought His guest from a glaring twitching state of terror and obsequious joy to her honest ordinary self.

'Ee-e-h,' she burbled, 'but I can never tell Your 'oly Majesty what I felt when I knew that You was going to let me come and see You. Oh thank You and God bless You, Sir. And I always knew You'ld come to it. And, O 'oly Father, ain't You very 'appy to think of all the good You're doing? Just fancy that ever I should say that to Your 'igh 'oliness and me sitting on one of your own chairs. God bless You Mr Rose, Sir, as if You was my own boy. Well now, I knew in a minute who it was that sent it me. Why 'oly Father? Why because Your 'oly 'ighness named that very amount years ago as what You'd give me if You was paid properly. Yes 'oly Father: I've done what You wished me. I got it cheaper than we thought because it's been empty so long. Thirteen 'undred pound cash on the nail for the 'ouse: a 'undred for doing it up: four 'undred and two for furniture and things: and please 'oly Father I've brought the change.'

She lugged out a great bank bag containing one hundred and ninety-eight English sovereigns.

'Oh but, you dear good soul, you shouldn't have done that. It was all yours.'

'All mine, 'oly Father? But I tell You I got it cheaper than we thought.'

'Well then you see you're a hundred and ninety-eight pounds to the good. You have the house and the furniture; and, if you can get the lodgers, you're safe for life.'

'If I can get lodgers, 'oly Father? Why I'm filled up, and turning them away.'

'Good! Well, put that in the bank for the winter.'

'But then I shall have oceans of money I've made in the summer, 'oly Father.'

'Look here, Mrs Dixon. Do you remember cooking two dinners one Christmas Day? One, we ate. The other, you carried under your apron to some carpenter who was out of work. Don't you remember who caught you pretending that you weren't spilling the gravy on your frock?'

'Oh, Mr Rose, Sir, how You do recollect things!'

'Well now, you stinted yourself then, didn't you?'

'Well perhaps a little.'

'Now don't stint yourself any more; and give away as many dinners as you like. See?'

The tears were streaming from her glaring eyes and running down her kitchen-scorched cheeks. She certainly was looking frowsy.

'See? I should think I did. Mr Rose Sir, if I say it to Your face, saint was what I always said of You. Dear! Dear! To think of me giving way like this. Well, well, You're too good for this world, Your Majesty. Oh and I've taken the liberty of bringing You a jar of pickled samphire like what You used to fancy. I've picked it and did it up myself with my own 'ands – and I thought perhaps You wouldn't mind 'aving this antimacassar which I've worked for You, 'oly Father. I knew all Your 'oly chairs'd be red, because I've seen pictures of them; and I thought that the grey and the orange would brighten up a dark corner for You.'

Hadrian thanked her kindly; and took her little offerings as though He prized them more than His tiara; and made her infinitely happy.

'Well now I won't detain Your Majesty, because I know there must be no end of grand people waiting about to see You, and me occupying Your time like this, 'oly Father. So I'll just ask You to pray for me and give me a blessing; and thank You Sir for all You've done for me, and I'll say a prayer for You every day as long as I'm spared.'

She got on her knees: and the Pontiff blessed her. Then He said,

'When do you go back, Mrs Dixon?'

'Well, Your 'oly Majesty, I was thinking of looking about a

bit while I'm 'ere, so as to have plenty to say to the lodgers: but I can't stay more than a week longer.'

Hadrian wrote on a card, *The bearer, Mrs Agnes Dixon, is Our guest. Receive and assist her.* He signed it; and gave it to her, saying, 'You know this place is full of lovely things, pictures and so on. And there are heaps of sacred relics in the churches. Well now, that card will admit you to see everything.'

'Will they let me see the fans?'

'Which fans?'

'Them they fan You with when You're glorified?'

'Oh yes. Show that card to the gentleman who is going to take you downstairs and tell him what you want to see.'

'Will they want me to give the card up at the door?'

'No. Not if you want to keep it.'

'Ah well, I'll see everything; and I'll keep the card till I'm laid out, 'oly Father. Oh whatever can I say! You'll excuse me Sir, and I'm an honest woman: but I must kiss Your 'oly Majesty's anointed 'and. Oh bless You, my dear, bless You!'

Hadrian paced through and through the apartment as soon as He was alone. 'Dear good ugly righteous creature,' He commented. Passing the safe in the bedroom, He let out with His left and punched the iron door. 'That's what use you are,' He said; and put glycerine on His bleeding knuckles. Catching a glimpse of His face in the mirror, 'Beastly hypocrite' He sneered at Himself.

Very disagreeable talk went on in Ragna's circle. The pontifical acts of Hadrian were vile enough, but His private ones were simply criminal. A Pope who asked you the hour and the date and the place of your birth, drew diagrams on paper, and then told you your secret vices and virtues, was a practisant of arts unholy. Doubtless that frightful yellow cat, which He took into the gardens every morning, was His familiar spirit. It had cursed Cacciatore in a corridor, almost articulately. Balbo, the chamberlain, was prepared to swear two things, which he had gathered from the gentlemen of the secret chamber. First, that His Holiness stood under a tap in His bedroom every morning

149

and evening, and sometimes during the day as well. Undoubtedly that was to allay the fervence of the demon who possessed Him. Secondly, that His Holiness sat up half the night writing or reading, and yet the pontifical waste-paper basket always was empty. Not even a torn shred of paper remained. But then, the ashes in the fireplace. Ah! The disposition was to refer to lunacy, or stupidity, or knavishness, or vileness, whatsoever was novel to the understanding. The Pontiff's aggressive personality, His ostentatious inconsistency, His peculiarly ideal conception of His apostolic character, His moral earnestness, His practical and uncomfortable embodiment of His views in His conduct, caused Him to be as loathed by Ragna's set as He was loved by the nine and the six. He was accused of an anarchistical kind of enthusiasm. When He heard that, He said,

'We are conservative in all Our instincts, and only contrive to become otherwise by an effort of reason or principle, as We contrive to overcome all Our other vicious propensities.'

That was considered an additional indecorum. His quaintly correct and archaic diction exasperated men who had no means of expressing their thoughts except in the fluid allusive clipped verbosity of the day. Objections were made to His hendecasyllabical allocutions, by mediocrities who could not away with a man who discoursed in ithyphallics. His autocratic dogmatism, which really was due to His entire occession by His office, shocked the opportunist, irritated the worldly-prudent. Outside in the world too, He was by no means a complete success. People, who were not of His Communion, thought it rather a liberty that a Pope should have the Authorized Version at His fingers' ends. At first, a lot of fantastic instabilities prepared to hail Him as a Reformer: but He gave dire offence to them, and to all pious fat-wits, by flatly refusing His countenance to any kind of Scheme or Society. 'The Church suffices for this life,' He said; and His sentence 'Cultivate, and help to cultivate individuality, at your own expense if possible, but never at the expense of your brother,' was highly disapproved of. Where did the Rights of Man come in? But then Hadrian was quite certain that Christians actually had no worldly 'rights' at all. Arraigned on the question of superstition by the stolidly common-sense Talacryn, He said 'Extra-belief, superstition, that which we hope or augur or imagine, is the poetry of life'; and His utterance was regarded as almost heretical. His utter lack of personal swagger or even dignity, His habit of rolling and smoking continual cigarettes, His natural and patently unprofessional manner, offended many outsiders who only could think of the Pope as partaking of the dual character of an Immeasurably Ambitious Clergyman and a Scarlet Impossible Person. He had enemies at home and abroad. And He remained quite alone, psychically detached: to a very great extent unconscious of, certainly uninterested in, the impression which He personally was creating; and altogether uninfluenced by any other mind or any other creature.

A parcel of curial malcontents waited on the Pope; and poured forth flocculent interrogations and sophomoric criticisms to their hearts' content. Hadrian sat perfectly motionless except for an occasional twinkle of His ears – a muscular trick which He had forced Himself to learn for the disconcerting of more than usually oxymorose fools. He was mute: He was grave. He looked, with large omniscient imperscrutable eyes, with the countenance open, with the thoughts restrained. Cavillers recited grievances – His refusal to wear the pontifical pectoral-cross of great diamonds, or any gems except His episcopal amethyst, was one – and appended sentences beginning 'Now surely – ' or 'And the scandal – ', or 'Ought we not rather – ' He was mute: He was grave: He was attentive. His intelligent silence had its calculated effect of causing errancy from points which primarily had been deemed important. Anon, only one objection remained: an objection to the new form of pontifical stole. No one complained of its colour. Red was canonically correct. But the silk should have been satin. Also, the pattern of the gold embroidery was uncommon. A rich design, of conventional foliage and grotesques enclosing armorials and keys, was what custom demanded. (Hadrian had no armorials. Years before, while discussing heraldic blazons with an aged clergyman, he had burst out with 'My shield is white'. 'Keep it so,' the other replied. And Hadrian's shield was Argent.) But this narrow strip, no wider than a ribbon, severely adorned with little fylfot crosses ('a Buddhist emblem' Berstein sneered) in little rectangular panels, with no expansive ends, and a scanty fringe, was hardly at all the kind of stole to inspire either the admiration or the homage of the faithful. Still Hadrian sat immobile, great-eyed, all-absorbent; and let them furiously rage, and imagine very vain things. And at the end of three quarters of an hour, He merely murmured 'Your Eminencies have permission to retire'; and stalked into the secret chamber.

It was felt that something ought to be done. Ragna put a case to Vivole and Cacciatore. The Oecumenical Council of the Vatican stood adjourned since 1870: but, if the Sacred College should demand – They found the notion excellent: communicated it to Berstein, and the French: plumed themselves; and went about mysteriously with their noses in the air. And there were intrigues in holes and corners.

Hadrian went up to the Church on the Celian Hill; and conferred diaconate on Percy Van Kristen. The Passionists liked that one for his stately shyness which did not wear away. It was the mark of a soul verisimilar to his patron's own, of a soul knit to no other: but, whereas the soul of Hadrian had been torn out of seclusion and bitterly buffeted by the world, the soul of Percy Van Kristen preserved its pristine tenderness. The Pope perforce went armed. His deacon remained by the altar.

The consistory was summoned for the twenty-fourth of May. That morning Hadrian woke just on these words of a dream, Oecumenical Council, Pseudopontiff, Heretic. A man with an active brain like His naturally suffers much unconscious cerebration. Very often it happened to Him vividly to dream some scrap or other of something apparently unconnected with the present. He used to wonder at it: mentally note it: generally forget it. Now and then, an event (of which it was the tip) immediately followed; and He scored. Hadrian named to the consistory the Lord Percy of New York as Cardinal-deacon of St Kyriak-at-the-Baths-of-Diocletian. His Eminency became resplendent in vermilion, tall, refined, reticent, with dark wide dewy eyes. He was admired in silence. The Pope by some accident turned His gaze to Ragna: he had such an aspect as caused His Holiness to look more intently. Ragna's great strong jaw moved as though to munch; and his glance defiantly shifted.

'Your Eminency is free to address Us,' the Supreme Pontiff said to Him.

'I wish rather to address the Sacred College,' Ragna answered, rising.

Hadrian had an intuition: His face became austere, His voice deliberate.

'On the subject of an Oecumenical Council where you may denounce Us as pseudopontiff and heretic?'

Ragna hurriedly sat down twitching. Berstein and Vivole muttered of divination and necromancy.

'That generally is done,' the Pope continued in the tone of one merely selecting fringe for footstools – 'That generally is done by oblique-eyed cardinals [He meant "envious" but He used the Latin of Horace] who cannot accustom themselves to new pontiffs. Rovere ululated for an Oecumenical Council when he found Our predecessor Alexander antipathetic; and there be other examples. But Lord Cardinals, if such an idea should present itself or should be presented to you, be ye mindful that none but the Supreme Pontiff can convoke an Oecumenical Council, and also that the decrees of an Oecumenical Council are ineffective unless they be promulgated with the express sanction of the Supreme Pontiff. Who would sanction decrees ordaining his own deposition? Who could? If We pronounce Ourself to be a pseudopontiff, what would be the value of such pronunciation? Ye were Our electors. We did not force you to elect Us. If We be Pontiff, We will not, and, if We be pseudopontiff, We cannot, depose Ourself. We are conscious of your love and of your loathing for Our person and Our acts. We value the one; and regret the other. But ye voluntarily have sworn obedience to Us; and We claim it. "Subordination", so the adage runs [He was citing the Greek to every Latin's disgust] "is the mother of saving counsel." Nothing must and nothing shall obstruct Us. Let that be known. And We should welcome cooperation. Wherefore, Most Eminent Lords and Venerable Fathers, let not the sheep of Christ's Flock be neglected in order that the shepherds may exchange anathemas.'

Mundo and Fiamma rose by impulse: went to the throne; and renewed their allegiance. The new cardinals mixed with the others and began to talk, while the rest of the Compromissaries approached the Pontiff. Orezzo moved that way with eight Italians. Then the seven brought each a companion. When, at last, the Benedictine struggled to his feet, opposition died. Ragna toed the line.

'His Holiness has averted a schism,' said Orezzo to Moccolo.

'One has to admire even where one hardly approves.'

'And to hobble after even when one cannot keep up with the pace.'

'Saint or madman?' Mundo repeated to Fiamma.

'One third saint, one sixth madman, one sixth genius, one sixth dreamer, one sixth diplomatist – '

'No. All George Arthur Rose plus Peter,' Talacryn put in. 'He said as much Himself to me once, whatever!'

Hadrian went out to take the air. Under His cloak He carried a pickle bottle, the label of which He had washed off and destroyed. As He went along, He picked up a trowel left by some gardener in a flower-bed. He found a solitary corner filled with rose acacias and lavender bushes behind the Leonine Villa. He looked up at the cupola of St Peter's and saw no Americans levelling binoculars. Then He dug a little hole; and buried pickles; and hid the bottle a few yards away beneath the beehives by the lavender bushes, mauve-bloomed, very sweet to smell. The solemn odour stimulated his brain; and He returned to chat with His gentlemen. They were engaged in physical exercises in a parlour. The Italian, who was one of nature's athletes, with so tremendous a power of chest-inflation that his ribs seemed unconnected with his sternum, interminably floated down and up and down to the floor on one leg, with the other leg and both arms extended rectangularly before him. The Englishman, a student, graceful and slim but not muscular, watched him and would imitate. His sinews had not the elastic force rhythmically to lower and raise him. He could get down but not up. He often lost balance, and rolled over in frantic failure. 'You must have thighs made of whipcord and steel to do it,' he was saying. Then they saw their visitor and attended. Hadrian asked what the exercise was and whence it came.

'*Santità*, from the *bersaglieri*,' Iulo responded. 'That they do, during an hour of each day for the fortification of their legs. From which they run.'

'It is beautiful. And are you going to emulate the *bersaglieri*?'

'My comrade goes to educate my mind. I go to discipline the physic of him,' the gymnast said.

'Oh, I'm going to help him rub up his classics as far as my poor knowledge lets me, Holiness: that's all,' the student added.

'Very good indeed,' Hadrian pronounced. 'Well now, something is going to happen to you. Go and escort the Secretary of State to the secret chamber.'

Ragna and the young men appeared within the quarter-hour. The Pope was seated; and a couple of Noble Guards stood behind His chair.

'Eminency,' He said, 'it is Our will to give these gentlemen the rank of Cavaliere – in English "knight" – '

'Nai-tah,' Ragna repeated.

'Your Eminency will cause letters patent to be prepared – '

'But this is the act of a sovereign!'

'And We, having no temporal sovereignty, exercise Our prerogative as Father of princes and kings.' He beckoned the gentlemen to kneel, took a sword from the guard on His left, struck them on the shoulder in turn, saying 'To the honour of God, of his Maiden Mother, and of St George, We make thee knight. Be faithful. Rise, Sir John. To the honour of God, of His Maiden Mother, and of St Maurice, We make thee knight. Rise, Sir Iulo.'

The cardinal retired mumbling. In the first antechamber, Sir Iulo cut a caper. 'Oh but that I should come to know such a one as this!' he chortled. Sir John went to his own room: opened an interlinear crib of Horace; and could not see one letter.

CHAPTER 9

HADRIAN knew that He was becoming confirmed in His pose of director. Not that He was inflated by His exaltation to the apostolature. He was conscious that people, except a few enthusiasts, were become indifferent to religion. He knew the danger of indifference to be so great that it was no time to strain at gnats. He could not trouble about rats in the ship's hold while the torpedo was approaching. He was thought to share the abominable heresy of Tolstoy, whose works He never would touch with tongs. He saw that most men lived in mist; and preferred it; that most men durst not see clearly, because their business and their social interest would not stand it. He was not absolutely certain that He Himself could see the remedy: but He was certain that blindness was no remedy. So He put forth the evangelic counsels for obedience. 'Strip; and obey those' appeared to be sufficient for the present; and He would not fiddle-faddle with human doctrines or empirical experiments. He had the big vision, the seeing eye, the hearing ear, wit, perverseness, daring, and the lonely heart, and the contempt of the world. The effect of His entire freedom of action was to inspire Him physically and mentally with the thrilling vigour of a pentathlete. He had the violent energy of the minute electron in the enormous atom. He felt Himself strong. He knew that His forces were tensely strung; and in their melody He was very glad. Sometimes He caught Himself wondering how long He could maintain the pitch: but from that thought He turned away. It was enough that He was able. He could not spare Himself. The night cometh when no man can work. 'Let it come,' he said to Cardinal Sterling: 'but while day lasts, We work.'

A splendid sentence of Mommsen's bit into his brain. *Caesar ruled as King of Rome for five years and a half...; in the intervals of seven great campaigns, which allowed him to stay not more than fifteen months altogether in the capital of the empire, he regulated the destinies of the world for the present and the future.... Precisely because the building was an endless one, the master, as long as he lived, restlessly added stone to stone, with always the same dexterity and always the same elasticity busy at his work, without ever over-turning or postponing, just as though there were for him merely today and no tomorrow. Thus he worked and created as never did any mortal before or after him; and, as a worker and creator, he still, after two thousand years, lives in the memory of the nations – the first, and withal unique, Imperator Caesar* – And Julius, also, had been Pontifex Maximus. Hadrian took a white umbrella for a walk as far as the black-lava fort on the Appian Way.

He considered the horrible condition of France and Russia. It was a menace to the world. Of Russia, He could learn nothing new. Thews and Thought together had abolished authority and gone mad in butchery. The information, which He had obtained from the French Cardinals, was not of a rather useful nature. Elements of emotional sentiment and archaic conven-tionalism rendered their opinions well nigh worthless. They were tolutiloquent in expressing horror at the impiety of mob rule which had deprived them of the right to military salutes ordained by the Concordat. They made the blood boil by their heart-rending descriptions of holocausts of priests and nuns – earnest heroic enthusiasts absolutely incapable of doing anything really practical in the way of eradicating that de-moniality of which they became the victims. Nothing would please Their Eminencies better than to hasten to their distracted native-land, to offer up themselves as martyrs to the devils of their dioceses. They were no cowards – if desire to rush on death be bravery: – but they were picturesque, and dithyrambic – mainly picturesque, with their long hair and their rabats edged with white beads. That would not do as an essential. Out of the mellay of matter laid before Him, the Pontiff extracted certain points. France, *qua* France, no longer was

Christian. The Devil was in power. Christians who were able to cross frontiers, did so. Spain, Italy, Switzerland, Germany, received them. England, America, Japan, blockaded Toulon, Brest, Cherbourg. Their liners tapped the coasts; and carried thousands into freedom. Poverty afflicted the emigrants: those left behind were butchers, or subject to butchery. Dom Jaime de Bourbon having perished, the Pope sent for the Duke of Orleans; and dismissed him with austere disgust. He subsequently withered away. His Holiness gave audience to a score of the French nobility; and spent some days picking the brains of emigrants fortuitously collected. Then, He again convened the French cardinals, and declared the pontifical will. They all were deposed from their episcopal sees, and nominated Apostolic Missionaries. Their charge was the cure, first of the bodies, second of the souls, of Frenchmen everywhere. The Cardinal-Missionary of Paris would go to London with the Cardinal-Archbishop of Pimlico, having powers to draw one million sterling from the pontifical treasure in the Bank of England: which sum, in halves, was to be the nucleus of two funds, an English and a German, for French Christians in their need. Each cardinal-missionary also received a breve authorizing him, and persons delegated by him, to collect money in every Christian country for the said funds. It was not to be a clerical charity. The Lord Mayor of London and the German Emperor were willing to administer it, each independently. Further, Their Eminencies were to use their own discretion about adventuring themselves in the diabolical dominion. If they best could serve God there, then in God's Name, and with God's Vicegerent's benediction, let them go: but they most straitly were bidden to keep one only object before them, viz. the service of God through the relief and comfort of His servants. Nothing was to prevent them in that.

The world began to concentrate the corner of its eye on Hadrian. Holland and Belgium fell into the arms of anarchical France. The vigorous bold brilliant young Sultan Ismail, having failed to win Morocco to his Pan-Islamic scheme, was intriguing for an alliance with the other great Mohammedan power, England. His Majesty's murderered predecessor, by the aid of Germany, had formed an army of a million and a half, full of fanatical valour and the wonderful natural adaptability of the Turk, the rawest recruit of which had a greater fighting value than was possessed by the conscripts of any other nation. This force was available for active service at fifteen minutes notice. The Turkish alliance was worth anyone's while; and was coveted. Germany had trained the Ottoman squadrons: but was not to profit thereby. Teutonic stolidity had been outwitted by the wily Oriental. Islam could only and only would mate with Islam – as might have been foreseen. The rest of the continent of Europe ringed frontiers under arms. Each nation feared the other; and all feared France and Russia.

Hadrian watched the diplomatic processes with interest. He knew that England was quite capable of taking care of Herself, with or without the Mussulman. He grasped the theory that Mohammedanism, arising six hundred years after Christ, justified the Wisdom of God in Judaism, proving that the Oriental mind could bear nothing more perfect; and He conceived a sort of sympathy with Islam. His conversations with ambassadors became known in courts (the King of Prussia's legate wrote amazing things to the German Emperor): from courts, descriptions of opinions, tastes, habits, descended until they were discussed in clubs and miscellaneous congeries. Hadrian's custom of walking about unattended, looking at the excavations in the Forum, visiting the sick in hospitals, sensuously delighting Himself with the glories of sunset seen from the Pincian Hill, were the themes of common conversation. And when, one evening, He got in a left hander (from the shoulder) on a socialist, who spat at Him in Borgo Nuovo; and then (on the filthy beast's bursting into tears and collapsing with the effects of the blow upon semi-starvation) pressing upon him His pectoral cross and chain, His gold spectacles, and all the coins left in His pocket after a couple of hours in Rome – then the English race began to find the Pope observable; and

English newspapers started columns called 'Rome Day by Day'. How the special correspondents spread themselves! She of the *Pall Mall Gazette* got the usual exclusive information of the Borgo Nuovo affair; and split nine infinitives in describing the myopic Pontiff narrowing His eyes to slits, groping His way along the colonnades with His fainting assailant; His passionate denunciation of the farce of organized charity, which had let a man become so degraded; His agitation until Cardinal Carvale came running with His spare pair of spectacles; His strangely pathetic thankfulness for the gift of sight which they afforded; His anguish at the defilement of His garment; and His tender invitation to the starving socialist to be His guest in Vatican. All this suited the English temper to a T – being English. But there created a profound and perdurable impression. The King of Prussia's legate wrote more amazing things to the German Emperor. Hadrian became regarded in cabinets and chancelleries as one who cared or strove neither for loss nor gain, neither for life nor death – as the one Potentate who rightly or wrongly knew his own mind – as a Power with whom a reckoning might have to be made. After all, it merely was the effect of simplicity upon complexity, of felinity upon caninity.

He was sitting alone, thinking, and carefully unravelling a woollen antimacassar. It had been crocheted in five bossy strips, three of orange hue and two of grey, alternately arranged. He had unravelled two orange and two grey strips; and had the wool neatly rolled in four balls beside Him. The next time He should go into the City, some little girl would be made happy with two nice balls of grey wool and a lira to buy knitting needles; and, the time after that, another little girl would have three balls of orange wool and a lira also; and pontifical eyes would not be scorched by ghastly antimacassars any more, nor would the kind heart of anyone be wounded. He finished the job; and went to talk to his socialist. That one turned out to be a goldsmith, with the ideals and the brains and the fingers of Cellini, but not the acquisitiveness. Hence straits, socialism, sophistries, starvation. They walked about the sculpture galleries for coolness; and spoke of Beautiful Things. Hadrian revelled. His guest was a man of taste; and talked on a trot with wonderful gestures, making and moulding ideal images which the mind's eye could see. They came to the Apoxyomenos: stood: raved; and became dumb, feasting on the lithe majesty of perfect proportion. The artificer first spoke.

'Holiness,' he said, 'can You see that body and those limbs crucified?'

Hadrian's mind caught the idea. The splendid forms of the marble seemed to rearrange themselves in the new pose. His eyes came slowly round to His questioner.

'Yes,' He answered: 'but soaring and triumphing, "reigning from the tree", not drooping and dying – and not the head and bust.' He took the goldsmith's arm and hurried him to the Antinous of the Belvedere; and began to speak very quickly.

'Sir,' He said, 'you will be pleased to stay here; and, with the materials which will be provided, you will make a new cross for Us. The cross will be of the kind called Potent, elongate: the Figure will combine the body and limbs of the Apoxyomenos with the head and bust of the Antinous, but posed as We have described. On the completion of this masterpiece, you will be offered an appointment as goldsmith in the pontifical household – '

'Ah, Padrone.'

Hadrian returned to the secret chamber, happy in anticipation of an emblem which would not offend His taste. True, He was glad (in a way) that a tangled life so easily could be made straight: but it was the visionary ideal of Beauty which really inspired joy.

CHAPTER 10

THAT aggregation of intellectually purblind and covetous dullards, who formed the socialistic sect of the King of England's subjects, presently began in their rough rude way to perpend the Pope of Rome. It had been a moot point with these discontented sentimentalists whether it would or would not be profitable to unite with French and Russian anarchy, and attain their ends that way: but one Julia, in the *Salpinx* screamed with such excruciating tales about slaughtered French babies, that that was 'off'. Also, it was remembered that a certain Comrade Dymoke, the only capable fighting man ever possessed by socialism, had been spunged upon for fifteen years by socialistic cadgers, sucked dry, ruined, and cast out, a victim of socialistic jealousy and treachery. In the plans laid for a Social Revolution, towards the end of the nineteenth century, that man had been named commander-in-chief. Now he was not available; and his place was vacant: for a military expert rarely errs into the purlieus of socialism.

But one thing had been done. The Social Democratic Federation had been induced, at the National 'Liberal' Club, to coalesce with the Independent 'Labour' Party. The coalition called itself the 'Liblab Fellowship': the *Salpinx* and *Reynards's* were its organs; and a parcel of Bobs and Bens and Bills and Bounders its prophets. It concluded that it would score by toadying the Supreme Pontiff. The brainless monster of socialism always was hunting for a brain to direct its forces. By some perverted process, it arrived at the feeling that a Pope, Who could indite the *Epistle to All Christians*, would be likely to lend Himself to the furtherance of its crude designs on other people's property. A week later, Cardinal Whitehead called Hadrian's attention to the current issue of the aforenamed journals, which contained an *Open Letter to the Pope* praising the 'enlightened humanitarianism' of His Holiness's recent utterance, inviting Him to have courage of His opinions, and to bring His *Epistle* to (what was called) 'a logical conclusion' by a formal authoritative declaration of the doctrine of Equality. Popes, as a rule, do not notice *Open Letters*. Hadrian, however, had learned from the *Pall Mall Gazette* that the fashion was for copious artists in words to lecture the Roman Pontiff. He anticipated the being told by that elegant journal that He knew as much about the true inwardness of Catholicism as a cow knows of a clean shirt. But He privately was of opinion that more harm may be done by leaving some things unsaid. But, Love – ! Was it possible that He could love, could like (even) hyenas who screeched such ditties as this on the same page:

'They will tax the baked potatoes,
    They will tax our blessed swipes,
They will tax our blooming hot pea-soup
    The leather, and the tripes,
They will tax the coster's donkey,
    They will tax the Derby 'orse
And they're going to tax the devil
    When he lives at Charing Crorse.'

Ouf! No. It was quite impossible. Yet – there were people whom He could like, if not love: people in His Own environment. These He would make easy, happy. To these He could set an example. They, in turn, would do as much for the rank below them: and so on, and so on. Thus, perhaps, by Nature's own method, might Love be brought down among men. So with a stern and trenchant rebuff He rebuked presumption. On the following Sunday, a Pontifical Breve was read from every Catholic pulpit in the Kingdom of England at home and beyond the seas. It proclaimed the dogma of Equality as scientifically, historically, and obviously false and impracticable: as a diabolical delusion for the ruin of souls. Hadrian did not soar away in metaphysical intricacies, but confined His argument to the broad highway whereon the ordinary man might walk at ease. Infinite difference, He said, was the note of the Divine Creator's scheme. Not equality, but diversity, of physique, of intellect, of condition, was man's birthright. One man was not as good as another: he generally was a great deal better – as every man well knew. The claim to equality was so indecently unjust that it only could emanate from inferiors who hoped to gain by degrading their superiors. Socialists, who claimed equality, solely were actuated by the lust of improving their own condition at the expense of their brother. That was selfishness, and unchristian, and (by consequence) damnable heresy. The servants of God were bidden to avoid it. The Vicar of Christ repeated Christ's commands 'Love one another – Love your enemies.' Only by Love could be attained the happiness which all desired. That the classes did care for the masses, futile and indolent though their method might be, was undeniable: but the attitude of the masses to the classes was unmitigated hatred. The accident of birth to poverty or wealth was not a fault, for it was inevitable. The principle of Aristos 'The Best' was to be upheld. The strength of Aristos was incalculable because it acted through the relations of private life, which were permanent: whereas the political excitement of socialism was essentially ephemeral. Rights, inherited, meritorious, conferred by legitimate authority, were sacred. Only the holders of such rights of their own free will could depose themselves or abdicate their rights; and, as Christians, they were expected to behave themselves Christianly: but to deprive them of such rights, at the will of those who did not confer them, would be an outrage. The socialistic idea, which suggested such iniquity, was essentially selfish and venal. Hadrian severely denounced the newspapers in which the *Open Letter to the Pope* appeared. He said that the thoughtful reading of a newspaper was one of the most solemn and painful studies in the world, for it was little more than a category of sin and suffering, of incitements to sin, of efforts to acquire filthy lucre honestly and dishonestly. He copiously quoted the advertisements, the Cyclorama page, the Motor Notes page, the Stageland, the Woman's Letter, and the Leaders, of the one, in order to show that the socialistic outcry by no means was the bitter groan of oppressed poverty, but rather the grumbling vituperation of envious discontented mediocrity anxious to affect an appearance, which was sham and not its own, and to wallow in luxurious conditions which it had not earned. Especially He noted the Socialistic Programme, '*We suggest that the nation should own ALL the ships ALL the railways ALL the factories ALL the buildings ALL the land and ALL the requisites of national life and defence,*' as a plain declaration that robbery of private property created by individual industry and genius – robbery, pure and unadulterated, was the basis of the socialistic scheme. He denounced the paper as being written for amateur agnostics by dilettante atheists. He pungently derided attempts made, by pseudoscientists of the obsolete school of Haeckel, to popularize among mistaken but serious secularists the science of yesterday and the destructive criticism of the day before that. As for the other paper, He likened it to a *cloaca* wherein filth of all kinds is committed and collected. The news of the day was reported only in so far as it was susceptible of filthy presentation. Pages were devoted to diffusing refuse from police courts; and (under the head of Secret History) to calumnious inventions or distortions of fact connected with any and every man or woman who was not of the dregs of humanity. As a method of earning a living by journalism, this pandering to the basest passions was disgraceful, and damnable in the full sense of the word. Not by such means were the bodies and souls of men to be improved or profited. Not by such means could happiness, here or hereafter, be attained, 'Let men raise themselves if they will; and let each man help himself by helping his brother to the utmost: there shall be no limit to your resurrection, well-beloved sons, if ye rise, not on other men but, upon your own dead selves,' the Pope concluded.

In accordance with instructions, the Cardinal-Prefect of the Congregation of Sacred Rites presented to the Pontiff certain completed processes and petitions for the beatification of the Venerable Servants of God, Alfred the Great, King and Confessor – Henry VI of Lancaster, King and Confessor – Mary Stewart of England, France, and Scotland, Queen and Martyr. Assent was deigned to these petitions; and pictures, each with a golden nimbus, were unveiled in the Vatican Basilica. The bull of beatification decreed the addition of the following words to the Roman Martyrology, the official roll of sanctity:

This day, in England, is kept the festival of the Blessed Alfred, King and Confessor, who by the acclamation of his own people is named Great: memorable as a father of his fatherland, a lover of his brother, a true servant of God.

This day, in England, is kept the festival of the Blessed Henry VI of

Lancaster, King and Confessor: memorable for meekness, for suffering, for purity of heart, for the gift of prayer.

This day, in Scotland, is kept the festival of the Blessed Mary Stewart, Queen and Martyr: memorable for womanly fragility, for nineteen years' atonement in prison, for choosing death rather than infidelity.

Semphill and Carvale had urged Hadrian to impose the Proper Office and Mass of the last upon England as well as Scotland. His Holiness would know why?

'Because Her Majesty was the rightful Queen of England as well as of Scotland;' Semphill responded with the air of one who has invented a new sauce.

'Display your premisses, Lord Cardinal,' said the Pope.

'They are simply historical facts, known to everyone.'

'But the conclusions which may be drawn from historical facts, mainly depend upon the sequence or method of arrangement of the said facts. Display yours, Lord Cardinal.'

'The Blessed Mary Stewart was heiress of James V, who was heir of Margaret Tudor wife of James IV of Scotland and daughter of Henry VII of England. Henry VII's heir was his son Henry VIII, who married Katherine of Aragona and had issue Mary Tudor. Subsequently, failing to obtain annulment of his marriage from Your Holiness's predecessor Clement VII, Henry VIII lived in sin with Anne Bullen and Jane Seymour by whom he had issue Elizabeth and Edward. Canonically this prince and princess were illegitimate and incapable of succession. Therefore, on the death of Henry VIII the crown of England demised to his sole legitimate issue, Mary Tudor –'

'But Parliament had passed an Act, 28 Hen. VIII c.7, giving the English Sovereign power to limit the crown by letters-patent or by his last will to such person or persons as he should judge expedient.'

'Surely, Holiness, that ought not to count. However, on the death of Mary Tudor without issue, I argue that the crown of England demised *de jure* though not *de facto* to the next legitimate Tudor who was Mary Stewart, heiress of Margaret Tudor.'

Hadrian turned to Carvale.

'Of course, Most Holy Lord, I feel with Cardinal Semphill. I think' – his beautiful blue eyes blazed with the fire of his dreams – 'I think that the time has come for doing justice to the memory of "that predestined victim of uncounted treasons, of unnumbered wrongs, wrongs which warped and maddened and bewildered her noble nature, but never quenched her courage, never deadened her gratitude to a servant, never shook her loyalty to a friend, never made her false to her faith". O think, Holiness, of all that the Stewarts have suffered!'

Hadrian Himself had a very tender and romantic feeling of attachment towards the Stewarts: but He responded, 'Our office is not to stir up strife. We Englishmen happen to have made an ideal of Elizabeth. With that delightful capability for making our own ideals and maintaining them in the teeth of realities, we have chosen to forget the fact that no sovereign of ordinary intelligence could have helped being gilded by the really abnormal galaxy of talent which illumined the age of Elizabeth. It was those gigantic geniuses who made the glory of England then. England happened to be personified by Elizabeth. Therefore, in English eyes, Elizabeth was great and glorious and all the rest. No one' (he turned to Semphill) 'can quarrel with your statement of blind and naked fact; and no one, who is right-minded, will. But, We desire to reconcile, not to exasperate, though we never will refuse to exasperate upon an apt occasion. Therefore We will not assert now that which need not be asserted. Be content that We raise your lovely martyred queen to the honours of the altars of your country. Ask Almighty God to look upon your land with favour for His Son's sake, and for the sake of her who in the Strength of that Son was faithful unto death. Call upon Mary in Heaven to add her prayers to those which ye offer to God on earth. Precious in the sight of The Lord – If it be His Will to confirm with signs and wonders these your invocations –'

Their Eminencies gazed at the Pope with ecstasy. That He,

whom they had known before, not always agreeably, that He – 'Oh, really,' said Semphill to Carvale as they left the Presence, 'I don't know whether I'm sleeping or soaking.' And Hadrian, alone, rolled a cigarette, saying to Another than Himself, 'Is that what You wish me to do in this case?'

Simultaneously with the beatificatory bull *Laudemus insignes*, was issued the *Epistle to the English*. The Pope affirmed that the English Race naturally was fitted to give an example to humanity. In particular, He categorically distinguished its solid worth, its dignified good sense, its deliberate tenacity, its imperturbable habit, its superb impassiveness in reverses, its stoical firmness under the most cruel deceptions, its unshaken determination to conquer under any circumstances. In general, He noted its faculties of self-restraint, of construction, of administration, and (among the upper and middle classes) of altruism. He indulged no vain regrets: but dealt entirely with the present and the future. He addressed the Race, as the Race would wish to be addressed, with perfect sincerity. In spite, He said, of the scum which floats, and is called 'Smart': in spite of the dreg which goes a-mafficking, and is called 'Hooligan' the English people at heart were as sound as ever. Millions, rich and not rich, gentle and simple, in town and country, led clean and wholesome lives. No newspaper paragraphs proclaimed that these good souls were bringing up their children to be ladies and gentlemen, were solicitous for the welfare of their inferiors, had respect unto themselves. No flaming headlines screeched, announcing that they were paying their way, marrying and giving in marriage, rejoicing and sorrowing, like the brave honest commonplace people that they were. No Society Gossip told of Robert and William and Nicholas and James and Frederick and Herbert and Percy and Alfred, day labourers for a too scanty wage, who never drank nor fought nor swindled nor yelled for their rights, but who led decent noble lives under circumstances often cruelly unjust and always rigorously hard. Of such as these, said Hadrian, was the English Race composed. He reminded England that she had received more from the Latin Church than any other nation: that her gains had been direct before 1534: indirect after that date, when her natural enemies were dragged down by the corruptions of Rome. (He thought they would enjoy that point.) He assumed nothing, not even a prejudice. He advised without commanding: He directed without trespassing. The latter half of the *Epistle* concerned those who owed Him spiritual allegiance: to these He spoke with all authority. He blamed their phrenetic anxiety to enter into worldly competition. He pointed out that the Penal Laws, which from 1534 to 1829 had deprived them of 'that culture which contact with a wider world alone can give', had rendered the Catholic aborigines corporeally effete and intellectually inferior to the rest of the nation. He did not blame noluntary defects: but facts were facts, and only fools would refuse to face them. These defects would find their remedy in the influx of new and vigorous blood and unexhausted brains. He quoted the words of a great critic who said that the religious movement of our day would be almost droll if it were not, from the tempers and actions which it excited, so extremely irreligious. It had taken four centuries to produce the present position of Catholics in England; and, as no man has a right to expect miracles, it might take four centuries more to restore them to a corporeal and intellectual equality with the average of their fellow-countrymen. To this end, He bade them to welcome and to comfort accessions to their number, not (as was the present custom) with slavering sentimentality giving place to slights, snubs, slanders, and sneers: but with brotherly love, putting in practice the Faith which they professed; and *letting* their light shine, instead of advertising comparatively paltry efforts at illumination. He reminded them that 'God made man right, but he sought out many abstruse reasonings'; and, for a society of Christians to pretend to be 'the world' or 'of the world' was an incongruous monstrosity. He warned them that the kind of conscience which they cultivated, the conscience which descends from its high personal plane, which consents to haggle and discuss how far resistance to temptation must be carried, which deigns to consider consequences, to weigh possibilities, and to guard against disaster, was the proximate occasion for the well-founded charges of hypocrisy and humbug brought against all religion by lewd fellows of the baser sort. As for those of the clergy, whose comportment elicited from outsiders testimonials to the effect that they were 'thorough men of the world having nothing clerical about them except their collars' or 'thoroughly good chaps who take their glass and enjoy a smutty story like ordinary beings' – His Holiness assured Their Right Reverencies, Their Very Reverencies, and Their Reverencies, that they completely misconceived their sacred character.

Our citizenship is in heaven (ἡ πολιτεια ἡμων ἐν οὐρανωι). If then in very truth, ye look for a city which is an heavenly, ye must esteem yourselves as being 'in the world' as strangers (ξενοι), or resident aliens (μετοικοι); and so ye ought not to be *curiosi in aliena republica*.

He ordained that married Anglican clergy (whose wives were alive and who possessed the grace of a Divine Vocation) on resuming allegiance to the See of Peter, should be admitted to the priesthood and serve secular churches: but faculties for hearing confessions were not to be disposed to married priests; and each such priest, having charge of a mission, must nominate and maintain at least one Regular as curate whose sole duty should be the administration of the sacrament of penance. Finally, the Supreme Pontiff commanded the sacrifice of that phantom uniformity which had been the curse of Catholicism for four centuries, and the retention and cultivation of national and local rites and uses. And He commended England to St George, Protector of the Kingdom.

The Archsocialists were bitterly chagrined by the pontifical denunciation of their *Open Letter*; but the *Epistle to the English* made them gnash their teeth. In print, they gibbered at first, and vomited after their manner. In congress, each one suspected his neighbour of being a 'traitor to the Cause' whose treachery had taken the form of urging his comrades corporately to attract the pontifical fulmination. There was a dreadful scene at West Ham and a free fight at Battersea. Comrade Pete

Quillet threatened to 'ave Comrade Bill Meggin's blighted ear; and had as much of the left one as twenty-seven unclean gorgonzola-coloured fangs could tear off, before he succumbed to six boots, a bottle, and a harness-buckle. At headquarters, the demagogues did behave with outward decency: not disguising their disappointment, but casting about for a new lead. The curious thing was that not one of them now but was more than ever anxious for alliance with the Power which disdained and damned them. It was the Power which they coveted – and admired, in the first intention of the word. Their attitude to the Pope was that of those who lick the hand that lashes them. The Pope was not a Penrhyn, against whose liberty they could invoke the laws at which otherwise they girded: He was to them something immense, intangible, potent, detestable – and most desirable.

While they were debating as to the precise posture in which they next should cringe, Comrade Jerry Sant communicated startling news. He was a delegate from the north: by profession, first a haberdasher's bagman, secondly a socialist; Socialism appearing to him an easy way of self-aggrandisement. As a rule, he did not push forward, working in the background, anonymously writing for the papers, watching for a chance to snatch. He whispered a word to his neighbour at the table.

'Rot!' said the latter.

'Rot yersel'!' Jerry retorted.

The other Fellowshipper guffawed. 'Here, I say, Mr Chairman, this Comrade says he used to know that old Pope!'

Jerry Sant became observed. He had the haggard florid aspect, the red-lidded prominent eyes, the pendulous lip of a sorry sort of man. He stood up and began to speak, sometimes dragging a sandy rag of moustache or fingering shiny conical temples, but generally holding on by the lapels of a short-skirted broadcloth frock-coat, protruding black-nailed thumbs through the buttonholes in a manner acquired during a week in Paris. His style was geological, so to speak, consisting of various strata deposited at various periods. The surface stratum, representing the Cainozoic Time, consisted of the platitudinous bombast characteristic of the common or oratorical demagogue. Below that, corresponding to the Mesozoic Time, came the ridiculous obsequious slang of the bagman of commerce. Below that again, corresponding to the Palaeozoic Time, appeared the gelded English which muscleless feckless unfit-for-handicraft little sciolists acquire in schoolboard spawning-beds. And these rested on stratum of the Azoic Time, to wit the native Pictish Presbyterian jargon of Mr Sant's sententious pettifogging spiteful self. These different strata occurred as irregularly as natural strata. They ran one into the other like veins in a fissure, causing displacements resembling those which technically are called Faults; and the tracing and stripping of the same is a task for the ingenious geophilologist.

'It's a gospel truth, comrades. I had used to fhat ye might call know the Pope a few years ago fhen he was just George Arthur Rose and not a pound note in his purse. I was running the *Social Standard* oot o' my own pocket, and many's the bit o' work I've let him have. He was trying his hand at journalism then, and gey glad to get it. I may take this opportunity of saying that he owes his footing to me; and most ungrateful he has treated me, comrades, as is the nature of him, proud aristocrat as he is. Not that I look for gratitude in such: but I've often thought when I've heard of him getting on – I mean before as he was fhat he is now – as perhaps he might like to remember him as gave him his first leg up. But no, not a bit of it though. I advised him of as much, once; and he rounds on me and cheeks me cruel. And I'm not the only one neither: I can tell you something else about him. There's a lady-friend of mine – '

'Here stop a bit,' the chairman interrupted. 'You're getting on a bit too fast. What did you let him write for the *Social Standard* for? Was he a comrade, I.L.P., or S.D.F., or Fabian p'raps? He seems to be rather a high sort from what you say.'

'A comrade! Tits, man! ma pairsonal opeenion is that he was nothing bit a . . . Tory spy. I always thought he was a Jesuit in disguise and now of course I know it. Fhen I knew him first he was pals with the traitor Dymoke – '

'Dymoke ! ! !' Teeth gritted; and the social equivalent for the Roman 'Anathema sit' was snarled.

'Comrades, it wasn't me that was to blame there you know. Wait a minute before we meaninglessly divide oursels. I have some most important developments to lay before the meeting as you'll all cordially endorse. Don't someone remember I was the one that stopped the traitor's letters and give information of his treachery? If it hadna have been for me he would have bought the bally show with his Tory gold. It was me as put my spoke in his wheel and got him expelled in time. Well, as I was remarking, fhen I knew Rose he was gey thick with Dymoke. Fhat for did I let him write for us? Wy, because he could write the verra blusterous epithets which'd make the enemy wince. Of course I went over all that he wrote though, just to see that he was economically correct. If I hadna have done that I might just as well have shut up shop. But I was going to say, comrades, there's a lady-friend of mine he's treated shameful – made love to her while her man was alive, borrowed twenty pound notes of her, had to be forbid the hoose, and then fhen she was left a widdy wumman with a family he cuts her dead at a picture gallery. That's fhat I mean by ungrateful, the swine, fit to make a man retch with his mumping cant. What I was about to observe – no, she's not a Fellowshipper yet. I met her in the way of business if you know what I mean: but I expect she'll join before long. I know she will if I can only bring off fhat I'm talking about. She's got a pension, and she takes paying guests, quite high toned and all. That's how I got to know her. I've put up there fhen I've come down to London these five year. Well, the moment I first come ben her best parlour I spots his photo on the cheffonier. 'Hech,' says I, 'I know that chap.' 'Then you know a very mauvy soojy,' says she, for she knows the French fine, and a' thing as genteel as you can think. So we had a bit crack; and fhat with fhat she told me and fhat I knew aboot him before, I may inform you that if we want to get anything out of him now I'm the man that can secure his entire acquiescence to any proposal we like to submit to him. Here's my plan, comrades, and if anyone's got a better let him out with it or else for ever after hold his peace and stand out of the way of them that has. Comrades, the hour has struck when tyranny will be no more for I've got the tyrant between ma legs and A'm going to squeeze him off my own bat, supposing as I'm properly supported. Cautious though, very cautious we must be: for Rose fhen I knew him was fine and slippery. Artful? E-e-e-e-e-eh! Dinna ye talk about his artfulness! Aye and proud too! He was the most haughty don't care sort of chap ye can think. I mind his eyes were like lowin' coals somewhens. You shouldn't nail him anyhow. Insolence I call it; and I'd have pulled his nose for him many times only he wasn't worth it. Starving I've known him: yet if you'll believe me he'd give himsel' a wash and a brush up and go out of an afternoon looking as smart as you please in his old clothes and with a fag always in his mouth like the masher he is. That fag! I'll let ye know it was aye the same fag. He hadna used to light it ever. He lit it once and put it out directly after; and then he used to stick it in his face every afternoon and show himself as usual, so that no one should know he hadna had a bit fhite fish, na naething to ca' a moothfu' o' flesher's meat wi' his piece the week past. He telled it me himsel' when I got to know him. And now, comrades, there's that feller sitting on the seven hills of Rome with three gold crowns on his head, as has been put in the papers, damning us for all he's worth. Comrades, fhat I wish to call the attention of this meeting to this evening is – I'll just speir if ye think that Rose should like to have his past life gave away by me and my lady-friend? Mrs Crowe, her name is.'

Jerry paused for a reply; and realized that he had possession of the meeting's ear: he mopped the lumps on his forehead: helped himself out of the chairman's whisky bottle: gulped a dram; and continued. His assumption of the rhetorical manner was consciously enormous now. 'Comrades, as in the east when the golden light of dawn shows that sunrise is about to come, so this poor feeble voice of mine shows that the tyrant's thrones are tottering to their overthrow. But, comrades, we maun beware. Snares beset our path. Once we have let oursel's be caught by his infernal Jesuitical machinations and he has scornfully

174

crrushed us to the earth. This is how Labor is treated, and thus shall Labor be treated as long as we go cap in hand and ask for our rights instead of demanding them and taking them as Comrade Matchwood says in the *Salpinx*. Comrades, this time we maun conquer or expire. If we want the former, we must fight our enemy with his own tools. Fhat are his tools? Comrades, his tools are Jesuitical Tory tools. His emissaries are everywhere, his spies beset our path on every hand I should say infest our road. Even in this hall tonight, a Tory eye may be upon us, a Jesuitical ear may be protruded to catch these whispers falling from this feeble tongue and pass them on to that arch-pariah in Rome who is drunk with the blood of working-men and battened on unearned increment. Comrades, we maun take a leaf out of his book: we maun hoist him up on his own Jesuitical petard. We oursels maun become Jesuitical for the sake of the Cause. Comrades, there in Rome sits the Abominable Desolation and I'll let ye know ye'll find him fhat ye may call a fikey customer. Day by day his satellites prostrate their forms before his so-called holy toe, and let him know a' things which they've found out by base and underhand sneaking means. That is whit way he is so powerful. His slaves tell him so much that he knows everything. Look fhat with an entire lack of consistency he said about the *Salpinx*. Could he have said that if he hadna been informed? No, I repeat, a thousand times no. Comrades we maun do the same. He knows our secrets and uses them against us most unfair. We maun worm his out too, and use them to bend his proud knee to the people's will. Comrades, I, me, know his secrets. I am the man and Mrs Crowe is the woman fhat shall shame him before all his silken harems and cardinals and potentates – upset his apple-cart if I may use a colloquious impression. We only have got to show the despot our two faces, and I'll let ye know he'll quail as sure's death. We shan't need say a word. At the mere sight of me and my lady friend the monster'll howl for mercy. Then we will be able to have our revenge for his recent most insulting remarks. We will dictate fhat he shall have to do to win our favour. All the starch and haughtiness shall go out of him like steam out of a toddy-jug when he sees us two; and he shall pay any price to gain our smile. And then I'll let you know what my plans are. Comrades, we're agreed aren't we that the only way in which the Cause can triumph over Capital is by having a Labor majority in the House of Commons. Fhat I mean by that is this. At that magnificent demonstration of Labor's irresistible electoral might, in the words of the *Salpinx*, we can make the Tories and our friends the Liberals pass our bills to pay us our proper salaries; and we will wrestle from the reluctant rich the mines and the railways and the mills and all the paying industries, and we shall even nationalize the land itself which our bloated aristocracy have robbed us of and mafficked in and wallowed in our gore. Comrades, I shall not detain you much longer for I see the hour is getting on. Fhat I mean to say is this is the point. There are, in this Great Britain and Ireland of ours the night, no less than 8,452,637 deluded papists with parliamentary votes. I obtained those figures carefully from statistics. You have to be careful about details like this if you mean to do yersel' any good at a'. Now, Comrades, all those 8,452,637 papists shall gladly drop their 8,452,637 votes into candidates' ballot boxes which will be put forward by the Liblab Fellowship. They shall do it at one word from their Pope, at one penstroke of his, such is the besotted state of slavery in which they exist. Refuse they dare not, or they should languish in the horrors of the Spanish Inquisition or light the Fires of Smithfield and the Massacres of the so-called Saint Bartholomew. Comrades, it is that one word and penstroke which the sight of me and Mrs Crowe shall squeeze out of their haughty Pope. We'd better have a proper deputation to go to wait on him with us for safety's sake; and happen we'd better have a sort of address to present, explaining how matters stand, just to make things look pleasant and polite as it were. That's only a matter of form though. The main thing'll be to see him fall back toes over tip on his judgement seat like him as was struck with worms when he sees who's in the deputation. Laugh? I won't ever have laughed like I will laugh at him then! Well now, comrades, I've said my say and I say no more leaving the matter to your esteemed consideration.

Comrades, think of all the insults which he and his myrmidons has made us groan under so long. Revenge is now at your disposal. This weak hand of mine has pointed out whit way. Seize it, oh seize it in the name of Freedom is all I ask. For myself I ask nothing, not a penny if you was to offer it me. Comrades, I'm fighting for the Cause. For the Cause I'd give my life as far as in me lies. That's my aim: that's my game, as the poet remarks. Comrades I shall not detain you longer I shall now sit down.' And the raucous gentleman panted into the next Fellowshipper's chair.

CHAPTER II

DEAR MRS CROWE,

Secret and Confidential.

Please burn it when you have concluded reading.

Referring to our numerous enjoyable conversations on the subject of Socialism in which you have evinced entire acquiescence, I am directed by the Council of the Liblab Fellowship to call your attention to the advantages obtainable from comradeship as per enclosed. The entrance fee is two and six and the subscription five shillings per ann. payable in June and Dec. I may add that those are special terms which I have exerted my influence to obtain in your favour and I trust I shall meet with your esteemed approval. Would you decide to join, kindly notify me of the same per wire for wh. I enclose six stamps. Yes or No will answer all purposes, but personally I feel sure that it shall be yes. On receipt of your anticipated favour will at once propose and have you seconded at our evening meeting to take place on the night of the same day when you get this letter. Should your reply be in the affirmative I am to let you know that you shall at once be nominated as a member of a deputation, which I have the honour to be a member of as well, which is about to proceed to Rome for the purpose of diplomatically interviewing our mutual friend the Pope. The expenses of the trip will be borne by the Liblab funds so there is no need to worry on that score. You are aware that travel especially to such a famous town as Rome is considered advantageous in every respect. The Italian sky the numerous old ancient edifices and the Romans themselves in their native monasteries cannot fail to amuse the eye of the beholder. The excursion is entirely gratis and so that difficulty is removed. But in addition to what I have said there is also the prospect of renewing our acquaintance with his so-called 'Holiness' ! ! ! ! And I may say for certain of having private interviews with him in the innermost recesses of his haunts. More I shall not now add. The mission of the deputation is strictly diplomatic and connected with political affairs, and I am of course not at liberty to divulge the details to anyone but fellowshippers, it would be hardly prudent. Ah would that you dear Mrs Crowe was one. But I may without any breach of confidence inform you in the strictest confidence that Rose alias Hadrian is in our power and therefore putting politics out of the question it shall go hard if you and me cannot do a little private business with him on our own account. Hoping to hear from you soon as per enclosed blank form and thanking you in anticipation

I remain
Yours truly in the Cause (I hope)
Jeremiah Sant

PS. Now burn this without fail.

Sant's lady-friend sat at the breakfast table, pondering this letter while her kidney grew cold. The four lodgers were gone to business; and she was alone except for the presence of her son. He was one of those beautiful speechless cow-eyed youths who seem born to serve as butts. Most people exercise some influence, assert some personal note. Alaric Crowe did neither. A course of female rule had produced him with about as much individuality as a cushion. He ate his breakfast in delicate silence. His mother was wrapt in thought. She found Sant's letter delectable. The consuming passion of her whole life was for George Arthur Rose. Next to him, she desired fame, notoriety, as a leader in suburban literary and artistic 'circles'. By perseverance, an undeniable amount of clever organizing power, a certain stock of third- or fourth-class talent, and any quantity of 'push', she had established a sort of *salon* where little lions hebdomadally roared. But she never had won the faintest regard from the man for whom she burned. The violence of her passion had caused her to make an irremediable mistake with him. She had not realized the feline temper which had caused him to repel advances as obvious as abrupt and as shameless as a dog's. He had ceased to be aware of her existence. Then she had

178

blundered further. Still ignorant of his peculiarity, she had treated him as the female animal treats the male of her desire. Finding him unapproachable by blandishments, she had turned to persecution. She would make him come to her and beg. Here, she also failed. In vain did she defame him to her followers: in vain did she libel him to the publishers from whom he earned his scanty subsistence: in vain did she force herself upon his few friends with stories of his evil deeds. He let those who listened to her leave him. He tolerated the ill-will or stupidity of Barabbas. He never said a word in his own defence. And he kept her severely and entirely at a distance, giving no sign that he even knew of her manoeuvres. It was galling to the last degree. Of course he was egregiously wrong. 'Neither in woes nor in welcome prosperity, may I be associated with women: for, when they prevail, one cannot tolerate their audacity; and, when they are frightened, they are a still greater mischief to their house and their city.' His feeling to women was that of Eteocles in the *Seven Against Thebes*. It caused him to make the tremendous mistake of his life. A woman of this colour never can be neglected: she must be taken – or smashed. That, he knew: but he would not take her, ever; and, a certain chivalrous delicacy, mingled with a certain mercifulness of heart, and a certain fastidious shrinking from a loathsome object, prevented him from prosecuting her with the rigour of the law. 'Wrong must thou do, or wrong must suffer. Then, grant, O blind dumb gods, that we, rather the sufferers than the doers be,' expressed his attitude. It annoyed himself: it made her fierce and furibund: and it was absolutely futile – And now, he had leaped at a bound from impotent lonely penury to the terrible altitude of Peter's Throne. He was famous, mighty, rich, and the idol of her adoration, despite the great gulph fixed between her insignificance and His Supremacy. Oh, what would she not give – for a curse, for a blow from Him. The emotion thrilled and dazzled her. Not one hour during twelve years had she been without the thought of Him. It was a case of complete obsession.

Her daughter flowed into the room in a pink wrapper,

finishing a florid cadenza. A touch on the teapot and a glance under the dish cover revealed astringent and coagulate tepidity. She rang the bell.

'Mother, why aren't you eating any breakfast?'

'I am eating it. I only just stopped a minute to read my letters.'

'A pretty long minute, I should think. Everything's stone-cold. Why you've only got one letter! Who's it from?'

'Mr Sant. He wants me to go to Rome with him.'

'Oh mother, you can't you know.'

'I'm sure I don't know anything of the kind. In fact I think I will go. There'll be a party of us.'

'Well, if it's a party – But what's going to become of the house?'

'I'm sure Big Ann is capable of looking after the house, Amelia. If I can't have a fortnight's holiday now and then I might just as well go and drown myself. I'm sick to death of Oriel Street. I want to go about a bit. Yes, I will go. And the house must get on the best way it can. Anybody would think you were all a pack of machines that wouldn't work if I'm not here to wind you up.'

'Oh, all right, mother, go and have a fling by all means if you like. But what about the cost? I'm sure I can't help you as long as I only get these three-guinea engagements. And I simply can't wear that eau-de-nil again. The bodice is quite gone under the arms.'

'You're not asked to help. Mr Sant pays all expenses. And, Amelia, if I can do what I'm going to try to do, you shall have as many new frocks as you can wear. We're going to see the Pope.'

'Going to see the Pope?'

'Yes, you silly girl – the Pope – Rose!'

'What do you mean?'

'Just what I say.'

'But you can't.'

'Nonsense. Of course I can.'

'Well I mean of course you can see Him the same as other

people do: but you'll be in the crowd, and He – I can't understand you at all this morning. Let's look at Sant's letter – How
vilely the man writes! Like a – You don't mean to say you'll
join these people? M-ym-ym. Yes, I see the game – Yes – But
d'you think you really could? – Well: if you like the idea still,
it's worth trying anyhow – Silly little mother! Why I believe
you're in love with Rose even now. Ah, you're blushing.
Mother, you look a dear like that!'

'Amelia, don't be stupid. Mind your own business.'

'Oh I'm not going to interfere. You needn't be jealous
of me. I'm sure I never saw anything particular in Him
myself.'

They spoke as though they were alone. Alaric went quite unnoted. He folded his napkin and rose from the table.

'A – and, mother,' he mooed, slowly, with a slight hesitation,
in a virginal baritone voice, resonant and low; 'if you go to
Rome, don't be nasty to Mr Rose?'

Both the women whirled round toward him. They hardly
could have been astounded if the kidneys had commented on
their complexions.

'Alaric! how dare you sir!'

'A-and I only say if you go to Rome I hope you won't be
nasty to Mr Rose.'

'Did you ever hear such nonsense, Amelia? Why not, I
should like to know?'

'A-and he taught me to swim.'

'So he did me. At least he tried to. And what of that?'
snapped the girl.

'A-and I don't think it's fair. I liked him. A-and father liked
him.'

'Yes indeed, he's just the sort of man your father would have
liked, unfortunately. He liked that sonnet man, too. A pretty
kind of person! All I can say is, Alaric, if I were to let you see the
letters I've got of his and the albums full – but there, you don't
know as much as I do about your father!'

The boy bellowed. 'A-and don't you dare say anything
against father! I won't stand it. Amelia knows I won't stand it

181

from her; and I won't from anyone, not even from you, mother. I won't, I tell you! I'll go right away if I have another word. Mother, I'm sorry: but you oughtn't. A-and I don't want you to be nasty to Mr Rose, because I liked him, a-and father liked him,' concluded Alaric departing.

Mother and daughter looked at each other. 'Who'd have expected Alaric to burst out like that? I'm sure it's very hard, after all I've gone through, to have my own children turning against me.'

'I am not turning against you, mother. I think – well of course I can't see why you care for Rose: but if you do you'd be a fool to miss a chance like this. What does Mr Sant mean about having him in his power?'

'I don't quite know. I suppose Georgie must have got himself entangled with these people somehow; and they think he wouldn't like it to come out. That's very possible. He's been mixed up with several shady characters in his time. However, we shall see. Amelia, do you know what I've been thinking? That mauve frock of my aunt Sarah's – now I believe I could make that up for myself for evenings and save a new one, you know. It's lovely silk. You can't get anything as good as that anywhere now-a-days.'

'What the one with the fringe?'

'Well, isn't fringe coming in again now? I think I know how to use every bit of it. The only difficulty'll be with the sleeves. I wish someone would invent a sleeve that only covers the lower part of one's arms. You see the best part of mine's about the shoulders.'

'Why don't you simply carry the fringe over the shoulders like straps; and wear long gloves?'

'Yes, of course I might do that. And Amelia, I really must have a new transformation; all things considered I think I will go to Du Schob and Hamingill's for it this time. I'm afraid they're rather dear: but when you look what a chance this is and how much depends ... Then there's another reason why I should go. People are beginning to neglect our Wednesdays. Well now, if I go to Rome with these whats-his-names it's sure to be in the papers; and then when I come back all our old friends are sure to want to know.'

So this precious pair of would-be blackmailers accompanied the deputation from the Liblab Fellowship to God's Vicegerent. Much of the formality prescribed for pontifical audiences had fallen into abeyance. Hadrian received ambassadors or personages with various degrees of ceremony: but, almost every day, He was to be found pacing to and fro in the portico of St Peter's; and then He was accessible to all the world. When, however, the Socialists applied for an audience, it was intimated that the Supreme Pontiff would deign to receive them at ten o'clock on the following morning; and the Vatican officials were instructed that the reception would be carried out with full state. It was George Arthur Rose's birthday. For twenty years no one had cared to remember it. Now there were scores who cared; and none who dared. Hadrian was more remote than George Arthur Rose had been.

A nervous little group of twenty obvious plebeians, male and female, awaited Him in the Ducal Hall. Superb chamberlains showed them the door by which the Pope would enter, and instructed them to approach the throne when He should have taken His seat. The great red curtains at the end of the Hall were drawn back; and cardinals, prelates, guards, and chamberlains, flowed in like a wave whose white crest was Hadrian. As the procession passed, Sant growled to Mrs Crowe,

'Does Himself well, don't He?'

'Oh isn't He just splendid!' she yapped.

Then chamberlains manoeuvred the Liblabs into position at the foot of the throne steps. Jerry by common consent had been chosen spokesman; and the united intellect of the Fellowship had drawn up the address which he, with ostentatious calmness, began to read. The Pope's ringed hand lay on His knee: His left elbow rested on the crimson chair and the hand supported the keen unfathomable face. He had prepared His plans: but He alertly was listening, lest unforeseen necessity for alteration should arise. He was watching with half-shut eyes and wide-open mind for an opportunity. None came. His prevision had been singularly accurate. The Liblab Fellowship really had nothing to say to Him, beyond turgid sesquipedalian verbosity expressive of its own disinterestedness, and fulsome adulation calculated (according to the Fellowshippers' lights) to tickle the conceit of any average man. It would have been funny, if it had not been terribly tiresome: impertinent, if it had not been pitiable. Sant's tongue clacked on his drying palate. To himself, his voice sounded quite strange in that atmosphere of splendid colour and fragrant odour. Mrs Crowe quivered; and wondered. The others were in a torpor. No one listened to the reader, except the Pope. The curia rustled and whispered, exchanging jewelled snuff-boxes. The guards resembled tinted statues tipped with steel.

'We have the honour to remain, in the cause of humanity,' concluded Jerry Sant, reciting the commonplace names of the signatories, 'On behalf of the Liblab Fellowship.' He refolded the foolscap sheets, and drew them through his fingers, looking as though he were about to hand them with a flourish to the Pope. A frilled black-velvet flunkey took them from him, gave them to a purple prelate, who passed them to a vermilion cardinal, who kneeled and presented them. The stately Cardinal Van Kristen moved from the side presenting a second manuscript. Hadrian unfolded it and began to read His reply. It was courteous and concise, distant and independent, simply an allocution on the distinction necessary to be drawn between Demagogues and Demos, the worthiness of the latter, the doubtfulness of the former. At the end there was a silence. Chamberlains discreetly made it known to the Fellowshippers that homage might be rendered by any who desired to render it; and gave instructions as to the customary manner. Twelve of the demagogues preferred a noncommittal pose, having fear of snorts of the *Salpinx*; and, of these, two found it convenient to glare uncompromisingly, letting it be seen that they regarded their host as the Man of Sin. But eight approached the throne. Five of them bowed, as over the counter: one kneeled on one knee and read his maker's name in his hat: Sant held his own elbows and looked along his nose; and Mrs Crowe laid her lips on the cross gold-embroidered on the Pontiff's crimson shoe. That was all. These people were bewildered, almost inebriated by the magnificence of the scene, by the more than regal ceremonial, by the immense psychical distance which divided them from the clean white exquisitely simple figure under the lofty canopy, by the quiet fastidious voice purring unknown words from an unimagined world, by the delphic splendour of Apostolic Benediction waved from the *sedia gestatoria* retiring in a pageant of flabellifers. On leaving the Vatican, they were thoroughly dazed: they knew not whether their diplomacy had been successful or unsuccessful. Jerry Sant had an indistinct notion that he might expect to be summoned after nightfall; and surreptitiously introduced to some pontifical hole or corner in order to be bribed. Mrs Crowe exulted in a new emotion. She actually had touched Him: and she thrilled: and she was sure that this was only a beginning.

When Hadrian was about to descend alone into St Peter's to say His night prayers, He observed one of His gentlemen practising a new and curious gymnastic in the first antechamber. Sir Iulo was in solitude; and he did not hear the feline footfall which came near. He had a longish knife in his right hand, held behind his back. Then, with his teeth clenched, and his eyes firmly fixed on an imaginary pair of eyes in front of him, and every sinew of him at its tensest, he suddenly whipped hand and knife face-high to the front hilt-upward, down to arms' length and forward up again point-upward, all with frightful force and rapidity. Hadrian watched him during five performances. Then Sir Iulo became aware of the Presence; and relaxed into upright stillness, grinning and glittering.

'What is this game?' the Pope inquired.

'Not game: but for the protection of You.'

'Protection? Protection from what?'

'From those most horrible peoples who have been today here pursuing some *vendettaccia*.'

'Do you mean those Liblabs?'

'But yes, those Libberlabberersser: especially a Libberlabber who has read, and a she-Libberlabber who goes with him. It is I who have seen of them both the eye. From which I vibrate a knife most commodious for the bellies of those. His Holiness can rest secure.'

'Do you mean that you are going to rip them up?'

'But yes, in the manner which I have learned of the chef from Naples. Now I watch them. When I shall have seen them make a movement, behold the tripes of them sliced *precipitatissimamente*!'

'Iulo. No. Understand? No.'

'There is not of dishonour! First like this, I demonstrate the knife – they view the mode of their deaths. There is in it nothing of sly – Next, I give them the death which they have merit. That is not the deed of a dishonourable.'

'You are commanded not to give death – not to think of giving death. It is prohibited. *O Viniti, quo vadis?* Understand? Bury the knife in the garden. *Sotterratelo nel giardino, Vinizio mio. Capisce?* Break it first. Then bury it in the garden – If you wish to be protector of Hadrian, learn to fight with fists – *pugni*. Understand? Tell John to buy a punching-bag – punching-bag – and practise on that.'

'Bai a punnertchingerbagger,' repeated the devout murderer-in-posse with disappointment, as the Pope left him limp.

A sign drew Cardinal Van Kristen to walk by Hadrian's side on the return from San Pietro and Vincula on Lammas Day. From time to time, his shy grand eyes turned to the Pope as they rhythmically paced along. From time to time, a blessing fluttered from the Apostle's hand to some stranger by the road-side.

'Holiness,' at length he said, 'do you remember that saint You used to worship on this day at Maryvale?'

Hadrian detached Himself from a reverie. 'Little Saint Hugh? Fancy your remembering that!'

And He again dived into silence.

'One would hardly fail to remember anything You said or did in those days, Holy Father.'

The Pope said nothing. He was thinking of something else.

'I put the picture you painted of Little Saint Hugh up in our refectory at Dynam House.'

No answer came. The cardinal's long eyelashes lifted a little as he looked at his companion. He was not sure that his attempt at conversation was welcome.

'Your Holiness does not care to be reminded perhaps. I did not mean to intrude. Sorry.'

Hadrian put out a hand. 'No, Percy, you don't intrude. We were wondering how long this King is going to be.'

'Which King?'

'Italy.'

'Oh. Yes?'

'Things are at a standstill.'

'For example?'

'Everything – at least in Italy – as long as something better than sulky peace is lacking. We want friendship, collaboration. See whether you can follow this. The personal influence of His Majesty is enormous. Although his acts are quite constitutional, yet, such is his magnetic force of character that he actually rules. No matter which party is in power, the King's Majesty rules. Practically he is an autocrat; and he, so far, has not made a single mistake, nor done a single unjust or even ungenerous deed. Now We also have some power, some personal influence. These people seem to like Us. They're charmingly polite. They run about after Us. We do not doubt but that they would obey if We commanded – if We ordained that no woman should cover her hair with a terrible handkerchief when she goes into a church – if We substituted silver sand for those abominably in- sane sponges in the holy-water fonts, for example – but how many of them would obey Us if We ordered them to cease from drying their linen at their windows, or to stop spitting? Do you follow?'

'No Holiness.'

'Our influence is over particulars, is sentimental, is ideal. The influence of the King's Majesty is over universals, is practical, is real – '

'Yes, I see that.'

'Well, then – '

'You mean that Your influence and the King's – '

'Could do a great deal more for this dear delightful country than – '

'Do you think that this King knows of Your desire for reconciliation?'

'Victor Emanuel is one of the four cleverest men in the world. It is impossible that he should not have understood the *Regnum Meum.* Besides, We addressed him by name. He owes Us the civility of a response.'

'Holiness, let me have that news conveyed to him. Guido Attendolo – '

'No. We Ourself have not yet seen clearly the next move. We believe that His Majesty of his own initiative ought to have approached Us – the son to the Father – before now. We have given him a token of Our goodwill. There the matter rests. He cannot have a doubt as to what Our purpose is. But – His Majesty must do as he pleases. We think that We have done Our part so far. At present, We are not moved to proceed further. When We are moved – and that is what occupies Us now. An idea seems to be forming in Our mind: but as yet – Percy, do ask Our friends to tea in the Garden of the Pine Cone at half past sixteen o'clock today.'

The same afternoon after siesta, Hadrian sat at one end of the great white-marble arc-shaped seat. A yard away sixteen cardinals spread their vermilion along the same seat. Little tables stood before them with tea, goat's milk, triscuits, and raisins. The Pope preferred to sit here where the pavement was of marble: because lizards avoided it, and their creepy-crawly jerks on grass or gravel shocked his nerves. He was sure that reptiles were diabolical and unclean; and His taste was for the angelic and the clean. He smoked a cigarette; and flung a subject to His Court, as one flings corn to chickens.

'Was not the question of requiems for non-Catholics settled two or three years ago?' replied Courtleigh.

'Yes:' said Talacryn. 'It was declared impossible, profane, inconsistent.'

'Why?' Hadrian's predilection was for the inconsistent, rather than for that undevelopable fossil which goes by the name of consistency.

'It would be inconsistent, Holiness, for the Church to proclaim, by the most solemn act of Her ministry, as a child submissive to Her, one who always refused, or certainly never consented, to recognize Her as a mother – one who, while alive, would have rejected any such recognition as a grave insult and an irreparable misfortune;' Talacryn responded.

'I don't follow Your Eminency,' said Whitehead: 'it's eloquent – but it's only eloquence.'

'Isn't Cardinal Talacryn rather begging the question, Holiness?' Leighton inquired. 'Who spoke of proclaiming as a submissive child one who never was submissive?'

'Holy Mass is the public and solemn testimony of visible communion; the *tessera communionis*, if I may use the term; and, therefore, the Church can only offer publicly for those who have departed this life as members of that visible communion:' Talacryn persisted.

'Holy Mass is a great deal more than that!' interjected Carvale.

'Yes?'

'Holiness, it is not for me to tell Cardinal Talacryn that Holy Mass is not only a sacrament for the sanctification of souls, but a sacrifice – the Real Sacrifice of Calvary, offered by our Divine Redeemer and pleaded in His Name by us His vicars. It is not another sacrifice, but the Sacrifice of the Cross applied. It is the Clean Oblation, offered to God for all Christians quick and dead, for all for whom Christ died.'

'Would not the bonafides of the non-Catholic in question come in?' said Semphill. 'Take for instance the Divine Victoria – '

'"Divine"?' queried della Volta.

'Yes, "Divine". You say "Divus Julius" and "Divus Calixtus", meaning "the late Julius" and "the late Calixtus". Very well, then I say "the Divine Victoria" for a more thoroughly worthy woman – '

'Well, but that would mean that on the death of such and such a non-Catholic, we should have to institute a process of inquisition, and adjudicate on his or her life and career:' Ferraio ventured.

Hadrian threw His cigarette-end at a lizard on the gravel, and laughed shortly. '"Pippety-pew, me mammy me slew, me daddy me ate, me sister Kate gathered a' me baines – "' He quoted with deliciously feline inconsequence. 'How you theological people do split straws, to be sure! Go on, though. You're intensely interesting.'

The Patriarch of Lisbon slapped his knee.

'Holiness, there are several decrees which are supposed to bear on the subject,' Gentilotto gently put in.

'Can Your Eminency remember them?'

'Innocent III ruled that communion might not be held with those deceased, with whom it had not been held when they were alive.'

'I concede it. But it doesn't touch the point. I distinguish. Holy Mass is more than mere communion. Besides, we don't communicate with, but on behalf of, the deceased. It's not a concession to the deceased. It's our duty to God and to our neighbour,' Carvale persisted.

'Then there was the case of Gregory XVI and Queen Caroline of Bavaria,' Gentilotto continued. 'The argument is the same: but perhaps it has been expanded a little. It definitely prohibits persons, who have died in the eternal and notorious profession of heresy, from being honoured with Catholic rites.'

'Another point occurs to me,' Talacryn went on. 'Supposing that we sing requiems for non-Catholics, we should imply that one religion is as good as another.'

'I guess I deny the consequence,' Grace retorted. 'Of course people would infer all sorts of things which ought not to be inferred: but I can't see that that need concern us.'

'One might imperil the salient and sacred aloofness which marks off God's Work from man's work, the Church's unmistakable contrast to the whole world,' said the Cardinal of St Nicholas-in-the-Jail-of-Tully.

'And her complete discordance from the world by all the difference which separates the Divine Institution from the human, the Church of God from the churches of men,' Saviolli appended.

'All the same I think I go with the Cardinal of St Cosmas and St Damian,' said Mundo.

'There would not be any real ground,' Sterling continued, 'for suspecting one of disloyalty to the Church, if one were to recognize the Invincibly Ignorant as the "other sheep" which His Holiness mentioned in His first Epistle. One is not going to take part in their worship, or frequent their services: because one knows better. And one is not going to accept the principle of a conglomerate Church of the "common-christianity" type any more than one is going to accept an Olympos of gods for a Divinity. But one confesses that one can see no reason why one should not pray for outsiders, offer Mass for outsiders, recognize them in short, as His Holiness seems to ordain. They don't know us; and, naturally, they invent a caricature of us, as things are. Yes, on the whole, perhaps one ought to support Carvale.'

'Well: if we're taking sides, I'll follow you,' said Semphill.

Their Eminencies rose and surrounded Cardinal Carvale. Talacryn was left alone at the other end of the seat; and Percy moved a few inches nearer to the Pope.

'Now Percy?' said Talacryn with invitation. The youngest cardinal shook his grand head in the negative.

'And will not you yourself join the majority?' Hadrian inquired of the single minority.

'I shall follow your Holiness,' Talacryn answered. The others looked their interest.

The Pope smiled. 'Note please, that We are not uttering infallible dogma, but the fallible opinion of a private clergyman, weak-kneed perhaps, or worldly. We know no more than this – that Christ died for all men.' Rising He began to throw on his white cloak, for it was the hour before sunset and the air was cooler. 'Eminencies,' He continued, 'We learn much from you. This discussion was an accident, due to Our negligence.

The case which We intended to submit to you was not the case of an outsider: but, while you have been talking, We have reached the solution of Our problem by another road. We request you immediately to publish the news that tomorrow at ten o'clock the Supreme Pontiff will sing a requiem in St Peter's for the repose of the soul of Umberto the Fearless King of Italy.'

An English Catholic painter came to paint the Pope's portrait. Hadrian knew him for a vulgar and officious liar: detested him; and, at the first application, had refused to sit to him. His Holiness was not at all in love with His Own aspect. It annoyed Him because it just missed the ideal which He admired; and He did not want to be perpetuated. Also, He loathed the cad's Hercomeresque-cum-Camera-esque technique and his quite earthy imagination: from that palette, the spiritual, the intellectual, the noble, could not come. But, He thought of the man's pinched asking face, of his dreadful nagging wife, of his children – of the rejection of all his pictures by the Academy this year, of the fact that he was being supplanted by younger grander minds. Ousted from livelihood! Horrible! Love your enemies! Ouf! The Pontiff would give six sittings of one hour each, on condition that He might read all the time.

The privilege alone was an inestimable advertisement. Alfred Elms looked upon himself as likely to become the fashion. Hadrian sat in the garden for six siestas; and He read in Plato's *Phaedo*, which is the perfection of human language, until His lineaments were composed in an expression of keen gentle fastidious rapture. Elms's professional efforts at conversation were annulled quietly and incisively. The Pope blessed him and handfuls of rosaries at the end of every sitting. Sometimes His Holiness was so elated with the beauty of the Greek of His book, that He even was able with a little self-compulsion to utter a few kindly and intelligent criticisms of the painter's work. That was startlingly real, mirror-like. The varied whiteness of marble and flannel and vellum and the healthy pallor of flesh, gained purity from the notes of the reddish-brown hair and the translucent violet of the amethyst. The clean light of the thing was admirably rendered. The painter could delineate, and tint with his hand, that which his eyes beheld, with blameless accuracy. What his eyes did not see, the soul, the mind, the habit of his model, he as accurately omitted. Hadrian made him glad with a compliment on the perfection of the connexion between his directive brain and his executive fingers. At the end of the last sitting also He gave him two hundred pounds, and the picture, and a written indulgence in the hour of death. The painter went away quite happy, and with his fortune made. He never knew how vehemently his work was detested, how profoundly he himself was scorned.

August was deliciously warm. The Pope moved the Court for a few weeks to the palace on the Nemorensian lake which the Prince of Cinthyanum lent. It was a vast barrack of a palace. Although three sides of it actually were in the little city, and a public thoroughfare pierced its central archway, yet it suited Hadrian admirably. Approached through numerous ante-chambers and picture galleries, there was a huge room frescoed in simulation of a princely tent. Here they placed a throne for receptions. There was a great balcony high above the porch, facing a two-mile avenue of elms. When the faithful congregated (as they often did) the Pope could show Himself. There were innumerable chambers of state and private suites, where the curial cardinals took up their abode. But high on the fourth side of the palace, with no access except by several little private stairs, Hadrian found an apartment of five small rooms which was quite secluded. From its windows (the palace stood on the crest of the cliff) a stone might be dropped into the fathomless lake three hundred feet below; and, beyond the lake, the eye soared to Diana's Forest of oaks and the spurs of the Alban Mount. A private stair and passage led to the incomparable (and almost unknown) gardens, which crowned the rocks with verdure and descended by winding paths to the mirrored waters of the lake. Here the Pontiff established Himself, with the noise of the world of men and its limitations on the one side; and, on the other, quiet and illimitable space wherein the soul might spread wings and explore the empyrean.

Half-way down the cliff, a little ruined shrine stood in the garden. The broken grey-brown tracery of the window framed an exquisite panorama of water and distant hills, brilliantly blue and green. The nook stood away from the main path; and was quite enclosed by sun-kissed foliage, and canopied with vines and ivy. Hadrian was spending a morning here, alone with cigarettes and the *Epinicia* of Pindar and His thoughts. The air was fragrant with the perfume of southernwood and the generous sun. He rested in a low cane chair, soaking Himself in light and peace. His eyes were turned to the far-distant shore where the great grove of ilex cast deep tralucid shadows in the water. A tiny slip of pink shot from sunlight to shade: another followed: two tiny splashes of silver spray arose, and vanished: two blue-black dots appeared in the rippled mirror. Hadrian envied the young swimmers. He remembered all the wild unfettered boundless sensuous joy of only a little while ago. Was the fisherman still down there with his boat and the brown boy who rowed it? He wondered what the world would say if the Pope were to swim in sunlit Nemi – or in moonlit. Ah, the mild tepidity of moonlit water, the clean cold caress of moonlit air! Not that He cared jot or tittle for what the world might say – personally. No. But – No. If He were to ask for the use of the boat, tongues would clack. And He could not go alone with the deliberate intention. Still – didn't Peter swim in Galilee. Weren't the Attendolo gardens private? Some night He might stroll down to the shore: the water was fathomless at once: there need be no wading with the ripples horribly creeping up one's flesh – Yaff! But the toads on the path, and the lizards and the serpents in the grass – oh no. Then, thus it must be: the Pope must not go to seek His pleasure: if God should deign to afford His Vicegerent the recreation of swimming, an opportunity would be provided. Otherwise –

Little footsteps pattered down the glade. His retreat was about to be invaded.

Three children burst through the shrubs – and stood transfixed. They were a couple of black-eyed black-haired girls, and a very pale-coloured very delicately articulated slim and stalwart baby boy with dark star-like eyes and brows superbly drawn. All Hadrian's fearful terror of children paralysed Him. These limpid glances made Him feel such a hackneyed old sinner. But He showed no outward tremor, looking gently and genially at His visitors, and wondering what (in the name of all the gods) He ought to say or do. Three nurses and an athletic tailor-made lady added their presence.

'A thousand pardons, sir,' a nurse exclaimed;

'*O Santissimo Padre*!' – Six knees flopped on the ground.

'Missy,' the boy announced, 'I have found a white father. Why have I seen a white father before never?' His utterance was very deliberate, and his English quite devoid of accented syllables.

The tailor-made lady rose to the occasion with an intuition which only could be feminine and a self-possession which only could be English. She bowed to the Pope, saying 'Your Holiness will pardon the intrusion. The children escaped us at the fork in the path – '

'But it is a pleasure,' Hadrian hypocritically put in: 'it is a pleasure,' He repeated, seeing that she was about to withdraw her charges; 'and it would be a greater pleasure to know the names of these little ones.'

'The Prince Filiberto, the Princess Yolanda, and the Princess Mafalda,' the lady replied: 'the Queen is giving a children's picnic in Lady Demochéde's woods; and we took the liberty of trespassing here in search of wild flowers. Of course we had no idea – '

'Missy,' said the boy again. 'I wish to speak to this white father.' He was standing with his exquisite fair little legs wide apart, his little body splendidly poised; and his glance was the glance of a young lion.

'Is it permitted?' Hadrian inquired of the governess.

'Oh surely;' she assented with perfection of manner.

'I wish to ask this white father whether he can speak English words like me;' the youngster proclaimed, keeping at a distance until he had reconnoitred the position.

'Don't be silly 'Berto, of course he can. This is Papa Inglese,

I think;' said the Princess Yolanda with the daintiest air of regality. She was a very stately little person, and quite aware of herself; and her great black eyes were wonderful. Her younger sister sucked a silent thumb.

'Then I wish to know whether I may kiss that ring – the big one. I always kiss rings when fathers wear them,' her brother continued. He quite ingenuously offered his little token of regard, giving reasons for the same in the manner of one who is too noble to take advantage of ignorance or even of blind good nature. Hadrian had not the faintest notion of what to say. He never in His life had spoken to a Royal Highness; and the childhood of the child had tied His tongue. He would not have hesitated for one moment to converse with an angel: indeed He would have been rather more than garrulous. But with a human baby boy! He extended His right hand.

The princelet took it: looked at it: looked from the great gold Little-Peter-in-a-Boat to the great amethyst; and pondered them. 'I think I will kiss them both;' he said at length. The full soft rose leaf of his lips flitted from the pontifical to the episcopal ring. He lifted his bright head; and boldly looked into the Pope's eyes, with a smile disclosing the most wonderful little teeth – with a gaze which told of a pact of friendship sealed.

'God bless you, little boy;' said the Apostle.

'Oh, He can speak my English words!' the youngster shouted with delight. 'Yolanda, come and kiss these rings, and hear Him say "God bless you, little boy" again – no – girl I mean, Missy dear;' with a side-look at the governess.

The princess came forward like a lady; and paid her respects. Her brother intently watched.

'God bless you, Princess,' said the Apostle.

'Oh but listen,' the Prince of Naples shrieked, jumping up and down; 'He knows all the words ezattually, just like my own father. He said to me "boy", and to Yolanda "princess". Now go you too, Mafalda, and I will listen again.'

The tiny maid went. 'God bless you, little Princess;' the Apostle said.

'That is right,' the boy cried: 'he said "little princess" because – ' There he stopped a moment. Then, 'White Father, why for have You – no – why did not You say "prince" to me? I am Prince Filiberto, aged five, Quirinale, Rome. Do You know that, White Father?'

'Yes, Prince. But you are a boy.'

'Well, I think so. Also I am a sailor, like Uncle Luigi. Cannot You see that, White Father? Do You know what thing is a sailor?' He stood by the chair, leaning against Hadrian's knee, deliciously rosily maritime in white flannel.

'Oh yes: We know many sailors:' the Pope responded.

'Are they English?' The question possessed importance. His Royal Highness evidently was by way of verifying certain information.

'Most of them are English.'

'My father says that all good sailors are English, or like English.'

'And are you a good sailor?' The Pope switched the argument away from the Majesty of Italy, for reasons.

'But yes, I am very good this morning. But I always am a sailor – even when I am – not quite good;' the candid baby said with a little hesitation.

'Do you like being "not quite good"?'

'Oh but yes – I should say, sometimes. I think I like it then: but not now. No – I do not like being "not quite good".' He settled the matter like that; and nobly lifted himself upon it.

'Won't you try to be a good sailor?' (Hadrian hated Himself for preaching. But such a chance! To make a white mark on the heir to a throne!)

'But of course I always try – except –' and there seemed to be the difficulty. The child drooped a little.

'You always do try to be a good sailor – and to give no trouble – '

'Give no trouble? What not to father?' the prince inquired, as though the very notion clashed with his preconceived idea of the uses of fathers.

'No: not to your father.'

'Nor to Missy?' The round face became a little longer.

'No: never to ladies on any account.'

'To whom then may I give trouble, if I may not give it to father nor to Missy?' He felt that he had put a poser.

'Don't give it.'

'What not to anybody?' This was a matter, a dreadful matter, which anyhow must be pursued to the bitter end.

'Not to anybody.'

The child's great brave eyes considered the Apostle attentively: then they wandered to his sisters, to the governess, to the nurses; and came back again. Hadrian returned his gaze, very gently, quite inflexibly. The boy must learn his lesson now. Prince Filiberto pondered the novel doctrine from all his little points of view; and at last he grasped the consequence like a man.

'Ah well, then I suppose I had better keep it myself. I am sorry that I gave it to you, Missy, yesterday.'

Hadrian experienced the strangest possible rigor of the throat. Another moment and something in Him would have spoiled all. He rose: blessed His visitors; and passed swiftly away through the trees to the left.

'Missy, I am liking that white father. When shall I see Him again?' came after Him in the incomparable voice of innocence.

He quickly went up the winding path, along the private passage, up the stairs to the terrace. He dragged a chair out there and sat down. 'God!' He exclaimed aloud, with tremendous expiration, to the wide expanse of water and earth and sky which yawned before Him. Tears welled in His eyes: and the constriction of His throat was relaxed. He took His handkerchief from His sleeve. Thank heaven He was alone! And He became calm and analytical and infinitely happy. Verses of Meleagros of Gadara streamed through his mind:

Our Lady of desire brought me to thee, Theokles,
me to thee;
and delicate-sandalled Love hath stripped and strewed me
at thy feet:
a lightning-flash of his sweet beauty!
flames from his eyes he darteth!
Hath Love revealed a Child who fighteth with thunderbolts?

> the splendour of twin fires did scorch me through and through.
> one flame indeed was from the sun, and one was love
> from a child's eyes.

His ecstasy was admiration of the lovely little person and the noble little soul. The clean and vivid candour, the delicate proportion, the pure tint, aroused in Him a desire to own. The frank self-hood, the unerring truth, the courageous tranquillity of self-renunciation, aroused in Him a sense of emulation. He, the Supreme Pontiff, was prostrate before the seraphic majesty of the Child. And, as though a curtain had been lifted, He had a peep into the human heart. Now, He thought that He could see and understand one cause, perhaps the chief cause, of human society – the ability to say 'This is mine, mine: for I did it'. He began to understand that the human mind must have external as well as internal operation – and much beside. As for Himself, He was making experiment of the first personal emotion of undiluted enjoyment of human society which He could re-member. 'Then I can love, after all;' He reflected. Though He mixed freely and absolutely independently with all men, yet, in the tender inner soul of Him, He shrank more shudderingly than ever from the contact. Every single act of urbanity, of courtesy, was a violent effort to Him. His feeling for His fellow-creatures was repugnance pure and simple. But, in the case of this yellow-haired mannikin, there was a difference. He would like to own such a radiant little piece of the Divine–Human as that fair Prince Filiberto. He would appreciate the honour and the joy of tending such a treasure. But He could not seek; and it never had been offered. Perhaps He would shrink if it were offered. That was His peculiar nature. Had He ever wished to exert for intimate relations with anyone? No: plainly no. He was a thing apart. More, He was a thing to be avoided. He re-membered how many times he aimlessly had strolled through London, watching His species gambolling in Piccadilly, or at the Marble Arch on a Sunday where the fierce lanky spiky sallow Anarchist raved, and the coy Catholic barrister cracked correct jests out of a shiny black exercise book, and the bright-eyed clean Church Army youth spoke with genuine conviction.

He had moved through partner-seeking mobs everywhere, lazily, vigilantly, studiously: yet no one ever had addressed him. He was seen. He was avoided. Yes, He was a thing apart. That was His trouble. And – what did the boy say? – 'I had better keep it myself'. The content of that saying was to Hadrian just like a thunderbolt. It was Love – yes, that was quintessential Love, from the clear eyes and the stainless lips of childhood – to keep one's troubles oneself. For in that way one relieved others. And the Servant of the servants of God must – He continued to sit in the sunlight in a sort of rapture. The lake and the hills and the turquoise sky faded from His vision. He was alone with His thoughts, His ideals, His soul. . . . After the noon angelus, He went in to His solitary meal. Later in the afternoon, when He had slept and washed, and put on fresh garments, He descended to chat with His court. His demeanour was observed to be more warm, more human. His eyes had an unusual and more usual glow. He did not seem to be so very very far away.

'I guess the air of this village suits you, Holy Father,' said young Cardinal Percy. 'You look like twenty cents this evening.'

'Yes, the air is delicious enough: but it is not the air.' Hadrian narrated the incident of the morning, ending, 'And We have recognized in Ourself a new and unknown power, a perfectly strange capability. We have made experience of a feeling which – well, which We suppose – at any rate will pass for – Love.'

He plunged again into business. He had noted three men for a purpose. Archbishop Ilario della Valla was a young and exquisitely polished prelate, son of an ambassador, thoroughly expert in the English language and habit. Signor Gargouille Grice was one of those nondescripts devoid of Divine Vocation, who fondly are believed to occupy an important place at the pontifical court (equivalent at least to the English office of Lord Chamberlain) but, which in reality is that of a flunkey. Prince Guido Attendolo was a young Italian of very generous birth, who, as younger son of a younger son not over-burdened with wealth, led an inconspicuous impotent uninteresting life. With the idea of giving these three a chance, the Pope dispatched them to America with the red hat for the American Archbishop Erin, whom He named Cardinal-presbyter of the Title of St Mary-of-the-People. It was merely an incident, intended to keep them from stagnation, to give them that scope which human nature must have if it is to do itself justice, if it is not to become a public nuisance. At the same time, He was satisfied that the sympathy of the prelate, the antiquity of the decurial chamberlain, and the urbanity (to say nothing of the perfect Greek profile) of the prince, would recommend them as ambassadors from the oldest power to the newest nation. On the arrival of the Apostolic Ablegate in New York, Hadrian published the *Epistle to the Americans*. He praised their exuberant vigour and individualistic unconventionality, while He warned them of their obligations to their race and of the evils of oligarchical tyranny. He begged them not to live in the desperate hurry which was instanced in their carelessness in details. He advised them not to be too proud to learn from the history of other nations, dwelling on the principle of the intermittent tendency of human nature. He pointed out that, as effect is due to cause, and as the scope and quantity of human ideas is very far from being illimitable, so, as human types recur, human ideas and the situations produced by them are bound to recur. 'Yet,' He continued, 'human nature itself, when inspired by Divine Grace, being so very fine and so very potent a force, is capable of immense development. It has Will, Free-will, which, rightly directed can rule itself, can control natural laws, can dispose events.' Wherefore, He admonished the Americans to divest themselves of juvenile arrogance and selfishness, in order that (having learned the causes which produce effects) they might know the rules and play the game. He spoke to them, not only with the authority of His apostolature, but with the affection of a comrade who wished to serve them from the experience (inherited and acquired) of a member of the older nations. He concluded with delicious slyness, 'The young ones think the old are fools: the old ones know the young ones are'.

America was openly delighted, not only by the consideration

which the Pope showed in addressing Her next to England but, by the pungent vivid validity of His remarks. She said that He had a dead cinch on things, that He was on to His job, that as a sky-pilot He suited Her to a gnat's bristle; and She began to regard Him with close attention.

The death of Francis Joseph, Austrian Emperor and King of Hungary, in September, had its not unexpected consequences. The confusion of Europe was worse confounded by conflict between Hungarian national sentiment and the Pan-Germanic League. Francis Joseph's successor did not inspire his multi-lingual subjects with the same respectful devotion as that which had been paid to the old Emperor on account of the triple prestige of his dignity, his long reign, his many sorrows. Hungary cried for a Magyar king. Bohemia cried for a Czech king. Russian Poland also cried aloud for a Polish king; and German Poland would have cried with her, had she dared. As it was, she opened longing eyes and waited. The Germans of Austria appealed to the German Emperor to come to their aid and take them into his mailed fist. The Habsburgh dynasty was tottering. Serbia was a small hell. Turkey and Romania viewed the prospect of Germany's expansion with favour: Turkey, because she found it easy to outwit the Teuton: Romania, because the power by whose favour she existed was possessed by devils. Albania, Montenegro, and Greece, strongly disapproved: they prized their individual national existence, and the idea of being reduced to dependency upon the Gothic Michael did not suit them. The distracted state of Austria, and her inability to keep her obligations to Germany and Italy, caused the lapse of the Triple Alliance. Yet Italy made no sign and Germany made no sign. There was an interval of intense and silent vigilance.

Hadrian read in *The Times* that Signor Panciera, Italian Ambassador at the Court of St James's, was leaving town for Rome for a few weeks. Cardinal Fiamma sought out His Excellency; and brought him privately and unofficially to the Pope's apartment. His Holiness was very happy to renew acquaintances with so genial and so solid and so trusty a man. (It was comparatively easy to love such an one.) The ambassador bowed; and wondered what was expected. The Pope put it patently. He was profoundly interested in affairs: He pried into no secrets: He did desire to collect facts and opinions from experts and secular statesmen: the six ambassadors left to the Vatican were sterile: if Signor Panciera could see his way to converse of current events, without betraying his sovereign's confidence, but simply as between two men whose motives were pure and patriotic, he would confer a favour upon (or, if he preferred it the other way, he would render a service to) the Pope. His Excellency bowed in reciprocation of the honour. Privately noting that His Holiness was concealing nothing, and (in fact) was unable to conceal, he thought that there would be no difficulty. This was not a matter of diplomacy or state-craft. The crystalline candour of the Pope made Him negligible as a statesman: as a mere man He was charming, perfectly transparent: He wanted, not state secrets but, the opinion of a man-of-affairs upon affairs. Signor Panciera was quite delighted. The state of Europe as revealed in the newspapers was passed under review. His Excellency thought that Germany was looking east and west rather than elsewhere. What could be expected? Naturally she would look that way where were her two natural enemies. As for Austria – peuh! – a secondary matter. Austria would not be touched by Germany as long as danger threatened from France and Russia. Italy? Well, Italy now was independent. No longer bound to Germany and Austria, Italy's attitude was that of the lion on guard (in the words of the immortal Dante).

'Naturally,' Hadrian interpolated, 'Italy would watch events and direct her policy in accordance with her interest.'

'But securely,' the ambassador responded.

The Pontiff spoke of Spain. Signor Panciera chopped his right wrist with his left hand. Spain was finished. Portugal? Portugal was English. England? England was England. The Pope and the ambassador produced a smile apiece: the one meant triumphant pride of race: the other, boundless and intelligent admiration. Hadrian swooped eastwards: the Balkan States? His Excellency began to discriminate: that little group of separate sovereignties was very difficult. He seemed to hesitate, to pick his words: of course the subject interested him very greatly. The Pope was quite singularly still. Now and again, as His massive dark guest passed Him in pacing, He plumped in a question. The Balkan States? Signor Panciera strode on toward the window, as though seeking the response there: came back: began a reply: returned to the window: came back again with a fresh half-dozen of unilluminating words. Hadrian went to one of his cupboards: took out two little brown bagatelle-balls; and placed them in the royal ambassador's hands. 'Your Excellency's aid to conversation,' He purred with a recondite smile. 'Don't be discomposed. All men have some trick of this kind. Ours is to play with Our rings or to push up Our glasses. Your friend Fiamma plaits the fringe of his sash. The Cardinal-Dean strokes the mother-of-pearl disk which stands on his wig for the tonsure. The Secretary of State munches his new teeth. And you like to click a pair of bagatelle balls, if We rightly remember. You were saying that that little group of separate sovereignties was very difficult. Because of their present autonomy?'

Click-click-click went the balls on the brown palm: and the ambassador tralated their clicking. 'Yes Holiness, for that reason: but also, I think, because they are racially distinct from the nations with which they expect to be incorporated.'

'Russia, Germany, Austria, Turkey, for example?' (Click) 'I think we may neglect Russia.'

'Yes? In the case of Romania?'

'I think that Romanian sentiment has veered round toward Germany.'

'Well now, let us ignore opinions; and go to these racial differences of which you speak.'

'I am of opinion that the Romanian people find themselves in sympathy with the German peoples,' Signor Panciera persisted.

'Bulgaria then?'

Signor Panciera took two or three journeys to the window and back, vigorously clicking the balls. 'Holiness, You do not ask for my opinion; and I only can give You the speculations of an amateur ethnologist.' (Click–click) 'I have – ' (Click) 'I can tell You what my studies have taught me – no more.'

'But that is most interesting, Signore. We are all students. Some are anxious to learn: some are not: but both are better off than the man who knows that he has nothing more to learn. Tell Us what your studies have taught you.'

'I really believe that the principalities south of the Danube contain the descendants of those Byzantines who were pushed northward by the incursion of Turks in the fifteenth century.'

'Why?'

(Click) 'First from physiognomy:' (click) 'second from the structure of their languages.'

'Wonderful! And you have noted points of similarity?'

'I will go further than that, Holiness. I ought to say that my attention was attracted to this subject by my Lord the King, who, you know, deigned to marry a Montenegrin Princess. His Majesty used to speak much at one time on this point to me and also to the Minister of Public Instruction – '

'That is Signor Cabelli?'

'Surely. We examined the matter for His Majesty; and our investigations all seemed to point to the fact that the Turks, in coming from Asia, swept across the Byzantine Empire in a westerly and northerly direction. Then, examining the outlets and the fringes, we found Byzantine characteristics all along the northern boundary of Turkey, that is to say not in Bulgaria which is Slav, but in Albania, Herzegovina, Bosnia, and Montenegro; and, more, we found them along the Adriatic coast of Italy. Your Holiness will see that these places are of a contiguity which would render them likely refuges for the Christians who fled before, or were expelled by, the Muslim.'

'Yes.'

'There is one thing more. We found traces of an earlier migration than the Byzantine. We believe that in Eastern Italy from Taranto to Ortona, and also in Southern Albania, may be seen the lineal descendants of the Athenians of Pericles' day.'

'But Greece, Excellency?'

'Holiness, the Greeks of today are degenerate from the dirty-knuckled Laconians crossed with the Ottoman Infidel, their *conquistadores*.'

'That is splendid, Signore. And it marches with an opinion which We formed some dozen years ago, at least in regard to your Italian Greeks. We have seen those with Our Own eyes. In Apulia, for instance, the Elgin Marbles have their living counterfeits: the charcoal burners and the fishermen look as though they had stepped out of the Frieze of the Parthenon. Once We heard a fisherman summon his boy by the word "Páddy" – to give it an English form. An Italian would have cried "*Putto*". But "Páddy," – what vocative is that but "Παιδε," pronounced as Alcibiades would have pronounced it? Oh, We see your point. And is your Lord the King still interested in the subject?'

'I believe that His Majesty is intensely interested. I hope I may venture to repeat the corroboration which Your Holiness has given me. I am sure that His Majesty –'

'By all means. Of course you merely will repeat the conversation. You will not intrude Us before the King's Majesty in Our apostolic character: but merely –'

'Your Holiness's wish shall be respected.'

'But to resume: We agree to identify those states south of the Danube with the Byzantines in general; and Montenegro and South Albania with the Greeks in particular. What about North Albania?'

(Click) 'That is Turkish.'

'All Albania is Turkish.'

'But South Albania is Christian. And all Albania, Christian and Muslim, reverences Madonna – "Panagia", Παναγια, "Lady of All", they call her.'

'How very extraordinary! Well now let us take their present situation. Suppose, Signore Panciera, that we reverse our positions. Instead of hearing your opinion, We will state Ours; and you shall comment on it. Is that fair? Is that agreeable?'

'Most fair: most agreeable. I always learn from Englishmen and I shall learn from Your Holiness.'

'Good. We believe that Montenegro is happy and contented under the paternal rule of Prince Nicholas.'

(Click-click-click) 'That is so, Holiness.'

'We hear that Albania is shaping well under Prince Ghin Kastriotis.'

(Click: a walk to the window and back; and more clicks) 'Since the murder of Abdul Hamid, and the erection of Albania into a principality, progress has been astounding. The beautiful country' (click) 'the splendid people, are a prize to any ruler. Sultan Ismail is the only cloud in the sky. He does not approve of the loss of that slice of his empire. But Albania will take care of herself.'

'Serbia, and her yearning for the restoration of the Serbian Empire?'

'Impossible. A nation which murders two kings in four years cannot be an Empire.'

'Quite impossible. Bulgaria, a country of heretics of the most notorious and dreadful kind, atrocious brigands to a man, ruled (or rather not ruled) by a foreigner who is a contemptible cur.'

'Your Holiness would propose –'

'The deposition of Prince Ferdinand – an easy task now that Russia has her hands full – and the annexation of Bulgaria and Serbia by Montenegro under the protection of Italy.'

(Click-click-click) 'There, Holiness, we come to the ground of high politics.' (Click-click-click-click) 'One must walk very warily.'

'Yes,' Hadrian mewed: 'until Italy and Germany have made up their minds.'

The ambassador bowed.

'Please leave the bagatelle balls, Excellency; and accept Our thanks for your very agreeable conversation,' said the Pope.

In giving an account of this interview to the king, the ambassador concluded 'And, Sire, His Holiness spoke like an Englishman'.

'Oh did He,' said Victor Emanuel. 'In what way?'

'Majesty, He was profound and limpid, He was large and particular, He was bold and careful.'

'*Basta!* Go again as often as you please; and let me hear more of this Englishman.'

'With the favour of Your Majesty.'

CHAPTER 12

THE Liblab deputation had returned to England: but Jerry Sant and Mrs Crowe hung on at a decent little hotel in Two Shambles Street, which was convenient to the English quarter. Their idea was to wait for an opportunity to push their scheme of blackmail. Most of each day, Mrs Crowe was in the Square of St Peter's, looking up at the Vatican, hoping for the apparition of Hadrian at His window. In the evenings, she saw Him walking to and fro on the steps of the basilica. There always was something of a crowd there. The poorest of the poor, by the common consent of the most courteous of nations, were placed in front; and she used to see the Pope giving words and gold to persons whom she deemed disreputable. She would have sacrificed her new wig for one of those coins. Once, she pushed into the front row and kneeled with the riff-raff. She heard a blind boy tell his miserable tale: she heard the Apostle's gentle words and saw the munificent careless gift. It was her turn. She felt the distant inflexible eyes on her bent head: 'God bless you, daughter; go in peace' dropped on her; and Hadrian passed on. The poor girl on her left bitterly wept – the police doctor had refused her certificate – her occupation was gone. Hadrian's kind of charity did not appeal to Mrs Crowe: she called it 'disgusting' and 'highly improper' to the *table d'hôte*. There were several quaint visitors at the Hotel Nike. They chiefly were English; and they listened in silence, with shy strange eyes, when she vented her views. Afterwards, though, she used to find herself the recipient of the confidence of weird old maids and worn-out matrons, who drew her into corners of the garden away from the cabin where Sant smoked, and nervously whispered, 'My dear, I'm sure you'll excuse me addressing you, but I feel bound to say I think I'm right in saying that I owe everything to Him Whom you're speaking about. I hope you don't mind me saying this but I feel sure you wouldn't wish to do anyone an injustice. You see I used to know Him years ago and, I hardly know how to put it, but a certain sum was named between us which would make me safe for life; and just now, since last April you see, that very sum, a regular income all my days, my dear, has come to me through the Bank of England; and I feel sure it's Him, for there isn't another soul in the world able, to do such a thing: and, my dear, although of course I can't approve of the indiscriminate charity you've named, I thought I'd just mention this to you because the fact is I've come here to try and see Him and let Him know how thankful I am.'

Tired wan clean men, with corns on their right middle fingers and jackets bulging along their lower edges, addressed her as 'Madam' and mentioned similar experiences; and, when two straight-limbed straight-eyed boys of sixteen, twins, orphans, were fierce with the same story, she began to feel uncomfortable, envious. That He should do these things for these scarecrows and nothing for her! People avoided her; and she was lonely. Sant, and the cosmopolitan bagmen with whom he fraternized, were no companions for her. She expected something a little more select in the way of society. She conceived the notion that she would stand a better chance of coming into contact with the Pope by means of some of the English in Rome. And – would it not be as well if she became a Catholic? The hotel people told her that very few English were in Rome: they began to come in October and to go away in June: July, August, September, saw no English except at the colleges and a few residents. She found her way to St Andrea delle Fratte, where she had heard of some Englishwoman's tomb; and saw no one who looked like an Englishman. She had the same experience at the church by the G.P.O. Then she discerned a little English affair in Little Sebastian Street, a convent of sorts; and she made herself conspicuous to the sisters. Those good creatures were only too happy to discover a chatty

Englishwoman; and, when Mrs Crowe quite accidentally let out that she had known George Arthur Rose, they precipitately produced candied fruit and orangeade. Mrs Crowe gossiped with discretion. She won hearts by listening attentively to monasterial rhapsodies. When she was permitted to slip in a word edgeways, she took care that it was a telling word. In all their lives the sisters never had heard anything so edifying as her description of the Holy Father's former predilection for white flannel shirts, white knitted socks and night-caps. They thought it heavenly of Him to have refused to wear any colours but white or black while He was living in the world; and the details of a black corduroy shooting-suit filled them with ecstatic rapture. In the course of these improving conversations it came out that Mrs Crowe herself was an agnostic – an unwilling agnostic, she whined – oh, if only she could believe what her audience believed, it would be such a comfort to her! Naturally the sisters gladly would help her to that kind of comfort. They gave her an aluminium medal; and promised prayers. She turned up regularly at mass and benediction; and they had great hopes of her. She thanked them so much. Now, wouldn't she just like to have a little talk with Father Dawkins – such a holy man? She would like nothing better. She had a little talk with Father Dawkins: that is to say that (frequently during the next few weeks) His Reverency exhorted for three quarters of an hour on end in the convent parlour; and she punctuated his discourses with 'Ah yes,' 'How true,' 'Why did I never hear this before,' etc. The sisters lent her *Thresholds*, and other violently cerulean books. She pronounced them quite convincing. And then she asked to be received into the Church.

She became seen at parties at the English pensions; and duly was slavered. She met cardinals and prelates at receptions. She was the excitement of the moment. Her pose of the interesting widow, fond mother of the dearest little girl and boy, clever writer of *vers de société* in the *Maid and Matron*, was much commended: but it was as the woman whose dear departed had been the Holy Father's most intimate friend that she chiefly scored. For His Holiness she always had had the highest admiration. He had been a peculiar man, certainly, but never anything but most distinguished. She remembered Him in poverty, going in the shabbiest of garbs: but His gait and carriage always had been the gait and carriage of nobility of soul. At all times, she herself had predicted some extraordinary fate for Him. She told the most adorable little stories of His wit, His humour, His pathos, and His dumb-bells. She dilated on a boil which had afflicted the back of His neck. She had heard that He slept in glycerined gloves for the softening of His chapped hands. Yes, He had been quite a friend of theirs. He was so earnest, so brilliant, so learned, that she never had been able to understand why a man of His ability should be a Catholic. Of course that was when she herself had been in outer darkness. Now that she was in the inner light, she perfectly could see why. Mrs Crowe was voted to be a very charming person; and became a great success.

Sant approved of her procedure. Neither he nor she could see their way to another direct approach to Hadrian. They must bide a wee. Meanwhile, no harm was done and much good might be done by cultivating the English quarter. And, perhaps it would be as well to keep socialism in the background for the present. Jerry would stay where he was; and she had better set up for herself elsewhere: they occasionally could meet to compare notes; and, if anything particular happed, why they could write. So Mrs Crowe took a little flat on Baboon Street, and displayed herself at the Spain Square tea shop and the English sisterhood.

At the back of her brain there was a well-defined desire. She kept it there to gloat over in private and at intervals: for she was far too clever a woman to let her passion master her at this stage. It was the mainspring of her acts, the goal of her thoughts, the ultimate of her existence: but she kept it well concealed and controlled. Now and then, in the lonely depth of night, it surged to her oppression: but dawn and the respectability of her temper, brought it within bounds. She played a careful game, adding to her counters as opportunity occurred. She had the Liblabs and their four pounds a week to support her: she had (what she called) the secret history of the Pope in her possession: she was capturing the pious English. And then, one evening she acquired quite a priceless item of scandal which, sooner or later, she would use for the procuration of her Georgie.

She had been wandering about alone in some of those new streets on the Viminal Hill, which Modern Rome built in imitation of the suburban residences of British merchants: streets where comfortable red-brick detached mansions stand each in a railed garden. As she was passing one of these fine but homely residences, the electric light sprang up in the drawing-room; and she was aware of three figures seated in the bay window. An afternoon-tea table was between them. They were two gorgeous white women with fair hair, evidently mother and daughter. Those she did not know: but the third was George Arthur Rose. She peered between the gilded bronze bars of the gate. It was dusk. No one but herself was in the street. And there, not twenty yards away, behind a pane of glass, was the man she worshipped. She gave up herself to her emotions during one minute. Then he and the women retired to the back of the room; and a decorous black-coated lacquey closed the curtains. For a moment, she felt like battering at the gate. Her heart violently palpitated. The connotation of the experience suddenly struck her. What was the Pope doing here? She knew that He went about everywhere: but they said that He never ate or drank in company; and she had seen Him finish a cup of tea. How dainty the elevation of that left little finger was! Ah! Why was He not dressed in white as usual? Disguised – taking tea in a private house – with two nameless women! Ah, why indeed! She focused her fury. The number on the gate – yes. She ran to the end of the street and read 'Via Morino'. She crossed the road and returned; and found a niche where she could hide in the shadow of a pillared wall. Here, she watched and waited as a terrier waits on and watches a kitten demure in a tree – yapping and yelping almost inaudibly, well-nigh bursting with suppressed impulse to pounce. Perhaps she waited half an hour. Then a couple of lacqueys came down to

212

the gate: opened it; and obsequiously bowed to an ecclesiastic who passed out into the street flinging the right fold of his cloak over his left shoulder. He swiftly walked towards Via Nationale; and she followed him. As he came into the more brilliant light, he drew the fold of his cloak closer across his mouth. That act decided her. She knew that her Georgie abhorred from every kind of muffling. That he should muffle now was natural enough. He did not wish to be recognized. He was incognito, for an evil purpose. That he should have chosen openly to walk through the biggest street in Rome, when he might have sneaked down byways, or might have taken a cab, only added to the evidence. Her Georgie was the most frantically daring of men, she knew. Precaution on the one hand, nullified by extreme audacity on the other, she had noted in him before. She nearly lost him as he made his way by the Austrian Embassy and the Gesù into Corso Vittorio Emanuele. At the Oratory he crossed and went by the little Piazza into Banchi, where he left a card with the porter of the Palazzo Attendolo. Again, he muffled his face and went on, crossing the temporary bridge, and going by Borgo Vecchio straight to the gate of the Vatican. Here, he was admitted; and Mrs Crowe was left alone in agony and in hilarity. She turned out of the Colonnade into the square cursing herself for not speaking to him, writhing because she had caught her loved one secretly visiting another woman. Then she laughed at the thought that she had found His Holiness the Pope engaged in vulgar intrigue. The barb of the one emotion lacerated her. The barb of the other she would save to dilacerate Him.

CHAPTER 13

O N the night of the second of October, the German Emperor sat in the Imperial box at the Berlin Schauspielhaus. They were playing *Wilhelm Tell*. William II looked on at the mummer portraying the audacious genius who, by skill and courage, delivered a people from tyranny. He looked on the presented incident with a humorous sense of its coincidence with his present intention: for, in the imperial mind – that agile predominant mind at which inferior minds (led by the *Pall Mall Gazette*) were used to mock – was stored certain knowledge of another scene yet to be enacted in which he himself would play the part of the deliverer. An aide-de-camp entered during the interval, while the house gave itself up to conversation, apples, nuts, *Pfefferkuchen*. He handed a locked portfolio to the Kaiser.

'The papers are all here?'

'Yes, Sire.'

'The manager attends?'

'He is at the door, Sire.'

'He has received my commands?'

'Your Majesty's commands have been executed.'

'Good. I will follow him. Go now to the newspaper offices; and bring the specials to me after supper. *Mahlzeit!*'

The curtain went up for the last act. The audience was stricken with sudden paralysed amazement. On the stage, actors, scene-shifters, the whole theatre staff, were grouped in an immense semicircle. In the chord of the semicircle, one figure stood alone, grimly dominant. At first, it was taken for a daringly realistic caricature of the Emperor; and fear of the penalties of lese-majesty dawned in the minds of the beholders. But the figure spoke, and doubt fled. It *was* the Emperor. Everyone knew that vigorous vocative 'Germans!' The said Germans were used to manifestations of their ruler's omniscience and omnipresence; and they automatically stood to listen. He quoted the assertion of Herr Bebmarck in the Reichstag, that every speech by the Kaiser against Socialists meant a socialist gain of 100,000 votes at the elections. Then he flung out a challenge. He said that the insuing elections meant war to the knife, not between him and his people but, between him and the handful of venal demagogues unworthy to bear the sacred name of Germans who led his people astray. He opened his portfolio. Socialism, he said, commanded four million votes. One third of the German Army was socialist. Socialism was the largest political party in the Empire; and increased each year at the expense of every other party. It was a vast and important body. A body needed a brain to direct its functions. Who, after all, was the head? The demagogues, or the Kaiser? At a moment like the present, when the Fatherland was menaced on both sides by anarchy and hereditary enemies, the glorious German nation must not be harassed by intestine feuds. Hitherto, a great part of his people had been taught to obstruct his schemes for German welfare. Thereby they had hurt themselves. They had had the pleasure of opposing him: but they had delayed their own betterment: for his alone was the will which should rule Germany. Yet, he would not blame his people. They had been betrayed by liars, deceived by treacherous pseudophilanthropists. He would not blame the tempted, but the tempters. The names of the tempters, the human Satans, were August Bebmarck, turner: Grillerbergen, locksmith: Raue, Bulermolken, Reistem, saddlers: Varmol, ex-post-official: Steinbern, lawyer: Volkenberg, territorial magnate: Singenmann, capitalist. He arraigned these men on a charge of having deluded the good heart of four million German people by professions of disinterestedness, of benevolence, by promises of universal betterment. He denounced their professions and their promises as false, and their practices as corrupt enough to have obtained the attention of the police. The socialist demagogues were traitors to the very cause which they professed to serve. Their object was not the improvement of the social conditions of the people: it was personal aggrandizement. He brought proofs from his portfolio. Bebmarck, Grillenberger, Varmol had accepted bribes of M. 100,000, M. 45,000, M. 40,000 respectively from the communist government of France. Raue, Bulermolken, Reistem had accepted the post of saddlery contractors to the French army. Each of the foregoing had given a written promise to influence the socialist vote. The Kaiser read and exhibited the promises; and continued. Steinbern had sold the minute books of various Socialist committees in Hanover for M. 300,000. (The books were produced by an imperial aide.) Volkenberg had scouted the proposal to municipalize his own vast possessions: Singenmann was proved to have derived his riches from ill-paid sweated labour.

'These be thy gods, O Socialism,' the Emperor cried: 'the mere possession of important private property, of what is called a stake in the country, has revealed their brazen faces and feet of clay. The mere offer of the price of blood has revealed the Iscariots of the Fatherland.'

He commanded his hearers to remember that in 1890 he himself had abrogated the laws against socialism and had dismissed the persecutor Bismarck, saying *Die Social Democratic überlassen sie mir mit der werdeich gang alleine fertig*. He said that his method had been to leave them free to work out their own salvation: but in vain. A bad tree does not bring forth good fruit. It had not been socialism, nor parliamentary majorities and resolutions, which had welded together the German Empire: but the army and he, the Emperor, the representative of that power in the state which, not only created German unity in the teeth of those who pretended to represent the people but, thereby carried into every German home the sense of national power. Finally, he demanded, did the innocent industrious great-hearted dupes of the socialist demagogues intend in this crisis of German history to follow and obey the behests of low-born traitors, never-sufficiently-to-be-damned-and-despised sweaters, infamous Rabagases: or would they give loyal allegiance to him, their divinely appointed and legitimate Kaiser, the heir of Friedrich the Noble and of Wilhelm the Good and of Friedrich the Great – to him, the Father of the fatherland, whose whole life and energy was devoted and consecrated to '*Deutschland Deutschland über alles*'.

With that, he left the stage and the theatre. The audience, a typically middle-class one, the very class of all others to which such an oration would appeal, was stirred down to the depths of its phlegmatic Teutonic soul. As the Kaiser departed, not a '*Hoch*' was uttered: but multitudes of stern-faced converts poured out, silently saluting him with the fire of loyalty lighted in their eyes. Germans are logical by nature. Display indefeasible premisses; and it is not a German who will err from the just conclusion. All night long, all the newspapers except the *Vorwaerts* issued special editions containing the Emperor's speech. During the next few days William II himself repeated it in the great cities of his empire. At Essen and Breslau his reception partook of the nature of an ovation. Everywhere the Press spread his epoch-making words to all who actually did not hear them. German good sense preferred honesty, vigorous masterly honesty, even hare-brained honesty, to the base treachery which is actuated by no motive except personal gain. German good sense could see that the Kaiser himself was the hardest-working man in the Empire: that his simply amazing diligence and toil were absolutely unselfish, absolutely impersonal: that he gained no tangible reward whatever: that his life, which quite easily might have been one of irresponsible pleasure and ease, was an incessant round of mental and physical exertion for the good of others. German honour admired and German generosity repaid. The fascinating personality of William II at last was recognized as the chief element of the nation's power. His splendid and unique confidence in himself and his imperial vocation inspired his subjects with confidence in him. The device of the secret ballot, and the now-unfettered ability of every German to vote according to his conscience, had the calculated effect. The elections showed that the enormous prestige of the Emperor had won the Socialist vote, and the Catholic vote, and the votes of the Right and the Left, in support of his paramount authority. The English newspapers ceased from jeering; and the *Pall Mall Gazette* split subjunctives as well as infinitives in applause of success.

The lay Major-domo of the Apostolic Palace found occasion to invite Cardinals Talacryn and Semphill to inspect certain accounts. 'I feel it my duty to call Your Eminencies' attention to the fact,' said he, 'that our Most Holy Lord consumes about seven and sixpence worth, of food and drink a week upon the average. It is shocking. Also it is ridiculous. Kindly cast your eyes over these documents. They are the accounts covering the past six months. Note how many times His dinner consists of three raw carrots and two poached eggs. Meat, you see, He eats not more than twice a week. Fish, He refuses. I understand that He will take the lean of beef, the fat of pork, the breast of a bird, and chew them for an hour.'

'That accounts for His magnificent digestion,' said Talacryn; 'and I know that He eats raw carrots for the sake of His white skin. But fat pork! Semphill, could you digest fat pork when you were His age? I can't even now.'

'Condescend to consider the wine,' Count Piccino added. 'His Holiness quite fails to appreciate fine wine –'

'All I can say is I can remember seeing Him thoroughly enjoy a teaspoonful of my peach brandy sometimes after dinner. That was twenty years ago though,' said Semphill.

'He used to enjoy peach brandy! Eminency, a thousand thanks. He shall have a bottle. I never thought of it. Until now, He has taken what we give Him: but He has no palate whatever for superior brands. He's quite content with a plain red wine from Citta Lavinia or Cinthyanum; and He drinks about as much of it in a week as another man would drink at a meal. But cream, and goat's milk – I believe He bathes in those.'

'No, no,' said Semphill; 'He drinks them day and night, that's all. He's got the digestion of a baby for milk. Shall I ever forget seeing Him drink a pint of thick cream – a whole pint – at a farmhouse once when we were out walking? I thought He'd die there. I begged Him to take some of my pills. I offered to make Him free of my collection. No. He laughed at me; and goes on rejoicing.'

'But, Eminencies, do you think His Holiness can live on this meagre diet?'

'*Chi lo sa?* I couldn't. He may.'

'He's a most incomprehensible creature whatever': Talacryn concluded.

Armed with the allegiance of an united empire, the Kaiser scoured away across the continent to Rome. He travelled incognito as the Duke of Königsberg and put up at the Palazzo Caffarelli. The world looked on and wondered. No news of his intentions was vouchsafed; and as a rule, journalists had the decency to refrain themselves from suppositions. The exception to the rule was French, of course.

Religion is the great preoccupation of William II. Beneath the spangled uniform of this Emperor there is the soul of a clergyman, or rather the visionary soul of an initiate of even vaguer mysteries. The Kaiser only waits for an opportunity to achieve in Rome what he has already achieved in the east, that is to say, to oust France,

shrieked M. Jean de Bonnefon in the Paris *Éclair*. *La Patrie* instantly yelled in comment,

Let Germany take the Holy See. It will be the end of Germany and the beginning of revenge for Sedan. The Paparchy is an acid which will dissolve the badly cemented parts of an empire which is still too new.

But it was not precisely religion which dictated the Kaiser's movement. He had the sense to know that religion is personal; and, though he never lost an opportunity of asserting his personal religious opinions, the idea of making them the rule for all men never entered his eminently practical mind. No: he had other plans; and he was seeking material wherewith to build. He conferred long and secretly with the King of Italy, a man after his own heart, a born ruler, a natural autocrat, who himself had been a slave. They discussed needs. William II wanted room for a population which had increased by twenty millions in thirty years. Victor Emanuel III wanted money and time – money to make easier the life of his people – time to mature improvements – give him those and he could laugh at Italy's enemies, the secret societies, and the clergy –

'Clergy?' the Kaiser demurred. 'Now are you really sure that the clergy are your enemies?'

'Yes, in their heart of hearts. Don't you understand that we robbed them? Don't you know that this very palace of the Quirinale, in which I am receiving Your Imperial Majesty, is stolen property?'

'Yes, yes. But this Englishman? Surely He makes a difference?'

'To some extent. But He cannot extirpate in a moment the

hatred and envy with which my House and I are regarded by the clergy whom we dispossessed. For nearly forty years, to hate us has been part of the clerical education. A weed of that kind cannot be rooted up at once. It is ingrained. Perhaps in another generation – *Basta!* '

'Meanwhile?'

'Meanwhile what?'

'Well, hasn't the Pope made things easier for you?'

'Yes, in a way. But what is His object? What concession, for example – '

'He doesn't seem to have left Himself any opening for extorting concessions.'

'But did Your Imperial Majesty ever hear of a priest who gave something for nothing?'

'One of my cardinals tells me that this is a madman, whose pose is to be primitive, apostolic.'

'Ha! For a primitive apostle He has a singularly dictatorial method. Have you read His *Epistles*, and His denunciations of the socialists, for example?'

'I have. I entirely approve of them. They have assisted me greatly in dealing with some rebels of my own.'

'Oh no one could find fault with His sentiments – so far. But they are so unusual, so extra-pontifical, that one wonders what they are concealing.'

'Is Your Majesty sure that they conceal something?'

'No, I'm not. Of course I have no means of arriving at certainty. That could only be obtained from the Pope Himself; and only from Him if He were willing to give it.'

'Has Your Majesty asked Him?'

'Certainly not. We continue to misunderstand one another. Your Imperial Majesty knows that there is no means of communication between my government and the Vatican. All we get is hearsay; and all they get is gossip.'

'Why do you not request Hadrian to receive you – you yourself? I imagine that He would not refuse.'

'Perhaps not. I believe that He has been preparing for me some such trap as that. But I distrust the Greeks even when they bear gifts. They say He says His prayers in Greek, by the bye.'

'I am about to request His Holiness to receive me.'

'Your Imperial Majesty's case is different. You are not likely to have fresh insults and fresh humiliations offered to you.'

'What do you mean?'

'I mean that I cherish the memory of all ecclesiastical pin-pricks which formerly were administered to my father and grandfather.'

'Pin-pricks? What do you call pin-pricks?'

'For example, in 1878, Pio Nono, from His Own deathbed, sent to reconcile my excommunicated grandfather, who was enabled to die in the Embrace of The Lord. A little later, died also Pio Nono. My father voluntarily returned the courtesy, sending his adjutant to offer condolence to the Conclave. Leone, who then was Chamberlain, ordered the Swiss Guard to refuse entrance to the royal envoy at the bronze gates – to refuse the message even.'

'Very clerical!' the Emperor said; and pondered a moment. Then 'Will Your Majesty go to the Vatican with me?'

'No, Sire: I never will go to the Vatican,' the King replied.

A telegram signed 'Wilhelm II. R.' addressed to the Prince-Bishop of Breslau brought Cardinal Popk to his sovereign at the German Embassy in Rome. On hearing the Kaiser's intention, he did his very best to persuade him away from it; and curtly was required to explain himself.

'Majesty,' said His Eminency, 'no good can come of such a meeting, and much harm may. Our Most Holy Father is English; and, being English, He has the English quality of cynicism. With Him it is "*Et Petro et Nobis*" in the highest degree. He is a man of strong likes and dislikes, fervently patriotic and therefore fervently anti-German –'

'Your Eminency knows that?'

'I have no explicit information: but, seeing the estimation in which those islanders hold us, I judge so. Sire, I beseech you to pause. I beseech you, I beseech you on behalf of your loyal Catholic subjects, that you will not expose your imperial person to the risk of an affront.'

'An affront, indeed!'

'Majesty, remember what happened when you first visited Pope Leo.'

William II laughed. 'Cardinal, you are a very good German, and a – well, queer Roman.'

'Sire, I distinguish. I implicitly obey Hadrian as Vicar of Christ: I dislike Him as a cynical Englishman. I am anxious that Your Majesty may not have occasion to dislike this Englishman who is the spiritual director of your loyal Catholic subjects.'

'Your Eminency's solicitude is most creditable. But I have met Englishmen whom I immensely admire for certain qualities which they possess and which we Germans lack. What you have said piques my curiosity. I wish to meet this particular Englishman; and I wish Your Eminency to arrange it. I promise you that, whether He affronts me or not, I will not afflict my Catholic subjects with another *Kulturkampf* – if that is what you fear. However, if you still hesitate to oblige your Kaiser, I will apply through my legation: or, better, I will apply through the Cardinal-bishop of Albano who used to be at Munich.'

The Cardinal-Prince-Bishop of Breslau went to the Vatican without any more ado; and the Supreme Pontiff consented to receive.

Hadrian endured an hour of terror. The task of dealing with an emperor – He was inclined to put it from Him as being too great a thing for Him. But He felt inquisitive to know what the Kaiser wanted. He Who sits upon the throne of Peter looks at all the world, knowing that He will see either enemies – or suitors. Hadrian also was inquisitive to see the person and the mind of the man whom He invariably had defended as being the only sovereign in Europe whose conduct indicated belief in his own divine right to sovereignty, and as being one of the few delightful persons in the world who can contemplate their own minds and behold they are very good. Hadrian was interested in William II as an extremely fine specimen of the absolute type. Yet – He hesitated to come to close relations with him, because – well, for one thing, because He disliked being domineered over, and this military Michael from the high Hohenzollern hill-top was certain to smack of the barracks. All the same, popes had received emperors before now; and it had not always been the emperors who had domineered. But could He love him? Well, at any rate, He could try to save him trouble. Then what was the Kaiser's object? He knew that something or other was wanted of Him; and He feared – feared lest He should say, as usual, more than He meant to say, and give, as usual, more than He need give. That, though, could be prevented. He would make this rule for the occasion: – Listen little, inquire less, affirm least, and concede nothing now. Good! It should be done. He had a couple of easy chairs placed in the throne-room, and a small table with cigarettes, cigarette papers, and tobacco, the Crab Mixture which George Arthur Rose had invented. He sat down in one of the chairs by the window: took out the little gold pyx from His bosom; and held it in His hands while He awaited the Emperor's arrival. His eyes became still and grave. His lips moved swiftly. A singular serenity inspired Him. . . . The introducer-of-sovereigns announced

'The Duke of Königsberg.'

'Your Majesty's visit gives Us great pleasure,' was the Apostle's greeting to the Kaiser, uttered in that clear young minor voice which was so well known in Rome. The two potentates took each the other's measure in a glance. The Emperor, smartly groomed in plain evening dress with riband, cross, and star, had that slightly conical head which marks the thinker and the single-minded obstinate man. The Pope, a year his junior, gave an impression of clean simplicity with His white habit and His keen white face. There was a distance, a reticence, in His gaze. He had remembered William's Teutonic osculation of His indignant predecessor; and, as the Kaiser approached Him, He took the imperial hand and shook it in the glad-to-see-you-but-keep-off English fashion. Spring-dumb-bells had given the Pope a grip like a vice and an arm like a steel piston-rod. The Emperor blinked once.

'I am grateful to Your Holiness for receiving me in this informal manner.'

The Pope inclined His head: motioned His guest to a chair; and offered cigarettes. He Himself rolled one: lighted it; and sat down.

'I have the pleasure of personally congratulating Your Holiness on Your Election; and I trust that God will grant You many years in which to rule Your section of His people wisely and well.'

'It is Our sincere hope that Our endeavour to feed Christ's flock may be acceptable.'

'I have many Catholics in my empire; and I may say that their virtues merit my fullest approbation.'

The Pope again inclined His head.

'I understand that Your Holiness has never been in Germany?'

'No. Our life hitherto has been an unimportant one. We are almost ignorant of the world and of men, except perhaps from the view-point of the outside observer and student.'

'My sainted mother used to quote an English proverb which says that Onlookers see most of the game.'

'All English proverbs, which are positive, have their correspondent negative – "Absence makes the heart grow fonder" – "Out of sight out of mind" – Your Majesty's proverb is contradicted by "Only the toad under the harrow has counted the spikes". We mean that We have learned much of what is done, but very little of the details of the doing.'

'Ah, that of course comes by heredity or by practice –'

'Or by occession.'

'I fear that I do not quite follow.'

The Pope suddenly was afraid that He had been guilty of a sort of appeal for this mighty emperor's pity and consideration toward His plebeian origin and inexperience. Was this keeping His troubles to Himself? He hastened to divert the conversation from Himself. 'Our predecessor St Peter was an illiterate plebeian of no importance: but, by the occession of Divine Grace, His Holiness was enabled to wield the keys of the kingdom of Heaven, and to win the unfading palm down there by the obelisk.'

'Ah yes. And I trust that Your Holiness may be similarly enabled. I have very little doubt but that You will be. The favour of the Almighty seems to be with men of our nation in a pre-eminent degree.'

'Our nation?'

'Yes. Surely Your Holiness remembers that, by birth, I am half-English?'

'Oh indeed yes. But, Majesty, in England you are thought of as being wholly German.'

'I am much misunderstood in England.' Again the head inclined in silence led the Emperor on. 'And also I have been much misunderstood in Germany. The English suspect me of plotting mischief against England; and my empire has been suspecting me of such leanings toward England as to interfere with my proper duty of attending to the interests of Germany!'

'And both suspicions are equally gratuitous.'

'Both. As a matter of duty, I think first of the interests of Germany: but, for the sake of those very interests, I am anxious to cultivate the friendship of England. Personally I have a great appreciation of many English qualities, as my many English friends know. And of course, although she was a somewhat terrible person, I had an immense and genuine admiration for my never-sufficiently-to-be-lauded grandmother, your great Queen Victoria. Now there was a Woman, a Queen – '

'In that matter Your Majesty's behaviour was magnificent. We Ourself saw you at her exsequies: We noted the signs of your countenance and your comportment; and We honoured your splendid piety. There only was one feeling in England towards Your Majesty then.'

The Kaiser was moved: his left arm twitched once or twice. 'Your Holiness's words' – he shook his ferocious eyes – 'are very grateful to me. But what have I done since – to lose – '

'Majesty, in the English mind, you are incarnate Germany.'

'I am Germany.'

'It is not Your Majesty whom England distrusts, but the Germans.'

'But why, but why?'

'Englishmen say, "It is all very well to dissemble your love but why did you kick me downstairs?" They don't believe in Your Majesty's friendliness because they commit the common error of confounding the particular with the universal. Your Majesty is the scape-goat. They lay upon you the sins of execrable taste on the part of your journalists and of shady diplomacy on the part of your statesmen; and they drive you out into the wilderness.'

'Is Your Holiness cognizant of the difficulties which I have to contend with?'

'We are perfectly astounded at the inertia, the stolidity, the volatility, the inconstancy of the material which rulers have to direct, to curb, to shape. We entirely sympathize with Your Majesty in the matter of the difficulties which fill your life. Also, to descend to particulars, We know and approve of your masterly method of dealing with demagogues.'

'I am very glad to hear this. I am pleased to know that there is one point on which I can agree with Your Holiness.'

'We trust that there are many points on which We cannot agree with Your Majesty.'

The Kaiser was taken aback. 'I do not understand,' he said.

'Complete agreement signifies complete stagnation. Disagreement at least postulates activity; and only by activity is The Best made manifest and approved.'

'Holiness, I beg Your pardon. I see the point. That is a very grand and at-all-times-to-be-remembered doctrine. I must try to remember Your beautiful words: for it is The Best which I am seeking for Germany.'

'And Germany never will find it in the socialism which aims at that ridiculous impossibility called Equality, meaning the acquisition by lazy B of that which active A has won. All history shows that Aristos only emerges from conflict. That is a truth which must be insisted on. At the same time, We rejoice to see that Your Majesty has been inspired to distinguish between the charlatans and their dupes. Much unrighteousness is done to suffering humanity by those who will not take the trouble to remember that, when the natural man is hurt, he howls and seizes the salve which is nearest. The wise ruler works to benefit his subjects by going directly to the root of the matter, removing the cause of injury. But We are not to preach to Your Majesty. You, no doubt, had some definite object in coming to Us.'

'Yes: I certainly had a definite object: but I had no idea that I was to discuss it with a Pontiff Who had so complete an intuition of my own imperial sentiments.'

'Our office is to become in sympathy with all who strive for The Best.'

'The kindness with which Your Holiness has received me, and the never-to-be forgotten truths which You so nobly have enunciated make my task much easier. I desired to consult Your Holiness, to obtain knowledge of Your feelings, in certain matters. At the present moment, You are aware, my eastern frontier is menaced by Russia, my western frontier by France; and, on my southern frontier there is a third and a more miscellaneous difficulty. The Germans of Austria have petitioned for admission to the Germanic Empire.'

'Can you admit – annex – them? Will it be well for you to do that?'

'Holiness, I must: as German Emperor, I must protect Germans. While Francis Joseph lived, his German subjects were content to live in Austria as Austrians. Now that Bohemia and Hungary are separating themselves from Austria, they no longer are content. Austria is no more. The fragments which composed her are for ever disunited; and –'

'Poland?'

'Holiness, in my empire there is no Poland.'

'No? Your Majesty believes that the German Austrians would be happier under your rule. Are you likely to meet with opposition if you annex them?'

'With tremendous opposition. France and Russia instantly will declare war.'

'With what chance of success?'

'With no chance of success. My glorious German navy and army will conquer France and Russia.'

'Majesty! Majesty! And yet – you have endeared yourself to hundreds of thousands of French refugees.'

'Thanks to Your Holiness's gracious initiative, You may take it that all Christian France is willing to become German – or English – out of sheer gratitude.'

'But Russia – Russia is immense – immensely powerful.'

'Pardon me, Holiness, but do You read the English newspapers?'

'Nineteen, studiously: thirty-seven, from which cuts are selected for Our perusal.'

'The English newspapers are well-informed, trustworthy?'

'Penny and threepenny dailies, threepenny weeklies, shilling and half-crown monthlies, generally are well-informed, generally are trustworthy.'

'So. Then I shall tell Your Holiness, from an English penny daily, that Russia is not powerful in a military sense. The large majority of her officers are abjectly incapable. The ranks are recruited entirely from the peasantry; and are, on the admission of their own generals, entirely unreliable. They have neither intelligence nor initiative; and they no more know how to obey than their officers know how to command. Russia's defeat by Japan taught her nothing. Also there has been for years among patriotic Russians, north, south, east, and west, a singular yearning for an overwhelming defeat by an European power. That way only, they say, can they be delivered from the crushing anarchic tyranny under which the whole country labours. Even supposing Russia to be united – which she is not – I say that she has no chance of ultimate success against the German navy and army. I say that her numbers have inspired a wholly unfounded and exaggerated apprehension of her military power. I say that bounce – Bounce, if Your Holiness will permit me to say it – bounce alone has served her purpose well. She will continue to use bounce until she is opposed by a resolute determination which there is no possibility of mistaking. Fear of Russia resembles the fear of a child at an ugly mask. If Russia were to cross my frontiers, she would march to her final overthrow. And, best of all, the Russians know that as well as I do.'

'Your Majesty appears to have made out a case. Well: you will conquer France and Russia. And then?'

'I shall annex them to my empire.'

'Are you likely to meet with any opposition then?'

'I do not know. I am about to proceed to discuss the point with my uncle. Meanwhile my ambassadors are consulting Mr Chamberlain and Mr Roosevelt; and I myself am consulting my royal cousin the King of Italy.'

'Ah – the King of Italy! – And what does Your Majesty desire from Us?'

'I should be glad to know the attitude which Your Holiness will prescribe for the Catholics of my empire, as well as for other Catholics, in the event of my engaging in these schemes.'

'Why?'

'Because at present my Catholic subjects are loyal. I should not permit any of my subjects to be disloyal. I wish to give them all freedom in religious matters: but I should not tolerate opposition to my state policy.'

'Touching the matter of Poland – '

'There is no Poland.'

The Pope put His hand on the table – pontifically. 'Will Your Majesty, for the purposes of argument, consent to imagine a place called Poland, partly Russian, partly German, inhabited by a race which is neither German nor Russian, a race very tenacious of its traditions. In the event of your annexation of France, and Russia, for example – and Austria which is composed of sixteen distinct races speaking thirty-two distinct languages, the various Slavonic nationalities of Parthians, Medes, and Elamites – '

'Parthians, Medes, and Elamites?'

'Well: Croats, Slovenes, Dalmatians, and the dwellers in Bosnia and Herzegovina, to say nothing of the Czechs and the Magyars – in the event of your annexation of all these, you would be obliged to have regard unto the racial characteristics of your new subjects. Now, at the same time, would you not be well advised to regard the racial characteristics of Poland?'

'In what way?'

'For example, would you concede to Poland, the Polish language, and a Polish king and constitution under your imperial suzerainty?'

'Your Holiness means something of the nature of federation, such as Your Own country so successfully has adopted?'

'Concisely.'

'I had not thought of it. It merits my profound consideration.'

'And what would happen to the other fragments of Austria, and to the Balkan States?'

'I do not know. The Sultan would have something to say.'

'And what will he say?'

'I must tell Your Holiness that I am much disappointed in Turkey. I looked upon it as the military power, whose ability to hold back Russia, and to prevent the political strangulation of Germany in Europe by keeping open the gates of the East, must be strengthened at all costs. Hence I practically rearmed the Sultan's forces; and passed numbers of young Turkish officers through my military schools. You may say that I made the Turkish Army. All to no purpose. The new Sultan has played me false. I am afraid now that Turkey will be more influenced by England and by Italy than by me.'

'Is that king blind?'

'My uncle?'

'No. Italy.'

'Not that I am aware of, Why does Your Holiness ask?'

The Supreme Pontiff stood up. 'We thank Your Majesty for the sincerity of Your conversation; and assure you of Our goodwill. We will ponder the matters which you have laid before Us.'

'I hoped to have had – ' But there was no mistaking the sealed face. And William II was one of the cleverest men in the world; and he also was half an Englishman. 'I should be greatly obliged if Your Holiness would write down that doctrine of Aristos. I should prize it greatly.'

The Pope went to a writing table and produced a couple of lines in His wonderful fifteenth-century script.

'I will make this one of the heirlooms of Hohenzollern:' said the Kaiser.

'May God guide you, well-beloved son.'

Hadrian walked that afternoon with Cardinal Semphill on Nomentana, as far as St Agnes-Beyond-the-Walls. It was one of those deliberately lovely Roman autumn afternoons, when walking is a climax of crisp joy with the thought of a cup of tea as the fine finial. They talked of books, especially of novels; and His Eminency asserted that the novels of Anthony Trollope gave him on the whole the keenest satisfaction. There was a great deal more in them than generally was supposed, he said. The Pope agreed that they were very pleasant easy reading, deliciously anodynic. His Own preference was for Thackeray's *Esmond*. He, however, would not commit Himself to approval of all the works of any one writer, simply because no man was capable of being always at his best. As they passed through Porta Pia into Venti Settembre, Hadrian pointed to the palace on the left of the gate, saying, 'Have you ever been there?'

'No, Holiness. At least, not since I've been wearing this.' He indicated his vermilion ferraiuola.

'Don't you think if we asked them very nicely they would give us a cup of tea?'

The cardinal mischievously chuckled. 'I am of opinion that the English Ambassador would be very pleased to make Your Holiness's acquaintance over a cup of tea.'

Hadrian rang the bell. 'Semphill,' He said as they waited at the gate, 'if there be any ladies about, will you kindly talk to them and leave the Ambassador to Us.'

Sir Francis was at home. And much honoured. So were two secretaries. And no ladies. And there was tea. Cardinal Semphill devoted himself to the secretaries; and told them funny stories about clergymen. They laughed hugely at the tales (which were witty) and at the wittier clergyman who told them. The Pope mentioned to the Ambassador that He had had a call from the Duke of Königsberg that morning; and drifted off into an inquiry as to where reliable maps were to be procured. Sir Francis named Standford of Longacre; and was much interested. Was there any map in particular which His Holiness desired to consult. They were fairly well off for maps at the embassy. Perhaps the Holy Father would condescend –

'No thank you, Sir Francis, They would ask questions about you in parliament if We were to borrow your maps. Why, Lady Wimborne will have a fit as it is, when she hears that you have entertained the Ten-horned Beast with tea.'

'I am not afraid of that, Holiness.'

'No, of course not. But Standford will give Us all the information which We need – unless you will tell Us' (the interest concentrated) 'what England is going to do in the present crisis?'

'I can tell Your Holiness one thing which She has done; and which will appear in tomorrow morning's *Times*. England and Turkey, the two great Mohammedan Powers, have entered into an offensive and defensive alliance today.'

'Which means that England's interests lie in Asia and Africa; and not in Europe.'

The Ambassador slightly started. 'May I know why Your Holiness thinks that?'

Hadrian rose and shook hands. 'Because of England's previous alliance with Japan: because of Her conscious sympathy with the barbaric. Read "success" for "sympathy" in the last sentence, if you prefer it. And please remember that this is not an infallible utterance.'

'It's an astonishingly smart one, all the same,' said the Ambassador with a genial grin.

'Thank you very much for your tea. Standford, you said? Good-bye. And, Sir Francis – there are no closed doors in the Vatican.'

Hadrian chattered at large during the remainder of the evening; and industriously dreamed all night, first of certain

232

portents connected with emperors' knuckles: then of tremendous maps on which one crawled: and finally His usual and favourite dream of being invisible and stark naked and fitted with great white feathery wings, flying with the movement of swimming among and above men, seeing and seeing and seeing, easily and enormously swooping. In the morning reaction supervened. He was listless: He wanted to be alone. They left Him alone; and during several days He was inaccessible, writing, and burning much writing. The palace, with its fifty separate buildings, its eleven thousand rooms, its fourteen courtyards hummed with the life of a population of a small town. Up in the series of small chambers under the eaves, in the large and lovely pleasaunce on the slopes of the Vatican hill, He found quiet and peace. He thought for hours at a stretch, smoking cigarette after cigarette, gazing out of the window or across autumnal lawns. Sometimes He remained rapt in contemplation of the perfect beauty of His new cross, gently stroking it with delicate finger. A portfolio of vast maps arrived from London. He pinned them on His blank brown walls and pored over them. In the night He often would rise and stand before them till His breast ached and His arms were stiff with the weight of the lamp. He sent a holograph letter to the King of Spain; and received a reply which lightened His brow. He concentrated His mind on the future. He began to form His plans.

At the beginning of November, He signed the decree of canonization of Madame Jehane de Lys, commonly called Joan of Arc; and simultaneously issued the *Epistle to the Germans*. Very few perceived the true inwardness of the paradox. Those Frenchmen who remained Christian were so overjoyed, at the honour accorded to their national heroine, that they failed to appreciate the significance of the *Epistle*. The Germans were so occupied with the contents of the *Epistle*, that the glorification of a Frenchwoman passed unnoted. In England, it was thought that the Pontiff was feeling his way. The *Worldly Christian* asked what you would expect of a Jesuit; and the *Daily Anagraph* compared Him to Machiavelli.

Certainly the *Epistle to the Germans* was remarkable not so much for its matter as for its suggestion. It was a masterpiece of what Walt Whitman calls revelation by faint indirections. The Kaiser did not know whether to be satisfied or dissatisfied with it. Hadrian praised the Teutonic race for its poetic (in the Greek sense of 'creative') and diligent habits. He dwelled with admiration upon the many benefits which civilization owes to the German constructive faculty. But He indicated the want of the 'open air and fresh water' element in all departments, physical and intellectual, of German life.

Scope is what ye need, free movement of mind and body. Stagnation breeds purulence, rancorous, suffocating, sour. Brooding never can bring satisfaction, nor can iron, nor can blood: but only the gold of Love. Wherefore, well-beloved sons, seek your salvation in Love. Love one another first: be patient, knowing that Love is manifest in obedience, and hath exceeding great reward.

CHAPTER 14

JERRY SANT saw Mrs Crowe driving in victorias with people who wore smartish bonnets. Professional experience enabled him to recognize real ospreys. Three or four times he met her in her mauve, going to an evening party. From this he deduced that she was enjoying herself; and, it being quite contrary to the principles of socialism that anyone should enjoy themselves except under socialist supervision, he put on a red necktie and paid her a visit. It was a wet day: she had nothing particular to do; and she was not unwilling to chat about herself. Looking at his florid sweaty vulgarity, it soothed her vanity to tell this plebeian of the patricians whom she had captured, the Honble Mrs This, the Baroness von That, and Lady Whatshername of the Other. They were so kind. Their kettledrums and bridge-routs were so chic. You met such thoroughly Nice people you know. And the American millionairesses were so amusing. They had such shocking manners. Mrs Crowe actually had seen one drinking soup out of a plate. Jerry had been getting more and more morose while she chattered; and now he burst out:

'I know better than to sup my soup out of the plate. I sup them with a spoon.'

'Of course you do, Mr Sant. But these American women have no manners whatever.'

'Ah weel now, we've had enough of that. Look ye now, I've been letting ye go your own way a bit; and I think the time's come when ye might introduce me to some of your gran' friens. A'm none to gey at the hotel; and besides that, it's me due.'

She found the man a sudden and accented nuisance: but she couldn't possibly quarrel with the keeper of the purse. 'I'm sure, if you think it advisable, I don't want to keep you back. I don't quite see though how I can take you with me, as you say. You see you don't know any of these people.'

'Well and fhat of that?'

'Why you silly man of course you've got to be introduced.'

'How did you get introduced yersel'?'

'Oh, why, I was converted, you see.'

'Imphm! Well, I'll let ye know I'm not for being converted, as ye call it.'

'No, I suppose not. I think it rather a pity, you know; because I'm sure you'd have no difficulty afterwards.'

'I willna!'

'Perhaps if I were to hint that you were thinking about it – '

'Ah weel, ye might do that now. Look here ma wumman. Why can't ye introduce me yersel'?'

'Oh I couldn't. People would want to know what you were to me – '

'I'm your paymaster.'

'Oh how can you say such things!'

'Because I am.'

'Yes I know you are: but you needn't say it out so bluntly. I'll tell you what I might do. You be at the tea-place in Piazzer Dispaggner every afternoon from four to five. I'm sure to come in tomorrow or the next day with a few friends; and, if you were to bow to me, I might recognize you and ask you to our table.'

'Wumman A'll dae't. Who pays for the tea, though?'

'Sometimes I do; and sometimes whoever I come with.'

'Well then I'm coming. And I'll let you know to have a good blow out, plenty o'scones and bit-cakeys an' a' that. I'll pay; and I don't mind if it costs me three shilling, so long as ye introduce me to some of these mashers.'

'Very well. But remember, you're thinking about becoming Catholic.'

'A'm not.'

'Dear me, Mr Sant, but you must be. Then they'll take an interest in you and ask you to their parties.'

'Ah weel then, I am.'

'Who *is* this Mr Sant?' said a Pict to an Erse (who called himself 'The' before his surname). The italicized question was asked at a reception in Mrs O'Jade's flat on Palazzo Campello, about a fortnight after the previous confabulation.

'I really don't quite know, beyond that he's a friend of that Mrs Crowe who was converted the other day.'

'Is he a convert too?'

'No, not yet: but they say he's likely to be. They're both Liblabs, you know.'

'Oh, yes of course, I read about them in the papers. What a score it will be for the Church! Well, what do you make of him?'

'Oh he seems earnest enough: but he's hardly got a word to say for himself. And I don't think he's quite a gentleman, you know.'

Hadrian sat at the end of one of His long bare tables. On both sides of Him were two great numbered baskets, At the other end of the table was a huge leathern sack containing the pontifical mail. At the sides of the table stood the two Gentlemen of the Apostolic Chamber with stilettos. The Pope unlocked the sack; and Sir John and Sir Iulo in turn drew out a handful of letters and displayed them before Him. He scanned the handwriting of each; and named a numbered basket into which the designated missive was cast. When the sack was empty, the contents of the baskets were dealt with. All the letters in the first were addressed 'To His Holiness the Pope, Prefect of the Holy Roman and Universal Inquisition'. Hadrian took the stiletto from Sir Iulo; and slit open each envelope which Sir John presented. Thus they were returned to the basket, and sent to be perused by the Cardinal-Secretary-of-State. The two gentlemen seated themselves at the table: cut open the envelopes of the second basketful; and pushed them within the Pope's reach. These were addressed in known handwritings. Hadrian read the letters, and sorted them in separate heaps before Him: each heap was weighted by a miniature ingot of pure copper, the colour of which He immensely admired. Two letters were placed face downwards by themselves. The envelopes from the third basket were opened, and the letters extracted by the gentlemen: Hadrian only looked at and arranged them. The fourth basket contained newspapers, which Sir John opened and examined for marked paragraphs. If any such were found, Sir Iulo folded the paper open and placed it: otherwise the paper was torn and returned to the basket. Meanwhile the Pope more closely inspected the letters which He had retained. The gentlemen placed a couple of phonographs on the table: inserted new cylinders; and retired. Hadrian got up and locked the doors. He took the little heaps of letters from under the ingots; and spoke into the machine formal acknowledgements of receipt and a short blessing, or definite instructions for detailed responses, until all had received attention except the two letters which lay by themselves, and three others. He unlocked the door. The gentlemen entered; and carried the instruments with the articulate cylinders to Cardinals Sterling, Whitehead, Leighton, della Volta, and Fiamma, who acted as pontifical secretaries in the ninth antechamber. Hadrian Himself wrote to His well-beloved son William, to His beloved son Edmund Earl Marshal of England, and to His beloved son A. Panciera. These being enclosed and addressed, He was left alone. He took the two remaining letters to the easy chair by the window; rolled and lighted a cigarette; and considered them.

Reverend and Dear Sir,

Since our late esteemed interview when I had the pleasure of addressing your lordship on the subject of Socialism I have been anxiously awaiting the favour of an acknowledgement of same. In case the subject has slipped your memory I should remind you that I informed you previously on behalf of the Liblab Fellowship that we were not averse to give our careful consideration to any proposal that you may see fit to make, with a view to cooperation with us against the horde of cosmopolitan gold-pigs who monopolize the means of existence production distribution and exchange in order to procure a complete change in the entire social organism. I am quite at a loss to understand on what grounds you have not favoured me with a direct reply unless there is anything on which you would like farther explanations, in that case I will be most happy to call on you per previous appointment for which I am now waiting at the above address neglecting my business at considerable expense and inconvenience to myself which a man in my humble position compared with yours (!) cannot be expected to incur and common courtesy demands should be made good. I therefore trust that in view of the not altogether pleasant facts that are in my possession your lordship shall see fit to send me a private interview at your earliest convenience. Hopeing that I will not have occasion to feel myself compelled to proceed farther in this matter if you leave me no option but to do so, and assuring your lordship that your valued instructions as to time and place of meeting will have my fullest and promptest attention.

I remain Sir,
Yours truly,
Comrade Jeremiah Sant, L.F.

ps. Perhaps I may mention by way of hint that we might be able to come to some arrangement for our mutual advantage not altogether on the above lines, and I beg to advise your most reverent lordship that I would be willing to meet your wishes if the terms are suitable. Asking to hear from you soon and hopping that any misunderstandings may presently be cleared up.

J.S.

Dearest dearest Georgie

For although you have no more the old sweet name my heart is ever

238

faithful and will not let me call you by any other. Does it not remind you of that day of long ago when the floods were out in the meadows and you and I and Joseph were coming home from the Bellamys, and you lifted me in your strong arms and carried me through the water that covered the path. How Joseph laughed. He never thought it worth his while to take care of me as you did. But I knew that it was because you loved me and my heart went out to you then and never has been my own since. If only you knew how deeply I regret the unpleasantness which arose since then I think you would pity me a little. Georgie do forgive me. It is my love which made me mad. I hate myself for what I did and would give the world to undo it. I was a mad fool then. I did not know what I was doing or how you would take it so seriously. Georgie you were always good and I was wicked. But haven't you punished me enough. Think of what I have suffered all these years apart from you. Every time you have refused to notice me has been like a stab in my heart. Georgie take pity on me. Do you know that I watch your window every day and watch you walk about the town. Several times you have brushed against me in the street without knowing it for I will do nothing to damage you any more, dearest Georgie. I know very well that ladies are not admitted to your palace for I have had myself made a Catholic in order to get a little nearer you, but all priests have housekeepers. Georgie do let me come and be your housekeeper. I promise on my word of honour that I will serve you faithfully in any and every way. We might be so happy. Nothing would give me greater joy than to work my fingers to the bone for you. Georgie do believe me when you see how I am willing to humiliate myself so for you. Of course I never speak of our former relations except that I say I knew you slightly when Joe was alive. But as for love I never mention it for it was nipped in the bud by my wickedness and never has been anything but a trial to me, and I should not wish my love to do you any harm. Don't think that last sentence means anything spiteful, it is not so indeed but I know you distrust me. I only mean that it would be better for both of us if you would not go on being so cruel heartless dreadful and neglectful of

> Your devoted and distracted
> N.

PS. I have a suspicion that the man who is with me is no friend of yours. Georgie, be wise and let me see you at least and tell you what I suspect. It is only your welfare I have at heart, don't refuse me Georgie don't.

Hadrian read these letters through two or three times

239

noting the yapping and the yowling of the one, the panting and the whining of the other, the barking of both. He returned to the window and looked at nothing until He had finished His cigarette. His thin lips stiffened in scorn and drew downward into the straight inflexible line. His impulse was to make an end of the male animal in a tank of aquafortis, if such a convenience only had formed part of the pontifical paraphernalia: as for the female, he remembered George Meredith's sentence, and would have liked to squeeze all the acid out of her at one grip and toss her to the divinities who collect exhausted lemons. The next minute, 'The dogs, the dirty abject obscene dogs,' He spat suddenly; and carried the letters to the safe in the bedroom where He locked them up. He prohibited Himself from taking further note of them. He was conscious that this course was quite wrong. But there it was. He had a busy afternoon before Him; and He diligently read in His breviary to prepare for Himself a convenient frame of mind. Pursuing His policy of emphasizing the difference between the Church and the World, He had summoned the generals of religious orders. To each of these He wished to say some words of admonition, words which would remain in the memory, and be passed from mind to mind, from mystic to thyrsos-bearer, from general to postulant. He rather enjoyed the sticking of labels on people and things now, because He could do it to some purpose. On the other hand, He had a feeling that He was only touching surfaces. Still, here and there the surface might be soft and capable of receiving impression: or here and there might be a crevice or a gap which He could fill with a cartridge. Somehow, anyhow, His words and acts must be made to penetrate to the roots of things, to influence fundamentals.

At fifteen o'clock He mounted the small throne. One by one the generals passed into the Presence: heard apostolic words; and passed out again – Servites, Premonstratensians, Augustinians, Cistercians, Carthusians, Oblates, Marists, Passionists, Carmelites, Dominicans. To the General of Trinitarians, He commended Africa; and ordained that twenty friars should preach as of old in the market places of England, Canada, and Australasia, for African missions. To the General of the Order of Charity, He would not say anything at present concerning the condemned Forty Propositions: but He would say Love your enemies the Jesuits, and 'turn not away thine eye from the needy and give none occasion to curse thee'. To the General of Benedictines, He gave command to keep his monks in their monasteries, and to prohibit them from appearing in the correspondence columns of newspapers, either under their religious names or their renounced secular styles. He reminded the Minister-General of Capuchins of the second minister-general, the apostate Ochino, who had preferred worldly things and had preached polygamy; and also of the fact that playing fast and loose with worldly things continued to produce apostate Capuchins. To the Minister-General of Franciscans, He commended Asia; and ordained that fifty friars should preach as of old in the market places of England, Canada, and Australasia, for Asiatic missions. Then He showed the grey scapular and cord which He was wearing next to His skin; and asked that the brotherhood should name Him to Blessed Brother Francis as a little brother who was not gay but sad, not lively but weary, and who had but little love. Hadrian, as Brother Serafino of the Third Order, kissed the Minister-General's naked feet, and begged a blessing. Returning to the throne, the Supreme Pontiff imparted apostolic benediction. And Brother Peter Baptist went out into the noisy antechambers with his clean bright face all-glorious, and light in his serene blue eyes. The Prepositor-General of Jesuits entered with ostentation of the knowledge that, if Hadrian the Seventh was the English White Pope, he himself was the English Black Pope. He had that benevolently truculent manner which women deem adorable. As he made his obeisance, Hadrian noted a little lacquered snuff-box in his hand and a frightful bandanna oozing from the pocket of his cassock. His Holiness instantly carried war into the camp, by reminding Father St Albans of the bulls of Urban VIII and Innocent X which prohibit snuff-taking on pain of excommunication.

'No doubt those bulls are obsolete: but Your Reverency will have the goodness to abstain from practising the filthy habit in Our Presence.'

The sallow General pocketed his snuff-box; and produced the stony mild smile which is used upon eccentricity. The Pope remarked that the Company of Jesus appeared to be in a verisimilar position to the Wesleyans, in that they had departed a very long way from the will and spirit of their founder. He used His slowly biting monotone, because He wished to save this General the trouble of misunderstanding Him. He said that, with the word 'Borgia' and the word 'Nero', the word 'Jesuit' perhaps was the eponym for all that was vilest in the world. That was very undesirable. Not that the good opinion of the world was desirable. Far from that. But Christians ought not to enjoy anything, not even an evil reputation, under false pretences. He wished to do something to rectify the erroneous opinion which the world had formed about the Company of Jesus, to straighten out the tangle, correcting and directing; and, as men were wont to judge more by actions than by words, He did not propose to beat the air with vain expostulations, explanations, expositions of virtue, and so forth. It had been done a thousand times before. Historic calumnies had been refuted from pulpits and in pamphlets with unanswerable logic: but still the man-in-the-street said 'Jesuit' when he meant 'a foxy wolf'. The Pontiff was not going to try to persuade the world away from its nonsense. He wished the Company of Jesus to give the world a proximate occasion of persuading itself. Therefore, He proposed to the General, in private, a return to the observance of the good old rule and a cultivation of the saintly spirit of St Iñigo Lopez de Recalde. He wished the Jesuits to reconsider the position, as it were: to surcease from the – not always mortally sinful – not always tangibly illegal – but perhaps – generally shady transactions –

The General intèrrupted. He was prepared to bully.

Hadrian froze him with a glance of blazing supremacy. 'Make no mistake,' the Pope said: 'We are not intending Ourself to punish your Company, nor to degrade your

Companions who so diligently degrade themselves, nor to confer fictitious and unmerited importance upon you by decrees of dissolution or suppression. We do not forget the badness of the agents in the goodness of the cause nor the goodness of the cause in the badness of the agents.' He was looking through His all-observant half-shut eyes straight at the bridge of the General's fine nose. That is the most exacerbating form of regard: for, while it holds the hearer rigid and intense, it effectually prevents retaliation. Much may be done with the eye in wordy warfare. You may challenge: you may intimidate: you may quell: but you may do none of these things while your opponent refuses to lend his eye to yours. So this sleek General found. The Pontiff held him with an eye which gazed so nearly into his, that he perforce was obliged to lie in wait for the flicker when his own could seize it. Hadrian knew the dodge. He had not watched and dichotomized men and Jesuits from the observatory and in the dissecting-room of His loneliness during twenty years for nothing. At the end of His sentence, His gaze swept right away. He rose and went to the window. Looking out over the roofs of Golden and Immortal Rome, He continued in a milder tone, 'We have cited Your Reverency only to hear Our paternal chiding of your naughty ways, to the end that ye may amend the same, returning of your own free will to the observance of the spirit as well as of the letter of those rules of life and conduct which your Father, St Ignatius, made for you.'

He paused. The General, who would have preferred wheeling manure in a barrow at the behest of a novice (A.M.D.G. of course) to listening to this rodent exhortation, took it that the audience was ended; and made shift to get on to his knees.

But the Pope went on. 'For, it is of the nature of all human things to deteriorate; and ye have made yourselves a scorn and hissing among men. The *Nouvelle Revue* states that ye are in great decadence. The statement may be one of your own devices for distracting the attention of the world from your nefarious machinations. Or it may be a fact. In both cases it is damnable and damnatory.' He paused again.

'*Jube, Domine, benedicere*,' the General intoned, with a determination to force the apostolic benediction, and to get back to the Via del Seminario as soon as possible. He felt that he had some very important things to say to his *socii*.

But the pitiless voice probed him again: 'Wherefore We admonish you that ye set your house in order while ye have time.'

The General's oval jaw took an extra lateral crease. His hands twitched and pattered down and up and down in a talpine manner. Suddenly the inflexible fathomless eyes flashed on him. Axioms like sleet tersely lashed him.

'Remember that ye only exist on sufferance. Dismiss delusions; and see yourselves as ye really are. Strip, man, strip. Search out your own weaknesses: lest, not the Father but, the Enemy discover the sores, and the diamonds, which ye are hiding. For ye do not merit the reputation, which is associated with your name, on the strength of which ye trade.'

The glossy black priest jerked to his feet: genuflected; and was backing from the white Presence. The Pontiff, whose mood had become quite pythian, stepped up to him, laying a firm hand on the bow of the ribbons of his ferraiuola. 'Wince not, dear son. Three fourths of you trade upon the reputation of your Company for cunning and learning. One fourth of you is the Christians of the world. At least be frank with yourselves. Let us have more of the flower of your Christianity. Let us have less of your false pretences. Your erudition is showy enough. Oh yes. But it is so superficial. Your machinations are sly enough. Oh yes. But they are so silly. Ye are not geniuses. Ye are not monsters either of vice or of virtue: but only ridiculous mediocrities, always pitifully burrowing, burrowing like assiduous moles, always seeing your pains misspent, your elaborate schemes wrecked, except sometimes, when – to complete the metaphor – quite by accident, ye chance to kill a king. This is not to the Greater Glory of God. Then stop. Stop. Here and now.'

They were by the door. The Black Pope had one hand under the blue-linen curtain, and was fumbling for the handle. The

White Pope quickly clinched His admonition. 'Don't pretend to be Superior Persons. Don't give yourself such airs. Don't gad about in hansom cabs quite so much. Don't play billiards in public houses. Don't nurture jackals. Try to be honest. Don't oppress the poor. Don't adore the rich. Don't cheat either. Tell the truth: or try to. Love all men, and learn to serve. And don't be vulgar.'

Father St Albans had got the door open. He looked like a flat female with chlorosis. He was green and quite speechless. But he bowed profoundly as the decurial chamberlains came forward to escort him through the antechambers.

'*Benedicat te Omnipotens Deus*. . . . Go in peace and pray for Us,' purred the Supreme Pontiff, rubbing His left hand with His pocket handkerchief and returning to the window.

CHAPTER 15

HADRIAN was mooning about in the Treasury one morning, wondering why people will persist in using diamonds by themselves instead of as a setting for coloured gems: grieving at the excessive ugliness of most modern goldsmiths' monstrous work: turning with disgust from huge brazenly vulgar masses of bullion shaped like bad dreams of chalices, pyxes, staves, croziers, mitres, tiaras, dishes, jugs, (not beds), and basons. He bathed in the beauty of sea-blue beryls, corundrums, catseyes, and chalcedonyx. A vast rose-alexandrolith mysteriously changed from myrtle-green to purple as He turned it from sunlight to candlelight. He moved to a great round table-moonstone, transparent as water one way: brilliantly clouded with the ethereal blue of a summer-morning sky, the other. These two stones had not the blatant ostentation, the inevitable noisy obviousness of rubies, emeralds, diamonds, and pearls. They were apart, chaste, recondite, serene, and permanent. He enjoyed them. His glance again passed over the flaring cupboards. A plan began to crawl out of one of his brain-cells. He took the alexandrolith and the moonstone in His two hands; and sat down profoundly meditating, gazing into the lovely silent mystery in the stones. So He sat for half an hour, while His plan unfolded its convolutions. To Him entered Cardinal Semphill, rather ruddier than a cherry, carrying the day-before-yesterday's *Times*. 'Holiness,' he said with some animation, 'I hope I don't interrupt You. Thank God we've got a King of England at last!' He read from the paper, '"The King's Majesty has been graciously pleased to send autograph letters to all the European sovereigns and prime ministers inviting them to assemble with the President of the United States and the Japanese Emperor at Windsor Castle, in order to concert measures for terminating the present lamentable condition of affairs."'

'That explains the length of the Japanese Emperor's visit to England, and Roosevelt's arrival last week. Yes, it's very king-like. Statesmanship is all very well up to a point. Then, its force seems to fade; and the kingship's chance comes. Lucky England to have a real King!'

'I thought Your Holiness would be pleased. And now what will be the outcome?'

'Who knows?' Hadrian thought for a minute; and then mounted an imaginary pulpit, and preached like a purposeful literary man. 'First, they'll quarrel terribly for certain: because five of them are distinct entities, and the others (the nonentities) out of sheer terror will make themselves a nuisance. Secondly, when the nonentities have been reassured, or squashed, the five entities will have to reach a common ground. If they do that, We shall be very much surprised. Thirdly, supposing an agreement to have been reached, Their Majesties and the President will have to get it constitutionally confirmed. Autocracy is supposed to be dead; and the usual constitutional farce will have to be performed.'

'Why do You say "autocracy is supposed to be dead", Holy Father?'

'Oh because the euphuism "constitutional monarchy" has taken its place. The twentieth century doesn't like the word Autocrat; and pretends that the thing does not exist. But it

246

does: not in the old hereditary form: but Aristos, the Strong Man, invariably dominates. It's in the order of nature. And Demos likes him for it, only the silly thing won't say so. That's all. Semphill, you might send a marconigraph to the Earl Marshal. We require news of this Congress of Windsor at least once a day.'

The Pope returned the gems to the *beneficiato* in attendance: took *The Times* with Him and went across the basilica into the gardens. A *tramontana* bit Him to the bone; and He tightly wrapped His cloak round Him, facing the wind and the blinding glare of the sun. He briskly walked a couple of miles, until blood-warmth stung his mind into activity. By Leo IV's ruined wall, He met Cardinal Carvale engaged in a similar exercise, his delicate cheeks fervid and flushed, and his grave eyes blazing. Good priests generally retain their bloom through the full five-and-forty years of youth. Hadrian invited his companionship and conversation for the return to Vatican. They were a pair, these two medium-sized slim athletic men, the one in white and the other in vermilion, both very brilliant in the sunlight, with vivid aspect and vivid gait. They looked like men who really were alive. Their discourse was just the vigorous rather epigrammatic talk of wholesome well-bred men. As they turned into the court of the Belvedere, His Eminency said 'Oh, by the bye, Holy Father, perhaps I ought to tell you that they cannot understand at St Andrew's College why You never have been to see them'.

'But you understand,' Hadrian promptly put in.

'Well – yes:' the cardinal responded. In his candid gaze there was intuition, sympathy – and something else.

The Pontiff read it. 'When did they tell you that?'

'Yesterday.'

'Oh. Do you often go there?'

'About once a fortnight, Holiness.'

'Carvale, do you like going there?'

'– Yes, on the whole I do. The youngsters are glad to see me; and the older men' (a radiant smile disclosed his exquisite teeth as he spread an arm) '– they like vermilion to take note of them.

247

And I think it does my soul good' (he spoke gravely) 'to visit the old place. I put it off as long as I could: I would have been glad to forget the horrors. Strange to say, I forgot them after I had been there a few times.'

Hadrian's heart informed Him. He understood it all quite well. 'Carvale let us go to St Andrew's now. We can get there in time for dinner.'

The cardinal instantly looked happy; and the two continued to walk swiftly through the City, going by Tordinona, Orso, Piazza Colonna, and the Trevi Fountain. As they passed the crucifix at the corner of an alley, Hadrian bowed. His Eminency did not. 'Why don't you salute our Divine Redeemer?' the Pope inquired.

'Well of course I always raise my hat to The Lord in the tabernacle when I pass a church –'

'And you bow to Us, and even to Our handwriting: but – Listen, Carvale: "It is idolatry to talk about Holy Church and Holy Father, to bow to fallible sinful man, if you do not bend knee and lip and heart to every thought and image of God manifest as Man –" Is that explicit enough? Well; it was a Protestant parson who wrote it – one Arnold of Rugby.'

'He was right, Holiness;' said the cardinal turning back and bowing.

They walked on in silence. The Pope was doing a thing which He could not away with. It might be thought that He, a former student, was come to the college (which had expelled Him) to swagger. Of course it would be thought. Let it be thought. Then the hateful memory of every nook and corner, in which, as a student, He had been so fearfully unhappy, surged in His mind: the gaudy chapel where He had received this snub, the ugly refectory where He received that, the corridor where the rector had made coarse jests about His mundity to obsequious grinners, the library where He had found impossible dust-begrimed books, the stairs up which He had staggered in lonely weakness, the dreadful gaunt room which had been His homeless home, the altogether pestilent pretentious bestial insanity of the place – He knew and winced at every stone of it; and wrenched Himself from retrospection. They were going up the narrow Avigonesi. Fifty yards in front, a double file of students in violet cassocks and black sopranos preceded them. A little group of raga-muffins shouted *cattivi verbi* at the file; and one caught hold of the conventional sleeve of a student's soprano which was streaming in the wind. Cheap cloth rent at a tug. The raga-muffin rushed off with his spoils. But the bereft one furiously followed: retrieved his streamer; and clouted a head which howled, resuming his place in the *camerata* all unconscious that his act had been observed.

'History repeats itself:' the Pope said, and laughed.

Carvale smiled in reply 'Fancy remembering that.'

'We forget no one thing of those days,' said Hadrian: 'also, the rape of Your Eminency's streamer was effected on one of the only two days when We were permitted to accompany the others to the University. Naturally We remember that. Besides, Carvale, you were in such a blind and naked rage; and We had deemed you such a virtuous little mouse.'

'Was I?' the cardinal said. 'One had to lie low, as a rule: but sometimes the old Adam –'

'We owe Our one moment of mirth in St Andrew's College to that old Adam.'

'I had to keep in coll. for a week though, afterwards. The boy's father was waiting for me with a knife.'

'Yes. Italy had not got over her taste for steel.'

'Will she ever get over it, Holiness?'

'Of course She will – when She has killed you – or Us. Nothing but a tragedy will break a habit of centuries:' the Pope said, as He rang the bell at the door of the college.

The old porter Aurelio opened, gasped, dropped on his knees. Hadrian and Cardinal Carvale entered. A long corridor extended right and left. In front, on the right, a wide stone stair ascended: on the left, another stair descended a little way to a glass door leading to a shabby shrubbery. Some students were on the stairs: others were in the shrubbery: two or three lingered in the corridor. At the Pontiff's entrance they all inquisitively turned, gasped, and flopped. It was awfully funny. They resembled violet hares on their forms, rigid, goggle-eyed, ready-to-bound. At the turn of the landing, a sturdy black-avised Gael fled upstairs to summon the superiors. The Apostle blessed the others with a shy smile, which would be kind, and a wave of the hand which emptied space – except for an obese little spectacled sharp-nosed creature like a violet sparrow who hopped about pertly obsequious. Down came flying the superiors as a bell began to ring and intonations sounded in the upper corridors. The rector was annoyed at being taken unawares: but he presented his vice-rector, a mild anaemic of thirty with the face of a good young woman.

'We are come to accept your hospitality, Monsignore, without any ceremony,' said Hadrian. They passed into the refectory to the high table. Twenty-nine students followed: and arranged themselves in two lines down the sides of the centre, and in a third line across the end. The dean-of-students intoned the Grace: the rest responded. The Pope placed Himself on the rector's right, with the vice-rector on his own right: Carvale supported the rector on the left. Soup, boiled meat, vegetables, baked meat, cheese, apples, appeared and disappeared. The rector conceded to Hadrian the right of signalling to the reader in the pulpit: the Pope kept him reading, because He did not want to talk platitudes, and because He did want to look at the men. He ate little. The food was abundant in quantity: indelicate in quality. They offered Him the best black wine from the college vineyards: but He preferred a student's little cruet of red, a coarse wine with some body and no bouquet whatever – an unsophisticate wine such as Fabrizio Colonna might have used at the end of the fifteenth century. Most of the diners assiduously and emphatically dined, with one eye on the high table, a nose in their own plate, and the other eye in their neighbour's. Hadrian noted all their physiognomies; and began to select those with whom He would have a word, He passed the weak young thin-nosed dean at the top of the right table, the tall quiet man in black

who looked already sacerdotal, the old bald amiabili
air of conventionality who might have been a pars
He would speak to him of the others – the blubber
gorger who mopped up gravy with a crumb-wedg
gulched the sop – no: the fastidious person who ate brea
drank water and looked so hungry – yes: the florid giant with
the fiery wiry mop – no: the dark man with the cruel face of a
Redemptorist – no: the sallow lath who had the manners of an
attaché – no. On the left, colourless mediocrities – no. Across
the end, youngsters: His Holiness distinguished a black-haired
white-skinned one with wet black eyes, certainly an Erse: a
crisp-brown-haired muscular hobbledehoy with shining grey
eyes and a tanned skin, who would look well in a farmyard: a
big bloom of boyhood yellow-haired, blue-eyed, scarlet and
moist-lipped, ardent and modest. The Pope tapped on the
table. The reader, to whom no one had listened, ceased; and
came down to his dinner. A low murmur of conversation
arose. Everybody began to think furiously of what he would
do or demand if he had a chance.

'This is a great day for the college, Holy Father,' the
rector said. The Pope slightly bowed. 'Had we known
that You intended to honour us, Holy Father, a proper reception –'

'Unnecessary,' Hadrian quietly interrupted. 'We do not
wish to disturb. Our children expect to see Us; and We are
here to be seen. They all shall be able to say that they have seen
and heard and handled Us, if they please.' He spoke lowly, and
(the rector perceived) unwillingly, but very officially. They
were eating wind-fallen apples. The rector offered an enormous
silver snuff-box. Hadrian passed it to the vice-rector, who took
a pinch with blushing alacrity. It went the round of the tables;
and returned on the rector's left. Hadrian carefully noted the
takers. Some took snuff perfunctorily, some customarily,
others horribly. The fiery wiry giant stood up and ostenta-
tiously absorbed it with a cringe to the high table. Those to
whom the Pope was resolved to speak took none: the fastidious
person disdained it. The meal was finished. The students ranked

for Grace; and all proceeded to the chapel to visit The Lord in the Sacrament. After five minutes' silent prayer, they emerged on the first corridor. There seemed to be uncertainty: the men congregated on the descent expecting directions. In the ordinary course of things, some would be going to Propaganda for lectures; others, to their own rooms for study or siesta: but, for the next few moments, perhaps a dozen would enjoy horse-play in the shabby shrubbery. A group of the last collected at the stairhead, by the reception-room (with the red-velvet settees and the sham Venetian glass chandeliers), into which the rector was endeavouring to entice the Pope. But Hadrian was looking at the students, mischievously smiling at them. 'It is to be hoped that you are not going into the garden to murder a cat:' He said.

Everybody instantly became as red as a scalding-hot capsicum, some with shame, one with disgust, others from sheer fear. Church students easily are frightened, because there generally is less grace than nature in them; and you only have to disclose a knowledge of the latter for them to desire (as phrenetically as possible) the predominance of the former. This makes for uneasiness, often for hypocrisy – in both cases, for mental and corporeal effort and a sudden flux of blood to the extremities.

'To murder a cat, Holy Father?' the vice-rector ejaculated. He was responsible for discipline.

'Yes. They used to murder stray cats here, just to pass the time. We have seen it. The one thing, which We remember in connexion with your shrubbery, is a rush of ramping infuriated boys with spades and pitchforks, chasing and smashing a poor stray cat. We can see the horror now, with its broken back, and one eye hanging out on its whiskers. We can hear its dreadful heart-rending yells. Boys, don't do such things – to cats of all creatures!'

He spoke with fervence. Some savages wondered what the blazes He was driving at. There was a little silence. No one seemed to know how to break it. Then the sparrow-like student appeared with a red chair which he had taken the liberty of extracting from the reception-room; and dragged it behind the Pontiff at the stairhead. It was a welcome interruption. Hadrian sat down; and dismissed Cardinal Carvale with the superiors. He was going to have the college to Himself for half an hour. The improvised throne stood alone in the bare corridor: the students clustered up the stairs below it. Hadrian perceived the inevitable odour of hot boy. He produced a sentence wherewith to address them.

'Dear children,' he said, feeling as old as Methuselah for the moment, 'do learn to love: don't be hard, don't be cruel to any living creature.' And that was all.

He beckoned the dean who came and kneeled before Him: laid His hand on the young man's head; and blessed him. The others followed in rotation. In a secret voice, He invited each one to ask a favour. Most asked Him to pray for them and held up their beads for a blessing: some asked for the apostolic benediction in the hour of death for themselves and their relations: the fastidious person asked for nothing.

'Nothing?' the Pope whispered.

'Nothing.'

'Nothing?' (very tenderly).

'Everything, O Sanctity:' the stoic responded with a sob and a stony glare. Hadrian inquired for the number of his room; and put a similar question to the other four whom He had noted. When He had blessed all, He sent them away, and sat alone for a minute or two. Then He went to visit the big boy: who looked at Him bravely, with tearful innocent eyes. To Hadrian, it was wonderful to see this great virile virgin of nineteen. He elicited a not unusual and simple tale: a little Gaelic farm, always Catholic through all persecutions, the third of eight sons, the Vocation at twelve years of age, the mother wanted to confess to her own son. It was idyllic. It would come exquisitely in the objective bucolic manner of Theocritos. The long shapely limbs trembled before Him; the grand shoulders bowed. He gave the boy His Own white sash as a present for his mother: bade him be a good priest; and left him wallowing in happiness. Hadrian stopped in the corridor, disappointed because the lad came from a farm: He had placed him beside the sea, and had conceived a mental image of him, bare-legged, in a blue guernsey, at the rudder of a fishing-smack. But the next, the muscular hobbledehoy, really did come from a farm: his skin had the unmistakable tan of the sun on a wheat-field: and his front was bovine. So was his manner. He was so frightened by the importance of his visitor that he spoke with surliness, and in the voice of a child of thirteen. Hadrian was astonished at the discrepancy between the voice and the speaker: He made him less uncomfortable by substituting an official manner for His friendly one (which the hobbledehoy could not understand) asking his name and the ordinary questions about his status and addressing him as Mr Macleod. It was a magnificent animal, incapable of the finer sentimental emotions, likely to conceal fat in a cassock (or in corduroy, if on a farm) before the age of thirty. Privately the Pope wondered what in the world was the sign of this one's Vocation. He Himself could perceive none: but then He was inexperienced; and the youth was secretive. Hadrian tried to draw him out. Was he happy? Oh yes. Did he want anything? Oh no. To what diocese did he belong? To Devana. When did he expect the priesthood? A look of wild terror came into the grey eyes. Hadrian perceived a clue; and pressed on, repeating his inquiry. 'I never will be,' the creature shrilled.

'Why not?'

No answer: but a rush to the bedside and a face hidden. Hadrian took him by the shoulders, and made an act of will. 'Why not?'

'I cannot:' and then the fountains of the great deep were discovered. His veneer of English peeled off: he spoke with the sibilate dental, the clipped deliberation of the Gael. No one ever had told him. He did not know till a month ago. No one knew. He had not mentioned it to his confessor, because it was not a sin. He read of it in Lehmkuhl and Togni. He would be obliged to go back and work on his uncle's farm where he had been brought up. They belonged to the Free Kirk there. He was an orphan. It was his uncle by marriage. Hadrian looked steadily into his eyes: 'Is this the truth, as though you were speaking before kings?'

'It wass the truth ass though she wass speaking pefore kings,' the response came in the strongest form of asseveration known to a Gael, deliberately selected and offered by Him Who knew so little, and so much of so many little things. Hadrian comforted him; and bade him pack his bag. His secret was safe. Vatican was the place for him, until some sort of useful happy life could be planned for him.

The Pope very slowly went up the last two flights of stairs to the top corridor. No man can come into a human tragedy without some vibrance of sentiment; and Hadrian's senses, keen by nature, were intensified by art. He entered the room of the black-haired Erse, who most certainly had kissed the blarney stone. Och! Blessins on the Howly Forther's blessid head and might the howly saints receive Him into glory. The Pope wrote a blessing in a garish birthday book; and got out of the room as quickly as possible. That such a lovely bit of colour and litheness should be so abject on the floor! His Holiness shut down the lid on memory; and knocked at another door.

'Come.'

He entered a large bare square room with a window which displayed the City from the Quirinale to St Peter's. He noted the bed, the chest of drawers whose top was arranged as a dressing-table, the writing-table, bookcase, and two chairs. A bath stood under the bed; and there were two large tin cans of water against the wall. The fastidious inmate offered a chair; and remained standing in the Presence. Hadrian signed to him to be seated also.

'Dear son, you are one of the unhappy ones. Will you tell Us your grief?'

'Sanctity, I have not complained.'

'No. But, complain.'

'I will not complain.' The Pope liked him for that; and for an air of distinction which was not breeding. Dialectic should be tried.

'How old are you?'

'Twenty-nine.'

'In which month were you born?'

'In July.'

'In England?'

'In England.' A rapid horoscopical calculation let Hadrian know the lines on which to proceed.

'You find your environment disagreeable?'

'All environments are more or less disagreeable to me.'

'All which you have tried up to the present, perhaps. Perhaps the future may be more propitious.'

'Sanctity, I earnestly hope so: but I do not expect it.'

'Why not?'

'I do not know.'

'Don't you find that your circumstances influence your conduct? Don't you find that they prevent you from doing yourself justice?'

'Always.'

'In this college, you have found no kindred spirit?'

'That may be my fault.'

'More likely your misfortune – and misfortunes are not faults, no matter what fools say. Note that. Note also that misfortunes may be overcome – But, they do not understand you here?'

'No.'

'They mock you? – They do. Why did they mock you to-day?'

'They did not mock me today.'

'Yesterday?'

'Because I carry those two cans full of water up two hundred and two steps every day.'

'Do you mean to say that there are no baths in this college yet?'

'We may have footbaths once a week, if we apply to the infirmarian. There is nothing else. And I like to tub decently.'

'No doubt they say that you must be a very unclean person to need so much washing?'

'Sanctity, You are quoting the rector.'

The Pope abruptly laughed. 'Have they ever put a snake – a snake – in your water-cans?'

'No they have not done that.'

'They did in Ours.'

The distance between the two now became considerably lessened. The fastidious person began to feel more at ease. His fastidy evidently was only a *chevaux de frise* for the discomfiture of intruders; and this delicate tender inquisitor was no intruder, but a very welcome – Apostle.

The Pope continued. 'Isn't it very absurd?'

'It is very absurd. Also, it is very disconcerting.'

'Of course you try not to let it disconcert you?'

'I try: but I fail. My heart always is on my sleeve; and the daws peck it. At present, I am trying to contain myself and to use myself in isolation.'

'That they call "sulkiness"?'

'Yes.'

'How much longer must you remain here?'

'Perhaps one year: perhaps two.'

'Can you persecute, can you hold out so long?'

'Oh, I will hold out. Nothing shall deter me. Sanctity, it is not that which makes me afraid.'

'Dear son, what makes you afraid?'

'The afterwards. These people are to be my superiors or equals – colleagues for life. I am not afraid of poverty or wickedness among the people to whom I am to minister: but, my brother priests – I shall be at the orders of some of these people, my rectors, my diocesans even. That makes me afraid.'

'Did you not know what kind of people –'

'Yes, I did know: but I did not realize it till I came here.'

'Yet you choose to persevere?'

'Sanctity, I must. I am called.'

'You are sure of that?'

'It is the only thing in all the world of which I am sure.'

'Do you always live on bread and water?'

'Yes.'

'Why?'

'I think the food beastly. I have been into the kitchen; and I have seen – things. I am afraid to eat anything except boiled eggs. They cannot deposit – sputum inside the shells of boiled eggs. But the servants complained of the extra trouble in boiling eggs especially for me. The bread is not made in the college. In order not to be singular, I eat and drink what I can eat and drink of that which is set before me; and I am deemed more singular than ever.'

'Have you said this to the rector?'

'Yes.'

'Do you like bread and water?'

'I think them both exceedingly nasty.'

'Does it affect your health?'

'Not in the least. It makes my head ache. But I am as strong as a panther.'

'Why "panther"?'

'I really don't know. It seemed to be the just word.'

'And you believe that you are able to go on?'

'I intend to go on.'

'You know that this college is not the place for you?'

'I suppose not: but my diocesan sent me here; and I intend to serve my sentence.'

'Dear son, what is your ambition?'

'Priesthood.'

'With a small patrimony, you would be on a more satis-factory footing here; and afterward you need not take the mission oath. The mere fact of the possession of a patrimony would purchase courtesy and consideration for you during your college life: and would give you an opportunity of culti-vating your individuality independently when you reach the priesthood.'

'Oh, yes. But I am a church student.'

'So were We.'

'And Your Sanctity persevered?'

'Yes.'

'So will I.'

'What is your name?'

'William Jameson.'

Hadrian took a sheet of paper and wrote the apostolic benediction to William Jameson. 'You will like to have this? Persevere, dear son; and pray for Us as for your brother-in-the-
Lord. And – do you know Cardinal Sterling? Well: come to
Vatican whenever you please and make his acquaintance. He
will expect you. Good-bye. God bless you.'

The Pope went down to the bald old amiability, who was
correct and mild enough in expressing a profound sense of the
honour. Hadrian spoke to him of himself; and found that a
public school, university, and Anglican parsonage had dulled
what capability of emotion he ever had had, or had taught him
the rare art of self-concealment. He was a capital specimen of
the ordinary man, stinted, limited: one whose instinct prevented him from asserting an individuality. But he was a
gentleman; and a Christian of a kind, actuated by the best
intentions, paralysed by the worst conventions.

'We wish to speak to you of Jameson:' at length the Apostle
said.

'Ah, poor fellow!'

'Now why do you say that, Mr Guthrie?'

'Well, Holiness, I'm afraid he's in a most uncomfortable
position. I'm sure this is not the place for him. You see he
doesn't get on with the men.'

'Does he quarrel with them?'

'Oh, dear me no! But he avoids them.'

'Perhaps he has his reasons.'

'Well, I'm afraid he has. But then it doesn't do to show them.
I often tell him so – try to chaff him into a more come-at-able
frame of mind, you know, Holy Father.'

'That hardly would be the way.'

'No I'm afraid it wasn't. He's so very sensitive, you see. Why
he actually got quite angry with me.'

'What did he say?'

'Well, he said that he really did think I ought to have known
better.'

'And what did you say then?'

'Oh I called him a – but I couldn't possibly tell You what I called him, Holy Father.'

'Why not?'

'Well really it was too dreadful. I've been regretting it ever since.'

'What did you call him?'

'Oh it's quite impossible that I should repeat it to You, Holy Father. I should never be able to hold up my head again.'

'Nonsense, Mr Guthrie. We desire to know it.'

'I'm sure I don't know what You'll think of me, Holy Father: but the fact is I went so far as to call him a – no, really I cannot – well – I'm sure I can't think what possessed me to use such an opprobrious term but I was excessively annoyed You see at the moment and the word slipped out before I was quite conscious of what I was saying –'

'What did you call him?'

'Well really if You must have it, Holy Father, I called him a Goose!'

'Oh. . . . And what did he do to you?'

'Burst into a roar of laughter and shut his door in my face.'

'Did you feel pained?'

'Well perhaps just a little at the time: but not when I came to think it over. You see I really can't help feeling sorry for him.'

'Why?'

'Well because really he must be very unhappy, You know, Holy Father.'

'In your opinion, Mr Guthrie, he himself is the cause of his own unhappiness?'

'Quite so, Holy Father. You see he doesn't seem to be able to rub along with the other men. He can't come down to their level so to speak. He keeps himself too much to himself: won't or can't conciliate the least little bit. Of course they all think it's pride on his part; and they pay him out with practical jokes of a rather doubtful kind I'm afraid. He's good and kind and clever and all that sort of thing; but he hasn't the slightest idea of making himself popular as a church student should be among church students. You see, he's what I may call (if I may be quite frank about him) such a Beastly Fool. The rector doesn't like it I'm sure.'

'Then perhaps it would be more accurate to say that the fault is not so much in the man as in his environment?'

'That's what I've always said, Holy Father. His present environment is quite unsuitable for a man of that kind. He must find it extremely unpleasant.'

'Mr Guthrie, won't you try to make it more pleasant for him? Bear with him: defend him: don't seem to form a party with him against the others: but don't give the others the idea that you approve of their attitude to him. Will you do as much as that?'

'I'm sure I'll do anything in my power, Holy Father.'

'That at least is in your power – God bless you.'

The Pope went on to the reception-room to fetch Cardinal Carvale. Not to neglect the superiors (although He was very tired) He allowed them to show Him rather dubious and very ugly treasures; and tolerated half an hour of vapid conversation. They thought Him so nice. He was bored to death. After conferring the usual favours, He obtained a whole playday for the college: notified the rector that He was carrying off a student: arranged for Mr Jameson to visit Cardinal Sterling; and took His departure. He put His acquisition into a victoria, and bade him drive to the obelisk in St Peter's Square.

'Dreadful place!' Hadrian ejaculated to Carvale as they turned down Tritone. 'Do you think you could make it decent if you were rector?'

'I would try, Holiness.'

'Well: We do not see how We can make you rector, because of Monsignor What's-his-name. But you might do something as protector –'

'Gentilotto is protector, Holiness. St Andrew's is subject to the Cardinal-Prefect of Propaganda.'

'Only for the present, Carvale. You will find that dear old Gentilotto is quite willing. And you yourself are a Celt. Yes, that's right! A Celtic college should have a Celtic protector.

Carvale, you are Protector of St Andrew's College from this moment, and you shall have your breve directly We get back to Vatican. Now, first of all, go to Oxford and ask Dr Strong to put you up for a week in coll.: and keep your eyes open. Do that with your first spare fortnight. Then come back and turn your rivers Peneios and Alpheios through that Aygeian stable. Give them baths and sanity, for goodness' sake; and try to get them into cleanly habits. You might make that shrubbery into a gymnasium and swimming-bath with a lovely terrace on the top. And, O Carvale, do make friends with them, and see what you can do to take that horrible secretive suppressed look out of their young eyes. Understand?'

'I think so, Holiness.'

'We give you a year. If We live as long as this day twelve-month, We will go again to mark your progress. Remember, you have a free hand. Now here's something else. Tell Sterling that a – but no – We Ourself will tell him.'

At the obelisk they picked up Hamish Macleod. Hadrian marched him straight up to the quarters of the gentlemen of the secret chamber. Sir John and Sir Iulo, stripped to the buff, were punching a bag.

'John,' said the Pope, 'Mr Macleod will be your guest for the present. Get him a room near your own and make him comfortable.' He drew the young man outside while Sir Iulo was lavishing his lovely English on the visitor. 'And John, reorganize his wardrobe on the scale of your own; and teach him your business.'

To Cardinal Sterling, who came to the secret chamber, Hadrian explained the case of William Jameson.

'You have your opportunity,' He said to His Eminency.

'And one will not repeat one's previous mistake, Holiness,' was the remarkable and thankful reply.

'No, for mercy's sake, don't. And now listen. The Treasurer will pay you on this order the sum of £10,500. You will invest it in the Bank of England on these terms. The transaction is to be secret. The interest on £10,000 is to be paid quarterly to William Jameson as long as he lives. On his death the capital is to revert to the Treasurer for the time being of the Apostolic See. Instruct the bank instantly to send £500 and the vouchers to Jameson, with a statement that it is his patrimony; and to give him no further information.'

Then Hadrian shut up Himself and rested, smoking and reading the *Reviews of Unwritten Books* in some old numbers of the *Monthly·Review*. One of them caused Him to think. It was called *Thucydides' Report of Pericles' Oration at the Incoronation of King Edward the Seventh.*

CHAPTER 16

JERRY SANT gnawed his rag of a moustache for a fortnight or so, till it was dripping and jagged. He began to have a notion that Mrs Crowe would like to have him elsewhere. That did not disturb him: for he knew that he always could compel her services, when he wanted them, by means of a pull on the purse-strings. The mildly elegant exiguity of the circle in which she moved, had no attraction for him. There were not many sax-pences there; and he felt out of his depth in a company which he could not lead by the nose. 'In the kingdom of the blind, the one-eyed man is king.' He knew himself to be 'a one-eyed man'; and, in the kingdom of the Liblabs, he naturally had been one of the kings. Here, among the English and Celtic Catholics in Rome, he was no more than tolerated – and awfully worried by people who offered him tracts, of which, for the life of him, he could make neither head nor tail. Further he really seriously was annoyed that the Pope had not accepted his handsome offer – had not even answered his letter. He thought it most rude. It is a fatal and futile thing to leave letters unanswered, especially impertinent letters. Silence does not 'choke off'; in ninety-nine cases out of a hundred, it breeds bile which is bound to be spurted sooner or later. It is a poor kind of a man who cannot indite a letter which is a guillotine, a closure about which there can be no possible mistake. By this means, uncertainty and its vile consequences are prevented.

Hadrian perfectly knew how to deliver Himself. His faculty for finding out other people's thumbscrews had provided Him with blasting powder, if He had desired to be dynamic; and He possessed Bishop Bagshawe's celebrated three-line formula, which never has been known to fail of throttling an importunate correspondent. But He no more could have touched Sant, even with a letter, than He could have touched tripe with tongs. His feeling for the man was ultimate antipathy, which led Him to commit the common error of ignoring what ought to have been annihilated. Hence Sant's sense of spleen. Finally Jerry had the Liblabs to keep quiet. Those extraordinary persons were asking for something definite in the shape of news; and he had no news at all to give them. That was the worst of it. Soon, some treachery or other would be hatched against him behind his back, in the most approved Liblab manner: he would be asked for explanations, for a statement of accounts: he would be hauled over the coals, and so on: oh he obviously could not let it come to that. He must make a fresh effort. The time had come for playing his next card. And for three days he sat at the Hotel Nike, writing press copy.

It was the Cardinal-Secretary-of-State who did himself the pleasure of acquainting the Holy Father with the result of Jerry Sant's manoeuvre. His Eminency, on the whole, never had had a more congenial duty to perform in all his life. He swirled into the Presence one evening at dusk when Hadrian was waiting for the lamps, sitting by the undraped window watching the dark figures passing over the grey square and the specks of yellow light springing in the houses of the Borgo. Ragna brought a newspaper which he thrust into the Pope's hands.

'See what a scoundrel you are!' he truculently snarled. 'Fly! All is discovered! The *Catholic Hour* is exposing you finely!'

'Oh,' said Hadrian, unimpassionately turning from the window, and speaking with extreme frigidity.

'Light some candles, please.' He took the paper: put up His left hand to shade His eyes; and looked at the sheet. As He read His pontifical name and His secular name, His blood began to tingle: for He still loathed publicity. As He read on, His blood began to boil. It was a frightful tale which He was reading – frightful, because He saw at a glance that it was quite unanswerable. It was unanswerable because there are some things of which the merest whisper suffices to destroy – whose effect does not depend on truthfulness. It was unanswerable because it was anonymous. It was unanswerable because He never could bring Himself to condescend. . . . Who could have attacked Him with such malignant ingenuity? The names of half a dozen filthy hounds occurred to Him in as many seconds: but He was not able to recognize any particular paw. He read on. He was conscious that His face was aflame with indignation: but it was in shadow. Coming to a clear chronological error, He chuckled. That taught Him that His voice was under control; and He remembered that the invidious eyes of Ragna were upon Him. From time to time thereafter, He produced a short contemptuous word or laugh by way of commentary as He came to excessive absurdities; and, so, gradually He possessed Himself again. Thus, He skimmed the article. At the end He looked up at the cardinal. 'Yes,' He said, 'We appear to be a very disreputable character. Now We will go through the thing again, and note the actual errors of fact.' He returned to the top of the first column: and began to read more analytically. In progress, He counted aloud 'One, two' – up to 'thirty-three absolute and deliberate lies, exclusive of gratuitous or ignorant mispresentations of fact, in a column and three quarters of print – Well?' He inquired, with a full straight gaze at the attendant cardinal.

'What are You going to do now?'

'We will ponder the matter which Your Eminency has submitted to Us; and at a convenient time We will declare Our pleasure. That paper may be left with Us. Your Eminency has permission to retire.'

Ragna strode towards the door. At the threshold, he turned and bayed, 'Abdicate!'

'No: We will not abdicate,' said Hadrian.

The Secretary-of-State rushed away. As he went swishing, snarling at all and sundry, through the antechamber where the gentlemen were in waiting, Sir Iulo suddenly shot out his arms straight and rectangularly level with his shoulders, swung up a stiff right leg in a verisimilar fashion, rigidly sank on his left toes till he sat on his left heel, recovered his first position with a jerk, changed legs and repeated the performance with the right. It was done in a second of time; and his white teeth glittered in a grin as his muscles relaxed. There are few more nerve-shattering spectacles than this of a lithe and graceful young gentleman in scarlet behaving, without any warning whatever, exactly like a monkey on a stick, manifesting the same startling descendent and ascendent angularity, the same imperturbable inevitable intolerable agility. Cardinal Ragna denounced him as a devil where he stood; and swirled away in a vermilion billow of watered silk.

As soon as He was left alone, Hadrian made the very firmest possible act of will determining neither to bend nor to break. This done, He ate His supper with careful deliberation; sent away the tray; and ordered a large potful of black coffee. Then He locked all doors and allowed Himself a period of disintegration preparatory to redintegration, a period of slackness preparatory to intensification. Now He severely suffered. He read the article on the *Strange Career of the Pope* again and again, till His head swam with the horror of it. This was the worst thing which ever had happened to Him. His previous experience of newspaper libels was as nothing in comparison. All through the bitter bitter years of His struggle for life, He had known Himself for a fighter. As a fighter, He had expected blows in return for those which He gave. And, when all was said and done, his fighting had not been to Him a source of unmitigated pain. For one thing, He had had pleasure in knowing that He scrupulously fought unscrupulous foes, that He fought a losing battle, that he fought a million times His weight, that He fought bare-handed against armed champions all the time. That knowledge it was – the knowledge that He had contended (not as a hero but) as heroes have contended – which alone had upheld him. And now – But this – It depicted Him as simply contemptible. Inspection of the image of Himself, which the *Catholic Hour*

266

with such ferocious flocculence delineated, brought Him to the verge of physical nausea. But it was not true, real. It was not Himself. No, no. It was an atrocious caricature. Oh yes, it was an atrocious caricature. Everybody would know it for that – Would they? How many had known the previous libels for libels? How many had dared to proclaim the previous libels for libels? One – out of hundreds – Oh how beastly, how beastly! He read the thing again; and dashed the paper to the ground. If it only had made Him look wicked – or even ridiculous! But no. He categorically was damned, as despicable, low, vulgar, abject, mean, everything which merited contempt. Only a strenuous effort kept Him from shrieking in hysteria, 'God, God, am I really like that?' He moaned aloud, with His palms stretched upward and outward and His eyes intent in agony. He lost faith in Himself. Perhaps He was such an one. Perhaps His imagination after all had been deluding Him, and He really was an indefensible creature. It was possible. 'Oh, have I ever been such a dirty – beast. Have I?' He moaned again. And then all the being of Him suffused – and whirled – and outraged Nature took Him in hand. The blow to His self-respect, the shattering onslaught on His sensibilities, were more than even His valid virile body could bear. He lay back in His low chair; and swooned into oblivion.

After the lapse of an hour, He began to revive. It would appear that He instantly knew what had happened: for He staggered to the open window that the cold night air might reinvigorate him. Full consciousness by slow degrees returned; and, with it, some measure of serenity. He took up the argument at the point where He had left it.

No: He was not like that. Before Jesus in the pyx on His breast, He was not like that. So He gradually calmed Himself. He had done desperate deeds and foolish deeds: but never ignoble deeds: stay – once – that had nothing whatever to do with the present matter: nor was that one ignoble deed ignoble in the esteem of anyone except Himself: it was 'smart' or 'clever' in mundane phraseology: no one had been injured by it: it had been atoned for: but, according to the ideal code which

He had made for His Own guidance, it was ignoble. However it was not known, except to Himself, and God, and His angel guardian: it was not even known to His confessor, for it was not even a venial sin. Well then – No. No. He had not merited the gibbet of the world's contempt.

Who had gibbeted Him?

He very carefully read the paper again. Who in the world could have collected such a mass of apparently convincing evidence? He was beginning to study the question from His usual stand-point of personal unconcern. His own written words were cited in proof of the allegations here made against Him. He knew them for His own written words. Who in the world so ingeniously could have distorted their signification: so skilfully could have mispresented Him? At some time in His life, He (perhaps inadvertently) must have trodden upon some human worm; and the worm now had turned and stung Him. He sought for a sign, a trace; and found it – Of course; and the motive simultaneously leaped to light. It was payment of a grudge, owed to Him by a detected letter-thief, a professional infidel, whom He had scathed with barbed sarcasms about ten years ago. There was something more than that. Again He studied the paper for corroboration. How came the *Catholic Hour*, of all papers, to publish a denunciation of Him? He noted that the *Catholic Hour* pretended its denunciation as being copied from the *Devana Radical*. And the letter-thief resided at Devana; and engaged in job journalism: also, he had access to more than much of the information here misused. Not to all of it though. Here and there in the article, Hadrian's literary faculty enabled Him to perceive a change of touch. Here and there were technical opinions and technical modes of expression which could not have emanated from that one. Who was responsible for these? The Pope, of all men on God's fair earth, was qualified to recognize 'the fine Roman hand' – the fine Roman hand at least of one of His Own contemporaries at St Andrew's College, whom He had afflicted with a ridiculous label, a harmless jibe simply composed of the man's own initial and surname joined together: the fine Roman hand of a pseudonymous editor with whom He had refused to have dealings. Yes, and there too was the obscene touch of the female. *'Spretae injuri formae'* over again!

At last, He summed up:

Material Cause. Information, possessed (the gods knew by what means) by the detected letter-thief and the female. Opinions, collected from (perhaps proffered by) Spite desirous of stabbing Scorn in the back.

Formal Cause. Calumny, that is to say Slander which is False.

Efficient Cause. The pontifical treatment of the representatives of the Liblab Fellowship now in the City.

Final Cause. (*a*) Intimidation. (*b*) Revenge.

It was as clear as daylight.

Hadrian sat back in his chair; and blamed – Himself. His mind went straight to the root of the matter. It was His Own fault. He had not loved His neighbour. He had been hard, unkind, austere. He had cultivated His natural faculty for rubbing salt upon His neighbour's rawest and most secret sore – salt in the shape of biting words, satire, sarcasm, corrosive irony, labels which adhered. But, He had done this when fighting, stark naked, and alone, against long odds! No matter. It was part of the struggle for life! No matter. But He would have been killed – not metaphorically but – literally killed, long ago – How did He know that? – Like all men, He had been trusting in Himself, not in the Maker of the Stars. As a matter of fact, He did not and could not know – In His Own eyes, as His Own judge, each point of His defence failed. He pleaded guilty. He had not loved His neighbour.

His soul fled up to the divinities who severely sit upon the awful bench: but there was no solace to be obtained from them. He took the beautiful crucifix from His neck: the pyx from His breast: laid them on the table; and knelt before the Sovereign of the seraphim. He made an act of contrition. He acknowledged His sin: acknowledged that He had merited condign punishment. He very humbly thanked God for giving Him His punishment in this world. 'O that my lot might lead

269

me in the path of holy innocence of thought and deed, the path which august laws ordain, laws which had their birth in the highest heaven, neither did the race of mortal man beget them, nor shall oblivion ever put them to sleep: for the Power of God is mighty in them,'

He prayed, in the verses of Sophocles.

He sent for His confessor.

It had been a dreadful experience. He was conscious of having been shaken seriously. He felt quite old. His youth and strength, His nerve, seemed to have been torn out of Him. The world seemed to have slipped away from under Him. Yes – the world – How should He meet the world? – With equanimity and fortitude. What should He say and do? Nothing. . . . Nothing. . . .

His confessor arrived; and He confessed that, since His last confession on the previous day, He had been guilty of the sin of anger. Also, He renewed His sorrow for a sin of His past life. He had not loved His neighbour. The bare-footed friar absolved Him; and commanded Him to say, for His penance, one mass for the present and eternal welfare of all whom He had offended.

Hadrian laid open the *Catholic Hour* on a table where it was not concealed and whence it would not be removed: tried to turn away His thought and to leave the incident behind Him. That the effect of it would become manifest, that the memory of it would recur, He knew: but neither memory nor effect ever should delay His progress. He spent the rest of the evening in meditation on the future. At bed time He did not go down to St Peter's: but said His prayers by His bedside with childlike simplicity and feebleness. And care-dispersing sleep lit on His eyelids, unwakeful, very pleasant, the nearest like death.

CHAPTER 17

IN the morning, Hadrian summoned Gentilotto, Sterling, Whitehead, Carvale, della Volta, Semphill, Van Kristen. He fancied that the gentlemen-of-the-chamber curiously eyed

Him. That was so. He guessed in a moment that now He always would have to stand the fire of curious eyes, to overhear the ostentatious whispers of people who wished to be known for nasty thinkers – of people who wished to see the Roman Pontiff wriggling on a white-hot gridiron. Very well. He would stand fire: perhaps, up to a certain point, He would answer questions of general (but not of particular) interest. But there should be no merely human contortuplications.

Their Eminencies came into the throne-room, where the Pope was sitting rather rigidly in a hieratic attitude, His hands on the arms of the chair, His feet and knees closed, His back straight and His head erect. He was a shade more pallid than usual. They each paid their respects in a different manner. Gentilotto's mild pure visage expressed compassion mingled with a sense of personal injury. The assailants of the Pope also had wounded him. Sterling's dark face was locked up with the look of one who is determined to be righteous under all circumstances, while willing to forward to the proper quarter a recommendation to mercy on behalf of the prisoner at the bar. The Cardinal of St George-of-the-Golden-Sail contained himself in personal innocence which precluded him from prancing to believe in the guilt of others. Della Volta's pose indicated ordinary but sympathetic curiosity. Carvale was white, and Semphill was red, with impatient indignation. Like Gentilotto, they both were hurt by the attack on their superior: but they were up in arms. Van Kristen was very very sad. His great melancholy eyes swam in a mist of commiseration; and Hadrian noted that his lips rested just an instant longer than usual on the cold pontifical hand.

Chamberlains placed stools for the cardinals and retired. The Pope began to speak in His usual swift and concise tone. By way of emphasizing the essential difference between the Church (a purely missionary association) and the World, He had determined to disperse the Vatican treasures. This was not at all what Their Eminencies had expected to hear; and they were rather taken aback. Hadrian gave them a moment; and then went on.

'Does anyone know whether dear old Cabelli is Minister of Public instruction now?'

Della Volta gave a negative.

'So much the better, because he will be at leisure to do Us a favour. And now' (His Holiness directly addressed the last speaker) 'We place this matter in Your Eminency's hands. You shall have a breve of commission; and this is what you will do. First, you will collect Cabelli and Longhi and Manciani as your board of advisers. Secondly, with their assistance, you will procure the services of the chief experts of the world – say five. Thirdly, you will cause these five experts to estimate the maximum and minimum values of each separate piece in the treasury. This list of values you will submit Us. Fourthly, you will have the pieces arranged (and the arrangement must be indicated on the list of values) in three divisions, the historic, the artistic, and the merely valuable on account of weight or character. Fifthly, you instantly will publish everywhere a note to the effect that the sale at fixed prices of these things will take place here from the first to the sixth of January following.'

He paused: for He saw that people wanted to speak. He conceded the word to Gentilotto.

'Has Your Holiness considered,' said the Red Pope, 'that most of the treasures are consecrated to the service of the Church?'

'Yes. We also have considered that the Church exists for the service of God in His creatures: that She does not serve either by keeping pretty and costly things shut up in cupboards: that the Church which set these things apart by consecration, also can restore them to usefulness by desecration. Technically things consecrate can become desecrate by tapping them with intent to desecrate: We soon will descend to the treasury; and will tap all the sacred things into gems and bullion.'

'That can be done;' the Cardinal-Prefect of Propaganda said. His heart pulled him one way: heredity and ecclesiastical prejudice, the other.

'There is one thing which I think it right to mention,' put in della Volta: 'the present officials of the treasury, and the buildings – what will become of them?'

'The officials will continue to enjoy the stipends of their benefices. They will have other and more useful occupation than the furbishing of plate provided for them. As for the building – when the cupboards are empty they will be removed; and, the treasury being no longer there, the building will remain the sacristy.'

'I should like to get a word in edgeways if I may;' said Semphill. 'Doesn't Your Holiness think that the Italian Government will interfere? Isn't there some law which prevents works of art from going out of Italy?'

'We should like to see the Italian Government interfere with Us:' Hadrian responded with a strong and illuminating smile. 'The Italian Government is neither a Fenian nor a fool.'

'No, but – ' the cardinal pursued.

'Your Eminency need fear no opposition from that quarter.'

'Is nothing to be exempted from this sale?' Sterling thoughtfully asked.

'There will be some exemptions.' The Pope turned to Cardinal della Volta. 'You will reserve one silver-gilt chalice and paten for every priest in the palace: one silver-gilt pyx for every tabernacle; and one plain set of pontifical regalia which We will indicate to you. Nothing more. Hereafter, the court can use ornaments which are the private possessions of individuals.'

'I must say that I think the pontifical regalia deserves a better fate than conversion into bullion and gems,' said Gentilotto.

'Nonsense,' the Pope sharply retorted. 'The pontifical regalia is not sacrosanct like the Carthaginian zaïmph.' The frayed edges of His nerves showed themselves.

'I concede it,' the cardinal admitted.

Hadrian rose. 'We have summoned the Sacred Consistory for tomorrow morning, when We will issue Our decrees in this matter.'

Semphill no longer could contain himself. He exploded with 'Of course Your Holiness has seen the *Catholic Hour*?'

Hadrian thought that He particularly liked this cardinal today for some reason. Yes of course, His Eminency looked better during Advent. The ordinary vermilion made his chubby rubicundity appear too blue. That was the reason.

'Oh, yes:' the Pontiff replied.

'Well really I never read anything more abominable in my life!'

'Nor did We.'

All the cardinalitial eyes were directed toward the Pope. He remained standing on the step of the throne; and seemed to be changing into alabaster. Semphill lashing himself to fury, continued 'I should like to think that something will be done about it.'

'So should We.'

Semphill prolapsed and stared. 'But surely Your Holiness will do something?'

'No.'

'What? Not answer them?'

'No.'

'One would have thought that there would be some canonical means of bringing the *Catholic Hour* to book for aspersions against the Pope:' Sterling said.

'There is the bull *Exsecrabilis* of Pius II. But it is not the Pope Who is aspersed. It is George Arthur Rose:' imperturbably said Hadrian.

'That's drawing it rather fine:' Whitehead said, looking up for the first time.

'Fine enough:' Carvale put in, with appreciation of the distinction.

'Excommunicate the editor, printer, and publisher, by name, I say!' ejaculated Semphill.

Sterling went on, 'One finds it difficult to understand what can have persuaded the *Catholic Hour* to insert – '

Hadrian interrupted, 'Just ask yourself this. Is it likely that an Erse periodical – and, when We say an Erse periodical, We mean a clerical periodical, (for, according to McCarthy, the Erse clergy hold the Catholic press in the hollow of their hand) – is it likely that an Erse periodical, which has the infernal cheek to dub itself the 'Organ of Catholic Opinion', and which once called Cardinal Semphill a – what was it, Eminency? – ah yes, "a scented masher" – could be expected to forego an opportunity of increasing its circulation at the expense of the Vicar of Christ?'

'Oh very good indeed!' exclaimed Semphill, with a hearty reminiscent shout of laughter.

'But, Holiness,' Sterling gravely continued, 'one knows that the statements are not true. One knows that the article misrepresents You entirely.'

'They are not wholly true; and the article entirely misrepresents Us.'

'One would recommend that that should be made known.'

'It is known. Hundreds know it. They are not prevented from saying what they know – If they dare.' Hadrian came down from the throne. A grey shadow hardened the sharpness of the face. The brows and the eyes were drawn into parallels, the latter half-shut; and the thin lips were straight and cruel. Their Eminencies mindfully retired. Van Kristen lingered till the others were gone. 'Holy Father,' he said, 'I guess that You're feeling it about as bad as the next man?'

Hadrian pressed the slim brown hand, on which the cardinalitial sapphire looked so absolutely lovely.

'Perhaps, Percy:' He said.

'I think I won't go back to Dynam House this fall,' the cardinal continued. 'They can do without me, Holiness. If I'm any good to You here, I'm no quitter so long as my eyes remain black.'

'You always are good and useful to Us, Venerable Father,' the Pope very stiffly said, as He quickly passed through the curtains of the secret antechamber.

Now the world had something to talk about beside the chances of universal war, and the inferiority of the present Pope. When the dispersal of the treasures of the Vatican was announced in the Sacred Consistory, five cardinals walked straight out to swear, four burst into tears, eight spoke their minds quite freely and (in the case of two) at the top of their voices, and the rest were dumb. Ragna, Berstein, Cacciatore, and Vivole came to the conclusion that Hadrian's new move was a pontifical red herring intended to divert the scent from the newspaper calumnies against George Arthur Rose. They went about trying to make people see the thing from their point of view. Celts and Catholics throughout the world set up howls; and compared Hadrian to Honorius to the advantage of the latter. 'From a Catholic point of view,' wrote one clerical gentleman (who in youth, as an attaché in Paris, had been known as La Belle Anthropophage), 'it is impossible to blame Hadrian too severely.' He was ruined, they said with unctuous rectitude; and He was going to sell the Vatican Treasures in order to provide an iniquitous provision for a disreputable and private old age. Naturally they judged by their own standard. All Catholics do.

The Liblab Fellowship congratulated itself on the possession of such a Fellowshipper as Sant. His diplomacy was thought cute. Socialists hourly expected to hear that the Scarlet Unutterable, in sheer despair, had asked to be allowed to seek a refuge in their ranks. Jerry Sant sat up all night at the Hotel Nike, in case the Pope should be moved to escape from a throne which had been made too hot for Him. In the event of such an escape, of course 'His Most Reverent Lordship' would come and try and make peace with them as He had put to so much unnecessary trouble and expense. So the Liblab cut and dried his plans. He would administer the oaths to God's Vicegerent: take His entrance fee and annual subscription in advance; and admit Him as a Fellowshipper. Then, as His senior comrade, He would order Him back to Vatican to use His popery for carrying out the schemes of Labour against Capital. Incidentally he would take the opportunity of transferring some of the pontifical capital from a man as didn't to a man as did deserve it. However, Jerry gave himself two sleepless nights for nothing. He would have been better, though perhaps not quite so comely, in bed. And then, on the third day, Mrs Crowe rushed in, displaying a tantrum which was a blend of joy and hate and fear.

'I suppose this is your work, Mr Sant?' she said, bringing a cutting from the *Catholic Hour* out of her chain bag.

'Imphm,' Jerry grinned like an oblong gargoyle.

'Oh how could you say such things about Him! I do think it shocking of you!'

'Wumman, hae ye nat telled me maist o' they things yersel'?'

'Yes of course. But I never thought you'd put it all in the papers.'

'A havena pit them a'. There's a plenty more – if He hasna had His paiks yet.'

'O but I'm sure He has, I expect you've simply stunned Him.'

'Maybe I have.'

'Haven't you heard from Him yet?'

'A havena. A'm expecting to hear the now.'

'Mr Sant if you've killed my George I'll – I don't know what I'll do: but I'll never forgive you.'

'Hech wumman, that won't kill Him: but it may make Him a bit sore and I'll let you know that He'll come here for His plaster.'

'I don't mind Him being sore. He deserves it after the way He's behaved to me. But – '

'Now just you tak' yersel' away. I can't have you messing about here when Rose comes. When I'm through with Him I'll forward Him to you. So you be off with you.'

'Clumsy beast!' said Mrs Crowe to herself when she stood in Two Shambles Street again. 'You'd much better have left it to me to arrange. I shouldn't be surprised if Georgie did something desperate now. It'd be just like Him. And I believe I could have coaxed Him – ' She hailed a victoria; and drove to St Peter's Square to have another look at the window.

The Pope gave the holy order of priesthood to Cardinal Van Kristen on Innocents' Day: His Holiness felt that the sacerdotal prayer of so innocent a one would benefit all. The English and American invasion of Rome beat the record for the winter season. At a carp-and-punch supper at Palazzo Caffarelli on Christmas Eve, it was remarked that the City just then contained all the world's multimillionaires. If war had been carried on in the antique manner, i.e. for ransoms and spoils, and if any power had possessed a sufficient military equipment, a new

277

sack of Rome would have been an exceedingly lucrative undertaking. However, as it was, Rome sacked the multi-millionaires. Despite the fact that the coming spring was likely to see the dawn of Armageddon, an astonishing number of people was unable to resist the temptation to purchase the treasures of the Vatican. The list of prices assigned by the experts had been submitted to Hadrian, Who struck the mean between maximum and minimum, greatly to the disgust of curialists who (when once the idea was grasped) were anxious to drive good bargains. They suggested an auction, which the Pope incontinently refused, saying that He was going to compete neither with tradesmen nor with brigands. He made it easy for museums to acquire historic specimens: the merely artistic chiefly went to private collectors; and the world acquired the valuables. The collection of lace alone fetched £785,000; and the total takings, amounting to four-and-thirty millions sterling, were deposited in the Bank of Italy.

Signor Panciera made it a great deal more than convenient to accept another invitation to the Vatican. This time, it was a short visit which he paid, and a fairly momentous one. The Pope did all the talking. His Holiness spoke dryly and concisely from a sheet of manuscript which He afterwards handed to the ambassador, and seemed to be consumed by some internal fire, the signs of which appeared in His white pain-drawn face. He said that He had noted with approbation the scheme of Signor Gigliotti, by which inoculated convicts were employed in the reclamation of malarious Apulia and Calabria. He wished Italy to establish and endow farm colonies in eucalyptus groves on the Roman Campagna, where a wholesome and industrious life could be found for inoculated boys and girls. He wished Italy to establish and endow almshouses for old people, and free schools where handicrafts would be taught to children. He wished Italy to establish and endow scholarships for the study of Italian archaeology, the idea being to foster a spirit of enthusiastic patriotism, by excavating and studying and preserving the buried cities and monuments and treasures of antiquity with which the sacred and glorious and inviolate soil of Italy simply teems. Lastly, He wished Italy to give rewards, say of a thousand lire in cash to every man and woman between twenty and thirty years of age, who had served one master or secular firm since Lady-day 1899, and who cared to claim such a reward. To give effect to His four wishes, He handed to Signor Panciera an order on the Bank of Italy payable to the Prime Minister of Italy for the time being. The value of the order was thirty-three millions sterling. It was an offering in honour of the thirty-three years during which God as Man had laboured for the Love of men. It was to be the nucleus of a national fund which was to be called 'The Household of Christ'. This fund was to be administered, on the lines stated, by one male member of the Royal Family of Italy, the Prime Minister, and the Minister of the Interior for the time being, and by nine trustees drawn in rotation from the list of nobles in the Golden Book. The first of these twelve was to hold his trusteeship for life, and was to be nominated by the King's Majesty within one year from the present date. The second and third were to be ex-officio trusteeships. Of the nine nobles three would retire each year; and the next three on the roll would succeed them. No ecclesiastics were to be concerned with the fund in any way, unless they were nobles eligible for trusteeship, or unless they were paid servants appointed as chaplains by the Trustees. Hadrian's particular desire was that the 'Household of Christ' should become in every sense a department of the government of Italy.

Signor Panciera came out reeling; and furiously drove in the direction of Monte Citorio. Here, he picked up Signor Zanatello; and the two carried their little basketful of news to the Queen-Regent in the Quirinale. Eleven minutes in Her Majesty's music-room sufficed to send the three quickly through the Hall of Birds, and upstairs to the marconigraph office, by which means they announced the scheme to Victor Emanuel at Windsor Castle. The Sovereign's reply was characteristically Italian, and (therefore) splendid.

'I add a million: the Queen adds a million: the Prince of Naples adds a million: all sterling.'

The Prime Minister sent the nation's thanks and asked His

Majesty to nominate himself as trustee. He got this gorgeous answer.

'The Trustees will be nicknamed the Pope's Twelve Apostles. The *Voce della Verità* and the *Osservatore Romano* instantly would assign to me the role of Judas.'

Signor Panciera sent this message 'Sire, there was a thirteenth apostle'.

The King retorted 'But he was an afterthought'. That made Queen Elena laugh. The King continued.

'Zanatello, take this money: give a receipt in the name of Italy. The Queen-Regent will issue a royal decree constituting the Household of Christ as a government department: I nominate the Duke of Aosta as the royal trustee: this scheme is just what Italy wants at this moment: give it effect at once.'

Zanatello implored His Majesty to become trustee.

'No,' came the final response. 'I will assist most strenuously in an unofficial capacity: when there is room for a thirteenth apostle, I will perpend: meanwhile I engage to double the fund within one year. The King of England will assist.'

Hadrian first read about the acceptance of the gift to Italy in the next day's *Populo Romano* -- one of the most respectable papers in the world, He used to say. He felt that He had achieved another step; and instantly proceeded to the next. He summoned the Syndic of Rome, and made over to him, as a free gift to the City, all the moveable sculpture, paintings, tapestry, and archaeological specimens then present in the Vatican. Simultaneously, He canonized Dom Bosco and Dante Alighieri and published the *Epistle to the Italians*. This document was mainly hortatory, and directed against disbelief and secret societies. He bade Italy to consider Herself as the temple of art in Europe; and to set Herself, by the contemplation of masterpieces of human workmanship already in her possession, or to be added to Her possession by future discovery, to produce Herself as a country and a people prepared for The Lord Who is Altogether Lovely. He spoke of the Mafia with admiration and with horror. It was a brotherhood rather than a society, He said. It was a brotherhood of individualists each devoted to the service of his brother. Its essential virtues were honesty, mutual help, self-restraint. Nothing could be better. But the Devil had distorted the operation of so excellent a scheme. His Iniquity tempted the Mafiosi not only to help each other in good deeds, but in evil – chiefly in evil deeds. They murdered and screened murderers; and forgot 'Thou shalt do no murder'. They robbed and screened robbers; and forgot 'Thou shalt not steal'. They alleged that Mazzini had welded them into a corporate body for political purposes; and had given them for a motto 'Mazzini Autorizza Furti Incendi Avvelenamenti', from the initials of which phrase they drew their corporate name. In place of that wicked and abominable sentence, He gave them 'Madonnina Applaude Fraternita Individualita Amore'. Let the Mafia flourish with that motto for its ruling principle.

Italy was seeing the burden of poverty removed from Her children, was seeing Her youth enabled to cultivate talents, was seeing the honest labour of Her manhood and womanhood rewarded, was seeing refuge and provision prepared for old age. Rome set herself nobly to work at housing the treasures of art which Hadrian had given. Immense and splendid palaces were planned for them and began to rise on the Esquiline and Celian Hills; and the gracious forms of the old gods were to stand beneath arcades of marble, white and pure as lilies without, mosaic of bright gold within, amid the groves upon Janiculum. Honest men came by their own. There were no unemployed. Consequently, no hearts were soured while hands were used; and anarchy began to fade away into the obscurity of bad old rubbish rejected. The *Epistle to the Italians* too! They were in the mood to listen to anything and everything from that dear little piece of omniscient omnipotent omnipresent aloofness whom they called 'Papa Inglese'. To the strong and simple Italian temper, His words carried conviction by reason of their own essential simplicity and strength.

'He speaks like one's own conscience!' said Caio and Tizio and also Sempronio.

'Hearken and obey Him, then,' invected Maria and Elena and also Margherita.

CHAPTER 18

ITALY was not first in the heart of Hadrian. She was third. He served Her, because He saw Her instant need. The second of His loved lands did not know Herself to be in need of Him: hence, He offered Her no more than courtesy. He did not want America to tell Him not to monkey with the buzz-saw. And England was first. And what could He do for England? The thought, that He might do something, alone sustained Him now: Life among the millions of articulately speaking men had become an everpresent horror to Him. He frequently wondered what prevented Him from hurling Himself from the windows on to the stones of Rome. He actually sent for a case of safety razors, and banished knives from the pontifical apartments. 'O for the wings, for the wings of a dove: then far away, far away, would I fly.' There was a boy named Roebuck who sang that, in New College Chapel in Commemoration week five-and-twenty years before. The golden voice, the incomparable young voice came back to Him in Golden Rome where He was longing to be at rest.

A scarlet arm held back the blue-linen curtain of the door, and Cardinal Leighton entered. 'I think we missed this, Holy Father,' he said, and offered a more-than-a-month-old copy of the *Catholic Hour*.

Hadrian in a moment dragged Himself erect physically and psychically: He took the paper and read:

We have received a long letter from 'D. J.' taking us to task for exposing George Arthur Rose in a way which he calls 'savagely cruel'. He says

'I thank God that I cannot appreciate the humour which speaks gaily of a man enduring eighteen months of semi-starvation, and at the same time struggling hard to earn a livelihood by his pen – for the honesty of his strugglings I can vouch. Whatever his past may have been – and I believe that your article is in the main erroneous – surely it is better to leave it as past. As a convert, he had to endure for the faith that is in him. Once before in his chequered career, at a moment when he had a means of living by his own hands within his grasp, a gratuitous newspaper attack snatched from him the support which he had made himself to lean on. At the present time he is leading an existence which is bitter enough to himself and quite harmless (not to say beneficial) to others; and I feel compelled to tell you that I look upon your onslaught as both criminal and disgraceful.'

Another correspondent writes, 'I was much grieved at your article called *Strange Career* etc. in your issue of Nov. 18th because I am a great admirer of some books which George Arthur Rose published before he was made Pope. Those books did more to convert me to Catholicism than any others and I am very sorry to read the account that you have printed of their author.'

Yet another correspondent writes, 'It may be well to inform your readers that the Austin White who wrote the very offensive letters headed *Rhypokondylose Religion* in the *Jecorian Courier* some few years back is the George Arthur Rose alias the Pope of Rome about whom your readers were so amply enlightened in the columns of your issue of 18th November.'

In reply to 'D.J.' we may say that we hold in our hand a letter which Rose addressed to an excellent priest in 1898. It concludes 'I regret for your sake the exposure which inevitably must take place when her brother-in-law, the bishop, becomes cognizant of the undue influence which you use in order to embezzle these sums from Lady Mostingham. I beg you to make amends and to withdraw from such degrading transactions before it is too late.' If our correspondent 'D.J.' still thinks it was not advisable for us to savagely and cruelly denounce the author of the last letter, we can only say we differ from him.

Hadrian read the screed with indignant scorn. It was the beastly English of the vulgar thing, more than the vile sentiments expressed, which put Him into such a violent rictus of contempt. He looked out of the window at nothing for a moment, to conceal His disgust. Finding that Cardinal Leighton waited, He controlled Himself; and turned round with a gaze of frigid inquiry.

'Yes?' He said.

'"Would to Heaven that You would grant me a trifling

favour,"' His Eminency quoted in Greek. It was a most artful and invariably successful dodge to approach the Pontiff in His favourite tongue. He recognized the quotation; and capped it with the succeeding verse.

'"Tell me as quickly as you can; and I at once shall know."'

'May I ask a question? Did You write that letter, Holy Father?'

'Which? The last? Yes.'

'What did You know?'

'Everything.'

'May I say that the amount of knowledge of men which You seem always to possess is quite extraordinary:' said the cardinal, blinking.

'No it is not. "To those who indeed suffer, Righteousness bringeth knowledge",' the Pontiff quoted from Aeschylus again. '"The greater the detachment from the world, over worldly things the greater power is gained," some true poet sings. We never were "a man among men". We had five senses and We used them. And all the men whom We ever met habitually and voluntarily came and told Us their secrets. We never sought them. They were laid bare before Us. And Our senses perceived them. That is all.'

The pontifical voice was hard and cruel: the face was harder and more cruel and also more terrible. The very Presence was like a candent flame. Good honest innocent Leighton looked at Him as at something inhuman: but he persevered.

'Holiness, I want to go on. Do You know who wrote the other letters?'

'Oh yes. D. J. was another "excellent priest". He was in philosophy when We were in theology at Maryvale. Why you know him too, Leighton – he took his B.A. with Ambrose.'

'What, "Gionde"? Yes, of course I knew him.'

'That's the man. We have not heard from him for years: but he evidently thought it right to defend Us. Poor chap! A snub rewards him. The *Catholic Hour* "differs from him".... A tipsy publican wrote the second; and the third was written by a Jesuit jackal, in return for the custom of, and most likely at the dictation of, the very detestable scoundrel to whom We wrote the last.'

'What became of him? The bad priest I mean?'

'He ruined himself, as We predicted. He persisted in his career of crime till his bishop found him out. Then he was broken, and disappeared – Maison de santé or something of that sort for a time. He's in one of the colonies now; and he might have been – Lord Cardinal, We have said too much. It is not Our Will and pleasure to move in this matter.'

'But the advantage I derive from hearing Your Holiness – if it is not impertinent – Holiness, I venture to assure you of my eternal fidelity –' Leighton stammered with emotion.

Hadrian showed him no face: turned to the window which displayed the panorama of Intangible Rome; and presently was alone.

'God! God!' He exclaimed, shaking the paper with terrific violence. 'Do you see this brutal cynical unrighteousness – pre-judged – condemned – the mere suggestion of defence derided and fleered at – in England, fair-minded England – England the land of the free –'

No: it was not England, but just a handful of the vicious vermin which infest her. England – the word summoned Him to His apostolature again. What was the mind of England now? That question occupied Him. He wished that England would declare Her mind to Him through ambassadors, the mind of the statesmen of England. He had no official acquaintance with any one of them. He could not ask for England's confidence: for, being English, He knew that asking slams the door. Humanly speaking, He had nothing to guide Him in the cosmic crisis of the present, the crisis in which He was certain to be consulted – as a last resort – but certain to be consulted. Of that, He was con-vinced. A short calculation displayed Jupiter passing through Aries, which signified immense benefit to England. Oh, very good. Then what should be His course of action? He got up and went round the room, looking at the maps and noting them, until it seemed that His mental horizon expanded and enlarged, and He had the whole of the orb of the earth within His vision. What should He say, or do, for England, when She was too shy, too proud, to give Him a sign as to what She wanted Him to say, or do? England, England! – 'Land of hope and glory – how shall We extol thee Who are born of thee? – wider still and wider shall thy bounds be set: God, Who made thee mighty, make thee mightier yet!'

He would say and do that which was given to Him to say or do. As an Englishman, He had His intuitions. And He required no confidences. England, the shy, the proud, should be served by Her shy proud son, the Servant of the servants of God. The divine afflatus of patriotism inspired Him, brightening His eyes, erecting His head. He sat down again: took His writing-board on His knees; and wrote. Anon, He rang the bell and gave some orders. Also, He sent some written slips of cyphers to the operators in the Vatican marconigraph office.

On the twenty-second of January, the Supreme Pontiff descended to the basilica of St Peter-by-the-Vatican; and sang mass for the repose of the soul of Queen Victoria, the Great, the Good. The same day, the English newspapers announced that His Holiness had sent a cardinal-ablegate to place the Golden Rose, the pontifical tribute to virtuose queens, on Her Majesty's tomb in the mausoleum at Frogmore.

CHAPTER 19

THE Italian Socialists having been won for Italy, and the German Socialists by the German Emperor, the British Socialists began to wonder where they themselves came in. The predilection for forming societies which is to be met with among all the degenerate and hysterical, may assume different forms. Criminals unite in bands, as Lombroso expressly establishes. Hence the British Socialists (in their quandary) held fatuous meetings hoping to generate a policy in an atmosphere of hot envious man. They really did want to know their exact position: for, in some indefinable way, they were beginning to feel that they were by no means as necessary to the universe as they had imagined themselves to be. It seemed as though this planet (for one) were moving quite easily without them, and (what was more annoying) on a path which was quite strange to them, a comfortable path and a desirable. They felt that they were being left out in the cold; and, as their nature was, they looked about for some safe person on whom to void their spleen. They began with the Roman Pontiff. That an archaic potentate of His calibre, should prove to be fresh and actual and vigorous, struck them as something of a nuisance. They had deemed Him hardly worth consideration, a decayed relic of antiquity, useful perhaps as a monument of the bad old days when the world was drowned in damnable idolatry: but nothing more. That any man whose reputation so publicly had been besmirched as His had been, should dare to hold up his head, to live and move and have his being, to dispose of millions of money and of the minds of nations, struck them as simply atrocious. He had refused the honour of their alliance, had scorned their overtures with contemptuous silence. They would return Him scorn for scorn: they would show Him what He had lost. If He flattered Himself that His so-called *Epistles* to this that and the other would have any influence, the sooner He was undeceived the better. The Liblab Fellowship soon would let 'an unhappy old drawler of platitudinous flapdoodle like Hadrian' know His place, quoth the blameless Comrade Bob Matchwood. All the same, amid all the rhapsodic rhodomontade of sound and fury signifying nothing, there remained among the fellowshippers just enough intellect to perceive one thing. Comrade Frank Conollan put on his pince-nez; and, with a spasm of jerks and twitches, was delivered of the opinion that the Liblab Fellowship could not hope to recover anything like a respectable position in the popular estimation as long as it remained where it was. He said that to blink the fact that Liblabbery had taken a false step in approaching the Pope of Rome, was not a bit of good. Liblabbery had courted a snub; and had been smitten with the snubbiest of snubs. If he might use a metaphorical expression, he would say that Liblabbery had been enticed into a bog and made to look unspeakably silly. If he might use a poetical expression from Shakespeare, he would say 'like unback'd colts they pricked their ears, advanced their eyelids, lifted up their noses, and calf-like follow'd through tooth'd briers, pricking goss, and thorns, which enter'd their frail skins, into the filthy mantled pool, where, dancing up to the chins, the foul lake o'er-stunk their feet'.

(It began to dawn upon the Liblabs that the Comrade was doing the very thing desired. He was leading up to the customary denunciation of some traitor. He was about to provide them with the name of the usual scapegoat. They prolonged pleased ears in his direction.)

He would go further. He would say, still using the expressions of the immortal bard of Avon, 'Your fairy, which you say is a harmless fairy, has done little better than played the Jack with us'.

(This was something like! The meeting's ears positively flapped.)

And then, being unable to keep on his pince-nez any longer by reason of a steamed nose, he brought his climax to an abrupt term by demanding the instant and public expulsion of Comrade Jerry Sant. That was voted nem. con. The Liblab Fellowship shook off the dust of its dirty feet at the traitor; and Comrade Mat Matchwood said some very slighting things about him in the *Salpinx*. No one is so facile and energetic about believing evil as a Pessimist, that is to say a Socialist; and, when one traitor is detected, what could be more natural than for others to be suspected. It happened so. The mutual jealousy, the flaring incompetency, the sordid selfishness, which always infected the socialist demagogues, and (of course) the essentially sandy foundation upon which the socialist system was based, led to further and more fatal dissensions. Suspicion mated with Baffled Purpose. Recrimination was the offspring of the match. The Fellowshippers, who had connived at the scheme of Jerry Sant, found themselves accused as his accomplices, and denounced and expelled in turn. From dissension it was no more than one step to disunion. Each demagogue, fearful lest he should have to take up an honest trade for a livelihood, devoted persuasive loquacity to the attracting of personal supporters. Burnson battened on Battersea. West Ham went a-whoring after strange Bills. Glasgow got into the galley of Kerardy. And Devana succumbed to a split-thumb-nailed and anarchistic plumber. Schisms within schisms insued. Dens and caves received the remnants of the Liblab Fellowship. Mutual damnation was the order of the day. The Socialists were almost Christian. The ranks were thinned by internecine war. Then came desertions. Socialism didn't pay; and socialists openly asked conservative agents for tory gold. When it was refused, they swore (after their kind). Labor (without the u) looked about for the patronage of Capital. And British Socialism was in a fair way to perish of its own radical fatuity, and instability.

Hadrian watched the process of disintegration from His tower in Rome, watched the natural absorption of the more respectable socialists by the more respectable community; and He was glad. Very soon now the silly obscene heresy would die and disappear, with the obsolete delusions of Gymnosophists, Anabaptists, Picards, Adamites, and Turlupins. Hadrian was glad. Then came *The Times*, announcing that Australia, Canada, and South Africa had armed all healthy males between the ages of seventeen and fifty; and that England was mobilizing the sea-and-land-forces of her Empire. Now the whole world was in battle array. He took out His pyx again, and prayed the prayer of the Danaides, 'O King of kings, Most Blessed of the blessed, Most Perfect Mighty One of the perfect, be persuaded and let this come to pass – avert from Thy race the insolence of men who (for a reason) hate it; and plunge the black-benched pest into the dark abyss.' It was a pagan enough prayer for a Pope to utter. It was a fierce enough sentiment for an altruist to express. It was an entirely comprehensible suggestion of a misanthrope and misogynist, tired by, impatient of, armed against, the tiresome divarication of little silly people. The thing which troubled Him most was the irreconcilability of the King of Italy. He had tried hard to give Victor Emanuel to understand that, not rebuff but, welcome waited for him. He knew the benefits which cooperation of Pope and King would bring. Yet the expression of the Persian fatalist in Herodotus – ἐχθίστη ὀδυνη πολλα φρονεοντα μηδονος κρατεειν – the bitterest of all griefs, to see clearly and yet to be unable to do anything, might have stood as the motto of His whole mind, as often before in His life, so most emphatically now. He recalled the Cardinal of Caerleon.

The blameless Sant and his companion were in a pretty pickle. Expulsion from the Liblab Fellowship included, not only the withdrawal of funds but also, a threat of prosecution on a charge of obtaining money on false pretences. The last they could afford to laugh at. No English court of law could or would convict upon the evidence producible. The first was tiresome: but of course they had a little put by. And with regard to the future? Mrs Crowe now was quite certain that Jerry had made a mess of things. She began to think with longing of her lodging-house. What was the good of staying on in Rome? Yes, and who was going to pay her expenses, she would like to know? She impatiently put that point before her paymaster. He did on a forensic air; and asked for time to advise himself of the matter. She demanded how long he would require. He remarked on the feminine propensity for kicking a man who has been knocked down; and ramped and raved till he thoroughly frightened her. Your Pict is a truly awesome figure when he is red with damp rage. She shrank into a corner whimpering, for she thought he was going to strike her. Instead of that he cooled to sudden wheedling; and anon he cuddled her. She permitted. It was better than nothing; and she felt as though she really needed something of the sort. How could she so misunderstand him? Of course he was not going to desert her. They both were in the same boat; and must sink or swim together. For his part, he intended to swim. She might have known that he was not the man to give up when matters had proceeded so far. But, she urged, what could they do? Do? They could do a fair lot of things. To begin with, they could go and wait on a lot of they old cardinals and mak' theirsels a nuisance. They went to Ragna, and told him very pretty stories. Their statements were as a treat of almonds to him: but he gave no sign of that. He was suave, polite: said that he would see what could be done; and bowed them away. They went to Whitehead and got no satisfaction. Caerleon thought that they had better let matters rest. Carvale denied himself to them. Sterling listened to them with judicial gravity and gave them no response. Semphill blazed at them; and dismissed them shattered as to their nerves. They returned to the Hotel Nike to wait for Ragna.

The cardinals discussed them with the Pope. The Secretary of State was insinuatory. He spoke of the terrible scandal; and let it be understood that, in his opinion, payments should be made to stop it. He hinted at the impossibility of defending the indefensible. Better to use that million, the balance of the sale of the Vatican treasure. That million had paid the expenses of the sale and of the restoration of the sacristy; and had endowed St George's College of historical researchers under the presidency of Dr Richard Barnett: it was accounted for in della Volta's balance-sheet, Hadrian put in. Carvale added that payment never stopped scandal. Caerleon earnestly hoped that nothing would be done: it would rake up the past and involve so many people. Semphill yearned for the good old days, faggots, tongue-tearing, hand-chopping, ear-cropping, head-cutting, eye-gouging, maiming, and stoning, and the groaning with much wailing of those impaled by the spine, and all that sort of thing out of the Eymenides. He loudly said so; and was silenced by a look from the Pontiff's scornful anguished face. Discussion languished. Then Hadrian said 'Bring them here'.

Sir Iulo pit-pit-pit-pitted across the City on a motor-bicycle, and burst into Via Due Macelli, a scarlet Hermes, with the annunciation, 'You are summoned to attend our Most Holy Father in the Vatican.' Mrs Crowe hiccoughed 'At last'; and bolted upstairs to put on her most fetching hat. Jerry Sant grinned spikily through a tattered moustache. The two got into a hired victoria; and followed the gentleman-of-the-secret-chamber.

Hadrian received them in the throne-room. He did not occupy the throne, but the central chair of a semi-circular group of five. Ragna, Sterling, Leighton, and Caerleon used the others. The latter had a pigskin portfolio on his knee. In front of the ecclesiastics were two chairs of equal importance. The man and woman lounged there. It was quite a family gathering. But between the Church and the World, Sir John stood by a little table furnished with the pontifical phonographs.

'We have summoned you, in order that ye may speak your minds to Us,' the Supreme Pontiff said: 'but ye shall know that We will not hold any communication with you except Our utterances and yours be recorded by these instruments.' His voice was very frigid: but there was neither menace nor offence in it. His quiet tone totally was at variance with the furious defiance of the matter of His words. The paradox disconcerted his hearers. Sant went magenta with wrath: remembered how much he had at stake; and was canny enough not to demur. With an attempt at an easy laugh, he said that it was a little unusual, not quite what he expected, but he didn't want to be unpleasant to His Lordship, and so he had no objection he was sure. And he lolled in his armchair, as who should say 'A'm fair easy'. Mrs Crowe bit her upper lip: but said that she had no objection either. Hadrian waved His hand; and the pontifical gentleman sat down and set the machines in motion.

The Pope put the woman to the question: 'Madam, what do you want?'

Face to face with that she failed to put her want in words. It was an acrid pungent permanent want, not-to-be-named. She bit at her upper lip again; and looked at Jerry for a lead. He proceeded 'I think, Reverend Sir, that it will be more advantageous for all parties if I was to speak for Mrs Crowe.'

'We will concede the point. Sir, what do you want?' the Pontiff said.

Then the virtuous Jerry also began to flounder. Want? Eh, but he wanted several things.

'Name them:' the Pope commanded.

'Well: reparation – damages.'

'For what?' the Pope inquired.

'For ma loss of time whiles I've had to be here and for ma

292

business which Ye may say's gone ta th dogs; and for the loss of ma Liblab Fellowship.'

'To what extent have you suffered?'

'To fhat extent? Well, I'll let Ye know. I've been here since last July, say eight months, say forty weeks, say three hundred days; and I take ordinarily a pound note per day on journey for expenses: but it's cost me a heap more than that this trip. Ye can call it five hundred pounds for out-of-pocket expenses. Then there's ma business which I've had to neglect, eight months, better say a year at one-fifty for salary, and commissions – say another fifty. There's eight hundreds. Then they've had the cheek to expel me as a Fellowshipper, as I suppose Ye've heard. Of course that's very damaging to ma prestige, say to the extent of a couple of thousands. Fhat's that come to? Two thousands eight hundreds – may as well call it three thousands. And of course there's fhat old Krooger named moral and intellectual damage – I don't know fhat tae pit that at, I'm sure – but Ye might tot it all up together and call it twenty thousands.'

'And your companion?'

'Aweel, Ye'd better double it and we'll both ca' quits. Forty thousands cash!'

The Pope cast a slight look round upon his cardinals. They returned it. 'You are demanding that We should pay you forty thousand pounds,' He said to the expectant Jerry.

'That's correct.'

'Why do you demand this sum of Us?'

'Why? Why because we've run into all these expenses on Your account. If Ye hadna have been here, neither would we have come and have had all this fuss and bother. Who's to idemnify us for that but Yersel', I'm asking Ye. I'll let Ye know we've fair ruined oursels – '

The Bald She interrupted. 'If I could have a private word with Your Holiness.'

The motive did not escape Hadrian's notice. 'Daughter, your conduct and your notorious proclivities debar you from a private interview with any clergyman, except in the open confessional.'

'Then in the confessional.'

The Pope rose and beckoned her to follow. He beckoned Sir John to stop the machines and remain: the others to follow. They descended into St Peter's. There, He turned out the English Confessor; and took his place, while the woman kneeled at the left side. Just out of earshot, the four cardinals stayed with Sant, who fumed in his inward parts. Fhat blathers was this going on under their very noses? The half-door and the window both were open: only the lateral partition divided the priest from the penitent. The grating was between their faces; and, though they were perfectly visible, they were visible apart and separate.

Hadrian in a low tone recited 'May the Lord be in thine heart and on thy lips'; and put Himself to listen.

Through the grating there came a whine – 'Georgie!'

'My child, there is no Georgie here, but only your Judge. Confess your sins, if you will – only to Almighty God. Show contrition. And, by His authority committed to me His minister, I will absolve.'

Then the Devil entered into her. She incoherently spluttered 'I have no sins – if I had, I wouldn't tell You – You reject me? – Oh I'll make You regret it – I'll make You suffer as I have – I'll show you up for what You are –' She stiffened and rushed across to Jerry 'Now do your worst,' she said; and her face was livid.

Sant gripped the lapels of his grotesque frock-coat and approached the white figure which emerged from the central compartment of the confessional.

'I should like to mak' an end of this matter,' he said.

Hadrian led the way to the throne-room: the phonographs were set to work; and the conference was resumed.

'Now,' said Jerry, 'I'm thinking that Your Right Reverence had better let us know definitely fhat Ye intend to do.'

The Pope spoke rather more slowly and with more singular mildness than before. 'You demand that We should pay you forty thousand pounds in reparation for damage which, you say, We have caused.'

'That's so.'

'It is useless to point out to you that We did not ask you to waste your time in Rome – '

'I should have been surprised if Ye had have.'

'And that We did not force you, or induce you, to neglect your business – '

'Nae! Ye never thought I'd have dared to face Ye as I have.'

'And that We were in no wise concerned with your expulsion from the Liblab Fellowship – '

'But Ye were! If Ye'd have had the civility to give the deputation a satisfactory answer, or even to have satisfied the Fellowshippers afterwards, or to have made it all right with me so as I could have settled them, then there wouldn't have been all this trouble and unpleasantness, my Lord.'

'Some men are gifted with an abnormal capability for making the greatest possible fools of themselves. For the credit of the human race, it must be said that indecent exhibitions of this kind are rare. Mr Sant, does it not occur to you that you are engaging in a very foolish and a very dirty business?'

'Dirty business Yersel'! Who're Ye talking to? Ma hands are as clean as Yours any day. Who owes twenty pound notes to this lady I'm brought with me?'

'We do not know.'

'Imphm. Well, suppose I was to say it was Yersel'?'

'You would tell an officious lie, Mr Sant.' The Pope turned to the woman. 'Madam, do We owe you twenty pounds?'

'You owe me a great deal more than that:' she barked.

'Mr Sant alludes to a specific sum of twenty pounds odd which was due to this lady's deceased husband for books, newspapers, and stationery, supplied some years ago when he kept a shop:' the Pope explained to the cardinals, with a gesture to Talacryn. The Cardinal of Caerleon extracted a slip from the portfolio; and read a receipt for the amount named plus 5 per cent interest. This document was dated the thirty-first of the previous March. The Pope continued, 'You know, Madam, that We paid this bill the moment We were in a position to pay it. You also know that payment was long delayed solely because you yourself, by calumniating and libelling Us to Our employers and to those who called themselves Our friends, prevented Us from earning more than a bare sustenance –'

Jerry burst in, 'Well, if Ye've paid her why shouldn't Ye pay me?'

'Because We do not owe you anything.'

'Then Ye mean me ta pit some more about Ye in the papers?'

'Listen, Mr Sant. We look upon you as a deeply injured man –'

'Hech! Now that's something like!'

'We look upon you as a deeply injured man, injured by himself. You have been your own enemy. You have suffered loss and damage simply because you have allowed yourself to persist in doing silly things and wicked things. Now, is it useless to ask you to change all that? Will you turn over a new leaf and begin your life again? You shall not be left alone. You shall be helped.'

'A want ma money.'

'If you wish to do well for yourself, if you wish honestly to earn a better living than you ever have earned, you shall have the opportunity.'

An appeal to a goodness which is not in him is, to a vain and sensitive soul, a stinging insult. Jerry's face became wetter and redder. 'And fhat about damages for the past?' he barked.

'You shall have a chance for the future.'

'Then Ye willna pay! Ye want me to show Ye up in the papers again?'

'You may put what you please in the papers. We will not pay even a farthing to prevent you, Mr Sant – not one farthing.'

'Then I'm not to get anything?'

'At a threat? No. Nothing!' Defiance hurled denial at the brute.

'Fhat are we waiting here for, wumman?' Sant snarled at Mrs Crowe. 'Here let's get out of this. He makes me fair sick with His holy preaching!' At the door, he turned round, bragging boldly like a cock beside his partlet; and waved his bowler hat,

'E-e-e-h but A'll mak' Ye squirm, Ye ... inseck!' he foamed.

Ragna was furious. 'Holiness, why don't You shoot them at once? You are Sovereign within these walls. Give order for their arrest before they leave the palace, Holiness; and have them shot!'

'It is Our will that they be left to the common executioner,' the Pope disdainfully ordained, sitting very hieratically in his chair, young, rigid, and terrific as the Flamen Virbialis. The audience had been a fresh phase of agony to Him: He had tried to merge His humanity in His apostolature, and had failed; and the failure was torment, physical, poignant. He was indignant; and He was dangerous. Their Eminencies inquiringly looked at Him. Leighton blinked; and thought it a dreadful pity. Talacryn was for running out and trying to persuade the blackmailers even at some cost – anything was better than scandal, he said. The Pope told him not to be a stupid fool with his infernal hankerings after compromise. 'Fancy paying for silence!' His Holiness scornfully adjoined.

'No but Holy Father, I think if You were to leave them to me, I could find some way of silencing them. Silence is what we want indeed, whatever.'

'Your Eminency is well skilled in the art of silencing people, bad and good. It is by no means an honourable art; and you are prohibited from practising it. We believed that you had ceased to practise it in 1899. Were We in error?'

'No indeed no, indeed, Holiness. It was merely a suggestion of mine, indeed,' the cardinal burbled.

'Drop it then!' the Pontiff slammed at him.

'Indeed I do, Holiness, indeed I do, whatever.'

'One would hardly have believed that such blatant wickedness could have existed in the world,' Sterling gravely meditated.

'Holy Father, it will all begin again,' Leighton sadly sighed.

'Let it begin again!' Hadrian challenged, white-flaming, irate, retiring to the secret chamber.

Their Eminencies went out through the other door. They were not at all pleased with the Pope. In the first antechamber several cardinals were congregated anxious for news, Orezzo and Courtleigh each in a sedan-chair, Percy, Fiamma, della Volta, Semphill, Carvale, and Whitehead. Ragna was of opinion that the charges ought publicly to be answered, that is to say if they could be answered: but – Could the accusations satisfactorily be disposed of? No one put the question: but the aroma of the idea of it was in the air.

'There was so much mystery about His Holiness:' Orezzo said.

'There always has been. He is a most incomprehensible creature, indeed:' Talacryn pronounced.

'One might expect anything, everything of Him: the height and depth of good and bad: extreme virtue, extreme vice: one almost could believe Him to be capable of anything:' Sterling adjudicated.

'Oh yes, until you have heard Him explain,' little Carvale put in. 'Did none of Your Eminencies ever watch Him in His talk? I have. Shall I tell you the difference between our Holy Father and ourselves? We see things from a single viewpoint. He sees things from several. We decide that the thing is as we see it. But He has seen it otherwise, and He presents it as a more or less complete coaction of its qualities. See this sapphire. Well, you see the face of it: underneath, if I take it off my finger, there are a number of facets to be seen and a number more which are hidden by the gold of the setting. Now my meaning is that our Holy Father has seen all the facets as well as the table of the sapphire, or the thing. Consequently He knows a great deal more about the sapphire, or the thing, than we do. You must have noted that in Him. You must have noted how that every now and then, when He deigns to explain, He makes mysteries appear most wonderfully lucid.'

'But, if one might venture to ask, how often does He condescend to explain – except to His cat?' Sterling interjected.

'I'm bound to admit that He opened my eyes considerably during that fortnight we spent together in town just before His election,' Courtleigh threw out of his chair. Ragna went to him and spoke of the desirability of capital punishment.

'Well, anyhow, I believe in Him,' Whitehead murmured.

'Yes:' Leighton energetically blinked. 'You'll excuse me if I'm shoppy, but I say with St Anselm, "*Neque enim quaero intelligere ut credam: sed credo ut intelligam. Nam et hoc credo quia nisi credidero non intelligam.*"'

The gong in the secret chamber loudly and suddenly sounded. The scarlet limbs of Sir John and Sir Iulo darted towards it. Talacryn was shaking an unwilling dubious head. Van Kristen gave him a tall look of disgust. 'Well, I guess Your Eminency will feel pretty small some day if you don't believe in Him too. There are no flies on Hadrian:' and he stalked away with the dignity of a grand boy honourably enraged.

'No no, Percy,' said Talacryn, running after him. 'Of course I believe in Him: but just for that reason I don't want Him to defend Himself. I want to keep Him quiet. I think it unwise to rake up the past. There would be so many frightful scandals, whatever.'

'Have you told Him that?'

'Have I not indeed.'

'And what did He say?'

Talacryn once more shook his head.

'Well then I advise Your Eminency to go "way back and sit down", as we say in the States.'

Newspaper tirades did begin again. The previous attacks on the Pope almost were forgotten (horribly pungently palate-tickling though they were) at a time when men's minds were filled with wars and rumours of wars. But the Fleet Street fishers, who knew their business, were aware that the public appetite is capricious and must be tempted with a variety of bait. Even wars and rumours of wars are apt to pall. One must not cry 'Wolf' too often. Tired of Black-gnats, trout must be tried with Mayflies: for newspapers must be sold, or the soap-and-cocoa people will quake; and newspapers will not sell unless their news are new. So, when the editor of the *Daily Anagraph* received a couple of letters from Jerry Sant and Mrs Crowe, proffering certain tasty information, and asking for an offer for same, he consulted his proprietors. The subject certainly was not entirely novel: but what had gone before merely had been so to speak an appetizer. This was the strong meat, the *pièce de résistance* in the banquet of garbage. Sant was in possession of exclusive information. The publication of it would mean a boom for the paper. Editors cannot afford to be curious about the morals of their contributors, or indeed of anything bar the quality of their contributions. Neither proprietors nor editor were actuated by any sort of malice, personal or professional, in defaming the Pope. Their motive was merely commercial. Therefore, they offered £4,000 apiece to Sant and his accomplice; and they invested a similar sum in amateur investigations. At intervals during the next few weeks, the *Daily Anagraph* published articles reflecting on the character of God's Vicegerent; and two columns daily were set apart for anonymous *ex-parte* statements concerning His career. Oh, it all began again! The points insisted on were that He was, and never had been anything but a lazy luxurious (the second intention was 'debauched') jesuitical machiavellian and false-pretentious ignoramus – Oh it all indubitably began again. Mediocrities, entrusted with power over their fellow-creatures, invariably develop into tyrants. All history proves it: the tyranny of the clergy was bad enough: but it was as nothing in comparison with the sordid tyranny of the Press which we now complacently tolerate.

Calumny culminated with a concoction of the calvous Crowe's. It was admitted that the high-water mark was reached. Hitherto, the very virulence of the assaults had engendered a certain amount of unexpressed sympathy among stock-holders, naval, Varsity, and other thoughtful men. 'Our Representative' had called at Archbishop's House, had interviewed Monsignor this and Monsignor Canon that, inviting the candid expression of opinion on the subject of Pontifical Infallibility, as viewed in the light of recent journalistic enterprise and research. The distinction between infallibility and impeccability had been impressed upon 'Our Representative': but that was all. No defence was offered either by the Pope or by His poor benighted papists. Then, by slow degrees, the elect, the intelligent, began to persuade themselves that, after all, the early misdemeanours of George Arthur Rose, if they were as stated, were altogether apart from the pontifical acts of Hadrian the Seventh. The latter distinctly were admired throughout the world: the former – well, they were a pity. So, public opinion was. And then came Mrs Crowe. She had a song to sing (oh!) of secret debauchery on the part of Hadrian the Seventh. She was concise in the matter of names and dates and places. She alleged that, at dusk on a certain evening in September, the 29th, she herself had seen the Pope, disguised in black like an ordinary priest, taking tea – He Who never ate in public – with two nameless women (far too beautiful to be respectable in her opinion) in a house on Via Morino. She was in the street. His so-called Holiness and His female companions were by the lighted window. Presently the blinds were closed; and she knew not what went on behind them. She watched the house for an hour and a half; and then the Pope came out muffling His face (a thing He never at any other time had been known to do, but necessary on this occasion to complete His disguise). He walked away; and she followed Him: saw Him stop at the Attendolo Palace, and (finally) enter the Vatican saluted by the guards at the bronze gates. She related the incident with such particularity and in such a manner, that a great many people fancied that they thoroughly understood. In a sort of way the good lady did more than most people have done towards effecting the Reunion of Christendom: for *The Cliff* deliriously discursed (from Revelations) of a great red dragon and seven heads and ten horns and seven crowns upon his heads, and of a beast rising out of the sea and seven heads and ten horns and ten crowns on his horns; and the *Catholic Hour* simultaneously washed its hands in innocency advertising unctuous rectitude in a leading article entitled 'The Third Borgia'.

CHAPTER 20

WHILE the dwarves were diverting themselves as aforesaid, their rulers were in council together. And one day Sir Francis Bertram found no closed doors at the Vatican. He was granted an audience which was friendly and unofficial and secret: so secret in fact that no news of it 'transpired'. It was treated as the return visit of an Englishman to an Englishman. He came in an electric brougham, quite unattended. No one noted that he brought a small dispatch-box with him: or that he did not carry it away with him: but some of the senior cardinals, who kindly came to discuss the latest effusions of the *Daily Anagraph* with Hadrian in the evening, found His Holiness brimful of gaiety. They remarked that the visit of the ambassador had done Him no end of good. His bearing was vivid, serene, and youthful: His conversation was witty, limpid, facile: no one would have taken Him for the person described in the newspapers. He read those which obligingly were handed to him: but showed no emotion whatever, although very eager expert eyes searched for some trace from which to lead theories and hypotheses. Nor did He utter any comment. He read: He laid down the paper; and resumed the conversation. Before Their Eminencies withdrew, He summoned the Sacred Consistory to meet at noon on the morrow; and that was the only noteworthy event of the evening.

Hadrian mounted the throne; and the vermilion college displayed itself before Him. A pigskin kitbag, which a gentleman-of-the-secret-chamber had placed by the pontifical footstool before the doors were locked, did not escape the notice of the more observant. The Pontiff Himself was in singularly good form: and this was incomprehensible, for He carried in His hand a copy of the very newspaper which everyone had read and retched over. That He should be so aggressively cheerful, so vividly dominant, with that in His hand, was considered hardly decorous. Even among those who firmly were determined to force themselves to believe in Him, that He should not bend His neck to the smiter now, did not tally at all with conceptions of propriety. With these sentiments, Their Eminencies composed themselves to listen.

After the formal opening of the session, a Consistorial Advocate (in garments of a violet colour and furred with ermine about the neck) was commanded to read aloud, from the *Daily Anagraph*, the account of the Pope's visit in disguise to the house on Via Morino. He was to read it, first, in English, then, in Latin. It was not a long lection: for journalistic instinct had perceived that the facts stated would be more damnatory in their nakedness. With that inscrutable incomprehensible vivid gleam of hilarity irradiating His face, Hadrian checked the Consistorial Advocate from time to time, preventing him from drifting into the monotonous gabble, which is used for the formal reading of documents whose contents already are known informally; and, if His object was to cause each deadly detail of the charge against Himself to come out clearly, with all the contours definite and all the tints brilliantly varnished, it must be admitted that His method was pontifically successful.

'*Ebbene dunque?*' muttered Cardinal Ragna.

Hadrian darted a word at the Cardinal-Prefect-of-Propaganda: 'Will Your Eminency have the goodness to describe, to the Sacred College, your acts of the afternoon and evening of the festival of St Michael Archangel?'

The naming of the festival of Michaelmas was like a touch on the latch of the Red Pope's memory. His pure and gentle face lighted up: for he perceived the connotation; and that inspired him with a joy so delectable that he paused to pick his words, tasting them deliberately, lingering over them. 'After siesta on the festival of St Michael Archangel – and that would be about 15½ hours of the clock, not later – I came to Vatican and was received by Your Holiness. I was admitted to the secret chamber. I sat opposite to Your Holiness, by the window. I remember that, for a reason. I spoke to Your Holiness on the subject of removing England from the control of Propaganda. I said that I had pondered Your Holiness's proposition. I said that it appeared to me, as it already had appeared to Your Holiness, that the necessity for treating England as a barbarous uncivilized savage country, in which the Faith is preached by missionaries, no longer existed. I added my own opinion, that to continue to treat England as a savage uncivilized barbarous country, now, amounted to perennial insult. I received Your Holiness's thanks. I am giving only the heads of this conversation, which was prolonged until the seventeenth hour. Then, the pontifical pages brought in a tray containing fruit and triscuits and some English tea. I told Your Holiness that tea astringed my nerves, remarking on the difference between English nerves and Italian. I was permitted to make a few jokes. In the midst of these very diverting burlesques, I ate a little fruit – perhaps a fig and a half – and I drank a little wine of Cinthyanum. Afterwards, I proceeded to discuss another case with Your Holiness. That case was the removal, from the spiritual rule of Propaganda, of the other countries which are under the secular rule of the Excellent King of England. It was a complication; and the discussion of it occupied some hours. I said, in sum, that sufficient information as to the nature and character and national history of the natives of those countries, especially Scotland, Ireland, and Wales, officially had not been laid before me. I requested Your Holiness to afford me longer time for the collection of information and investigation of the subject. I permitted myself to note that, while we were talking, Your Holiness made and smoked nineteen cigarettes. I remember that, when at length I rose to pay my respects, Your Holiness drew me nearer to the window by which we had been sitting; and deigned to indicate the image of St Michael Archangel which poises itself on the summit of the Mola. The metal of which the said image is formed appeared to be burnished, owing to radiance from the lights of the City. I said that it resembled an angelic apparition in the obscure sky of night. I remember that Your Holiness said "May the Prince, of the angels who do service in heaven, succour and defend us on earth". I responded "Amen". Your Holiness added some words in the Greek tongue, which You deigned to explain as signifying "O god of the golden helm, look upon, look upon the City which thou once didst hold well-beloved". To that prayer, I also responded "Amen". And I was permitted to retire at the same moment when the pages were bringing in Your Holiness's supper, which was at 20½ hours of the clock.'

Cardinal Gentilotto sat down; and the eyes of the Sacred College twinkled like talc. The Pope, Who had receded to His more usual distant reticent gravity, gave them a silent moment for appreciation; and then darted a verisimilar word to Cardinal della Volta. 'Will Your Eminency have the goodness to describe, to the Sacred College, your acts of the afternoon and evening of the festival of St Michael Archangel.'

The ex-Major-domo of the apostolic palace hemmed; and prayed for permission to send for his diary. Then he bravely proceeded. 'M-ym-ym-ym: Twenty-ninth September. At 15 o'clock, I drove by the Fort of Monte Mario to the Milvian Bridge: and walked a little in the fields. The sky was cloudy. Afterwards I drove by Via Flaminia and Pincio to Countess Demochede's villino; and sent away my carriage. I obtained news of the German Emperor. Her Excellency's daughter the Princess Neri was there. Tea and very agreeable conversation. The Princess expatiated on the virtues of pedestrianism. She and her beautiful mother derided me when I said that I was about to walk to Vatican. I went to Palazzo Attendolo to inquire for Don Umberto. He had bought a new horse, a straw-berry-roan, and was gone to Cinthyanum to try him. That young man always is buying horses – m-ym-ym. Returned to Vatican at 19 o'clock. Said Mattins and Lauds. Wrote to – m-ym-ym – wrote four letters, Holiness. Supper, *capretto ai ferri* and *zuppa inglese*. Gave my news of the German Emperor to our Most Holy Lord. Read Chap. IX, 1, of Matthew Arnold's *Literature and Dogma* with Δ Semphill. Conversed with that deacon about it till bedtime. He says that it is not a book to fear. In my opinion it is a wonderful book but shocking, and likely to cause misunderstanding except among the English: but it is not damnable, though many will think so. *Sancte Francisce, ora pro me.*'

He was about to sit down; and the College was about to open

twenty-three mouths: but Hadrian with the left hand signed him to approach the throne, and with the right simultaneously beckoned a master of ceremonies in a red habit and a violet cloak.

Cardinal Berstein interpolated with a recondite sneer, 'The phenomenon of bi-location, as exemplified in the case of St Philip Neri, is well-known. But this is not the case of a saint.'

Hadrian wiped the floor with the sneerer. 'Nor was the case of Samian Pythagoras, divine, golden-thighed (if Your Eminency ever heard of him), the case of a saint. Yet, inasmuch as Pythagoras was heard to lecture at Metapontion and Tayromenion on the same day and at the same hour, he would appear to have been an exemplification of the phenomenon of bi-location. However, this is neither the case of a saint, as you so acutely have observed: nor a case of bi-location, as you so hilariously would pretend.' He flung the retort at the cardinal with such force that Berstein sought his seat with not innocuous concussion.

'Lord Cardinals, the voice of the snake and the voice of the goose are one and the same. They both hiss:' the Pope added before moving again.

A feeling that His Holiness was dynamic, picric, dangerous, pervaded the assembly. Each most eminent lord wondered who would be the next victim of that quiet shrill velvet claw which tore the brain. The Pontiff bent His head to the master of ceremonies, signifying that he should remove the mitre. Also He unclasped the morse of His cope; and addressed Cardinal della Volta.

'Can Your Eminency remember what habit you wore during the afternoon and evening of the twenty-ninth of September?'

'Yes, Holy Father, I wore the plain habit which we commonly wear.'

'Like this?' Hadrian stooped and opened the kit-bag; and drew from it a black cassock with red buttons, a red sash, and a black cloth cloak, and a black three-cornered beaver-hat with thin red cord and tassels.

'But yes: precisely like that.'

'Would Your Eminency do Us the extreme favour of putting on these garments now?'

Della Volta smiled: but he made the change, and stood on the throne-steps pulling out the folds, stretching his arms in the new sleeves. The Pope took another and a similar suit from the kitbag; and changed His Own white for black. Then He descended to the cardinal's side; and faced the college. They were as like each other as two blots of ink. And the college roared. Of course, everyone instantly remembered Courtleigh's allegation that della Volta was the Pope's Double: but no one until now had seen the two side by side and garbed alike. And the college roared – roared chiefly with delight at dismissal of tragedy by comedy.

The Pope and the Cardinal resumed their proper habits; and Hadrian again enthroned Himself. His aspect had become very cold, very hard. He spoke a few words in the dry incisive tone which slapped like sleet, from the far distance of His misanthropic soul snatched away to that remote place shared with wounded beasts who creep to die alone. He began swiftly; and intensified the value of His words by gradual monotonous deceleration which marked their close. 'Lord Cardinals,' He said, 'know that, if We desire to intrigue, Our experience of the extreme stupidity of intriguers has taught Us to avoid their pitifully trite folly. Know also that intrigues, disguises, tricks, artifices, stratagems, and deceptions, are repugnant to Us. And finally know this, that We never will derogate Our pontifical paraphernalia or authority to another.' After a moment, He changed His manner; and in a formal tone announced that the Congress of Windsor had invited the intervention of the Roman Pontiff as Supreme Arbitrator. It was the appeal of Caesar to Peter. He made known the contents of the dispatch, which Sir Francis Bertram had brought; and read the names of sovereign and presidential signatories. And, without waiting for comment, He uttered the ceremonial form which closed the Consistory; and was borne away.

Acclamations followed Him. Vermilion tumbled over ermine in an effort to get at Him. What a number of things everybody urgently desired to know! What was He going to do? Would He not take this magnificent opportunity of re-claiming Peter's Patrimony? He could not be denied it now. That was Ragna's notion. The two Vagellaii agreed with it: Italy could be compensated by the cession of Italia Irredenta, said Serafino. Little minds expatiated on an infinity of little things. Then, some began about the calumnies. What was He going to do about them? Oh, for certain He had disproved the charge made against Hadrian the Seventh; and most likely he could disprove the others. 'Could He?' Berstein cynically guffawed. Well, was He going to publish this disproval? 'Who knows?' asked Fiamma. The English and American cardinals energetically asseverated that, for their part, they neither were going to consult His Holiness on the subject, nor to consider themselves bound to secrecy in regard to the refutation which they had heard and witnessed. It was Carvale who hurriedly collected and expressed the opinions of his colleagues. 'What d'ye mean?' neighed the long faced Capuchin. 'I'll tell you what we mean:' said Semphill. 'With the help of my friends here, we'll have an authentic copy of the acts of this Consistory sent to every newspaper on earth.' 'And, you can bet, right now!' Van Kristen cried. The Cardinal-Archdeacon and nine Italians vociferated approval of the scheme. Talacryn trum-peted with the others, gambolling gaily along. Then he put down an elephantine foot – he was not quite sure that it was advisable: down at the back of his heart he felt the old distrust of Hadrian – he did not want to be involved by seeming to support – His Holiness was a most difficult man to get rid of, if one wanted to get rid of Him, whatever. But, still, the Cardinal of Caerleon trampled along with the others. Their Eminencies surged upstairs, chattering like a tygendis of magpies; and flowed along galleries, screeching like a muster of peacocks, until they reached the approach to the pontifical antechambers. The approach was closed, guarded by skewbald harlequins of Swiss with halberds. Before it stood the two gentlemen-of-the-apostolic-chamber, who formally responded to inquiry, 'Our Most Holy Lord is in secret'.

They had to make what they could of that. Those with sense went about their business without ado. Some, however, lingered to resent rebuff: or in the hope of obtaining quasi-accidental admission by bribery. Ragna panted up to four thousand lire in Sir John's ear; and departed cursing. The door was barred by 'Our Most Holy Lord is in secret'.

In secret Hadrian was kneeling upright in His chapel.

'God, I am very worldly. I have enjoyed the triumph.' That was the confession which He made, not precisely with sorrow but, with a consuming contempt for Himself. He had done such an ordinary deed: He despised Himself for doing it. He remained in contemplation of His disgusting humanity for some time.

By degrees, His mind detached itself from that; and attached itself to the next subject which He had prepared. He went into His workshop: covered the chairs around His armchair with sheets of MS. notes: drew the writing-board on His knees: laid out blank paper: rolled and lighted a cigarette; and began to read and amend His notes. From time to time, He sat back in His chair, gazing out of the window at nothing, working at problems in His brain. Now and then, He scribbled a note, a word, a phrase, a sentence.

At length He began to cover sheet after sheet. He wrote for hours and hours together, day after day: burning most of what He wrote, amending more, rewriting much. Anon, an acrid torpor astringed and benumbed His right arm from elbow to finger-tip, announcing the advent of scrivener's palsy. It was evening, about two hours after the Angelus. He put down His pen; and summoned the first gentleman-of-the-secret-chamber. Sir John sat in front of Him: rolled up the sleeve; and gave the arm and hand a gentle friction. Hadrian silently watched his busy hands. They were beautiful hands, very white, very slim, very soft – yes, singularly soft and soothing. Yet they were strong hands, firm and lissome. They did not tire with that continued searching movement, moulding and defining tired muscles and aching sinews, working the fatigue and ache gradually downward to dismissal at the finger-tips. Also the bent head was a good head, small and round, covered with close-cropped hair, black-purple, hyacinthine. And the healthy pallor of the face, the delicately cloven chin, the extremely fine grey eyes, the vigorous form, the exquisitely chaste and intelligent aspect – fancy expecting such an one to roll pills and fill capsules for ever in a chemist's shop! No: he was better as he was.

'John,' the Pope inquired, 'how do you get on with Macleod?'

'Oh, very well. I think I like him very much.'

'Is he comfortable?'

'Oh I think so. He seems so at any rate.'

'Has he got anything to say for himself?'

'Oh yes: now. He was a bit frightened at first: but he's got over that now.'

'To whom does he talk most freely?'

'Oh to me. Not but what he has plenty to say to Iulo too. But he'll tell me anything.'

'What do you mean by "anything"?'

'Oh everything about himself.'

'John, look up into these eyes a moment.' The shy grey eyes readily soared into the shy brown eyes.

'How much has he told you about himself?'

'Oh everything: that's all.'

'Everything?'

A fine flush tinged the fresh ivory face with coral: but the grey eyes did not waver. 'Oh yes, everything.'

'Can he sing?'

'Oh no, not a note – thank Heaven.'

Hadrian withdrew His gaze. 'And you think you like him very much?'

'Oh yes – I don't think: I know. I'm so awfully sorry for him.'

'And pity is akin to – '

'Oh but it's not pity and it's not love. It's something else altogether. It makes me in such a rage. I don't think I can make You understand, that's all.'

'Try.'

'Oh well – do You remember Max Alvary?'

'The singer-man? Yes. Why?'

'Oh, don't You know what I said when I saw him in *Siegfried*. You see, first I saw the splendour of his beauty; and then, when it came to the "Idyll", I got into a rage and I said "and that voice too".'

'What did you mean?'

'Oh it seemed so abominably unrighteous – all that beauty, and all that voice as well. That he should have two gifts; – and that others – I, for instance – should have not one!'

'What has this to do with Macleod?'

'Oh, a lot, in a topsyturvy kind of way. Look what a fine chap he is to look at – just like that lovely Figure on Your cross. And he's clever too. Well, You'd think him fortunate enough, wouldn't You? Then comes Fate and spoils him – spoils him completely. That's what makes me furious. To have to class him with Mustafa. I wonder he doesn't kill himself.'

'Go gently with that wrist, please. Have you told him that?'

'Oh no, I should hope not. Sorry. I want to do everything in the world to keep him from knowing what I think – to keep him from hitting on that line of thought by accident, by himself, even. It would drive the poor chap mad: that's all.'

'John you're a brick. Now listen to this. Thoughts you know, are things. If you think such thoughts, they'll be in the air about you; and it's as likely as not that Macleod's senses will perceive them. So you'd better extirpate them *hic et nunc* – if you like him and want to help him.'

'Oh do You think so? Well, I will then: because I really do want to help him.'

'Good. And now what's to be done with him?'

'Oh but why should anything be done with him? He's very happy here.'

'Thanks to your goodness, John. Silence! But first of all We must give him a reason for being here: and then We must remember that "here we have no continuing city". Now listen attentively. When you have finished that hand, you will go to

311

the Secretary of State, and tell His Eminency to issue a patent to Mr Macleod as third gentleman of the chamber – emolument half yours – no knighthood. Will that do?'

'Oh finely!'

'Good. Well now let's go back a bit. Suppose Macleod wasn't here. Where, in your opinion, would he be best?'

'Oh I hardly know what to say to that.'

'You know your Meredith? Well then, favour Us with the outline of your ideas. Pour them out pell-mell, intelligibly or not, no matter. We undertake to catch hold of something.'

'Oh well, I think he'd do well in a garden. He's quite learned about flowers; and, if You ever saw him handle one, You'd wonder however a chap with a chest and arms like a blacksmith, as his are, could be so tender. There's a lot more force and there's a lot more gentleness in him than You'd think. Same with trees. He looks at them as we look at other chaps – just as though he could speak to them and make them understand him if he wanted to. He'd do well at anything out of doors, farming perhaps. I did think at first of the sea –'

'Because of his wonderful eyes?'

'Oh yes I suppose that was the reason. Did ever You see such a blue, a blue that makes you want to strip and dive – just the eyes for a sailor, aren't they? That's simply my romance though. But I haven't talked to him much about the sea. Do You know what I should like to do? I should like to go a long sea-voyage with him in one of those old sailing-ships, and take the Pliny and the Sophocles which You gave me, and a lexicon, and a dictionary, and read them with him, right away from – of course I don't mean what You think I mean.'

'No: of course you don't. And then, when you come back from your long sea-voyage in a sailing ship, you think that Macleod could be useful and happy on a flower farm, with orchards, and all that sort of rot, while you could sit in the shade of medlar trees and rose bushes, and look after him so that no one should insult him, and read books (write them too perhaps) and dream dreams (and certainly write those) and live happily in a dear old-fashioned farmhouse ever after –'

'Oh You're laughing at me now!'

'Not at all.' The bright brown eyes became grave.

'John, what are you going to do with yourself when Hadrian is dead?'

'Oh but You're not going to die –'

'How do you know? Answer the question.'

'Oh I haven't thought about it. I don't want to think about it: that's all.'

'Nonsense. Think about it; and be done with it. John, when We are dead, if you have a place like that, and means to work it, means to move about and use yourself – will you use yourself? And will you take Macleod and be a brother – not a real but the Ideal Brother to him?'

'Oh of course I would: but –'

'Will you promise?'

'Oh yes, I promise You most faithfully. But I hope to God I'll never have the chance –'

'Well, no one knows when you will have the chance: but you shall have it. Bring the pen here, and the writing-board.' Hadrian pulled down His sleeve, and stroked the cat for a minute or two, thoughtfully looking out of the window. Then He wrote, putting what He wrote into an envelope which He gave to the shaking sprig of virtue who stood before Him. 'You will take this to Plowden, after you have been to Ragna. You will obtain his formal acknowledgement. See that it is made out in your name; and keep it secretly till the time comes for using it. On Our death you will present it; and Plowden will pay you five thousand pounds, and take your receipt for it. With that sum, you will buy, and stock, such a place as We have described. As long as you and Macleod live, Plowden will pay you a regular income, so that you never can come to want, and always can have something to give away. Every quarter day he will pay a hundred pounds to you, and fifty to Macleod; and you can make as much more as you like out of your farm. That, remember, is yours; and you may do what you please with it. When you both die, the capital which provides your incomes will return to the pontifical treasury: so if you want to marry, and beget a family, and leave something more than real property – the farm – behind you, you must earn it. We give you a chance, and perfect freedom. Do you follow?'

'Oh I never shall forget a single word. Holy Father, I can't take it. What have I done to deserve it? What could I ever do to deserve it?'

'Boy, you have done this to deserve it. You have wished to bear or to share another's burden. You shall have your wish; and you shall have a little reward here and a very great reward – there – if you carry out your wish. That's what you have done and what you can do. You are good, and you are trusted. And that's all. Now go away at once because We have a lot of writing yet to do.'

'John,' cried Hadrian, just before the door closed. 'By the bye, you had better tell Macleod of his appointment; and see about his uniforms at once: but keep the other matter to yourself till – you know when. Oh – and please make him understand that We shall call him "James". That Gaelic "Hamish" is a little too much. And he had better be Mr James to the others.'

Outside the closed door, Sir John struck his own hands together. 'And the maddening thing is that there is nothing in the whole world that I can do for Him. If I were to give Him a little present, like a baccy-pouch, ten to one it wouldn't be precisely to His taste – anyhow it'd only be like giving Him a calf of His Own cow. Oh damn! It's like a wax match offering a light to the sun.' He suddenly faced to the door again; and his words came in the form of a solemn pledge. 'Lord, I promise.' He remained entranced for several moments: and anon went on his way with steadfast brow.

CHAPTER 21

THE Cardinal-deacon of St Cosmas and St Damian did it. The acts of the Consistory, in so far as they related to the calumny against the Pope, duly appeared in *The Times* and the *Globe* and the *New York Times* as news which was fit to print. Innumerable other papers lifted them with acknowledgements. No comment was made. The collared-puppy-in-the-Tube, and the spectacled-person-in-the-motor-car, and the female-with-the-loaf-coloured-hat-at-the-bargain-sale, forgot all about George Arthur Rose: paid no attention whatever to the Pope; and violently sat up on their hind-legs regarding the Supreme Arbitrator. France and Russia emitted caricatures and howls; and prepared to invade Belgium and Sweden, with the intention of descending on Germany from three sides.

Mrs Crowe became conscious that she had lost rather than had gained by her connexion with Jerry Sant. The English Catholics treated her as they are wont to treat converts after the first three months; and showed her the cold shoulder. The refutation of her latest calumny had made her look foolish – and something dirtier than foolish. She was mortified: she was angry with herself; and she naturally yearned to tear and mangle everybody else. She thought that the best thing which she could do would be to pose as a much deceived woman, to break that disastrous connexion with the Liblabs, and to return (if possible) to the *status quo ante*. So she went and fell upon Jerry, vituperating him for the accented failure of his schemes – for leading an innocent lady astray with his nastiness, and his pig-headed stupidity, and all that. She frankly told him that he had gone too far. The precious pair 'had words'; and finally separated. Jerry remained at his hotel, dumb and dangerous, brooding. As for the lady, respectable mediocrity allured her by the prospect which it offered of a not unfamiliar obscurity, where she might try to piece together the shreds and tatters of her reputation. She had a little money left – and with economy – She would stay just a little longer. Who knew what might happen?

One by one, cardinals received summons to the secret chamber. Their brains were picked and their opinions heard. Nefski of the ashen pallor and the haunted eyes admitted that Poland might be happier as a constitutional monarchy and a member of a federation. Pushed to it, he promised to use all his influence to persuade. Mundo, cleanly, rotund and sparkling, spoke of Portugal's long and illustrious alliance with the Lord of the

Sea. His compact vivid nation had no grievances. Grace looked silently vigorous; and praised the Munroe doctrine. If only – The French cardinals chattered: were aghast: sobbed: were quite limp; and became picturesquely and dithyrambically resigned. Oh they were so excellent: and so futile! Courtleigh pleaded age, infirmity. Circumstances had become more than he could manage. He had begun to think that he never had been anything but a decorative figure-head: that he never once had gripped the rudder of affairs since the Prince of Wales had been so – well, rude to him. He was old: he was garrulous: craving for greetings. He begged leave to go and end his days in the college which he had founded, if the Holy Father would but deign to relieve him of his archbishopric. Hadrian did deign; and summoned Talacryn, to whom He said 'We are about to fulfil the ambition of Your Eminency's life by preconizing you to the archbishopric of Pimlico.'

The cardinal said something about being unworthy of the honour.

'That of course,' the Pontiff responded: 'but We place you there because you know or ought to know more of Our mind than any man: and your task is to make that known to England. It at least never can be said, if you should err, that you erred through ignorance of Our will. You have health, you have youth, you have a dominant presence. People will listen to you. Your danger and your fault are due to your national habit of suspicion. That can be conquered. Act up to your name: be frank: suspect no one: be ready to renounce – but your heart should tell you all that We would say. Now for Caerleon. Whom would you like to succeed Your Eminency there?'

Talacryn said something about the right of the clergy to elect: but that was swept aside. Then he dwelled on the difficulty of finding a suitable priest who could speak the native language.

'That last is not essential,' said Hadrian: 'you yourself cannot speak and cannot even learn that frightful jargon, although you are a native of the dreadful place: and, after your habit of suspecting people, and – yes, it had better be said – a slight tendency to the habit of officious lying, – (the cardinal went purple) –

'there, it is said and done with: you have had your lesson, and you know better now: – after those things, the only reason why your episcopate has not been a very brilliant one is that you started with the false idea of the necessity of speaking that corrupt and obsolete dialect.'

'But does not Your Holiness think that a foreigner – '

'No: England is the dominant race: her language is the language of all her colonies. Why a triplet of little conquered countries should refuse to learn English – should be permitted to insist on their barbarous and unliterary languages, We never could understand. They are conquered countries, annexed to their conqueror. They have lost their national existence for centuries. They have no national existence, or any kind of existence apart from England. No. Nationality does not come into the question of your successor at all. That is where the Church of Christ differs from all religions. Rome can do, and does do, what no other ecclesiastical power durst do. Our predecessors sent an Italian to Canterbury, and even a Greek, Theodore; and We are sending a Celt to Pimlico. As for Caerleon – do you remember John Jennifer, the priest of Selce? You do – he was a white man at Maryvale – and since? Good. He is Bishop of Caerleon.'

'He speaks the language, Holy Father,' said Talacryn, laughing.

'The merest accident. We selected him for his steadfast sturdy goodness under great difficulty at Maryvale. Oh, we remember – '

And the Pope's gaze went far away into the past.

Cardinal Talacryn mentioned that the Secretary of State desired to know whether His Holiness would require the services of the Patriarch of Byzantion at the present juncture.

'The Patriarch of Byzantion?'

'It was thought that as he had negotiated with England during the reign of Your Holiness's predecessors – '

'Oh. Then, no. The services of the Patriarch of Byzantion are not required. When His Grace is not smirking in ''black'' drawing-rooms, or writing defamatory letters to duchesses – '

'Defamatory letters, Holy Father!'

'Yes: defamatory letters, such as this one which he wrote in 1890.'

The Pope got up, took off His episcopal ring, unlocked and dived into an alphabetical letter-case, and handed a most ingeniously suggestive and lethific note to the cardinal. 'Well, when His Grace is not engaged in these disedifying pastimes, he has his patriarchate to attend to. In fact unless he can see his way to become a resident patriarch in Byzantion within the month, he may look for a decree of deposition.' The Supreme Pontiff's aspect was austere. 'Your Eminency will convey that response to Cardinal Ragna's obliging suggestion.'

Talacryn made haste to kneel. 'Give me a blessing, Holy Father, and I will immediately proceed to my new see, whatever.'

Hadrian smiled. 'God bless you, son. But do not go yet. Pimlico has been in the hands of the Vicar-General and the Coadjutor for years; and the Vicar-Capitular can manage for the present. Stay here a little while. We shall need you. We shall not need you long.'

And Talacryn went out from the Presence, glad, yet grave.

During a few days, questions and answers incessantly passed between the Vatican and Windsor Castle. Hadrian consulted sovereigns: discussed difficulties with statesmen. Baron de Boucert expressed the opinion that it would be futile to oppose the inevitable expansion of Germany. Signor Barconi himself officiated at an instrument installed in the apostolic antechamber, until he was carried away in nervous collapse. Hadrian envied him: and forced Himself to resist temptation. He had much to do yet. Messages, messages, study of maps, collation of MS. notes, filled a score of each twenty-four hours. There was need of profound thought, so that the clairvoyant undazzled eye like a diver might reach the bottom of deep-preserving thought. The four hours which remained chiefly were spent at the tomb of St Peter in the basilica. The Arbitrator slept not at all in these days. He ate while at work; and only sought refreshment under the ice-cold tap in the bathroom. A squadron of

English cruisers escorted a procession of royal yachts and battle-ships, which conveyed the Congress of Windsor to Golden and immortal Rome.

Then came the issue of the *Epistle to the Princes*, in which the Apostle reiterated the evangelic counsels, predicating a scheme of utter self-sacrifice and non-resistance in imitation of the 'sweet reasonableness of Christ'. This would mean, said He, the deliberate loosening and casting away of all conventions which bound society together. It was right: it was straight: it was the most direct road to heaven. But it was not in accordance with the human will: it would be called utopian, and unconven-tional; and it would be derided more than followed: it would cause confusion inconceivable if it were attempted on the grand scale. Truth more quickly emerges from error than from con-fusion. Men, being what they are, i.e. bound to err, would be better for having their errancy guided. They would diverge from the road: but they should not leave it out of sight; and, properly guided, their movement at least could be made to tend towards the Point Desirable. Individuality so long had been suppressed, that its efforts required administration. Therefore the Pontiff showed, as well as an unconventional, a conven-tional way of approaching that Point Desirable. He maintained the aristocratic and monarchic principle in strict integrity. A rebel was worse than the worst prince, and rebellion was worse than the worst government of the worst prince that hitherto had been. He proclaimed the anarchy of France and Russia to be a manifestation of diabolic ebullience, which ought to be restrained and stamped out by all right means, even the most stringent. France and Russia, having forfeited the right of being deemed capable of ruling themselves, henceforth must submit to be ruled. Satan finds mischief for idle hands to do. Occupa-tion and scope for occupation, alone will enable individuals and nations to work out their own salvation humanly speaking. Men *must* use themselves – for good or ill. Most human ills were caused by the lack of scope for energy. Sitting on, or screwing down, the safety valve invariably was fatal – a doctrine which He enforced on the attention and obedience of the clergy.

These principles involved a rearrangement of various spheres of influence. The Ruler of the World, Peter, the Supreme Arbitrator, decreed that the only nations, in which the *facultas regendi* survived in undiminished energy, were England, America, Japan, Germany, Italy. Some of the old monarchies, however, had not yet reached that point of decay when their extinction would become desirable: they were Norway, Sweden, Denmark, the German kingdoms and principalities and duchies, Spain, Portugal, Greece, Romania, Albania, Montenegro, the republics of Switzerland and San Marino. These were to be maintained as sovereign states and to preserve their national characters. Some also of the old monarchies, which had tolerated unmerited suppression, were to be given an opportunity of proving themselves worthy of corporate existence. These were Hungary, Bohemia, and Russian and German Poland. They were revived as kingdoms; and required to provide themselves with constitutions (after the manner of England), and to elect their respective monarchical dynasties. Switzerland and San Marino were confirmed as republics. The Sultan at the instigation of England, his ally, would move his capital to Damascus, in order to concentrate the main force of Islam in Asia. Serbia was added to the Principality of Montenegro. Turkey-in-Europe and Bulgaria would become merged in the kingdom of Greece. So far for particulars.

Hadrian denounced, as bad and idle dreams, the plans of recent political schemers who had adumbrated ideas of a federation of the English-speaking and the Teutonic races. He dwelled upon the essential differences which divided Germany from America, and both from England. No blend was possible between the English and the Germans; and Americans were not qualified for bonds. Each one of the three was unique; and each would stand alone. Three such enormous powers must have each its own separate and singular existence and sphere of action. Three such spheres must be found, in which the three nations independently might thrive. It was room for independent development which must be sought out, and assigned.

He stated the case of the continent of Europe. Belgium had 228 inhabitants to the square kilometre: Holland, 160: Germany, 104: Austria, 87: France, 72: Russia was so sparsely populated that only a migration of 109,000,000 people from the rest of Europe would raise her to the European average. Hence, the Pope proclaimed the instauration of the Roman Empire, under two Emperors, a Northern Emperor and a Southern Emperor; and confirmed the same to the King of Prussia and the King of Italy as representatives of the dynasties of Hohenzollern and Savoy respectively. He ordained that this instauration should not be deemed 'the ghost of the dead Roman Empire sitting crowned upon the grave thereof, but its legitimate heir and successor, justified by the ancient virtues of the Romans, the beneficence of their rule', and the vigorous aspiration to well-doing which characterized their present representatives. The Northern Emperor William would nominate sovereign dynasties for Belgium and Holland. He might replace the present exiled monarchs on their respective thrones: or he might depose them and substitute members of his Imperial family. He then would extend the borders of Germany, eastward to the Ural Mountains by the inclusion of Russia, westward to the English Channel and Bay of Biscay by the inclusion of France, southward to the Danube by the inclusion of Austria. At the same time, he would federate the constitution monarchies of Norway and Sweden, Denmark, Holland, Belgium, Hungary, Bohemia, Poland, Romania, and the republic of Switzerland with the other sovereign states already under his suzerainty: while the Southern Emperor Victor Emanuel would federate the constitutional monarchies of Portugal, Spain, the extended kingdom of Greece, the principalities of Montenegro and Albania, and the republic of San Marino, with the kingdom of Italy, which last now was to include Italia Redenta. The frontier dividing the Northern Empire from the Southern was to be formed by the Pyrenees, Alps, Danube, and Black Sea.

The case of America was defined. The United States were to be increased by the inclusion of all the states and republics of the two Americas from the present northern frontier of the United States to Cape Horn.

The Japanese Empire was authorized to annex Siberia.

All Asia (except Siberia), Africa, Canada, Australia, New Zealand, and all islands, were erected into five constitutional kingdoms, and added to the dominions of the King of England, Ireland, Wales, and Scotland. The title 'Emperor' being anti-pathetic to the English Race (on account of its primary signifi-cance 'War-Lord'), the official style of the Majesty of England, Ireland, Wales, Scotland, Asia, Africa, Canada, Australia, New Zealand and all islands, henceforth would be 'The Ninefold King'.

Thus the Supreme Arbitrator provided the human race with scope and opportunity for energy. The provisions of the *Epistle to the Princes* were drawn up in the form of Treaty divid-ing the world, till midnight (G.T.) of 31 December (N.S.) of the year 2000 of the Fructiferous Incarnation of the Son of God, into the Ninefold Kingdom, the American Republic, the Japanese Empire, and the Roman Empire. This Treaty was signed, in the Square of St Peter's at Rome, by the Pontiff, the Sovereigns, and the Presidents, on the Festival of the Annuncia-tion of Our Lady the Virgin; and the armies and navies of the signatories instantly set about the pacification of France and Russia by martial law.

CHAPTER 22

APRIL brought to Hadrian an experience of one of those periods of psychical disturbance which are incidental to the weakness of humanity, and inevitable by a man of His particu-lar temper. Things lost their significance to Him, persons lost their personality, events their importance; and time was not. He kept a straight face, and forced Himself to courteous demeanour: but He was living in a world in which He felt Him-self to be just off the floor and floating, a world in which every-thing was strange and everybody was quite strange, a world where nobody and nothing mattered the least little bit. He had the sense at the beginning to include Himself in secret behind guarded doors; and also to hold His tongue when His attendants were in the Presence. He simply sat and wondered – wondered who He was, how He came there, who dressed Him like that, and when; and decided that it did not matter. He nursed His cat, cooing and mewing and talking cat language in a most enjoyable manner. When the creature went away – it did not matter. He used to gaze at His cross by the hour together, planning combinations of lights and shades and backgrounds of book-backs: placing the golden symbol there, and revelling in the supple splendour of the Form, its dignity, its grace, the majestic youth of the Face, noble and grave. He would close His eyes and learn the lovely planes and contours with delicate reverent touch. It pleased Him to think that He had created a type of incarnate divinity, which neither was the Orpheys of the catacombs, nor the Tragic Mask of the Vernicle, nor the gross sexless indecencies wherewith pious Catholics in their churches insult the One among ten thousand, the Altogether Lovely. That thought brought Him back to Space and Time. Indignation at images at least eleven heads long, proportioned like female fashion-plates, visaged like emasculate noodles whom you would slap in the face on sight, simply for their tepid attenuate silliness, if you met them in the flesh – this drew down Hadrian to realities and life. He felt utterly exhausted. An exposition of sleep seized Him. He was always drowsy; and would fall asleep in the daytime over the writing and reading which He put Himself to do, in His armchair by the window, in His favourite seat by the old wall in the garden where He spent the vivid afternoons of spring. Only toward nightfall, was He able to write that beautiful clear script of His, to bring any of His usual alertness to bear upon affairs: even then that alertness was extraordinarily diluted. His intellect was nebulous, uncertain. He could not select saliencies, could not concentrate his thoughts: His constructive faculty was in abeyance: His imagination was in chains. He spent a long time over His scanty meals, chewing, chewing, reading, reading, and remembering nothing which He read. In an inert perfunctory way, He blamed Himself for waste of time; and continued to waste it. No doubt it was divine nature's will. Let it be understood that He was not slothful in the confessional sense of the word. He was merely lethargic, dulled, blunted, listless, eager for nothing, except to flee away and be at rest – at rest.

From this stupor, He awoke in panic, as though nympholeptose, lymphatic, driven to frenzy by some unknown external agency. He became inspired with an appalling consciousness of the absolute necessity for instant active continuous exertion – if He were to continue alive upon this earth. He felt that, if He were to permit Himself to relax for one instant, if for one instant He were to abdicate command of His physical forces, to let Himself go – that instant would be His last. With this in His mind, He prepared for momentary unconscious lapses from violent activity. He posed with care, so that, if Death should seize Him unawares, He might not present a disedifying or untidy spectacle to the finders of His corpse. He carefully avoided postures from which, when He should be reft from the body, His form would fall indecorously. He did not trouble His confessor more often than twice a week as usual: but His one prayer, His incantation, always was on His lips, 'Dear Jesus, be not to me a Judge, but a Saviour'. He was losing hold of the world. Continually, through every hour of the day and night, His head rang with the reverberating boom – boom – boom – boom of His strong heart's beating. The rhythm was maddening. He used to count the pulsations, wondering, after 'fourteen', whether He would be able to say 'fifteen': after 'ninety-seven', whether He would be in Rome to say 'ninety-eight': expecting the sudden wrench of self from body: conjecturing the nature of that unique experience. Once, He put Himself to the question 'Was He afraid?' He answered, No, because He dared to hope; and, Yes, because He had not been there before. But Socrates had said that death was our greatest possession on earth; and Seneca said that death was the best of the inventions of life; and Seneca's friend St Paul said 'to die is gain'. On the whole, He was not afraid, afraid, of death. But,

He did not dare to go – to go – to sleep now. At night, He used to lie in bed, first on His right side, then at full length on His back with the pillow under His neck, and His hands crossed on the breast which had been tattooed with a cross when He was a boy, and His ankles crossed like a crusader, rigid, as He wished to lie in His coffin – and His brain active, active, counting physical pulsations, meditating on the future, scheming, planning, counting each breath, and waiting for the last – and death.

Sometimes He wondered whether it was all worth while: whether it was in accordance with God's Will that He should be so wilful. He decided to risk an affirmative to that, on the ground of the existence of His will. He knew that He tried rightly to use it. He hoped for mercy on account of lapses. One point He determined. With all due respect to Socrates and Seneca, Death came by Sin, and Sin was God's enemy, and God's friends must fight God's enemies to the bitter end. To relax was suicide, and suicide was sin; and, tired with conflict as He was, eager for rest and peace as He was, it certainly was not worth while to add to His tale of sin: it was not worth while to exchange tiresome earth for untiring hell: to lose, what Petrarch calls 'the splendour of the angelic smile'. He had no steel in His possession except safety-razors: knives and scissors He had abolished long ago; and now He had light strong gratings fixed to all His windows. He would not go into temptation. 'I am fawned upon by hope. Ah, would that she had a voice which I could understand, a voice like that of a herald, that I might not be agitated by distracting thought,' He said to Himself in the words of Electra at the tomb of Agamemnon. Had He been trained in boyhood at a public-school, in adolescence at an university, had His lines been cast in service, He would not have had to put so severe restraint upon Himself. The occasion would not have arisen. A simple and perhaps a stolid character would have been formed of His temper, potent and brilliant enough to distinguish Him from the mob, but incapable of hypersensation. Instead, His frightfully self-concentrated and lonely life, denied the ordinary opportunities of action, had developed this heart-rending complexity: had trained him in mental gymnastics to a degree of excellence which was inhuman, abominable (in the first intention of the words) in its facile flexible solert dexterity. He was not restrained by any sense whatever of modesty or of decorum. He had no sense of those things. He knew it; and regretted it. He was Himself. He distrusted that self, rejoiced in it, and determined to deal well and righteously with it. Dr Guido Cabelli, at length summoned, found Him positively furious with the pain of physical and intellectual struggles. The physician exhibited Pot. Brom., Tinct. Valerian. Am., Tinct. Zinzil., Sp. Chlorof., Aq. Menth. Pip., once every three hours. It made the Pontiff conscious that He stank like a male cat in early summer: but He heard no more boom-booming in his ears. It strung up His nervous system for the time. He put on His pontifical mask; and addressed Himself from the ideal to the real.

He put the affairs of nations on one side. They, the nations all were tumbling over one another in their eagerness to rearrange themselves upon the pattern which He had devised for them. If He adopted the Pythagorean role of an uninterested spectator, either He would be annoyed by something ugly or something silly, or He would have a chance of glorifying Himself on account of some success. And He wished to do otherwise than that. 'In this world, God and His angels only may be spectators.'

The affairs of religion, as far as He could see, amounted to the service of others and the cultivation of personal holiness, the correspondence with Divine Love. Someone had told Him that – yes, Talacryn in confession, of course – that the key to all His difficulties, present and to come, was Love. That was all very pretty and theological on the part of the bishop, the Cardinal-Archbishop: but it was the baby who had taught Him the secret of the method. He would, He really would keep His troubles to Himself. His office was the office of leader and exemplar. Nothing must interfere. He put Himself to review the first year of His pontificate: and a black enough tale it seemed to Him. Without surprise, without emotion, He noted the blurs of impatience, pride – pride – humanity. Retrospection was the most wearisome most fatuous banality. Onward!

Leader and exemplar! One thing was clear. He must come down among the led and following. He must be seen of men. And He was not seen. No. Peculiar personal preference kept Him apart, mysterious. He rather enjoyed (not the being misunderstood but) the not being understood; and, at the same time, He had been doing a lot of people the gross injustice of crediting them with the possession of intelligence similar to His Own, of perspicacity equal to His Own, of the ability to keep up with His rapid pace and abrupt manoeuvres. That was unrighteous. No doubt it had been all very fine and noble and so forth to sit down silent under calumny, for example. One could afford to do that when one was innocent. But, when millions of people (to give the devils their due) actually wanted to believe one innocent, and would be grieved and perhaps injured because the opportunity to believe innocence was withheld, was it righteous to refuse to condescend? No, such a pose was mere pride. The Servant of the servants of God must not fear to soil the whiteness of His robe in any kind of ordure. Also, to save others was the best way of retrieving oneself.

He sent for the nearest cardinals. Ragna, Saviolli, Semphill, Sterling, Talacryn, Carvale, Van Kristen, Gentilotto, Leighton, Whitehead, responded to the summons. Hadrian received them in the throne-room, but without formality; and contrived to give them an easy and genial greeting. They thought Him to be looking seriously ill. There was the dead whiteness of a gardenia in the hue of His face and hands: His reddish-brown hair was going grey over the left ear: His intense and rigid mask was the sign of pain. His whole aspect also was diaphanous, wasted. But His manner was vivid: He was not inaccessible. Their Eminencies gave Him their attention; and wondered what He was going to bring out of the dispatch box by His side. He was extremely glad to see the Secretary of State: for He knew how antipathetic He was to that one; and now He was going to try to give him satisfaction. At least it should not be His fault if Ragna's ordinary attitude of discreet and convulsive brutality remained unmitigated.

'Lord Cardinals,' the Supreme Pontiff said, 'it has occurred to Us that ye have many things to say: that there be many things which ye desire to know. We, on Our part, are ready to hear; and We are willing to respond to questions.'

Questions instantly were born in each man's brain. Ragna was the first to deliver Himself of his. 'Holiness, will You answer a question about the *Epistle to the Princes*?'

'Yes.'

Ragna collected himself. 'I am curious to know why the rights of France in Egypt were not even named. I can see that the very nature of Your Holiness's counsels demanded that Africa as a whole should pass to England: but I cannot understand why Germany, in taking over France, should not also have taken over the condominium of Egypt. Why did that fall to England; and why did Germany consent to its falling to England?'

Hadrian made an effort to conquer His natural incapacity for coming near a subject at the first attempt; and put Himself to be concise. 'Your Eminency knows that since – We forget the exact date – but since a very short time ago, no international obligations have existed which could restrain Egypt from legitimate attempts at emancipation. Nothing but Ottoman firmans held her. Very well. We discovered that when the King of England and the Sultan, last October, made alliance, the latter issued a firman in which England was named Protector of Egypt. Then' (the speaker slightly smiled) 'when the task of arbitration was submitted to Us, We found that the German colonies in Africa, not only did not pay their way but, required a yearly subsidy of £1,500,000; and therefore, taking one thing with another, We arranged to give Germany sufficient employment for a century nearer home. She promptly recognized that *megli' è fringuello in man' che tordo in frasca*. The fact is that she was only too glad to be rid of her own parasitic colonies, which had severed their connexion from the parent stem, and derived their nutriment from other states: while the colonies of France which were epiphytic, having no existence apart from the source from which they sprang, were wiped out (as French colonies) when France was wiped out.'

'And no doubt Germany, in her pretty Gothic way, was in such a desperate hurry to grab France, that she forgot all about Egypt. D'ye know they say she's going to call her conquest Gallia again?' Semphill put in with a sniff. 'And now I'll ask a question. Holy Father, may I smoke?'

'But smoke!' Hadrian assented with pleasure; and held out His Own hand for a cigarette. Some of the others did likewise; and the gear began to run much more easily. Van Kristen expressed joy that the Germans were not to have chances of doing more monkey business on the Erechtheum and the Acropolis at Athens.

'Yes,' Ragna meditatively continued: 'I suppose I ought to have understood all that. But now, Holiness, there's another thing: why did the Sultan consent to evacuate Europe?'

'Simply because, with all the examples which he has had lately, he goes in mortal terror of assassination. He has managed to persuade himself that he only can be warranted against that, as long as he is under the aegis of England. Well: seeing England and Turkey allied, We moved England and England moved Ismail. The former had sense: the latter, sentiment. But Ismail really is not half bad: in fact he's rather decent. If we only had another dear charming child-like naked Christian like Blessed Brother Francis – '

'What?' said Carvale with animation. He happened to have noted that, when Hadrian rioted in superlatives, it meant no more than positives: but, when He negligently drawled comparatives, 'not half bad' or 'rather decent', the ultimate of praise was signified. 'What?' the cardinal repeated.

'We would send him to give points to Ismail's mollahs and dervishes.'

'St Francis has innumerable sons, Holiness,' Saviolli put in.

'And We only know one who in the slightest degree resembles his father,' the Pope responded, waving away the subject.

'One would like to know,' said Sterling, 'whether Your Holiness is not really of the opinion that the *Epistle to the Princes* was perhaps a trifle too sentimental and – '

'Sentimental? Yes. The Ruler, who rules sentiment out of his calculations, ignores one of the most potent forces in human affairs. Too sentimental? No. And what else was Your Eminency about to say – a trifle too sentimental and – '

'One would have said perhaps a trifle too arbitrary.'

'Dear man – ' the Pope gleefully began.

But Ragna interrupted 'Nothing of the kind. That particular *Epistle* was replete with pontifical dignity: it was the finest thing – '

Hadrian stopped him 'We were about to remind Cardinal Sterling that when the Ruler of the World geographically rules the world, He is accustomed to do His ruling with a ruler. Our predecessor Alexander VI used a ruler on a celebrated occasion on the Atlantic Ocean.'

Everybody burst out laughing: laughed for a few moments; and returned to a serious demeanour. There was a question, an important question, which sat upon all tongues, wing-preened, ready to fly. But His Holiness already had refused to discuss it. Those, who had tried to persuade, so seriously had been hurt by His icy reticence or by His blunt aloofness, that no one now was temerarious enough to attempt the reopening of so unsavoury and so personal a matter, except upon explicit invitation. Knowing what he did of men, Hadrian had expected hesitation: but, seeing that His purpose was likely to fail of completion; and, being determined that it should not fail, He slowly and significantly drew off the pontifical ring from His first finger, and put it in His pocket. 'Gentlemen,' He said with quite a change of manner, 'some of you would like to put George Arthur Rose to the question?'

They would indeed. They would whatever. They would like it so much that they all spoke in unison. The sum of their words amounted to a request that George Arthur Rose would give them some sort of statement concerning newspaper calumnies, some sort of statement by way of support to their contention that he had been grossly wronged and mispresented.

It was George the Digladiator who responded. He seemed to step down into the arena, naked, lithe, agile, with bright open eyes, and ready to fight for life. 'Very well,' he said – 'I will give that statement to you: but understand that I will not defend myself in the newspapers. If I were a layman, I should have whipped in a writ for libel, and have given my damages to Nazareth House. I should have preferred to trust my reputation rather to an English judge and jury, than to the nameless editors of Erse or Radical newspapers. Fancy having one's letters edited by the *Catholic Hour*, for example: fancy having one's letters, which are one's defence, nefariously garbled by a nameless creature who is one's prosecutor, and one's judge, and one's jury, all in one! However, not being a layman, I cannot go to law; and I will not condescend to have dealings with those newspapers. Understand also, that I tell you what I am about to tell you, not because I have been provoked, abused, calumniated, traduced, assailed with insinuation, innuendo, mispresentation, lies: not because my life has been held up to ridicule, and to most inferior contempt: not because the most preposterous stories to my detriment have been invented, hawked about, believed. No. Please understand that I am not going to speak in my own defence, even to you. I personally, and of predilection, can be indifferent to opinions. But officially I must correct error. So I will give you some information. You may take it, or leave it: believe it or disbelieve it. You shall have as photographic a picture as I can give you of my life, and of the majestic immobility by which you clergy tire out – assassinate a man's body – perhaps his soul. You are free to use it or abuse it. When I shall have finished speaking, I never will return to this subject.'

'Of course we shall believe what you say,' Semphill rather nervously intercalated. 'I'm sure we believe it unsaid. We take it as said, you know. But if you could see your way to give us details, say on half a dozen points, that would be quite enough.'

'The *Daily Anagraph* has not apologized for its latest slander,' Carvale put in.

'Why should it?' George inquired.

'Well, I sent an authenticated account of what happened in the last Consistory. The other papers printed it; and I should have thought the least the *Daily Anagraph* could have done would be – '

'Carvale, you're making a mistake. The *Daily Anagraph* has no personal grudge against me: although the last editor had, because I once innocently asked him whether historical accuracy came within the scope of a Radical periodical. That was years ago, at the time of the second Dreyfus case. I know that he was furious; because Bertram Blighter, the novel-man, told me that that editor in revenge was going to put me on the newspaper black-list, whatever that may be. No, it is not a personal matter, a matter which an apology is customary. It's simply an example of the ethics of commercial journalism. The man wanted to increase the sale of his paper. I happened by chance to be before the world just then. And he took the liberty of increasing his circulation at my expense. Actually that is all. You can't (at least I don't), expect an editor, who is capable of doing such a thing, to apologize for doing it. The case of the other papers is verisimilar: except of course the *Catholic Hour*. That simply exists on sycophanty by sycophants for sycophantophagists, as Semphill knows.'

'Yes I know,' said Semphill. 'And I don't allow the thing to enter my house.'

'But the others – in their case it's not lurid malignance, but legal malfeasance. Did you say that they apologized?'

'No. None of those, which printed the calumnies, apologized. They just kept silence. But all the respectable papers, which had not calumniated you, printed my refutation of the *Daily Anagraph*.'

George made a gesture of scorn, of satisfaction, of dismissal. 'Then the Pope is clear;' he said. 'Now I will try to tell you, as briefly as possible, what you want to know about the other person.' He produced a sheaf of newspaper-cuts. He was in such a white rage at having to do what he was about to do, that he wreaked his anger on those who listened to him, piercingly eyeing them, speaking with swift fury as one would speak to foes. 'The *Catholic Hour* states that in 1886 I was under an under-master at Grandholme School: that I had to leave my mastership because I became Catholic. That is true in substance and absolutely false in connotation. I was an under-master: but as I also had charge of the school-house, I was called the house-master. You also perhaps may be aware that there is only one headmaster in a school; and that all the rest are under-masters. But, when slander is your object, "under-master" is a nice disgraceful dab of mud to sling at your victim for a beginning. Well: I resigned my house-mastership of my own free and unaided will for the reason alleged; and I have yet to learn that the becoming Catholic is an extraordinarily slimy deed. Further, note this, far from my resignation being the dishonourable affair which the *Catholic Hour* implies, the headmaster of Grandholme School remained my dear and intimate and honoured friend through thick and thin, for more than twenty years, and is my only dear and intimate friend at this moment.'

Semphill and Carvale looked up, and then down. Sterling looked down, down. Van Kristen looked up. The others, anywhere. Talacryn looked annoyed. The taunt was flung out; and the flying voice went on. 'The *Catholic Hour* thus casts its diatribe in a key of depreciation. Next, I am said to have gone to a school for outcasts, to have quarrelled with the two priest-chaplains; and presently to have been "again out". The idea being to infer evil, it is rather cleverly done in that statement of the case. But here are the facts. The school perhaps might be called a school for outcasts. But I, a young inexperienced Catholic of six months, was lured by innumerable false pretences, on the part of the eccentric party who offered me the post, to accept what he called the Headmastership of a Cathedral Choir School. He did not tell me that he was forcing the establishment on the bishop of the diocese, nor that the Headmastership had been refused by several distinguished priests simply on account of the impossible conditions. I bought my experience. That I quarrelled with the chaplains is quite true. I did not quarrel effectually though. They were a Belgian and a Frenchman. They drank themselves drunk on beer, out of decanters, chased each other round the refectory tables in a tipsy fight, defied my authority, and compelled the ragamuffins of the school to do the same. I naturally resigned that post as quickly as possible. Then follows a pseudo-history of the beginning of my ecclesiastical career at Maryvale. Talacryn knows all about that; and can tell you at your leisure. Afterwards, I came across (I am quoting) "came across a certain Pictish lairdie, and was maintained by him for three or four months – "'

'And I know all about that,' Semphill interrupted: 'You gave a great deal more than you got.'

'The fallacies connected with my career at and expulsion from St Andrew's College are known?'

'Thoroughly,' assented Semphill, Talacryn, and Carvale in a breath.

'The statement that I contracted large debts there – '

'What about those debts?' Ragna asked.

Carvale told him. 'They all were contracted under the personal supervision of the Vice-Rector. They were quite insignificant. Besides that, they would not have been contracted but for the promise of Archbishop Smithson and the advice of Canon Dugdale – '

'And the advice of me,' Semphill added in a low tone.

'Oh, you at length acknowledge it?' George fiercely thrust at him.

'Yes, I acknowledge it.'

'Well then, we're quits now:' George quietly and mysteriously mewed.

'One confesses that the question of the pseudonym interests one,' Sterling judicially said.

'I had half a dozen. You see when I was kicked out from college, without a farthing or a friend at hand, I literally became an adventurer. Thank God Who gave me the pluck to face

334

my adventures. I was obliged to live by my wits. Thank God again Who gave me wits to live by.'

Cardinal Leighton was standing up, blinking and blushing with indignation which distorted his honest placid features. 'Holy Father, don't say another word.' He twitched round towards his fellow-collegians. 'How can you torture the man so!' he cried. 'Can't you see what you're doing, wracking the poor soul like this, pulling him in little pieces all over again? Shame on ye! – Holy Father don't say another word.'

'Oh if I had only known!' cried Van Kristen.

'You did! I told you myself; and you didn't believe me!' George fulminated.

The youngest cardinal wept into his handkerchief, shaking with sobs. George neither saw nor noted anyone. He was glaring like a python. Demurrers to Leighton's remarks arose. No one wanted to wrack anybody. Questions had been invited. Of course no one believed. But it would be so much more satisfactory – Ragna added. George sat violently still in his chair while they talked: let them talk; and prepared to resume.

'If Your Holiness would condescend –' Carvale began.

'There is no Holiness here,' George interrupted, in that cold white candent voice which was more caustic than silver nitrate and more thrilling than a scream.

'If you would do us the favour of just noticing a few heads.'

'As you please,' George chucked at him: 'agree among yourselves as to those heads; and you shall have bodies and limbs and finger-nails and teeth to fit them.'

Their Eminencies began agreeing. George meanwhile went into the secret chamber for ten minutes or so: and returned with his cat on his neck, and his own tobacco-pouch. He was beginning a cigarette; and his gait was the gait of a challenged lion. Sterling presented him with a pencilled slip of paper. He read aloud 'Pseudonym: begging letters: debts: luxurious living: idleness: false pretences as to means and position'.

'I think it right to say that I myself am perfectly satisfied on all those points,' said Semphill. 'I've read the calumnies – and I

335

call them dastardly calumnies – in the light of my own knowledge of the facts; and I can only say that the worst thing which they've alleged against you is that you've been used to go about bilking landlords. All the rest is excusable, not to say harmless.'

'Gracious Heavens!' George exclaimed in a rictus of rage. 'Do you suppose that a man of my description goes about bilking landlords for the sake of the fun of the thing? It's no such deliriously jolly work, I can tell you. However, I've never bilked any landlords if that's what you want to know. Never. They saw that I worked like nineteen galley-slaves; and they offered to trust me. I voluminously explained my exact position and prospects to them. I was foolish enough to believe that you Catholics would keep your promises and pay me for the work which I did at your orders. So I accepted credit. I wish I had died. When at length I was defrauded, legally, mind! – for, as my employers were Catholics and sometimes priests, I trusted to their honour, and obtained no stamped agreement: – when I was defrauded of my wages, my landlords lost patience (poor things – I don't blame them) harried me, reproached me, at length turned me out, and so prevented me from paying them. I dug myself out of the gutter with these bare hands again and again; and started anew to earn enough to pay my debts. Debts! They never were off my chest for twenty years, no matter what these vile liars say. Debts! They say that I incurred them for luxurious living, unjustifiably – '

His passionate voice subsided: he became frightfully cool and tense and terse, analytical, quite merciless to himself. Their Eminencies never before had seen a surgical knife at work in a human heart and brain. They all sat vigilant and attentive, as self-dissection proceeded. 'They say that I gorged myself with sumptuous banquets at grand hotels. Once, after several day's absolute starvation, I got a long-earned guinea; and I went and had an omelette and a bed at a place which called itself a grand hotel. It wasn't particularly grand in the ordinary sense of the term; and my entertainment there cost me no more than it would have cost me elsewhere, and it was infinitely cleaner and tastier. They say that I ate daintily, and had elaborate dishes made from a cookery book of my own. The recipes (there may have been a score of them) were cut out of a penny weekly, current among the working classes. The dishes were lentils, carrots, anything that was cheapest, cleanest, easiest, and most filling – nourishing – at the price. Each dish cost something under a penny; and I sometimes had one each day. As I was living on credit, I tried to injure no one but myself. That's the story of my luxurious living. Let me add though that I was extravagant, in proportion to my means, in one thing. Whenever I earned a little bit, I reserved some of it for apparatus conducing to personal cleanliness, soap, baths, tooth-things, and so on. I'm not a bit ashamed of that. Why did I use credit? Because it was offered: because I hoped: because – That I did not abuse it you may see, actually see, by my style of living – here are the receipted bills – and by the number and quantity and quality of the works of my hands. I never was idle. I worked at one thing after another. The *Catholic Hour* admits my skill; and mispresents that as a crime. At the same time, I myself don't claim my indefatigability as a virtue. Nothing of the kind. It's something lower than that. It's comical to say it: but my indefatigability was nothing but a purely selfish pose, put on solely to make philanthropists look unspeakably silly, to give the lie direct to all their idiotic iniquitous shibboleths. It wasn't that I *couldn't* stop working: but that I *wouldn't*. The fact is that I long, I burn, I yearn, I thirst, I most earnestly desire, to do absolutely nothing. I am so tired. I have such a genius for elaborate repose. But convention always alleges idleness or drunkenness, or lechery, or luxury, to be the *causa causans* of scoundrelism and of poverty. That's a specimen of the *Eidola Specus*, the systematizing spirit which damns half the world. People never stop to think that there may be other causes – that men of parts become rakes, or scoundrels, or paupers, for lack of opportunity to live decently and cleanly. Look at François Villon, and Christopher Marlowe, and Sir Richard Steele, and Leo di Giovanni, and heaps of others. Well: I resolutely determined that you never righteously should allege those things of me. Simply to deprive you of that excuse for your failure to do your duty to your neighbour – simply to deprive you of the chance of classifying me among the ruck which your neglect has made – I courted semi-starvation and starvation, I scrupulously avoided drink, I hardly ever even spoke civilly to a woman; and I laboured like a driven slave. No: I never was idle. But I was a most abject fool. I used to think that this diligent ascetic life eventually would pay me best. I made the mistake of omitting to give its due importance to the word "own" in the adage "Virtue is its own reward". I had no other reward, except my unwillingly cultivated but altogether undeniable virtue. A diabolic brute once said to me "If I had your brains I would be earning a thousand a year". I replied "Take them: tell me what to do: give me orders, and I implicitly will obey you. Then, take that thousand a year, and give me two hundred; and I'll bless you all my days." He said nothing; and he did nothing. He was just a fatuous liar. I mocked him: caught him stealing my correspondence – there is his written confession; and, he wrote these anonymous calumnies in long cherished revenge.' The dreadful lambent voice flickered for a moment; and more rapidly flashed on. 'I repeat, I never was idle. I did work after work. I designed furniture, and fire-irons. I delineated‘ saints and seraphim, and sinners, chiefly the former: a series of rather interesting and polyonomous devils in a period of desperate revolt. I slaved as a professional photographer, making (from French prints) a set of negatives for lantern-slides of the Holy Land which were advertised as being "from original negatives" – "messing about" the *Catholic Hour* elegantly denominates that portion of my purgatory. Well I admit it was messy, and insanitary within the meaning of the act too – but then you see I was working for a Catholic. I did journalism, reported inquests for eighteen pence. I wrote for magazines. I wrote books. I invented a score of things. Experts used to tell me that there was a fortune waiting for me in these inventions: that any capitalist would help me to exploit them. They were small people themselves, these experts – small, in that they were not obliged to pay income tax: they had no capital to invest: but they recommended me, and advised me, to apply to lots of people who had: gave me their names and addresses, dictated the letters of application which I wrote. I trusted them, for they were "businessmen" and I knew that I was not of that species. I quieted my repugnance; and I laid invention after invention, scheme after scheme, work after work, before capitalist after capitalist. I was assured that it was correct to do so. I despised and detested myself for doing it. I scoured the round world for a "patron". These were my "begging letters". – At that time I was totally ignorant of the fact that there are thousands of people who live by inviting patronage; and that most of them really have nothing to be patronized: while the rest are cranks. I knew that I had done such and such a new thing: that I had exhausted myself and my resources in doing it: that my deed was approved by specialists who thoroughly knew the subject. I was very ashamed to ask for help to make my invention profitable: but I was quite honest – generous: I always offered a share in the profits – always. I did not ask for, and I did not expect, something for nothing. I had done so much; and I wanted so little: but I did want that little – for my creditors – for giving ease to some slaves of my acquaintance. I was a fool, a sanguine ignorant abject fool! I never learned by experience. I still kept on. A haggard shabby shy priestly-visaged individual, such as I was, could not hope to win the confidence of men who daily were approached by splendid plausible cadgers. My requests were too diffident, too modest. I made the mistake of appealing to brains rather than to bowels, to reason rather than to sentiment. I wanted hundreds, or thousands – say two: others wanted and got tens and hundreds of thousands. A cotton-waste merchant could not risk fifteen hundred on my work, although he liked me personally and said that he believed in the value of my inventions: but, at the same time, he cheerfully lost twelve thousand in a scheme for "ventilated boots". I myself was wearing ventilated boots, then: but the ventilated-boot man wore resplendent patent leather. Cardinals' secretaries could live at the rate of two thousand two hundred and ninety pounds a year and borrow three thousand and sixty pounds, on a salary of two hundred pounds a year; and they could become bankrupt for four thousand one hundred and twenty pounds with one hundred and eighty pounds' worth of assets. But I – I could not get my due from that man, one of whose secretaries wrote his business to me on the franked notepaper of the late Queen of England's Treasury: while the other, the bankrupt, gave me a winter of starvation, because his lord had altered his mind, quoth he, about the job on which I was working, and had determined to put his money into a cathedral. No. I never accomplished the whole art and mystery of mendicity. I perfectly could see what was required of him who would be a successful swindler. I was not that one. I was playing another kind of game – unfortunately an honest one. Take that "unfortunately" for irony, please. I mean – but you perfectly know what I mean. I made nothing of my inventions. By degrees, I had the mortification of seeing others arrive at the discovery which I had made years before. They contrived to turn it into gold and fame. That way, one after another of my inventions became nulled to me. I think I am right in saying that there are only four remaining at the present moment. Finance them now? Engage in trade like a monk or a nun? No. No. I shall give them to – that doesn't matter. It shall be done today. Idle? Idle? When I think of all the violently fatuous frantic excellent things I've done in the course of my struggles for an honest living – ouf! It makes me sick! Oh yes, I have been helped. God forgive me for bedaubing myself with that indelible blur. I had not the courage to sit down and fold my hands and die. A brute once said that he supposed that I looked upon the world as mine oyster. I did not. I worked; and I wanted my wages. When, they were withheld, people encouraged me to hope on; and offered me a guinea for the present. I took the filthy guinea. God forgive me for becoming so degraded. Not because I wanted to take it: but because they said that they would be so pained at my refusal. But one can't pay all one's debts, and lead a godly righteous sober life for ever after on a guinea. I was offered help: but help in teaspoonfuls: just enough to keep me alive and chained in the mire: never enough to enable me to raise myself out of it. I asked for work, and they gave me a guinea – and a tacit request to go and agonize elsewhere. My weakness, my fault was that I did not die, murdered at Maryvale, at St Andrew's College. The normal man, treated as I was ill-treated, would have made no bones whatever about doing so. But I was abnormal. I took help, when it was offered gently. I'm thankful to say that I flung it back when it was offered charitably, as the Bishop of Claughton offered it, and Monsignor – you know whom I mean, Talacryn – and John Newcastle of the *Weekly Tabule*. I'll tell you about the last. He said that, being anxious to do me a good turn, he had deposited ten pounds with a printer-man, who would be a kind friend to me, and would consult me as to how that sum could be expended in procuring permanent employment for me. I took seven specimens of my handicraft to that printer-man. He admired them: offered me a loan of five pounds on their security. With that, I fulfilled a temporary engagement. Then I consulted the printer-man, the "kind friend". He proposed to give me a new suit of clothes (I was to do without shirts or socks) to accept my services at no salary, and to teach me the business of a printer's reader for three months; and, then, to recommend me for a situation as reader to some other printer. But, I said, why waste three months in learning a new trade when I already had four trades at my fingers' ends? But, I said, what was I to live on during those three months? But, I said, what certainty was there at the end of those three months? But, he said, that he would "have none of" my "lip, for" he "knew all" my "capers"; and he bade me begone and take away my drawings. Those were ruined: he had let them lie on his dirty office floor for months. Oh I admit that I have been helped – quite brutally and quite uselessly. Helped? Yes. Once, when they told me at the hospital that I was on the verge of a nervous collapse, a Jesuit offered to help me. He would procure my admission to a certain House of Rest, if I would consent to go there. By the Mercy of God I remembered that it was a licensed mad-house, where they imprisoned you by force and tortured you. Fact! There had been a fearful disclosure of their methods in the *P. M. G.* Well: I refused to go.

Rather than add that brand to what I had incurred through being Catholic, I made an effort of will; and contrived to escape that danger: contrived to recover my nerves; and I continued my battle. Regarding my pseudonyms – my numerous pseudonyms – think of this: I was a tonsured clerk, intending to persist in my Divine Vocation, but forced for a time, to engage in secular pursuits both to earn my living and to pay my debts. I had a shuddering repugnance from associating my name, the name by which I certainly some day should be known in the priesthood, with these secular pursuits. I think that was rather absurd: but I am quite sure that it was not dishonourable. However, for that reason I adopted pseudonyms. I took advice about adopting them: for, in those days, I used to take advice about everything, not being man enough to act upon my own responsibility. Also, the idea of using pseudonyms was suggested to me; and the first one was selected for me. As time went on, and Catholic malfeasance drove me from one trade to another – for you know – Talacryn – Carvale – Semphill – Sterling – that two excellent priests declared in so many words that they would prevent me from ever earning a living – legal assassination, you see definitely was contemplated – I say as Catholic malfeasance drove me from one trade, I invented another, and another; and I carried on each of these under a separate pseudonym. In fact I split up my personality. As Rose I was a tonsured clerk: as King Clement, I wrote and painted and photographed: as Austin White, I designed decorations: as Francis Engle, I did journalism. There were four of me at least. I always have thought it so inexplicable that none of the authorities – you, Talacryn, with your pretended confidence in me and your majestic immobility towards me – that none of you ever realized the tremendous amount of energy which was being expended, misdirected, if you like. Certainly no one of you ever made a practical attempt to direct that energy. I was like a wild colt careering round and round a large meadow. You all looked on and sneered "Erratic!" Of course I was erratic, for you all did your very best, by stolidity, hints, insinuations, commands, to create obstacles over which I had to jump, through which I had to tear a way; and there was no one to bit and bridle me, to ride me, and to share his couch with me. And of course my pseudonymity has been misunderstood by the stupid, as well as mispresented by the invidious. Most people have only half developed their single personalities. That a man should split his into four and more; and should develop each separately and perfectly, was so abnormal that many normals failed to understand it. So when "false pretences" and similar shibboleths were shrieked, they also took alarm and howled. But, there were no false pretences. I told my name to everyone whom it concerned. I am not the only person who has traded under pseudonyms or technicryms. Take, for example, the man whose shop I am said to have offered to buy. He himself used a trade-name. He begged for my acquaintance when I was openly living as a tonsured clerk, about a couple of years before my first pseudonym even was thought of. Take, for another example, those priests, Fr Aleck of Beal, and the Order of Divine Love, who are alleged to have "charitably maintained" me. By the way, they never did that. They always were paid for my entertainment, in hard coin, and their own price – always. And the Fathers of Divine Love refused me shelter for one night in 1892 at the very time when they are said to have "charitably maintained" me. They did suggest a common lodging-house at fourpence, though; and I flung back the suggestion in their faces and walked the streets all night. But all these people knew all about me and my pseudonyms. In fact, the very priest who suggested the common lodging-house, was the man on whose advice I adopted my first pseudonym. It was invented by an old lady who chose to call herself my grandmother: she was that priest's patron and penitent. It was approved by him and adopted by me. And there you have the blind and naked truth on that point. It now is pretended that "King Clement" was a jesuitical machiavellian device of mine, implying royalty, dominions, wealth, and interminable nonsense. I think that the pretension is due to malice and imbecillity. It is malignant now: but I firmly believe that it began by being imbecile. I confess that the name, taken together with my

343

domineering manner, my pedantic diction, my austere and (shall I say) exclusive habit, was liable to misconstruction by the low coarse half-educated uncultured boors among whom I lived. It's an example of the *Eidola Fori*, the strange power of words and phrases over the mind. I think it really was believed, in some vague way, that I was an exiled sovereign or some rot of that sort. I believe that I perceived it; and laughed to myself about it. But I did my best to disabuse the fools of their foolery. That made things worse. Liars themselves, they could not conceive of a man speaking truth to his own detriment. My disclaimer was taken for a lie; and they honoured me the more for it; and chuckled at the thought of their own perspicacity: that is to say, when what I said was intelligible to them. You see I used to be a great talker. I have had many experiences; and I used freely to talk of them. It amused and instructed; and I like to amuse and to instruct. You will understand that my voice and my manner of speech did not resemble the voice and the manner of speech of the ruffians with whom I worked and lived. Live as poorly as I would, dress as shabbily as I would, the moment I opened my mouth I was discovered to be different to those people. They perceived it; and I never could disguise my speech. Also, I'm quite sure that they could not understand my speech – follow my argument. I used words which were strange to them to express ideas unimagined by them, while their half-developed minds were more than half occupied, not in listening to me but, in contemplating me, and in trying to form their particular idea of me by the aid of the *Vulgi sensus imperiti*, the imperfection of undisciplined senses, at their disposal. I called that Imbecillity. Perhaps Ignorance is the apter term. The Malice is to be found among people who ought to know better: people to whom I have told the exact truth about myself, exact at the time of telling: people, who being possessed by a desire to think evil, think evil: people who read between, instead of on, the lines: people, prone to folly, whom I have not helped to avoid their predilection. I tried to be simple and plain, to sulk (if you like) in my own corner by myself. It was no good. Anyhow, I told no tales of realms or wealth as mine. I made no false pretences. I myself was grossly deceived: barbarously man-woman-and-priest-handled. I was foolish to try to explain myself. I was foolish to try to work with, to live with, to equal myself in every respect with, verminous persons within the meaning of the act. I ought to have died. But I did not die. That is all. It is not half. Now you know. Make what you please of it.' –

'Tell me,' Gentilotto instantly said: 'Why did you never go to the Trappists?'

'Because I went to something worse, to something infinitely terribly more ghastly. Trappists live in beautiful silent solitude; they have clean water, beds, regular meals, and peace. I went to live in intellectual silence and solitude in an ugly obscene mob, where clean water was a difficulty, food and a bed an uncertainty, and where I had the inevitable certainty of ceaseless and furious conflict.'

He hurled the words like javelins, and drew back in his chair. The old bitter feeling of disgust with himself inspired him. He feared lest perhaps he might have seemed to be pleading for sympathy. So he angrily watched to detect any signs of a wish to insult him with sympathy. But he really had gone far, far beyond the realm of human sympathy. *There was not a man on the earth who would have dared to risk rebuff, to persist against rebuff, to soar to him with that blessed salve of human sympathy – for which – underneath his armour – and behind his warlike mien – he yearned.* Pity perhaps, horror perhaps, dislike perhaps, might have met him. But he only had emphasized his own fastidious aloofness. He had cleared off the mire: but he had disclosed the cold of marble, not the warmth of human flesh.

The cardinals remained silent for a minute. Then Ragna said '"An enemy hath done this!" Who is it?'

George blazed with vigorous candid delight. 'That is the first genuine word which I have had from the heart of Your Eminency!' – He returned to his repellent manner. 'I gave the names of my calumniators to Cardinal Leighton.'

'Jerry Sant the Liblab, aided by the woman and a clot of worms who had turned;' Leighton said to Ragna.

345

'Let them be smothered in the dung-hill. *Anathema sint.*' Ragna growled.

Again there was an exposition of silence in the throne-room. George was frozen hard and white. Ragna and Leighton continued to look at each other. Carvale's eyes had the blue brilliance of wet stars. Saviolli, Semphill, Talacryn, Whitehead, were as though they had seen the saxificous head of the Medoysa. Sterling gazed straight before him, in the manner of the sphinx carven of black basalt. George was watching them with half-shut eyes from the illimitable distance of his psychic altitude. Presently, the pure pale old face of Gentilotto and the pure pale young face of Van Kristen simultaneously were lifted; and their eyes met His. He blushed: slowly drew out the pontifical ring: and put it on His finger.

'Lord Cardinals, it is Our will to be alone:' the Supreme Pontiff said.

They came one by one and kissed His ring: and retired in silence.

CHAPTER 23

WHEN the door was shut, Hadrian remained quite motionless on the throne; and set Himself to review what He had said. He wondered whether He for once had got down to and laid bare the root of the matter: whether He for once had made His argument clear and convincing. Good God! Who ever could hope to be convincing? – He flung the thing away from Him; and for ever closed that volume of the book of His life.

He rose; and went straight into the bedroom. Here He stripped, and stood erect, knees and feet close: gripped a pair of ten-pound dumb-bells; and swung them with the alternating gesture of a right and left overhand bowler, rhythmically swaying from the hips. He counted up to a hundred; and went to another movement: a full round overhead sweep of both arms together, expanding the long-breathing lungs, quickening the pulses, brightening the eyes. His skin became moist and warm.

He washed His face and hands in oatmeal water with no soap; and went into the bathroom, turning on the high tap and letting the cold soft water rain down upon Him until He was numbed. He quickly dried Himself; and put on completely clean clothes, rolling up those which He had discarded and thrusting them into a linen bag. Then, He emerged all flushed and white and fresh; and summoned Sir Iulo to the secret chamber.

'And so you are thinking of marriage, *carino*;' Hadrian said, putting the young man into a chair and bestowing fumificables.

Sir Iulo went almost as scarlet as his uniform: his eyes and teeth gleamed. Hadrian handed to him a sheet of paper containing six stanzas of passionate expression in rhyme, under the heading '*Vorrei che tu ascoltassi la mia voce*'.

'Don't leave your sonnets about. And don't be so terrified, you silly boy. Well: is it true?'

The lover's face twitched rather. 'I l-o-v-e her,' he said with an enormous vocal expansion of the middle word. 'But I will not to abandon You, *Santità*:' he added with fixed eyes.

'Who is she? Is she good? Has she any money?'

'She is the little daughter of the dentist. But good? But, yes. But no money:' was the categorical reply.

'Does she love you?'

'Oh, but how she loves me!'

'How long have you known her?'

'Since Christmas, *Santità*, when the father of that has scaled the my tooths.'

'Have you spoken to "the father of that" about "that"?'

'Oh, but not yet, *Santità*. Nothing of less, he knows. I gave him to know without the word.'

'And he didn't drive you out of the house?'

'But no: for behold me not the assassin of that dentist.'

Hadrian laughed. 'Can you describe her?'

'Oh that I might to describe her to one who is so dear, so wise –'

'Describe her.'

'Is named Evnica. Is example of goodness, of intellectuality.

For example: yesterday with the favour of the Most Holy I make a visit. I am entering the saloon in the manner of cat, softly, softly. Behold in a book reads the Signorina Evnica – not book of novels, not journal of *Don Chrisciotte*. No, I look over her shoulder, reading titles. Behold, book of piety entitled *Office to the Proximate* –'

'*Office to the Proximate?* What book of piety is that?'

Sir Iulo repeated the title in Italian.

'Ah yes, *The Duty towards our Neighbour*. Yes: a very good sign in a girl. Go on.'

Sir Iulo fixed his bright green eyes upon a mental image; and described each point as he observed it, using his gorgeously florid Tuscan idiom. 'Has a face to make burn Jove, and to return to ram, eagle, or bull; and to make scorn to medals old and new. Blonde she has the hair like thread of gold. The cheeks appear like a rose damasked. The mouth and the eyes are worth a treasure. Has looks angelic, divine: but in the effects and all the motions, human; and the her excellencies not have end. She has what they call a good and fine hand: is white like snow of mountains. Is literate; and makes to talk Tuscan; and in life not a flaw can be found. There is not who better to a swan understands me. Does great things, enough facts, little eats: not drinks never in the middle of eating and not at afternoon tea (*merenda*). More, I say. She is in her proper acts so learned, that all I have in the world, or small or great, I should have given to her pleasure at a stroke. The more beautiful to my day I never saw: none more servitial: none more prudent: nor acts in a girl more courteous and gay. Has Petrarch and Dante in her hand; and, at time and place if I command, she vomits a little sonnet lightly. Girl of all perfect qualities; and holds me in pledge there if mine –'

'Well now: suppose that you marry her, will you be good to her?'

'Oh, that she shall be the my life and the my delight, dressed in velvet, guarded as a queen, for fear that if she goes about too much should not be robbed by some little hypocrite: that she shall live on collops and bread of baker –'

'How amusing you are! Well: marry that paragon, and be good and happy. You must have an apartment in the City for her, you know; and, about your duties here: you can come when you like. You are not dismissed: but John and James will suffice. Understand, boy, you are wanted, wanted here, always.'

'I am here always, *Santità*.'

'No. Go away and marry. "The most certain softeners of a man's moral skin, and sweeteners of his blood, are domestic intercourse and a happy marriage and brotherly intercourse with the poor." Always remember that. By the bye, what are you going to live on?'

'If I am always a Gentleman of Hadrian, I am having a plenty of money.'

'Ah, but you always will not be a Gentleman of Hadrian, because Hadrian will not be always; and, when He is not, His successor will say "*Via! Via!*" to you.'

'And then I shall do some things?'

'Ah, but what things?'

'Who knows? But I shall do things.'

Hadrian went to the safe in the bedroom: then to the writing-table, and wrote. He came back with some papers in His hand.

'Attend! Take this note to Plowden by the post office. He will give you a thousand sterling. That is a marriage gift to you, so that you may get an apartment in the City and marry that little daughter of the dentist. Don't be silly. Listen. What do you know about photography?'

'About photography? But I know to use that Kodak, the gift *della Sua osservantissima e venerabilissima Santità*.'

'And you do it very well. You are one of the few men now alive who perceive the right moment for pressing the button. Understand?'

'I see with eyes.'

'But there is something beside seeing with eyes. There is a mind which ponders and selects.'

'Too much of honour.'

'No. No honour at all: a stated fact. Well now: think of

negatives. They are dense in places: clear in places; and, in other places, more or less dense. Understand? Under the negative you put a certain paper; and expose it to light. Light goes through the clear places and stains the paper black: it partly goes through the more or less dense places; and stains the paper grey in various gradations of tint. It fails to go through the dense places and leaves the paper white. There is your photograph, a little black a little white and many different greys. Understand?'

'Yes, *Santità*.'

'Your photograph is an image of the form, the contours, the modelling, the *morbidezza*, of the object before your lens. It lacks one thing. It has not colour. The process has tralated colour into monochrome. Do you see that?'

'Yes, *Santità*.'

'Now white means a blend of all colours; and black means the absence of all colours. Then grey should mean some colours, of this quality or that, of this quantity or that, according to the clarity or the density of the grey. Understand?'

'Yes, *Santità*.'

'Your negative is black and white and many greys.'

'Yes, *Santità*.'

'Then understand that all colours lie hidden in the black and white and greys of the negative. In the black, lie all colours: it produces the positive white. In the white lie no colours: it produces the positive black. In the various greys, lie various colours – why are you jumping about? Keep still and listen, wriggling lizard that you are! What do you want to do?'

'To liberate those poor colours.'

'So does everybody. At least, everybody wants to photograph in colours: so they paint on the backs of the films; and they play the fool with triply coloured negatives. Only one man in the world knows that the colour already is there – already is there, my boy – stored in the black white grey negative; and that the black white grey ordinary negative will give up its imprisoned colours to him who has the key. Well now: take the second envelope. The key's there; and it's yours.

(Don't stare like that!) There are three other things as well, which may be useful. (Don't say a word!) Read all those papers until you understand them. They're quite simple. Then practise. When you can do the trick, you will want a little help to do it greatly, to make it useful. (Get off the floor!) Then take the third envelope to Plowden – it's mentioned in the first – and he will give you two thousand sterling. (Don't touch that foot!) That will be enough if you are industrious. Now you are trusted, *Iulo mio*. Be good always; and be kind to everybody. No don't move. We are going into the gardens with Flavio. You stay here till you feel better. – Ptlee-bl ptlee-bl ptlee-bl,' Hadrian mewed to His delighted and excited and persequent cat.

CHAPTER 24

It was the festival of St George, Protector of the Ninefold Kingdom. Hadrian noted with pleasure that it was what the Italians call one of His "fortunate days". His head was clear, His limbs were supple, His body lithe: He felt young, exuberant, potent. His soul seemed balanced, elevated. His whole poise was one of gentle incisive simplicity. He had that upright rather dominant gait, by no means arrogant, which marks the happy able man. The Sacred College came early in the morning, directly after His mass, to congratulate Him on the anniversary of His pontificature; and Ragna took occasion to whisper that the Northern Emperor left Palazzo Caffarelli for the Quirinale at dawn. Everyone knew what that meant.

When, later, Hadrian descended in state to the Sala Regia, He was on the alert. The introducer-of-sovereigns announced: the Ninefold King – the President of the United States of America – the Northern Emperor – the Japanese Emperor – and a posse of subsidiary kings, princes, and sovereign-dukes, who came with the world's congratulations. The pontifical paraphernalia lay on the high red throne: but Hadrian stood at its foot to receive His guests. His garb was white, absolutely simple and fresh; and His pose was apostolic, frank, and genial. These enormous potentates towered above Him in the splendour of their grandeur; and, as Cardinal Carvale, the fantastic dreamer, said to Cardinal Van Kristen, they radiated from Him as from a source of light.

After the ceremony of reception was finished, Their Majesties, Augustitudes, Highnesses, and Honours, lingered, chatting with the pontifical court. Some of them had a few words with the Supreme Pontiff. The Northern Emperor came and said, 'I know that Your Holiness will felicitate me on a dispatch which I have just received from my brother Prince Henry, who announces that my glorious German navy has taken Kronstadt.'

Hadrian replied; and added 'Be merciful, Augustitude.'

William then did a politely ferocious scowl, intended to indicate imperial impatience; and continued in a lower tone, 'I am also anxious to assure Your Holiness that I myself deeply regret the absence of my cousin and imperial brother, Victor Emanuel. All that I could say has been said to persuade His Augustitude to join me on this auspicious and never-to-be-forgotten occasion. I wish that to be known.'

'It only is a personal obstacle, not a political, which prevents the Southern Emperor from coming here?'

'Most Holy Lord, it is not even a personal obstacle. Victor Emanuel has the most profound and much-to-be-admired and pre-eminently well-merited veneration and reverence for Your Person. It is – well, really it seems almost childish – but he has persuaded himself that –'

'That the Roman Pontiff owes the King of Italy a visit?'

'Precisely, Holy Father. There is some history of an approach which His Augustitude's royal and martyred father made to the Conclave of 1878 –'

'And for a mere idea, Victor Emanuel will continue alienate from Us! Yet, ideas are very fine things, to be respected, to be cultivated, in this material age. They are so rare, so singular. And constancy, fidelity to an idea, above all things is singular and rare, in this age of compromise from which the world only now emerges. Victor Emanuel is not to be blamed, but praised.' Suddenly a bright light came in the Apostle's eyes. 'Well, then, the next step is obvious. If the son will not come to the Father, then the Father must go to the son.' And an impulse to instant movement appeared to urge Him onward.

The Northern Emperor splendidly rose to the occasion. 'It would be one more grand deed added to Your Holiness's many grand deeds. I trust that I may have the never-sufficiently-to-be-valued honour of accompanying You.'

'But We walk:' said Hadrian.

'I also will gladly walk:' said William.

The Pope darted a rapid glance round the hall. The King of Portugal was talking to the Japanese Emperor; and the Basil of the Hellenes was listening to the Prince of Montenegro-and-New-Serbia. The Ninefold King, with one arm paternally resting on the shoulder of the young King of Spain, was telling (as his own) an extremely funny story (which he had heard five minutes before from Cardinal Semphill) to the President of America. Cardinals and sovereigns clustered round them, ploding with laughter at each admirably detailed jocosity. 'We can escape this way;' the Pope said to the Emperor. Outside the hall, a pontifical page ran for the white three-cornered hat; and the two descended the Scala Regia, with its Ionic columns flanked by pontifical guards, and made their way into the Square of St Peter's. There was a cleared roadway; and they quickly walked between long lines of magnificent Italian soldiery. Rome occupied the side-walks; and sank to its knees as the Supreme Pontiff, shedding benedictions, went swinging lightly and swiftly by. The German Gentleman made no attempt to take salutes until Hadrian said, 'Oh do notice these dear Romans. They will be pleased. And you know that you profoundly admire the *bersaglieri*.'

The Emperor responded, 'I am as proud to salute the Romans as I am to salute the noblest Roman of them all – to use the words of Your Holiness's divine Shakespeare.' And he strode on, saluting, while the Pontiff blessed.

As they passed the Palazzo Venezia, Hadrian said, 'Victor

Emanuel really behaves extremely well. Three-quarters of his army are in the field; and here is a parcel of foreign sovereigns practically occupying his capital in – no, not homage – in courtesy to Us –'

'And also out of respect, Holiness.'

'Out of respect then and courtesy to Our Apostolature. It is no affair of his; and yet he lines the streets with troops, while he himself – oh, it's really very decent of him!'

'Victor Emanuel is a truly great man;' the Emperor commented. The Pope assented.

They entered the Palace of the Quirinale; and went straight through the ambassador's hall to the Southern Emperor's study. William remained in the ante-chamber. Victor Emanuel in a light-grey flannel suit was reading proofs of his numismatic catalogue. He stood up pale and stiff, when his groom-of-the-chambers came in and whispered a word. Hadrian followed on the instant, entering with candid gentle dignity, extending an English hand. Not a word was said. Victor Emanuel, shining with the light of the purple which he had not yet worn, took the outstretched hand: held it: felt his own gripped and held. He bent his head – then his knee. Reconciliation was complete.

'May I have the honour and the happiness of presenting my wife to Your Holiness?' he said, a minute later. He went along the corridor and gave two raps on a further door. 'Darling,' he cried; 'please come.'

The exquisite Empress Elena appeared. She started slightly at first: but bravely came on, imperially mysteriously pale and radiant as 'the chorus of nightly stars and the bright powers which bring summer and winter to mortals, conspicuous in the firmament'.

Hadrian at once won her with 'And the lovely children'.

'Oh yes, the kiddies!' Victor Emanuel said.

'Do you know that We owe one immense emotion to your boy?' and Hadrian narrated the incident in Prince Attendolo's garden.

Mother and father proudly laughed. 'Yes, we heard about that, of course; and I wondered what would happen if ever we ourselves should meet Your Holiness by accident, as the children did:' the Empress said.

'Well, we have met, and now Your Augustitudes know:' laughed Hadrian.

'Filiberto is a queer little chap,' Victor Emanuel continued: 'he says the most extraordinary things; – came running into the stables the other morning crying because some dog had barked and startled him. "Stamp at 'em," I said; "and after all, you can run faster than a dog," said I to hearten him. "Yes" says he "but you see, father, when I do run, I'm always putting out one leg at the back for the dog to bite!"'

'But I can tell you something better than that,' the Empress put in. 'He was a bad boy in the chapel at benediction on Sunday. I'm afraid, Holiness, that this is rather a naughty story –'

'Tell it instantly and relieve your sinful soul, daughter;' the haughty pontiff commanded.

How the three roared! She continued, 'He persisted in trying to balance a pile of prayer books on the ledge of his chair-back; and every now and then they came down with a crash. At last I took him on my knee; and told him that the holy angels were looking at him, and that they would go and tell the Lord God what a wicked little ruffian he was. And then he said – he said, "Dirty little sneaks!"'

'Oh, oh, the exquisite boy!' Hadrian shouted with laughter.

'Well, I'll go and fetch him;' said the Southern Emperor, running out of the door, just as the Northern Emperor came in by the other, prepared to play the part of peace-maker. That, now, was not necessary; and England, Germany, and Italy, chattered like children till the children came. Their father did not return. His men were having a bad time, trying to beat the record for getting a sovereign into his habit of ceremony.

The fair Prince Filiberto solemnly approached the Pope. 'Are You the White Father which formerly I have seen in somebody's forest?'

'Yes,' said Hadrian.

'Are You quite good now?' the boy continued, with great black basilic eyes.

'No,' said Hadrian, feeling the horror of the end of youth confronted with the flower of innocence.

'Are You truly contrite for having been a naughty boy – no, man I mean?'

'Yes,' said Hadrian.

'Are You sitting on my father's sofa because he has forgiven You?'

'Yes,' said Hadrian, thinking what a frightful old fool He must appear.

'I liked You when I saw You in that forest; and I like You now: but mother told me that the White Father was not my father's friend.'

'Mother made a mistake, little son;' said the Empress, leaning forward in sudden confusion. 'The White Father is father's best friend.'

'Oh, how I am glad for that: because now You can be also my friend!' the prince cried, scattering his deliberate English to the four quarters of the globe.

'Most willingly,' said Hadrian, taking the rose-brown hand, and drawing the child towards Him. Innocence put up its pretty lips. The Apostle lost one breath; and stooped and kissed the stainless brow. Then He turned to greet the girls.

'This child once asked my husband a very awkward question,' the mother said, presenting the Princess Yolanda. 'The King of England was coming here; and Victor was showing her His Majesty's incoronation portrait. Ah, but how she admired it! And she said, "Father why don't you wear a hat like that king?"'

The Supreme Pontiff looked at the blushing child. 'You would not call it a "hat", Princess, now that you are grown up?'

'No, *Papa Inglese* – a crown.'

'You would like your father to have a crown? Tell him that there are two waiting for him, one at Monza, and another in the Lateran.'

The Roman Emperors escorted the Pope returning to Vatican. On the way, carriages met them, and disgorged sovereigns: state coaches met them, and emitted cardinals: courtiers alighted from horseback and emerged from motorcars. The return became a procession of the powers, led by the Power of the Keys. They had crossed the Ponte Santangelo, and were about to turn to the left by the Castle, when a dishevelled man in black contrived to break out from the ranks of the people. He got through the *bersaglieri* and stepped into the middle of the road: pointed a revolver at Hadrian; and fired. The bullet struck His Holiness high up on the left breast, piercing the pulmonary artery just above the lung.

The slim white figure stopped – wavered – and sank down. The whole world seemed to stand still, while the human race gasped once.

A frantic woman in a fox-coloured wig pitched out of the opposite crowd; and grovelled. 'Love, Love,' she howled hideously: 'oh and I loved Him so! Oh! Oh! I really did love Him. Yes I did, I did, I did, I did. . . .' she yelped to the sun in the firmament of heaven. The discord resembled the baying of a dog which breaks the cadence of Handel's *Largo* on arch-lutes.

God's Vicegerent moved – looked at her from a distance, gently, even curiously 'Daughter, go in peace,' He said and turned away. She remained there grovelling, longing to touch Him, forlorn, gorgonized.

The Roman Emperors also kneeled to right and left, fiercely looking among their aides for the help which did not come, which could not come, from man.

The assassin was in a hundred tearing hands. Screeches shot out of his gullet when they silently and inevitably began to tear him to pieces. Roman knives flashed over the parapet; and slid into Tiber: hooked hands, like the curving talons of griffins, were the weapons for this work. But the Supreme Pontiff beckoned him; and the gesture was unmistakable – universally authoritative. Shaken and violently shaking, jagged, lacerated, a disreputable wreck of Pictish ready-made tailoring, Jerry Sant staggered forward, staggered like one fascinated.

357

Cardinals and sovereigns drew away from him, and the mob hemmed him in.

' . . . for they know not . . . .' The Apostle raised himself a little, supported by imperial hands. How bright the sunlight was, on the warm grey stones, on the ripe Roman skins, on vermilion and lavender and blue and ermine and green and gold, on the indecent grotesque blackness of two blotches, on apostolic whiteness and the rose of blood.

'Augustitudes, Our will and pleasure is –'

'Speak it, Most Holy Father –'

'Augustitudes, We name you both the ministers of this Our will.' And to the murderer He said, 'Son, you are forgiven: you are free.'

Down Borgo Nuovo came guards, chamberlains, curial prelates, cardinals, from Vatican. The English and American cardinals took their vermilion on their arms, and ran like lithe long-limbed schoolboys. The faithful young Sir John outran them all. He kneeled to Hadrian, Who said,

'Dear John, take this cross – and Flavio.' The Southern Emperor unclasped the chain and rosy pectoral cross; and handed them to the gentleman-of-the-apostolic-chamber, who took them and fainted away. Out of Santo Spirito, came one with the stocks of sacred chrism. Cardinals Van Kristen and Carvale, panting, kneeled before the Ruler of the World. Percy drew out the hidden pontifical pyx: took the Sacred Host therefrom; and held It. 'The profession of faith, Most Holy Lord,' he bravely whispered.

'I believe all that which Holy Mother Church believes. I ask pardon of all men. Dear Jesus, be not to me a Judge but a Saviour.'

Cardinal Sterling gravely intoned the commendation of a Christian soul. The splendid company of angels, the senate of apostles, the army of white-robed martyrs, the lilied squadron of shining confessors, the chorus of joyful maids, patriarchs, hermits, Stephen and Lawrence, Silvester and Gregory, Francis and Lucy and Mary Magdalene, Mary – God's Own Mother, all the saints of God who daily are invited to attend the passing of the poorest Christian soul, were invoked for the Father of Princes and Kings. 'And mild and cheerful may the Aspect of Christ Jesus seem to thee – ' The singer's voice failed. Cardinal Carvale went on with no interval: imparted absolution, and the sacrament of the dying. 'Saints of God advance to help him: Angels of The Lord come to meet him, receiving his soul, offering it in the Sight of The Most High.' The splendour of mortal words reverberated from the ancient fortress wall, in the great silence of Immortal Rome.

When the Earthly Vicar of Jesus Christ had received Extreme Unction and Viaticum, when He had had done for Him all that which Christ's Church can do, He required to be lifted on His feet. The Roman Emperors rose, raising Him. The vehement ferocity of their aspect terribly contrasted with their tender movement. The torments of powerless power, of intimidation inflicted in the supreme moment of exultation, rent these grand strong men – and graced them. The bloodstain streamed down the Pope's white robes with the red stole of universal jurisdiction. The slender hand with the two huge rings ascended. The shy brown eyes fluttered; and were wide, and very glad. Then the tired young voice rang like a quiet bell.

'May God Omnipotent, ✠ ✠ ✠ Father, ✠ ✠ ✠ Son, ✠ ✠ ✠ and Holy Ghost, bless you.'

It was the Apostolic Benediction of the City and the World.

The hand and the dark eyelashes drooped, and fell. The delicate fastidious lips closed, in the ineffable smile of the dead who have found out the Secret of Love, and are perfectly satisfied.

So died Hadrian the Seventh, Bishop, Servant of the servants of God, and (some say) Martyr. So died Peter in the arms of Caesar.

The world sobbed, sighed, wiped its mouth; and experienced extreme relief.

The college of Cardinals summed Him up in the brilliant epigram of Tacitus. '*Capax imperii nisi imperasset.*' He would have been an ideal ruler if He had not ruled.

Religious people said that He was an incomprehensible creature. And the man on the motor said that the pace certainly had been rather rapid.

Pray for the repose of His soul. He was so tired.

FELICITER

MORE ABOUT PENGUINS
AND PELICANS

A HOUSE AND ITS HEAD
Ivy Compton-Burnett

In 1935 a reviewer wrote of *A House and its Head*, 'It is as if one's next door neighbour leaned over the garden wall, and remarked, in the same breath and chatty tone, that he had mown the lawn in the morning and thrust his wife's head in the gas-oven after lunch.' Here, through stark dialogue and a finely integrated plot, Ivy Compton-Burnett writes about an upper class Victorian family, piercing the facade of conventionality to reveal the human capacity for evil . . .

'No writer did more to illumine the springs of human cruelty, suffering and bravery' – Angus Wilson

THE STORY OF THE EYE
Georges Bataille

Widely regarded as the greatest sexual/pornographic novel of this century, *The Story of the Eye* was first published in 1928, and in it Bataille explores his own sexual obsessions.

This edition also includes Susan Sontag's essay, 'The Pornographic Imagination', which discusses this and other erotic classics, together with Roland Barthes's essay on *The Story of the Eye*.

A LIFE
Italo Svevo

First published in 1893, *Una Vita* and its author remained in obscurity for over thirty years until James Joyce hailed Svevo as a major literary discovery. As in all his works, Svevo is concerned here with the bourgeois soul, and its inability to will or act. His heroes are typically men of business, but with cultural pretentions and he depicts them in their free time when they are not working. It is less important to Svevo whether they have spare money or not: the important thing is that they always have time to spare. How they lose it, use it or kill it forms his major theme – worked with all the quixotic genius of which he was capable.

Penguin Modern Classics

THE TRAGIC MUSE
Henry James

Henry James published *The Tragic Muse* in 1890 at the beginning of his intense, but disastrous, flirtation with the theatre. Its themes reflect those preoccupations and, although this is the most 'English' of his novels, James concentrates his debate on the artistic life, in a masterly example of the 'all dramatic, all scenic'.

JOSEPH AND HIS BROTHERS
Thomas Mann

As Germany dissolved into the nightmare of Nazism, Thomas Mann was at work on this novel. This epic recasting of the famous biblical tale is a magnificent reconstruction of the ancient Near East. It stretches back past the days of the patriarchs to the dawn of civilization itself, and constitutes one of Thomas Mann's major achievements.

THE HOUSE OF MIRTH
Edith Wharton

First published in 1905, when it profoundly shocked society, *The House of Mirth* is a novel of manners that helped to carve out for the author an area of social fiction into which not even Henry James could trespass. 'A passionate social prophet' wrote Edmund Wilson, 'is precisely what Edith Wharton became. At her strongest and most characteristic, she is a brilliant example of the writer who relieves an emotional strain by denouncing his generation.'

Elizabeth Bowen

Elizabeth Bowen has been described as the most distinguished novelist of the century. Penguin are proud to include the following titles in their list:

FRIENDS AND RELATIONS

In *Friends and Relations*, through nuances of drawing-room comedy, the absurd – potentially explosive – interplay of propriety and passion, Elizabeth Bowen richly earns V. S. Pritchett's tribute: 'Daring by nature and intellect and passionate in imagination, compassionate in heart, she saw to it . . . that her people faced the secrets from which society no longer protected them.'

THE LAST SEPTEMBER

Basking in the late summer sunlight, the old family house casts a long shadow over the figures strolling in the grounds.

The ambushes and burnings of the Irish Troubles of 1920 seem far removed as up at the 'Great House' tennis parties and dances continue to divert and flirtations with English officers from the local garrison amuse. Yet a sense of brooding, nostalgic melancholy pervades – the sense of a tragedy coming to its climax in the calm, opulent sunlight of an Irish autumn.

'Miss Bowen is amusing and satirical . . . her biting little sketches of social awkwardness or shallowness, her rendering of character by the idiocies of abbreviated conversation, show extraordinary discernment and are extraordinarily funny' – *Observer*

Olivia Manning

Olivia Manning's *Balkan Trilogy* and *Levant Trilogy* form a single narrative entitled *Fortunes of War*, which Anthony Burgess described in the *Sunday Times* as 'the finest fictional record of the war produced by a British writer. Her gallery of personages is huge, her scene painting superb, her pathos controlled, her humour quiet and civilized. Guy Pringle is certainly one of the major characters in modern fiction.'

THE BALKAN TRILOGY:

THE GREAT FORTUNE
THE SPOILT CITY
FRIENDS AND HEROES

THE LEVANT TRILOGY:

THE DANGER TREE
THE BATTLE LOST AND WON
THE SUM OF THINGS

Also published in Penguins

SCHOOL FOR LOVE

In wartime children have to grow up quickly. One small boy, waiting to return to England, finds himself in Jerusalem in the care of Miss Bohun whose house offers a refuge to others washed up by the freak tides of destruction. There he can watch the unaccountable, wayward progress of the feeling called love – and there his real education in life can begin.

'Through the clear light of Miss Manning's sympathy . . . we feel for this horror [Miss Bohun] some of that emotion, part amusement, part revulsion, part admiration for a triumphant assertion of life, that we feel for other comic horrors in literature, Tartuffe, Squeers, Mrs Proudie' – C. P. Snow in the *Sunday Times*

The biobraphy of
an extraordinary and complex man

THE QUEST FOR CORVO
A. J. A. Symons

The public attitude to Fr. Rolfe (Baron Corvo) has altered
completely in recent years. As the literary merits of *Hadrian
the Seventh* and other works have come to be appreciated,
there has been a growing interest in the bizarre character of
their author. The life of this uncouth, lonely, arrogant genius,
who bit the hands that fed him with unprecedented venom,
was first put together by A. J. A. Symons over thirty years ago
in an extraordinary piece of biographical research. And the
modern reader will find that *The Quest for Corvo* still reads as
excitingly as any story of crime and detection.